Polychrome

Ryk E. Spoor

Polychrome
A Romantic Fantasy

Iris Mirabilis Press

Polychrome: A Romantic Fantasy

Published by Iris Mirabilis Press

Cover art by Bob Eggleton

Other Books by Ryk E. Spoor:

Atlantaea Universe:
Digital Knight (2003)
Phoenix Rising (2012)
Paradigms Lost (2014)
Phoenix in Shadow (May 2015)
Phoenix Ascendant (date not set)

Boundary Universe (with Eric Flint):
Boundary (2006)
Threshold (2010)
Portal (2013)
Castaway Planet (February 2015)
Castaway Odyssey (date not set)

Arenaverse:
Grand Central Arena (2010)
Spheres of Influence (2013)
Challenges of the Deeps (date not set)

Other:
Diamonds Are Forever (with Eric Flint; part of the anthology
Mountain Magic, 2004)

Acknowledgements:

For his help in both setting up the Kickstarter and bringing *Polychrome* to actual publication, a huge thank-you to Lawrence Watt-Evans;

For providing an awesome cover, a big cheer to Bob Eggleton!

For lovely interior illustrations, applause for Morineko-Zion!

For her laser-guided editing, thanks to Barb Caffrey!

And for encouraging me until I had the guts to do this, my beta-readers!

Dedication:

This book is dedicated to two people:

First, to L. Frank Baum, whose vision of the far-distant lands of Faerie became the single largest written influence in my life from the time I was about six until I was in junior high, and whose images and characters remain some of the most beloved of all in my heart.

And second, to Kathleen Moffre-Spoor, who had to put up with the competition from a phantom rainbow-dancing girl for months... and whose marriage to me gave me the understanding of what a romance really is.

Foreword:

The written universe of Oz is immense, complex, often contradictory, and known well only to a few, now. This was not always the case; in its heyday, the Oz books were the equivalent of Harry Potter — constant bestsellers, translated into fifty languages around the globe, eagerly awaited by legions of young — and not-so-young — fans. But today, most people who know of Oz at all know it from the classic MGM movie starring Judy Garland.

Polychrome is based, not on the movie universe (which is, in fact, still in copyright) but on the fourteen original Oz novels written by L. Frank Baum, and mostly illustrated by John R. Neill. Those who are curious about the original stories, and wish to see what Baum wrote — and what I have worked from — can find the original fourteen novels for free on Gutenberg (www.gutenberg.org) .

The major difference between the movie and the book is simple: in the movie, Oz is a dream, a psychological tool for Dorothy to deal with her frustration surrounding her Kansas life.

In the book, it is all entirely real. Dorothy Gale really is whisked away to the fairyland of Oz, endures hardship and the very real threat of injury or death, and gathers a group of staunch friends who help her win through despite all odds, and in the end she confronts adversaries head-on with determination, stubborn will, and — perhaps her most powerful weapon — kindness. In short, she grows up, despite being a very young girl at the time, and returns home to Kansas to rejoin her bereaved aunt and uncle as more than a dependent — she becomes their support and friend, though still young and innocent.

Dorothy returns to Oz multiple times, having many adventures and meeting even more strange and wonderful people, before eventually settling there forever with her Aunt Em and Uncle Henry.

Other mortals, too, become adventurers in the fairylands surrounding Oz and eventually visit that central fairyland itself: Betsy Bobbin and her mule Hank, Trot and Cap'n Bill, the eternal lost boy Button-Bright, and more, as well as natives of Oz and the other surrounding lands such as Ojo the Lucky, Prince Inga of Pingaree, the jolly King Rinkitink, and more sinister figures such as the Nome King (and yes, "Nome" is the correct spelling in Baum's works)... and, of course, the Daughter of the Rainbow itself, the beautiful and ever-cheerful Polychrome.

In *Polychrome* I have attempted to write a story of Oz as Baum depicted it... adjusted for the fact that Baum was both human, and writing for children, not adults, and thus some things had to be understood, or re-interpreted, in view of what an adult would have seen and known. I don't think it is *necessary* to have read the Oz novels before reading *Polychrome* — several of my beta readers were not readers of Oz — but if you have been an "Ozite" in your heart, I hope *Polychrome* will help you enter that realm once more, if in a slightly older fashion.

Come then, and visit Oz anew... or for the first time.

Ryk E. Spoor
September, 2014

Polychrome Glory

Prologue 1.

The grey Dove, slightly larger than the others, sat silent on the branch, a branch tinged with the color of twilight shadows and pre-dawn sky. Despite the mildness of the day, the perfect time of near-awakening of the world, it did not join with its brethren in the cooing, mournful yet soft and comforting sounds that such birds usually made.

The other doves paid him no heed. They had long since learned that he was not at all like they, and while he took some small comfort in their presence, he spoke little and sang not at all. They cooed and chirruped softly, filling the air with sleepy morning sound.

The large Dove abruptly sat up higher. There was movement there, through the deserted Gillikin forests where few ever came, carrying with it a flash of green brilliance rarely seen in these purple-tinged lands.

For the first time in...years? Decades? He had long lost track of time, but it had been long, long indeed; but now the Dove gave vent to a laugh, a rippling chortle, as the moving creature came full into view.

And it was well worth a laugh or two; shambling through the undergrowth with a rolling gait, sometimes on two splay-footed feet, sometimes making use of knuckles at the end of long arms, was a brilliantly green monkey or ape, covered with soft silky emerald hair, with a face as comical as a circus clown.

But the glint in the dark green eyes was far from amused, especially as the other doves took up the laugh and sent it rustling through the forest, a chorus of mirth. "Oh, now, do I look so amusing, little doves?" The voice was soft, gentle, unexpectedly feminine.

"Coo! Coo! You do, do!" they chorused.

1

"Then I wonder if you find this amusing, as well," the Monkey said gently. With surprising speed and viciousness, it began whipping stones and branches from the forest floor up at them. These were not small objects of rebuke, either, but large, well-aimed missiles, meant to knock their targets from their perches, to maim or worse.

Two doves were smashed from the branches with screeches of astonishment and pain; the others took flight in terror and consternation, unable to comprehend the violence so rarely seen in Oz.

The large grey Dove, having read those dark eyes in the moment before, had merely moved to the other side of the trunk. He now peered back around, to find the Monkey already regarding him speculatively.

"Now you're a strange one, Dove," the Monkey said. "Not only do you not fly from me, you seem familiar with violence, so that it frightens you not at all."

Seeing no missile forthcoming, the large Dove hopped back onto his accustomed branch and studied the green Monkey curiously. Finally, he said, "Had I been born a dove, it would be otherwise."

"Oh-HO!" cried the other, and did a short, capering dance. "So you *are* one transformed as I!"

"Transformed?" The Dove could not quite keep the sound of envy from his voice. "At least your shape leaves you hands, Monkey, hands and a shape which can live something of a civilized life. What of me, bereft of all but speech that was formerly mine?"

The Monkey's smile was humorless, an unsettling and half-mad expression which made the Dove almost decide to flee. "Oh, how very reasonable that sounds, little Dove-who-is-not, yet how little it shows you understand. Those who did this to me knew well what they did. As a Dove, you have no way to attempt anything you did as a Man — for a Man you were, I think? Yes, of course, you were. Yet as a Monkey I have hands, yet not the delicate and sure hands I had once, hands that could weave and sew, and make gestures of supreme power and control. They taunt me, misshapen and useless

2

things, fit only for feeding me... or," its eyes glinted with sadistic humor again, "throwing missiles at those who mock me."

The Dove shrugged its wings. "With hands such as those I could manage, at the least, to end this transformation and return myself to human form. Nor do I particularly worry about mocking others, as it is one of the few amusements remaining to me."

"Indeed? Yet you hid from my little barrage. I think you speak loudly but not so honestly, little Dove."

For answer, the Dove darted down and grasped the Monkey's tail in its beak and gave an effort, lunging upward. The Monkey gave a howl of pain and astonishment as it was hurled upwards into the trees by a strength vastly greater than any Dove should possess. "I speak as I wish and act as I wish, within these pathetic limits, Monkey. Now your amusement begins to pall, and I wish you would leave me to myself."

But the Monkey's expression had faded from pain and anger to intense interest. "Such strength...even an ordinary human being could not have done that. Who were you, Dove? Who were you, that even in this form you have such power, and who was it that managed to transform you to this harmless-seeming guise?"

"You would know? Very well, I will tell you, for all of this has made it come clear for me again, after years of trying, trying to forget. Once I was a man dwelling in the land of the Herkus, a humble and ordinary cobbler, a shoemaker by trade. But that was a trade I despised, for my forefathers had all been mighty wizards, and that *should* have been my trade as well. Instead my father, accursed be his name, went wandering away, leaving me behind with no instructions, no knowledge, and nothing to my name but our house. I was forced to find a trade that was both needed and which I could do, and in shoemaking I found it — something requiring attention, and focus, a delicacy of touch, yet strength as well. But I hated it, for I should have been great and respected.

"But finally fortune smiled upon me — or so I thought — and I found a hidden cache of magical instruments and recipes within my own home. I quickly mastered these, and discovered many other secrets known to no others; I thus gave up my old profession and withdrew to a mighty and solid Wicker Castle which I constructed

3

through magic alone. I then discovered that the great and wise Ozma," and never had words been uttered in so venomous and sarcastic a tone as the Dove spoke the last four, "had decreed all magic save that of herself and her two lackeys, Glinda the Good and the Wizard of Oz, was forbidden. As I recognized that one day they would come against me unless I stopped my practice of magic — and as I had no intention of doing that at all — I resolved to prevent them from acting against me by striking at them first.

"I arranged to steal all of the objects of magical power they owned, and their notes and recipes, so that they would be effectively powerless. Ozma's power comes from being a fairy princess, and of course cannot be removed, but she cannot use her power for injuring others, and I judged that she could be of no threat to me if I could neutralize the others. By bad fortune she happened to discover me as I was removing all of her mystical treasures, and I was forced to kidnap her. After she began to drive me to distraction with her insistence that I surrender and be punished, I transformed her to a form both silent and distant."

The Dove looked bitter and pensive for a moment. "But all my cleverness was for nothing. Two expeditions, through coincidence and luck — and, I will admit, perseverance and a certain cunning — eventually tracked me down. The Wizard, though bereft of much of his power, was still educated in magic and helped them through my defenses to the Castle.

"But *still* I would have defeated them, for I trapped them in my throne room; but there remained to them one magical device which — having been acquired only recently, as we of Oz tell time — I had known nothing of. That was the Magic Belt of the King of the Nomes, captured by the mortal girl Dorothy Gale; she had somehow acquired some small control over its vast powers and used it to first undo my enchantment, and then to transform me to the shape you see before you." He glared at the Monkey defiantly.

The Monkey gave vent to a surprisingly lilting laugh. "Oh, my dear Dove, how very entertaining a story! I have heard something of it before, in the rumors of tales that echo back to us from the Mortal world. Yet I had heard you reformed and repented of your evil."

It gave a screech more appropriate to a diving hawk than a Dove. "Repented? Of being deprived of my birthright and desiring only to ensure I could live as my ancestors had? All I regret is that I had not the knowledge to turn that thrice-accursed Dorothy Gale to stone and all her friends with her, ere she came to my door!"

"Oh, my dear, *dear* Dove, you cannot imagine how lovely those words are to hear. For know that I, too, am a victim of the mighty Ozma and her so-called justice.

"Once I was a simple housewife — a homemaker with no concerns or interests outside of my little valley. As I was also a Yookoohoo –" the Monkey smiled again as the Dove gave a start of surprise, "—I had no need of anything outside my valley. I kept to myself and invited no visitors.

"So when visitors did intrude on my valley — on my property — I felt it was not at all wrong for me to use them to assist me, since they had intruded upon *my* privacy without permission or warning."

"Oh! Oh!" the Dove cried triumphantly. "I, too, have heard rumors of you in the same way, but it seems perhaps those were more clearly translated. You were once the Giantess, Mrs. Yoop, who captured two of the heroes of the realm, the Scarecrow and the Tin Woodman, as well as a mortal boy and one of the Fairies, and when they escaped was herself transformed — into a shape, it was said, that can never be shed."

"You speak near enough the truth, Dove." The Monkey studied him intently. "Yet no enchantment is truly unbreakable, and I know of ways it might be done. I cannot work the magic of a Yookoohoo in this form, for I have never taught myself the trick of working that magic in a form not that of a Giant or a Man. But other forms of magic I might, if only I had access to the tools thereof."

The Dove was silent for long moments. Finally it shifted uneasily on the branch. "And if you had such access...?"

"Then," the Monkey said softly, "I would be very grateful and willing to assist the one who could give me such access, and thus a form able to work that magic that is mine by right."

The Dove shook his head. "Many are those who have tried this, including myself — the opposition of Ozma and her champions. They fail. They always fail."

The Monkey chittered in frustration. "Yes. And Glinda... she would read of it in her Book."

The Dove suddenly looked up. "Not true. Not true. So long as neither of us wore the form of a man or woman. The Book of Records sees only the actions of men and women, or Fairies and such that are very much like men and women. Of beasts it records not a word."

The Monkey narrowed its gaze. "But as soon as we regained our forms..."

"Yes." The Dove paused.

After a moment, the Monkey said, and its voice was soft, insistent, urgent, "But...if we made plans before we changed back..."

"We would have to repeat my original plan," the Dove said slowly. "But this time we would have to prevent any from *un*doing what we have done." He was tempted, but at the same time reluctant. *I have spent so very long making myself accept what I have become. Dare I hope? Dare I act again?*

"Could it be done?" The Monkey's voice reminded him that this had once been a woman. A giantess, but a woman nonetheless.

"Oh, yes." His voice grew stronger as things became clearer, as acid-strong hope burned away the acceptance of years. "Oh, certainly. They looted my castle, of course, but I was no more a fool than my ancestors. Copies I made of instruments and recipes, hid them in secret areas of my castle. They left the castle itself...and with your help, I could retrieve them. And then..."

"And then," the Monkey said, so quietly it was like the whisper of his own thoughts, "and then we could regain all we have lost... and more."

Prologue 2.

The door to the throne room was flung open. Framed in that huge portal was a delicate figure of a girl, fair hair wild and tangled in an unwonted manner, cap askew, gossamer garments actually rent, torn, grimy and smeared with red-brown stains that spoke of a grimmer origin.

The Rainbow Lord shot to his feet and started forward. "*Polychrome!*"

His eldest daughter walked — not danced, *walked*, with a heavy foot so unlike the tread that normally could leap from a blade of grass and leave the dew on it barely marred. "Father...Iris Mirabilis, my lord...I have returned...from the mission...on which you sent me." She clasped a bundle to her with one arm, gripped it to her like death.

He caught the exhausted girl as she staggered; fairy princess or not, she had clearly reached her limits. His heart was filled with dread, and he truly knew fear; he had hoped the thefts, so like others in the past, had been something easily dealt with...but now...

"Forget the formalities, daughter mine. Are you injured? Be these stains of *your* blood?" The thought filled him with both rage and horror. None had dared truly injure one of his children for time out of mind — not that many even had the power to attempt it.

Polychrome managed a weak smile. "No...no, Father. Any blood...is from those who pursued me."

"You *fought* them?" He knew his daughter was...unorthodox. She danced to Earth often, forgetting the Rainbow, wandering the world below until she wearied of it. Her dances were more than mere dancing, for she had modeled many of them on the training of his Storm Legions, a ballet not merely of beauty but of wind and lightning. But the thought that she not only could, but *would* fight...

"In a manner of speaking." Her voice rasped faintly, but with a touch of humor. He called immediately for wine. "I led them on a

7

merry...chase, through angered trees and invisible hazards. And evaded them many times, despite their weapons. They harried me, even to the skies above the Desert, and beyond, Father. Oh, Father!" She suddenly pressed herself into his chest and began to sob. "Oh, Father, it is all too terribly true! The Emerald City...is gone!"

For a moment his mind simply refused to accept the words. Finally he said, "What do you mean when you say 'gone,' my daughter?"

A servant appeared and proffered a goblet; Polychrome seized the Cloudwine and drank the entire goblet in one long series of swallows — something startling and worrisome, for a fairy princess who could normally subsist on a few dewdrops and mist cakes for a day or more. When she spoke again, however, her voice was smoother, and a touch of color was returning to cheeks that had been pale as morning mist.

"Grey stone, Father." She shuddered. "Grey, cold stone, all of it. For a mile and more around to the very towers of Ozma's palace, solid grey stone, and soldiers of stone and metal commanded by those who now rule from that grim mockery of what was."

He nodded slowly. The disruptions in the very essence of the air had given him much cause to worry, and the rumors had been terrifying. But to hear it from his own child... "Go on, Polychrome," he said gently. "You did not take so long, or suffer so much, only seeing this transformation. The theft of things magical, that was how this began. Was it as they believed?"

Her violet-blue eyes met his, and he saw the answer there before she spoke. "Oh, yes, Father. But far cleverer, far more dangerous. And not alone."

"And none resist this...abomination?"

"Why do you think I *stayed*, Father?" Polychrome's voice was sharp, angry, and he drew back in surprise. "Many of them were my friends! I sought for them, through the Quadling Country where I found the Palace of Glinda in ruins, to the Munchkins, fleeing in terror from the armies sent to subdue their lands. I saw the Gillikin Forest in flames!" Tears burst out anew. "Most of my friends were *in the Emerald City* when it happened! A Council of War, to determine how to locate their enemy — something their enemy had already planned upon! Ozma, Dorothy, the Cowardly Lion, the Wizard, Glinda, the Scarecrow, the Tin Woodman, all of them, all of them were there! I..." she almost broke down, but in a show of discipline and strength that almost forced tears from the Rainbow Lord's own eyes, she took hold of her voice and heart and refused them the chance to retreat. "I saw through the windows of the Palace, Father, saw the grey stone statues of the heroes of the realm, mortal girls and metal men, all stone, dead, dead stone."

"And Ozma herself?"

She nodded slowly. "Father, she is sealed within a crystal pyramid at the very doorway to the Castle, facing the great Courtyard, where she must have been caught by whatever hideous spell they used."

He was silent for a long moment; he watched as Polychrome took another goblet and sipped from it. Finally, he spoke. "You say 'they,' Polychrome Glory." He rarely used both of her names, saving that for times of great import or great tenderness...and this, he judged, was a time for both, for his favorite daughter was sorely wounded in the heart, if not in body. "Who *are* they?"

For answer, Polychrome looked down and slowly loosed her grip on the bundle she held, with a wince from the pain that comes when loosing a near-deathgrip. She brought out the oddly-shaped lumpy bundle and looked down at it. With a sigh, she reached in and removed first a long grey envelope, sealed with green wax. On it was inscribed "Iris Mirabilis, Lord of the Rainbows" in a spidery but elegant hand. Wordlessly she extended the envelope to her father.

He regarded the envelope for a moment, then broke the seal and withdrew the letter, which he read.

> **To Iris Mirabilis, Lord of Rainbows and the Seven Hues of Heaven**
> **Greetings.**
>
> **As your lovely and accomplished daughter Polychrome has seen fit to visit our realm, newly acquired, of Oz, and as there may be some confusion as to the status of this land, we send you this missive.**

9

Be it understood that all of Oz is now under our rule, and shall remain so; and that we have under our control all of the power of that land and can direct it as we will, even unto the power once belonging to Ozma its ruler, the sorceries of Glinda, the enchantments of the Wizard, and all other manner of power held here.

As Oz was and has always been the core of true Faerie power, since its blessing by Lurline ages agone, you will recognize that we are now a greater power than any other. We do not seek warfare with you or the others of Faerie or the enchanted lands above or below, but make no mistake: we shall tolerate no interference in our affairs. Leave us to ourselves, and all shall be well. Meddle, and whosoever has challenged us shall be destroyed. Each of us was vanquished once; we shall not be defeated again.

We remain, sir,

Ugu the Unbowed
King of Oz
and
Amanita Verdant
Queen of Oz

The Rainbow Lord knew his face looked like a thundercloud as he set the letter down. "So quickly has it happened...and they claim to control the power itself. But...who is this 'Amanita,' Polychrome?"

She gave another shudder, and he realized that Polychrome — his brave, undaunted, ever-cheerful daughter — was truly afraid of this unknown woman. "Who is she? I have never heard this name before, my daughter, and yet you seem afraid of her, as though you knew who she was."

"Oh, I know her, my Father. She it was who captured me once, held me prisoner, stripped me of my form and most of my power, kept me as a plaything and a pet, and would have done so perhaps forever had not others come who gave me a chance at freedom."

Shock caused him to draw in a breath. "*Her?* That monstrous Giantess, the Yookoohoo? She has taken a new name? But I thought that Princess Ozma had sealed her powers away in a form from which they could never be recovered."

"Perhaps...perhaps her old form cannot be recovered, Father. But she has a new one, a beautiful Human girl with hair green as emeralds; but I knew her when she laughed as the letter was given to me, for I had heard that laugh many times."

He remembered discovering how his missing daughter had been imprisoned. The thought of that monster loose again... "But something still seems amiss. They caught you spying, and sent you away with this letter. Why chase you and harry you near to death?"

Now Polychrome laughed, a laugh as joyful as a sudden ray of sunshine, and at the same time bright as a blade unsheathed; and he wondered at just what sort of girl he had fathered.

"Oh, not for that, Father. But for the fact that I sought allies and friends not yet imprisoned, and in the Winkie Country I found a few still fighting; but they were falling, and their King gave to me a final charge...and..." Now, for the first time, she hesitated.

"Polychrome... what is it?"

Her jaw set for a moment, and then her shoulders slumped. "He made me promise to give my charge only to you...but that I must leave the room, and am only to be told...whatever you feel I must know."

An unnamed dread began to creep over him. He held out his hand; slowly, unwillingly, the girl let him take the bundle. He removed the wrappings.

Within lay a pink stuffed bear, a small crank protruding from one side.

Others might not have recognized the significance, but the Rainbow saw many places indeed. This innocent, even silly, looking object was one of the most potent mystical objects...or beings, depending on how one viewed it...in all of Oz. The Pink Bear was a seer, a prophet, blessed or cursed with the ability to live only whenever the crank in its side was turned, and to think, and speak — and see into some place where the future, past, and present were all

11

one, where distance was meaningless and walls nonexistent, and speak of what it saw there.

"And the Lavender King..."

Polychrome turned her face away. "They torched the forests."

An appalled silence fell over the throne room. Finally he stood. "You gave your word, my daughter. You must leave the room...while I hear the last words of one monarch to another, on the fall of his allies and the loss of the greatest of the Faerie lands."

After a moment, Polychrome nodded. He gestured to the servants, who immediately came forward and helped Polychrome out; her sisters, he knew, would help tend to her as well.

He placed the Bear on the arm of his throne and placed his magic upon it; the Little Pink Bear would at least not have the indignity of relying on someone to turn that crank; it would turn itself until the Bear desired it to stop.

The little head turned jerkily, and one paw came up. "Hail, Iris Mirabilis!" the Bear said in a high, childish voice. Then its head sagged, and the eyes sparkled as though with tears. "My King is destroyed. My...father is gone."

"I know," he said softly. "And I have no words of comfort for you now, I fear. Your King and father sent you to me, in the hands of my daughter, risking her life and giving his own that she might escape, I would guess. Why?"

Answering questions was what the Bear had been created for; its duty might not be warming, but it was familiar, and easier than feeling and grief. "To guide you, to show you the way."

"There is a way to defeat these people? To restore Oz to what it should be?"

"It has not been what it should be for a long time. Mistakes were made." The little Bear's words were more complex and cryptic than normal.

"Explain, Bear."

"Much power prevents me from speaking plainly. Some is my own; I am a prophet, prophets speak as they must." The little Bear paused, then spoke again. "Balance was lost here. Balance is also lost without, in the human world. Both must be regained. Both are needed."

The Rainbow Lord nodded. The Faerie had always relied on mortals for certain things, and the mortals had in their turn been supported by the Faerie in much of their essence — even though these days they knew it less and less. "Then tell me what must be done."

"Two paths before, and the way never clear." The Bear's voice was cold and hard now, the voice of a speaker of destiny. "One brings you joy, the other filled with fear. All will hinge on the choice of one, a choice only made before it has begun."

The words continued, and as the Rainbow Lord heard the Prophecy unfold, his face became more and more grim. There were no certainties. Even the best path was fraught with danger and potential for mishaps. And in the end...it would cost him the most precious thing in all the world.

But that was the price that true Kings paid; all that they had. And more.

Chapter 1.

They're close now.

She was astounded by their speed. Over cloudscape and through brilliant ways of the sky she had met few that were her equal and none her master; even her own father could not match her in fleetness of foot across the skies.

But these were no natural beings, not even in the sense that she, a princess of Faerie, could be considered natural. Forged from spirits of dark power and bound in chains of Faerie magic, constrained to the will of others, they were living aspects of wild storm — alive, yes, thinking, yes, but not creatures that were ever meant to be. *Father had his Storm Legions, trained warriors of the heavens, and so they made their Tempests.*

Despite the peril, she laughed joyously. *At last I'm doing something. The waiting is over!*

The clouds were valleys and hills, dark-tinted with hints of storm and rain, white with touches of sun, and she danced along them, pretending she did not see the blue-black flickers of motion in the deepest shadows, the sparking crackles of hidden lightning. They were closing in, hoping to cut her off.

As she rounded a great white-blue crested cliff-face of smoke and dreams, two Tempests flowed from within the clouds depths, moving on tendrils of sickly green-tinged black, the hue of tornado and destruction. "Halt –"

Instead of pausing or slowing, she gave a great leap forward, springing high, the lowering rays of the evening sun catching her fair hair and making it flame like molten gold. The Tempests were caught unprepared, not expecting her to act so decisively and dangerously, and she landed fully six feet on the other side of them and danced onward, laughing. "I halt not until I reach my destination, you poor bound stormcloud-spirits, and I have no time to play tag with you today!"

15

Three more leapt from a slow-curling arc of white above her, slashing with crackling lightning and jagged-edged talons of night-dark mystic cloud. More serious now, but still wearing a half-pitying, half-mocking smile, Polychrome whirled aside, turned, bent like a willow; lightning missed, cursed talons caught only air, and she dealt the nearest a gentle slap that somehow unbalanced it, sent it reeling into its fellows, gave her an opening.

I have to make it to the proper point. She had to watch now, for the time was growing very near. She repeated the words of the prophecy to herself again:

> *Where three cloud-castles stand and face the sun*
> *There the Rainbow Princess ends her run;*
> *Cloud-wall ahead, dark storms behind*
> *At last the fated place she'll find.*
> *Down the Rainbow all is changed, there is no familiar ground;*
> *Only when her name is spoken shall she turn herself around*
> *And when she sees the speaker, know your hero has been found.*

It had been a job memorizing the prophecy; especially since the Little Bear would sometimes reword things when repeating it, saying that the future itself could shift. She also suspected that there were parts her father had never told her. She just hoped she remembered it all correctly now, as the future of everything might depend on her getting all of the words exactly right.

Focus on what you're doing! she reminded herself as she barely evaded two more Tempests; there were a dozen behind her now, trying to close the distance, and failing — but not failing nearly so easily as she had hoped. *There are many steps to victory, Father always said, but you can only take one step at a time, and anyone trying to take more will only trip over her own feet.*

A crackling bolt of lightning hooked just past her ear, cutting a strand of her hair, leaving it to flutter through the cloud to the ground below. Black-tendriled octopus shapes loomed through the mist ahead; she ran up the side of the billowing clouds to her left, bounced down and literally danced her way over the Tempests' stunned heads before they could react. She laughed again, the exhilaration of risk and of hope combining in a heady brew like the finest Cloudwine.

Before her clouds blazed brilliantly, reflecting the light of the setting sun... *There!*

Just to her left, she could see three mighty thunderheads in a perfect row, triple towers throwing back the light of the sun that, as she altered her course, was directly behind her — perfect conditions for a Rainbow. "And there surely are dark storms behind," she muttered.

A clear space, wisps of cirrus trailing gossamer bridges; she paused in her flight, sent a shockwave of Faerie power across, the bridges shattering behind her, Tempests plunging downward; they would recover, but they had lost precious time. *Not all of them, though...*

Now the cloud-walls loomed up like the bulwark of the world, so she would need to crane her neck to see the top, and the Tempests were coming faster. "Father!" she called. "Father, now!"

A blaze of light appeared and grew before her, a mighty bridge of seven colors forming in midair, with a second slightly dimmer but no less spectacular arch above, a bridge that Polychrome danced onto mere inches ahead of the Tempests; but no creation of dark magic could set foot on the Rainbow, and the Tempests knew it all too well. With screeches and howls of frustration and rage like hurricanes at a window, the dark and twisted beings faded away, returning to the clouds and, Polychrome knew, eventually to their Master and Mistress in Oz.

But let's not think on that, she told herself. *We're going to rescue all of Faerie soon!* Her feet knew the curve of the Bow as well as they knew the clouds of home, and she danced her way down the Rainbow. *Things* do *look different...great jumbles of buildings like I've never seen...so* many *houses...streets...what's all those things* moving *on them?*

There wasn't much time to study it, though, for her descent was fast, down the Rainbow nearly as fast as a stone might fall, to come to rest on a hard, black surface, a strange, exciting odor lingering in the air.

17

She landed in the middle of a ring of people, already staring even before she arrived. *Of course. For them, the rainbow recedes ever away, can never be caught. It's been...centuries?...since the last time Father's Rainbow came to rest with one end fully in the mortal world, centuries since I set foot here. Ever since Faerie truly began to separate itself.*

It was a bit of a jolt to realize how long it had been. She remembered that day well — the day her father had been told that the mortal and Faerie worlds would separate for some unknown time. She herself had been younger — young enough to still have sisters that were more babies than girls, and as mortals counted time that would be a long time indeed.

The Rainbow lifted up and faded, only moments after her foot touched the black surface, and the murmur of the surrounding people increased. She looked back eagerly. Which one of these would recognize her? *They all look so...strange.*

It was a warm summer's eve — though it still felt a bit brisk to Polychrome when she wasn't moving — but even so, some of the women were positively indecent! Exposing the entirety of their legs and arms wasn't enough, it seemed — they even had exposed their midriffs! And the men were not dressed that much differently. Shorts like those worn by boys, loose shirts... but no, not all of them were at all the same. She saw a couple of young women who had hair of a color that would have made more sense for Faerie, not for the mortal world. Another...man? woman?...was dressed so oddly, and wearing such makeup that Polychrome couldn't even decide which he or she was. And *black* lipstick?

She also noticed that — however much things might have changed — there were some things that hadn't. Many of the men in the circle were looking at her in a way she always thought of as "hungry." It was sometimes annoying, sometimes useful...but one difference was the openness of the gazes. Gentlemen tried to conceal it — the Wizard, for instance, had been so subtle about it that it had taken some time before she was sure he even noticed. This was much more direct...and unsettling.

A somewhat more...normal-looking man, wearing what appeared to be work pants with boots and a checkered shirt, stepped forward. "Excuse me...miss...did I just see what I think I saw?" His eyes only occasionally met her own, being busy surveying the rest of her.

She laughed. "Not being in your mind, sir, I have no idea what you think you saw, so I cannot say." The laugh chimed around the huge black expanse, which was filled with peculiar brightly colored metallic shapes — *carriages of some sort,* she realized, as she saw some of them moving in and out of the black expanse. A quick glance showed that the black lot, covered with regular lines of a bright yellow, was in the center of a U-shape of buildings — storefronts, she decided. Some kind of a market area.

"She came down out of the sky with the rainbow!" someone else said, and that seemed to break a dam; suddenly all of the people surrounding her were talking, a Babel of voices that was filled with words she couldn't recognize, many disbelieving, some overjoyed, some hostile, and a few in tones she did not like at all: "...impossible, the rainbow can't..." "...saw it, you can't deny it, a visitation..." "...like me a piece of that..." "... hey, who're you shoving?..."

The ring of faces began to contract around her, and for the first time she felt a twinge of...well, not *fear* exactly, but concern. The crowd had grown, they surrounded her five deep, six, more, and she wasn't sure she could clear all of them in one leap if it got much deeper. And she had no idea where to go now that she was here; none of this was familiar in the least. She *thought* she was somewhere on the eastern coast of the country Dorothy called America, but she wasn't even sure of that.

"...angel would have wings, wouldn't she?..." "...care what she is, she's hot..." "...people all sound crazy, and what the hell is she *dressed* in? Ought to call..."

Across the black lot she saw one of the carriages slow and turn in the direction of the crowd; her eyesight, closer to that of an eagle in some ways than of mere mortals, could make out the word *Police* on the side. *I'm not sure I want to speak to their officials; do they even* believe *in Faerie any more?*

And then, from behind her, an incredulous voice said, "*POLYCHROME?*"

19

It was a warm, deep baritone voice; she liked it immediately, and her heart seemed to leap within her. *At last!*

A smile broadening on her face, she turned to see the speaker.

Chapter 2.

I snapped the computer case shut and locked down the screws. "All set."

"Thanks, Erik." Lisa said with a tired smile. "You didn't have to _"

"No, I didn't, but it wasn't a big deal and you need that thing running tomorrow. Don't we finish the next big volume for State Legal this week?"

"Yes, you're right. But _"

"No buts." I was actually exhausted myself — repairing three machines that had chosen to, as an English acquaintance of mine used to say, go "tits up" all at once was a pain in the butt. And not, technically, my job, though at Pinebush Publishing I sort of got all the technical jobs that weren't technically mine, whenever I was around. But the exhaustion probably contributed to my being honest. "You're one of the few people I've managed to keep from offending at one point or another, so it's worth it."

Lisa blinked at me in surprise. She was a very pretty, very tall young woman of thirty, which I suppose wouldn't be young for some, but was for me — with hazel eyes and short brown-blond hair. "You've muttered things like that a couple of times before, Erik, but I honestly can't understand why. You've almost never said anything offensive in all the years you've been here."

I sighed and sat down. "Maybe *offended* isn't the right word for a lot of it. But..." I glanced at her, noticing the purse in her hand. "Do you really want to hear the answer, or do you want to get home?"

"Is it really that long?"

"That's a rather personal question, sir!" I said in a Monty Python voice, and she gave a rather unladylike snorting chuckle in response. "There's the Reader's Digest version, I guess. When I came here I had just started... growing up. Yeah, I know, I was thirty and now I'm staring at the big Five-O. Only relationship I'd had for any

21

length of time had blown up just a bit before. I had about twenty years of being a rebellious angsty teenager before I decided to reach my twenties, so I actually never figured out what the hell I wanted to do with my life — so I didn't do anything." I didn't want to go into the details — it would sound like self-pitying whining. Probably would *be* self-pitying whining. Might even be already.

"You? Angsty? Erik, I've known you since I started working here six years ago, and one thing I admire about you is that I didn't think angst and you even *knew* each other."

"Okay," I amended. "Not usually angsty, at least not where other people could see it. But interested more in having fun — of the pretty quiet geeky kind — than doing Serious Work, and..." I shook my head. "Ahhhh, never mind. I wouldn't have said anything about it if I wasn't so tired. I don't want to complain about my life; for everything bad, I've ended up with at least as much good. And what's the point of stewing over it anyway? If you don't believe in things basically working out, you'd have a pretty bleak life, I'd think. I don't understand people who walk around thinking 'the world is a dark and lonely place,' to quote something you won't know."

Lisa shook her head. "You're right, I don't, but at least let me tell you that whatever anyone else thought you should've done, everyone here is damn glad you ended up working here."

"An opinion I intend to keep earning by doing the work I can do whenever I'm around. Now get going. I'll lock up."

"All right. Will you be in tomorrow?"

"I don't think you'll need me as long as these little monsters stay fixed. See you on Friday."

She waved as she left; I grinned back and then went to wash up.

The conversation had stirred up some of my old, rare regrets. Well, no, not rare, but rarely indulged. I generally didn't see the *point* in regretting things that were past, or at least of agonizing over them. Changing the past wasn't possible, and so going back over what I should have said, or not have said, or done, was...well, like picking a scab off. There might be some strange fascination in it, but in the end you were just hurting yourself and interfering with the healing process.

I locked up the offices and went out to my car. Which didn't help, because it *used* to be my father's car, which reminded me of the whole conversation again. My dad had died not too disappointed in me — at least he'd seen I had a stable job and a reasonable chance at living out my life on my own — but my mom hadn't seen enough to know that I'd started to turn things around before she'd died during a routine examination. My brother was married, had kids, a real career, and I hadn't really managed to do anything of significance even on the family scale, despite having been the genius of the family. Not even a steady girlfriend. Or these days not even an unsteady one; all the female possibilities in my small circle of friends had already paired up, and I had no experience of how to look — and a general, gut-level aversion to *looking*, in that sense.

"Oh, bah. Cut this crap out," I said out loud to myself as I pulled out of the parking lot onto the Washington Avenue Extension and turned right. "You *did* finally get your own life, and a job you like, which is more than a lot of people manage. You don't *have* to work all that much because you've got a big cushion you inherited — which even fewer people have."

I managed a smile, which stopped feeling pasted on as I noticed the magnificent view dead ahead of me: three immense thunderheads towering over Albany. I love storms, always have, and these looked like they might be delivering a doozy to the Capital Region.

And, I continued to myself, *you may not ever have achieved your pipe dream of being a writer, but you still give people some fun through your imagination as a gamer. Which, again, is more than a lot of people manage.*

A part of me would always feel I was a failure, I knew, but I wasn't going to let that part dominate. I had a decent life, and it was stupid and nonproductive — and ultimately self-destructive — to insist to myself that I should have Done Something Special. Especially since *that* part of me wouldn't even be satisfied if I'd done everything my parents had hoped for; no, *that* part of me was the part that had never finished growing up and wanted to change the world in the kind of way that simply didn't happen.

23

"There *isn't* any magic in the real world." I reminded myself, and then with a sudden grin, corrected myself. "Except *that.*"

"That" was one of the most magnificent rainbows I had ever seen, now looming over the city in the almost-setting summer sunshine slanting over the city. Rainbows *were* pure magic to me, whispering in my mind of the Bifrost Bridge and Hermes on his messenger duties, of promises of gods and leprechauns and other things, some very near to my heart. And this was an amazing rainbow, fairly blazing against the dark undersides of the clouds beyond, a second, nearly as intense bow paralleling it, a hint of a third visible at points. One end looked as though it came down in Watervliet, the other much nearer, not far from the side of I-90 — somewhere around Westgate Plaza. I drove homeward towards that brilliant arch, pretending that I would be driving under it.

Then I almost drove off the road as I realized two things:

The setting sun was *ahead* of me...and so was the rainbow. And the rainbow *was* getting closer.

Impossible, I thought, staring even as I forced myself back into one of the driving lanes. *Rainbows are only visible with the light* behind *you! They're products of light reflected back at you. They're an illusion, they can't ever be caught up to! If the rain got more intense, it* might *make a rainbow look like it was getting closer for a few moments...but* look *at that thing!*

The mighty rainbow's arch now rose so high that I had to crane my neck to see it — while constantly glancing back down to make sure I didn't hit anyone — and the colors were so strong and *real* that they obscured even the brilliant white of the thunderclouds' tops behind them. *It's impossible, but I'm* seeing *it.*

And I found myself passing *under* the rainbow, one end disappearing in trees to the left, the other coming down not half a mile off... *My God, it* is *in Westgate!*

I took the Everett Road exit at a dangerously high speed considering the wet pavement, but the little Subaru only skidded a bit. More dangerous were the other gawkers. Most people might not understand *why* the rainbow can't get closer or why it's only visible with the sun over your shoulder, but most people *do* know it can't happen, and there were quite a few people following this same route to find out what was going on.

The end of the bow was off to the right now, huge as the Golden Gate Bridge and awesome as Niagara Falls, stretching up into the infinite sky. I was at Central Avenue, turning, but now the bow was fading. "No, no, no, *no, NO!*" I shouted hopelessly, as I saw it lifting, dwindling, disappearing, gone. I was at the entrance to the Plaza, but the rainbow had disappeared, leaving everything once more dull and ordinary and the same.

No, wait, not quite. There was a ring of people gathered in the middle of the parking lot — I couldn't even imagine what it must have been like to be standing around the rainbow's end — and...

I skidded the car to a stop, sitting across two spaces diagonally, and practically leaped out. There was something or someone in the middle of that circle. I couldn't make it out, but...

"Excuse me...sorry...Let me *through!*" I muttered as I bulled my way into the ring of spectators, which seemed to be at least five or six people deep by now. Whoever it was in the middle — it *was* a person — they were not very big...moving around a lot, rhythmically, almost dancing –

No. It can't *be.*

I felt a terrible chill of awe and joy, and terror that I might be utterly insane, that only grew worse as I drove through the crowd, now not even hearing the protests around me, drawn forward. It simply wasn't *possible*...

But there was a flash of violet-blue eyes as she spun, laughing, answering some question, a face seen in that moment of such beauty that I could not even imagine words to describe it, golden hair drifting like rays of sunshine around a gauzy-veiled body I didn't dare look at, hair bound only by a simple black cap, and delicate feet dancing, moving, following a phantom music that seemed in turn to follow her own motions.

I slowed and stopped at the edge of the crowd, unable to approach closer for fear that to approach would shatter the impossibility into the dull awakening moments of morning. But the feelings could not be restrained, and I heard myself speak, my voice strained with wonder, and awe, and a pure incredulous joy:

25

"POLYCHROME?"

I saw a radiant smile dawning on her face as she turned towards me. Then her gaze reached me, and the smile... faltered. It did not... quite...go away, but it was clear that she'd been expecting someone, and that someone wasn't me. *Well, big surprise there. Of course she wasn't expecting some overpadded, over-the-hill Oz fanboy.*

The real question — assuming that I wasn't dreaming or totally nuts — was what the hell she was doing here at all. I couldn't remember any instance of Polychrome showing up outside of Faerie at all.

She took a step forward, towards me, and even though the fading of the smile had thrown a little cold water on my original dizzying elation, just that motion brought a lot of it back. "Sir? Do you...know me?"

"As surely as I know Dorothy and Ozma and Button-Bright, Lady Polychrome," I answered, feeling that some faux-formality would at least allow me to keep from babbling like a loon.

Her lovely brow wrinkled — just a touch — as though she were thinking, trying to work something out. Then her face smoothed out, and I caught a tiny movement of her shoulders, a shrug. "Then I must speak with you, sir. Might I know your name?"

The crowd was starting to look at me, too. *Oh-oh. And there's a cop getting out of his car to see what's going on.*

"In a moment — for now, I think we need to go somewhere quieter!" I prayed she'd understand.

Fortunately, her quick gaze showed she was already thinking along those lines. "Surely, sir."

Suddenly her hand was in mine; I felt my heart stop as it prepared to leap out of my chest, but then I forgot that as I found myself leaping for real, carried by a spectacular jump that cleared most of the crowd. I landed slightly off and stumbled, but recovered. I realized she was just going to run, and pulled back; given how easily she'd seemed to lift and carry me, I was startled by how suddenly she jolted to a halt, as though I'd been stopping a toddler. "Not that way — here!"

She blinked at the car — *Of course, she probably never saw one in her entire life* — but when she saw me yank open the door on my

26

side, she simply nodded and leapt to the other side, pulling the door open and sliding into the passenger seat in a single fluid motion like a leaf settling to the ground. *Thank God I cleaned the car this weekend. It's still kinda messy, but at least there's room in the passenger seat.*

I started the engine and put the car in gear. The crowd had started to follow but none of them seemed inclined to get in the way, and the cop was just running around the side of the crowd...

I pulled out fast, heading for the main exit. For once, I was lucky with this light; it was pure green, and I went straight through. I could get into a maze of streets in that direction pretty quick, and *this* wasn't something I wanted to explain to anyone. I heard Polychrome give a delighted laugh as we accelerated, apparently enjoying the novel sensation of a self-propelled vehicle. Glancing in the rearview, I could see that there were no cars following me.

With the immediate crisis over, it finally began to sink in. *What the hell have I just gotten into?*

Erik Medon

Chapter 3.

It does make sense, in a way, Polychrome thought as she studied the man who had recognized her. *The prophecies may be vague, but there is quite a bit in there about the lack of certainty of success, about the hero having to find himself.*

She felt a slight chill that had nothing to do with her usual need for warmth, a chill running through her heart. *And a lot about the possible paths of failure, starting with the first day we meet.*

He wasn't *all* that bad-looking, she supposed. A bit too heavy, hair unfortunately retreating — though not nearly so much as the poor Wizard's, which had effectively given up the fight except at the perimeter of his head — but under that a square jaw, some solidity to the shoulders. The face looked nice — some small worry lines, but it looked like his face creased more often in smiles. Behind the rather thick glasses in bright silver frames, the eyes that occasionally glanced at her but were focused mostly on directing the course of this strange vehicle were a clear blue. But he *was* rather a great deal older than she had expected. Most people who found their way to Faerie were young; the few older ones had some connection to Faerie before they arrived — even the Wizard, though he had never guessed it; the Shaggy Man had his Love Magnet, and the other older people she knew of had been brought there in the company of, or due to the actions of, younger people.

But from what her father had said, it was utterly impossible that this man had any connection with Faerie. He *couldn't*, or all their hopes would be for nothing.

Seeing that they were now moving (at a very impressive speed) steadily along some very wide roadway, she decided it should be safe to speak. "And now that we are safely away, sir, may I have your name?"

At her voice, she saw a paradoxical expression: he smiled, yet a tenseness lurked at the corners of his mouth, along with almost a hint of fear; but she didn't think he was afraid of her — no man she'd ever known was, unless she meant them to be.

"My name is Erik Medon, Lady Polychrome." He spoke formally, his gaze flicking to her face and then away. *He's making a very great effort, now that I think of it, to look nowhere else. Well, he's trying to be a gentleman, even if it seems that this is rare here.*

"Just Polychrome, if I may call you Erik," she said with a small laugh. *Yes, the laugh was right. Worries are not my province, nor things to concern one of Faerie.*

"Please do...Polychrome."

She heard the echo in his voice of the same disbelieving joy that had filled it when first he spoke her name. *I like that.* "Thank you for your timely arrival, Erik. I am not sure I liked the looks of all those people." *How to bring us to the right discussion...I need to understand him. But there is so little time!*

He chuckled and his smile looked more natural. "Mobs are not comfortable things to be around, and people don't always react well to things they don't understand," he said, tacitly agreeing. "But, if you'll pardon me for jumping straight to the point, you said you needed to speak with me. And you seemed to be expecting someone when I spoke, though — obviously — you weren't expecting *me.*"

Well, that solves that problem. Polychrome nodded. "I was expecting you, actually...I just didn't have any idea who you were."

He frowned in thought for a moment, and then his brow cleared. "I see. You were following a prophecy."

That startled her. "Well-thought, Erik! You have hit exactly upon it!"

Another surprise was the slight blush that touched his cheeks at the compliment. "Oh, that didn't take much thinking. Seen the scenario enough in the books I've read. You came here with the knowledge that you needed to meet someone at a particular place... hmm...and obviously it had to be whoever it was that first recognized you, since as soon as I spoke your name you knew it had to be me." The vehicle was crossing over a very high bridge now, and she looked down from a dizzying height at a great brown river below. Erik continued, "So...what is it you need to find me for? And of course the other question is, when am I going to wake up?"

"As to the second, you are very much awake right now. Is magic and Faerie so much forgotten now that you think this could only be a dream?"

"Forgotten? As far as people today are concerned, there never was such a thing. The few people who do believe in magic...well, they believe in something very different from anything even *vaguely* like the Faerie of Oz, and nowhere is there any real evidence it ever existed. To be honest...even the Oz books themselves are fading from most people's memories. Most people who know the word associate it with a single movie that wasn't even an accurate adaptation of the book."

He turned them onto a ramp leading to another street. "And as far as the world I know is concerned, the Oz stories were just that, stories, no connection to any reality. With you *here*, of course, I now know that isn't at all true. Baum, and possibly Neill, had to know *something* about the reality of Faerie. Assuming I'm not dreaming this whole thing, which is something that I am hoping is not true with a desperation you could not even begin to imagine."

The intensity of the last words demanded a reassurance, and she laughed. "You are not dreaming, Erik Medon, and there will be no awakening to a world in which you have not met me in that strange black field of horseless carriages. Although," she continued more soberly, "you may well come to wish that you would awaken, for in the end this may be more nightmare than dream."

"Having met you and learned that Faerie is real?" Now *he* laughed, loudly, a cheerful, free sound that seemed to lighten the air around her. "Polychrome, that would take something much darker than I can imagine." He turned the wheel and brought the vehicle to a stop in a driveway next to a small white house. "And I can imagine quite a bit." The last part sounded almost as though he was quoting something.

Erik came around to open the door and hand her out — though in a way that showed he was utterly unused to this sort of formality or courtesy. "Thank you, Erik. So this is your home?"

He nodded, looking slightly worried. "Um, realize that I live here alone, so, well, I don't keep things very neat most of the time. Okay, just about *any* of the time."

31

This was something of an understatement, she found, as the door opened and he turned on what appeared to be electric lights. The rooms were *cluttered*, mostly with books and papers piled here and there. It wasn't, as she'd momentarily feared, a place of unhealthy litter, and as she wandered, dancing idly, through the various rooms, she suddenly recognized it as the same kind of disorganized, omnipresent clutter she'd seen in the Wizard's private rooms on occasion, or those of other men of education and no family; the sign of a thoughtful man, though not a very *organized* one. *Maybe the mess...isn't a bad sign*, she thought. *He reads a great deal; he thinks and writes, I can see. His mind is quick. Maybe...*

He blocked her entry to one room. "Definitely *not*."

She giggled. "Ah, your own room. Fear not, I will not invade such a secret lair." She danced back to what was clearly the sitting or living room; he stepped ahead of her and removed several stacks of books from a large, overstuffed chair.

"Now that we're here, Polychrome...& he said slowly, watching her sit (and still clearly keeping his eyes locked on her face, though she suspected that he had not managed to keep his eyes so elevated while following her), "what brings you here?"

"Well..." To her surprise, for a moment Polychrome found herself speechless. *How in the world do I begin?*

Surprisingly, he seemed to understand. "Let me see if I can help a little," he said. "You know I've read the Oz books — how else could I have known who you were? — but realize, I'm not so naïve as to believe that every detail in those books is accurate. My guess is that Baum toned some things way down — because they were children's books — and a lot of other things got tweaked either for the sake of a story, or to fit his own beliefs. So don't worry about shocking me with facts that don't fit those books." He stepped towards the kitchen. "I know you don't eat much at all, but I need to grab me something."

I just don't know how to start. She looked at the faint shadows moving as he rummaged through the...refrigerator?...that seemed to store a lot of food. *Especially when I have to eventually get to the part where I tell him...*

But *that* wasn't something to dwell on. When she got to that part, she'd just have to go straight through and say it before she lost her nerve. Which wasn't at *all* usual with her, but then, this whole thing was very unusual.

As he came back in, eating a rather thick sandwich of some sort, she decided abruptly that it was best to go straight to the heart of things. "Oz has been destroyed."

With a comical widening of the eyes, Erik gasped. This was unfortunate as he also had a large bite of sandwich in his mouth at the time. He gagged, tried to speak, and in a panic Polychrome ran over, pounding him on the back. *Oh, by the Seven Hues, what could I tell Father? "I'm sorry, I accidentally made our hero choke himself to death?"*

Suddenly the food dislodged, he swallowed and took a deep breath that had a strange, whistling undertone. "Sokay, okay," he said, waving her back. From his pocket he took a yellow, shiny object shaped something like the letter "L" and stuck one end in his mouth, pressing with the other; there was a quick *hiss* and he inhaled, then held his breath for a few seconds. "Sorry," he said finally, "that kind of thing sometimes triggers an attack. Asthma," he said, as she shot him a questioning gaze. "My lungs don't always like to do their job and will choke up on me." He shook his head, then sat down in a nearby, smaller chair. "What exactly do you mean, Oz is *destroyed?*"

"The land itself is still there." She tried to find the right words. "But it is no longer the Oz you have read of — even allowing for what those books did not tell you."

He had an odd smile for a moment as she spoke, then his expression grew more serious. "Was this a...natural change, for want of a better word?"

To her own surprise, she found herself hesitating. She *knew* that it hadn't been natural in any sense of the word... yet he clearly had a very good reason for asking... And a part of her felt that there might be something important behind that question, something her father might have understood better than she. But she shook her head.

"No. Conquest. And you need to realize that Oz...is the center of Faerie. Those who hold it are more powerful than the rest, and

33

the condition of Oz can affect the rest of us. And perhaps rebound upon your own people."

The blue eyes narrowed as he nodded his head, and for a moment she saw a strategist, leaning over a map. "Or, perhaps, what is done here rebounds upon your own."

That...is not far from something Father said. "There are... connections between our worlds, according to my Father. So you may be right."

"Okay, Polychrome." He spoke with a new tone, someone listening to a problem and looking for understanding. "Start from the beginning. Tell me how it happened, who was responsible, and then how I come into all this."

Maybe...maybe he can *help.* She drew a deep breath. "It began when there were...thefts..."

Chapter 4.

Focusing on what Polychrome was telling me wasn't easy at first. I may not have *had* many lady companions, especially in the last few years, but I was very, very far from unaware of the attractions of the opposite sex; given my commonly-noted lack of maturity, perhaps overly much so in some ways. And there was no girl or woman I'd ever met who could compare to Polychrome.

I think I had managed a heroic feat in keeping my eyes fixed on hers most of the time we talked, and never letting them drop below the neckline, but the couple of times I'd followed her I had lacked such a clear focal point and I had studied that view much more intensely than was probably proper. And, of course, I have excellent peripheral vision, so even her frontal view was fairly clear — too much so, in some ways. Neill had captured much of Polychrome's *essence* correctly in his pictures, or I'd never have recognized her — the ethereal delicacy of her basic build, the sunshine-golden hair that floated unconfined yet never in the way, her curiosity, her joy — but the real Polychrome was not the almost fainting hothouse flower that the pictures conveyed. Her stormy-violet eyes were merry and bright and intensely *alive*, her face beautiful but far *stronger* than Neill's artwork had allowed, her figure much more... intriguing than I suspect had been *permitted* when those pictures were drawn.

It did not help *at all* that Neill's drawings had been *entirely* accurate in depicting her gauzy, near-transparent, diaphanous clothing. It wasn't — quite — transparent, but as most guys know, sometimes a tantalizing *hint* of a view is as riveting as a full exposure. Even her scent was maddeningly distracting, a combination of flowers and thunderstorms, and a nigh-subliminal *song* seemed to follow her, a phantom music that echoed her actions and moods.

It was also not helping that I was terribly aware of how poorly I compared to her or any men she must know — both in general appearance and in the semi-squalor of my bachelor existence. Only

Ryk E. Spoor

the oddities of the high-tech era managed to make my place look different than she might have expected. But she was talking and serious now, and with another supreme effort I drove all those thoughts to the background and focused every mental faculty on her problem. *For whatever incredible reason, she has come here to find you. This is that impossible chance you've been waiting for all your life. Don't blow it.*

The initial *modus operandi* of the unknown attackers was clearly familiar, and she confirmed it shortly. The immediate aftermath was grim.

I nodded. Of the various so-called villains in most of the Oz books, these were the two who — once I allowed for the shifted imagery in the children's versions — were undoubtedly the most formidable, intelligent, capable of long-term planning, and of nursing an intense grudge against all Oz. "Yeah, the ending of *Lost Princess* never rang true to me, even as a kid. I just couldn't see Ugu suddenly reforming that way. He never showed any sign of really caring about other people, and I think that level of reforming takes a lot more than just a few weeks of thinking," I said. Another thought struck me. "I'm betting they also got themselves a few more allies, among others that Ozma's regime had stepped on."

"You go fast, and well." The quick smile she gave, lighting up the grave face, and the swift *glissando* of bright notes amid the muted, somber background strains sent another spurt of joy through my heart all out of proportion to the words. "But they reserved the vast majority of power for themselves, and none would be foolish enough to gainsay them."

"Why didn't they change Ozma to stone also?"

Her smile was suddenly more cynical. "Because Ozma is the true heart of Oz, granted that power through her birth line, in direct descent from the Faerie Queen Lurline. Turning her to stone would weaken the power of Oz overall, reduce the value of their prize. Imprisoning her in that mystic cage leaves her helpless, trapped in a dream that permits her only the vaguest awareness of the situation, her power sealed such that it can only be used by her captors — and even that indirectly, in that she cannot prevent them from making use of Oz's power."

36

"So she wasn't actually in Lurline's band to begin with? I was always confused about that — Baum's tales didn't leave it clear."

Polychrome shook her head. "Ozma is a child from the point of view of any Faerie. It was required that there be both mortal and Faerie blood on the throne of Oz, so that both sides were represented at this, the core of all Faerie. She is descended of a line of rulers." She smiled again. "And as I think you have already guessed, his early tales oft held more of truth in them than the latter tales."

"It did strike me that way — no money? A perfect socialist state? And all the evil gone except in out-of-the-way benighted places?" I grinned, then grew serious. *I think we've still been dancing.* "But you still haven't told me...where do I come in?"

Now I saw real worry on her face, and the sound was of foreboding horns far off in a darkened fog. "Well...you know I was following a prophecy. A man of your talents already guessed that the prophecy led to you."

"Hard though that is to believe — and I can imagine your disappointment."

She flushed, a lovely rose hue that if possible made her even more beautiful than she had been. "Well...I..."

"Don't try to apologize, Polychrome. I would never have picked *myself* for hero material — as opposed to *dreaming* of it — and if you *weren't* surprised and disappointed, well, you would have been seeing things *I* don't in myself."

She was silent for a moment, as though she wanted to protest but couldn't think of any convincing way to do so. Then she sighed. "Yes. But as I have thought on the prophecy – or *prophecies*, for really it's more than one, a string of several pieces more than a single epic of foretelling – I think I see that someone like you was exactly what the Little Bear was describing." She stood and turned away from me toward the window, gazing into the darkness. "And there isn't any certainty, yet. Or, really, none until the ending. The prophecies make clear that we can fail. That, perhaps, we are far more likely to fail than to win through. And..." she hesitated.

I had a feeling I wasn't going to like the answer, but I asked, "And? What is it?"

"And the first chance to fail is...tonight."

I had a feeling there was more to it, but that was bad enough. "*Tonight?*" I glanced around involuntarily, wondering if something was lurking in the shadows already. "No offense, but what the hell will I be able to do in the next few hours that will determine ultimate victory or defeat?"

She looked sincerely sorry, pained, a touch of mourning violins. "It's...the prophecies, Erik. Now that I've found you, the next part has to be fulfilled, and as it was told me, that is:

> *To the Rainbow's Daughter a beauty will be shown*
>> *Might and mortal glory as she has never known*
> *Set her feet to dancing, until they've skyward flown*
>> *Through the skies and homeward to stand before*
> *the Throne.*

I blinked. "So let me get this straight. *I* am supposed to show *you* beauty such as you have never known?" I could not keep total incredulity from my voice.

She bit her lip. "I...don't see any other way to read that prophecy, Erik. And the following stanza was:

> *If no joy by dawning, if no dancing glory felt*
>> *Hope is gone now, shattered, lost*
>>> *Like first snow's fading melt.*
> *Return you to the palace and prepare you for the end*
>> *For mortal heart has withered*
>>> *And Faerie has no friend.*

"Oh. Okay. So in the next..." I checked my watch. "Um... lessee, it's about nine, and the sun rises tomorrow at around 5:40, so in the next, oh, eight or nine hours all I have to do is show you some incredible beauty that sets you to dancing, or I've doomed all Faerie. No pressure."

She gave a sympathetic giggle. "No, none at all."

Holy Jesus. I was utterly appalled. How was it *possible* that someone like me could be the key to this mystery? Even worse, how could it be that by *not* meeting this criterion I'd doom all Faerie? "...for mortal heart has withered,. and Faerie has no friend." The whole thing implied that there was in fact something special about *me* that would be difficult or impossible to duplicate — that is, finding another person that would fit those qualifications would take too long, or — worst case — there simply *wasn't* anyone else with those qualifications.

One good thing about this new wrinkle was that I was finding it a lot easier to concentrate. "'When a man knows he is to be hanged in the morning, it concentrates his mind wonderfully,'" I said, slightly misquoting Johnson. "Poly — you don't mind, I hope, if I call you that?"

"Not at all. My friends mostly do."

"Poly, that last verse...that means that there has to be something specifically about *me* that's unique. Trivially that's of course true — my genetic structure, exact personality, all of that is unique — but I find it hard to believe that it's *that* which is so important. Do you know any more about what about *me* is supposed to be unusual?"

She looked as though she were having an internal debate, then nodded. "First...Erik, understand that there are things I know that I can only tell you at particular times. And there are things that *I* haven't been told, and won't be maybe ever, or only whenever I'm supposed to. My father is the *only* one who's heard the whole of the prophecies of the Little Bear, and the way the prophecies work..." She sighed again. "Just telling the wrong person the wrong part could ruin the entire thing. I suppose it *might* end up making things better, but I would be very unwilling to risk it."

I nodded. "Just as long as all of you also remember the old, old problem of prophecies biting people on the, er, nether regions because they took actions trying to either avoid the prophecy or make it come true too literally."

"Oh, believe me, Erik, we are all too aware of that. It's one of Father's biggest worries, and the Little Bear can't clarify things too much." She followed me as I started sorting through books, looking for something that might give me an idea as to what kind of "beauty" I might show her that she wouldn't already have seen. "But there are a few things I can tell you. The most important is that you're supposed to be pure mortal, not more than the faintest trace of Faerie in you."

I glanced at her. "That's unusual? You've had people like Dorothy, Cap'n Bill, all of them there –"

"Most of them aren't pure mortal. Most people who end up in Oz or other parts of Faerie have at least *some* trace of Faerie in them. Often quite a bit."

"Really? You mean most of the mortals in the Oz books are–?"

"– part Faerie, though often a very, very *small* part. It's one reason many of them didn't have parents or were missing at least one parent. Such people often get...lost, between worlds, especially if something distracts them from their anchor in this world, or if they encounter some passing magic. The cyclone that picked up Dorothy on her first venture had some spirits playing in it – against the laws of Faerie, I'll note! – and that brought her across."

"So I'm supposed to be purely mundane, then."

Poly smiled. "Don't sound disappointed. There's nothing wrong with it, and according to Father you should find it an advantage in many ways, though exactly *what* those advantages are he's not discussing until you arrive."

The thought of "arriving" at the palace of the Lord of Rainbows was still mindboggling. But that wasn't going to happen if I couldn't figure out what I could show her.

I was connected to the Internet, which gave me access to an awful lot of possibilities. Computers themselves were pretty impressive. But *impressive* wasn't the key here. I shrugged. Nothing for it but to try to find something.

I showed her pictures of just about everything I could think of. I showed her television and modern sculptures and paintings of old masters, video games and clips of movies, parades and models, clothing old and new, mountains and jungles and ancient ruins.

A lot of things she found silly, quite a few were fascinating, others nothing special; after all, as I should have realized, in her past visits to the mortal world she'd probably seen every type of natural wonder *we* had. It was the newer material that interested her at all – things invented since the era of the early Oz novels. But none of them really touched her sense of *beauty*.

There were a couple of moments where I thought there was *something*. She spent a fascinated moment looking at a picture of the Twin Towers, marveling at how huge it was, a chiming of wondrous bells echoing for an instant in her sourceless following themes. A picture of the gaudy Las Vegas Strip held her attention for a few seconds. But nothing *quite* managed.

I knew I was missing something, something crucially important, not just to me or her, but everyone in the world, if my guess of the connection between Faerie and the mundane world was anything like the truth. There were moments I *almost* had it, but in desperately grasping for that clue it evaporated, disappeared like morning mist or like a dream that seemed so clear upon awakening, but as you try to remember the details they become less and less until you are left with nothing but a vague memory and disappointment.

I glanced at the clock on the wall. *12:55.* "Poly...look, I know you don't need much rest, but you've had a busy day, and you might as well get some. I'm the one who has to figure this out, and maybe I'll do that better alone. I'll come get you if I get any ideas."

She gave me a grave look — mixed, I thought, with sympathy as well as concern — but nodded. I showed her to my one guest room (which was, fortunately, clean, as I rarely used it), then went back to my study.

Think, man. The prophecy makes it clear that there is *something you* could *show her. You just have to* find *it.*

The problem was that I was running out of ideas. Oh, there were things I could *envision* that might do the trick, but they simply weren't available here. "Damn me for being such a *geek*." I muttered. "It may have made me able to recognize her, but almost everything I have or do is on a damn computer or in a book. And there's nothing around here more impressive than she's already seen. I don't have *TIME!*"

I started taking books off the shelf, flipping through them, but it was a measure of desperation. Books wouldn't do it. Videos wouldn't, either. There was something completely different about seeing something on even the best wide-screen and seeing it in person, but what I was missing I didn't know. Walking quietly so as

41

to not awaken Polychrome, I went through the house one room at a time, seeking some clue, something that would bring out that vague, half-formed idea and make it solid. Minutes passed. Tens of minutes. An hour. Two.

I wandered through the attic, seeing dusty packed boxes that I hadn't opened in years, standing in the barely adequate gloom of the streetlight like an abandoned city under a dead moon. I turned, seeing the flash of the light against the darkness, then froze.

That's it. Almost it. What am I...

The buildings. she'd looked at buildings. But no, that couldn't be it. she'd *seen* Albany as we drove across the bridge on our way here. But...somehow, that was it. *The Las Vegas Strip...*

And suddenly I had it. The one chance I had, the one possibility in the real world that I had ignored, that she *couldn't* have ever seen, the one thing that just might work. I was downstairs in a flash, throwing things into a backpack, checking my pockets — keychain with light, mini-laser pointer, Swiss Army knife, wallet, couple of inhalers — thinking desperately fast, writing a note to leave on the table for whoever finally came in after me. *After all, if this doesn't work out, I can always just come back this morning and go back to normal. No one else will read it if nothing happens.* I looked up at the clock. *3:30.*

I rapped gently on the door; it opened almost immediately. My memory had already started to fade the immediacy of her own beauty, and seeing her again made me momentarily speechless. "Yes, Erik?"

"Um." I shook myself. "Come on, Polychrome. I have one possibility. You have to promise to just do what I say for the next few minutes. Will you trust me?"

She studied me for a minute, then gave me the smile that seemed to go straight through my heart. "Yes. I will."

"Okay. Then I want you to close your eyes and keep them closed until I tell you to open them. I'm going to take you to the car, and we're going somewhere. It's not far away, but I want you to promise to keep your eyes closed until I say. Okay?"

"Understood, Erik."

42

Taking her hand to lead her into the car was almost too much. I was so charged with adrenalin, loss of sleep, hope and worry that just touching her sent a tingle up my arm. Her hand was silky as rose petals, yet I could feel a strength in it, the strength that had carried me over the heads of a crowd of people, delicacy combined with immortal power. *Don't lose focus!*

We got to the car and I made sure she was properly buckled in, then put the car in gear. I knew where I was going, heading up Route 4, to the point where the bridge over I-90 gave one of the best vantage points. The road streamed by, black in the headlights, streetlights flicking regularly by.

"Still keep my eyes closed?" Polychrome asked.

"Still. Just a few more minutes." *Just ahead...*

I pulled off to the side shortly before the bridge. "Hold on. I'll get you out."

The night air was cooler, and I knew that to her it would be cold, but either way it wouldn't be long now. I led her to the best location, took a deep breath and gave a wordless prayer to whatever powers there might be. "Okay, Polychrome. Open your eyes."

She opened her eyes...and gasped.

Before her was the city of Albany — but not the city as she'd seen it in the light of day, an impressive but somewhat dingy-grungy pile of masonry, buildings jumbled together, showing all the warts all too clearly in the sunlight. This was a magnificent blaze of light in the darkness, the mighty five hundred foot main tower of the South Mall alight with a thousand brilliant tiny squares of luminance, four smaller towers shining next to it, the curve of the Egg outlined in reflected glory, the rest of the city adding to it, standing against the surrounding night, a mighty beacon of edges and beams and hard-cut stone defying the power of darkness. In daylight it had been merely a city; with the cloak of night and the infinite brilliance of electricity, it became a symbol.

"Ohhh..." she sighed, eyes wide, harps and bells beginning to resound in the remotest distance. Slowly, hardly able to take her gaze from the city, she turned. "You...you *built* this?"

"*Me?* No, I only wish. But *we* did, my lady Polychrome. THAT is the power and the glory of my people, Poly, and if that will not suffice than there is nothing more I have to give."

"*Suffice?*" she repeated, and I heard tears in her voice, saw a glitter in her eye, and a rising crescendo of trumpets and drums, a chorus of triumphal voices, resounded in her words. "Oh, Erik, it is *beautiful!*"

And, surrounded by the ethereal music, Polychrome began to dance.

Chapter 5.

He *did it. He DID it!* For a moment, Polychrome was so filled with joy that she could do nothing but dance in the darkness, the song in her heart echoed by the Music of the Spheres, trying to give to her dance the ascending glory and defiant, mortal pride and courage that glorious City represented. She laughed, and saw his face looking up at her as she floated lightly in the air, and for a moment, she wondered at what she saw there; he seemed transfigured by her own joy, his blue eyes exultant yet wide and filled with something she could not quite recognize, something that made her miss a step, stumble subtly, an uneven movement that a mortal might not notice, but that was the clumsiest motion she had made in centuries.

But there is still so far to go, she reminded herself, and took hold of her joy. It was still there — at long last, they could at least begin, the hope was not gone — but they had to move, and move swiftly. She extended her hand. "Dance with me, Erik."

He stared at her and blushed. "Um... Dance? I wish I could, but me dancing with you would be like trying to get a hippopotamus to do acrobatics with a dragonfly — the hippo would look ridiculous and the dragonfly might get squashed by accident."

She laughed and took his hand. "Oh, I am *sure* you are not quite *that* bad, Erik, even if you have never danced in all your life. And really, it's necessary."

He took her hand gingerly, as though afraid to break her, and she extended her fingers, gripped tightly. "I am not a porcelain doll, Erik Medon, nor a dragonfly to be crushed easily. Now follow the motions."

He's definitely never danced as I know it, she thought, as he tried to follow her steps. *But he does have some sense of rhythm, not entirely unschooled in musical beats...*

Erik seemed to finally recognize the movements, at least in essence, following the music as it followed her. Not perfect, not

45

nearly so graceful as even one of the Storm Guards, but not so bad as she had feared or he had implied. "So...this is necessary?"

She smiled at his puzzled expression. "Very necessary. You see, only by dancing our way through the sky will we be able to reach my Father's realm. He cannot send another of his Bows here to the mortal realm, not so soon after the last; there are many reasons for that. But I have my own magic that — if you allow it, if you are part of it — can bring us where we need to go."

"Dance through the sky?" he repeated incredulously, eyes still fixed upon hers as they had been ever since he took her hand. "Poly, really, there's just no way that could happen. Not with me, two left feet and all."

She giggled and swept one hand outward. "But Erik... you already *are* doing it."

He glanced down and gasped, stopping for a moment, forcing her to continue to dance around him. Beneath them a ghostly, circular rainbow light rippled like a spectral dance floor, but beneath that lay air, hundreds, thousands of feet of air, sparkling lights like Faerie itself dusting the land below. She laughed aloud at the wonder in his face, and again as she saw neither fear nor denial but a blaze of joy like the dawn in his face. "We're *flying!*"

"Air-walking, dancing in the clouds, yes, even flying, Erik, that we are, on and within that which is my middle name, as long as you have the heart to see it with wonder as I hear in your voice."

"Within...the glory," he said, wonderingly. "Polychrome Glory..." His eyes met hers again for a bright needle-sharp moment, and then he seized her hand and *led* her in a dance, a crude dance but one of energy and sincerity that she cheerfully threw herself into wholeheartedly. "Oh, Polychrome, you – you have no idea. To fly among the clouds...this is one of my dreams. Since I can remember!"

His joy was contagious and echoed her hope, and she saw the glory following his feet as it followed her own, resonating between them as though he had, somehow, always known. Erik glanced ahead and his own smile broadened. "Can we dance to the top of that tower, Lady Polychrome? Will I be able to make it that far?"

In the silver of moonlight and the approaching deep rose of dawn, a mighty thunderhead loomed in the distance, an argent mountain of misted rubies. "That far and farther, Erik, for beyond that a thousand miles and ten lies the castle of my Father — a thousand miles, and closer than a few heartbeats."

He said nothing, but his eyes shone, and for a moment she saw how he must have looked ten, twenty, perhaps even thirty years before, sharp gaze filled with wonder and a happiness unadulterated by any doubt or fear.

But as they climbed the misty billows, leaping from one height to the next in a dreamlike series of leaps, she saw a flicker of light to one side, far away. Dim and small, but the violet-against-darkness was unmistakable. *A Tempest.*

"Erik...we must keep our eyes open. Remember what I said about my journey here."

It was odd; for a moment, she could have sworn that his face lit up *more* as he realized the implications. But it might have been her imagination, for his expression became grim almost instantly. "You saw something?" He glanced around, eyes scanning the area.

"Only one, and far away. It may not have seen us yet. And they would be scattered far and wide now, knowing that I may travel far from my landing spot ere I return. But I am afraid we need be on our guard. You...are not a warrior, I can see, and I will have to defend you if they catch us."

His jaw set, his mouth opened as if to argue; but, despite the pride she saw in his face, she also saw him force it down. "I guess you would."

That was not easy for him. He probably thinks of me as a fragile mortal girl. "But I'd rather we not have to worry about that." She led the dance, off to the side of the thunderhead, now reaching the crest. "The sun will rise soon, and while they can function in daylight, their senses will be dulled and — with luck — we shall be able to evade their notice." She took stock of the situation, the distance they must travel, what songs and steps she might take to find the shorter path between the mortal and Faerie worlds, nodded. "Just promise me — no matter what you think is the proper or right course — that you will do as I say if the time comes."

47

Reluctantly, he nodded. "All right."

She stood still for a moment, looking to the East; the bright line of sky abruptly brightened and a single beam of sunshine speared out, illuminating them and warming her, casting their shadows like arrows into the vast Western distance. "Then," she said, with a sharp smile and hearing the music echo her resolve, "let's go!"

Chapter 6.

We leapt from cloud to cloud, the white mists undefined at close range, yet giving springily underfoot like deep, deep turf, little puffs of mist following every step. *If I die right now, I'll die happy,* I found myself thinking. It was clichéd, it was corny, but it was true. I'd met Polychrome, I'd actually found a way to show her beauty, and I'd flown and danced through the clouds themselves.

But I wouldn't die a success, and the problem wouldn't be solved, so I hoped that dying wasn't in the cards for a while yet. The warning of danger and that sharp, perilous smile Polychrome had flashed me added an edge of excitement that was almost too much to bear. Part of me had *wanted* to hear that there was danger, even though I was very far indeed from being ready to face anything. It was a little galling to recognize that I'd have to depend on Polychrome to defend me, though.

I knew my eyes weren't nearly as good as Poly's, but having had good reason to learn to sense movement and oddities in a background — both as an amateur astronomer and as one who had, in his past, been frequently bullied — I was pretty good at noticing things that might pass others by, at least when I was paying attention. I was paying attention now, and a tiny flicker of motion caught my eye.

"Poly –"

A single glance in that direction and her face hardened, suddenly more Valkyrie than fairy. "Yes. We run now, Erik. Do not let go, do not falter."

The dark shape was terribly small in the distance, yet somehow it had the same eerie implication of deadly power of a tornado; in the sunlight I could see the same green-black color that was unmistakable to anyone who'd ever seen such clouds.

But there was no time to look back, because Polychrome was pulling me along, forcing me to run, run as I hadn't in years. I had mastered long walks, gained some endurance that way, but effort-triggered asthma was not something that encouraged distance running.

I ran, though, holding Polychrome's hand as her power helped turn my heavy mortal steps to inhuman bounds, clearing a hundred yards, two hundred at a step, sprinting at a speed to rival a jet, yet leaving hardly a wake behind us. It was a terrifying but exhilarating experience, and in some ways I wished it could go on forever.

But my lungs were not cooperating. The air was not nearly as cold around Polychrome as it should have been, nor so thin, but my air passages were closing themselves off. I heard the thin, shrieking whistle in my chest, felt the pressure. My ribs began to ache and I stumbled, almost falling, forced myself to continue, but now my thighs and calves were beginning to protest, pain of fatigue starting to radiate through them, stiffening my legs and throwing my stride off. "P–Poly..." I gasped, but my voice was a thin whisper and the wind of our passage tore the word away, cast it backwards.

Then I staggered again, tripped, reflexively reaching out. But Poly had already begun the next leap, and as she did, the rainbow glory that surrounded her passed out from beneath me.

A shockwave of deadly cold washed over my body and my ears screamed and popped as pressure equalized, explosive decompression at 35,000 feet. For a moment, even the strangled ache in my chest was forgotten in the ice-bladed agony.

And then I had something even worse to worry about, as I plummeted like a stone. Ice crystals tore like microscopic claws of miniature demons over my face, and I screwed my eyes shut to keep the wind from possibly freezing my eyeballs solid. *35,000 feet... terminal velocity maybe 120mph...reached that or close to it by now...about seven miles...I've got three, three and a half minutes before I hit. Ouch.*

An apocalyptic blue-white flash and a *BOOM* like the shattering of a mountain let me know that I might have a *lot* less than that. Or more, if I got into an updraft. I was buffeted by turbulent winds and freezing rain soaked me. I was wheezing and shivering and the only reason I wasn't screaming is that I couldn't spare the breath.

I've still got my inhaler on me. Got to wait until it's warmer, though...can't suck this stuff in deep...too cold. I might be dead a couple minutes later, but if anyone could save me, I sure didn't want to suffocate to death afterwards.

A blast of warmer air, a splatter of rain that was probably still cold, but felt like a warm shower after that last bit. It was pitch black...but no, wait, something light...which direction? *I'm going towards it, so it's down. Oh boy, get ready...*

The grey-black mist thinned, lightened, and suddenly I burst out into clear air, the thunderhead still rumbling above me, wrinkled carpet of the earth below. Already I was very far from home, I could tell; none of the geography looked familiar, and I'd done quite a number of airplane flights over the years. *A minute or so left...*

I pulled out the inhaler, took a shot. It was a feeble first try, but the tightness began to loosen. I waited a few seconds, spreading myself as wide as possible on the winds... *Not that this will help much... even if I hit water from this altitude it'll splatter me like concrete, even if I slow myself to a mere 90 miles per hour or so...* Another puff on the inhaler, and that — plus all the adrenalin from the fall — seemed to finally force my lungs to give up on the suicide attempt. I felt air rushing back into me, my brain clearing, as the details of the ground began to resolve, showing that I had only a few thousand more feet to go...

And then I saw a spark of rainbow light above me, dropping from the cloud like a diving hawk. It plummeted towards me, closing the distance... but I was still falling. I glanced down, saw the Earth rushing closer with terrifying speed, looked up, and I could see Polychrome now, a look of grim determination on the beautiful face, drawing nearer, nearer, reaching out...

And our hands touched.

Instantly I stopped, enveloped by warm air and standing on rainbow glory. I looked down.

Polychrome had caught me with about two hundred feet left to go.

I looked at her, trying to smile, while my legs shook from the reaction to near-death, seeing her own pale face mirroring my own. "Cut it...a...a little fine there, didn't you?"

For a minute I thought she was going to slap me, but suddenly she giggled. "You...don't you ever do that again!"

"Believe me, I didn't plan on it. But I can't keep running like that for long; I stop breathing." I was glancing around now, looking for a speck the color of gangrene and storm.

She looked concerned. "Are you–"

"All right...for now. But what about our pursuers?"

She gave a shaky laugh. "Your...unexpected maneuver, Erik, probably surprised them more even than it did me. And I did not use my power to pursue at first, merely dropped, so they had not a trace to follow. I hope – I hope that we have lost them, at least for now. Can you walk, at least?"

"I can. Maybe even jog a bit."

She watched me with concern, but led us upward, away, back into the sky. By the time we reached the heights again, the stormclouds were gone, and fluffy cumulus floated in every direction. "Well," I said finally, "against *that* background I think I could see one of those things a *long* way away."

"And I could see them even farther, and there are none to be seen." She gave the first real, relaxed smile she'd given for hours, and that ethereal music rolled out again.

"What *is* that?" I asked.

"What?"

"I keep hearing music."

She laughed, and that helped loosen the tightness remaining in my chest and body, just hearing her laugh again. "The Music of the Spheres! It follows all the Faerie in one way or another. 'Tis the song of the world we inhabit, the spirits and powers that are associated with all Faerie and, perhaps, those above us as well."

"Above you?"

We landed atop another cloud and saw more stretching before us, a curious formation of one cloud higher than another, almost like steps. "Something had to lay the foundations of the world, chart the direction of the winds, place the stars in their courses.

52

Some even say my Father is descended of these. He might be. I have never asked. But call them the Great Spirits, the Powers, the Gods, what you will, I do not doubt they exist."

I chewed on that as we hopped from one cloud to the next. *I suppose that wasn't the sort of thing Baum would even want to have touched with a forty-foot pole, especially not in the early Twentieth Century.* It did give a deeper level to what was happening, and I wondered how these...gods...might be, or get, involved in the current events.

Wind buoyed us up, the Spheres sang, and we rose higher and higher. And finally, leaping once more to another cloud through a level of even higher mists, I beheld...

"The Fortress of Rainbow." Polychrome spoke with dramatic flair and a deep pride as she gestured upward.

The clouds here *were* steps, there was no more mistaking it, as they became more and more immense oblong risers, great stairs a hundred feet high and just as broad, reaching to a Brobdingnagian edifice that made the words fortress or castle utterly inadequate — a mighty palace with invulnerable walls of polished grey-crystal stormcloud, tumbled rose-quartz mists made solid rising as pinnacles, azure crenellations defining the tops of amethyst keep towers within, bridges of gossamer-white fog joining each to the next, and a shimmering aura of all colors shining out from behind it.

I stared at it for many minutes, speechless as we rose higher and came closer to the Fortress of Rainbow. "If you live here, Lady Polychrome," I said finally, "I can only say that you did our poor mortal city far too much honor, for nothing save your own beauty have I ever seen to compare to *that.*"

Was it my imagination, or did she actually blush for an instant? "You are far too kind, but I am sure my father will be pleased to hear your words."

I am going to meet the Lord of the Rainbow. I'm really going to meet the Lord of the Rainbow. I can't believe I'm even thinking that. "And when will I have the pleasure of saying these words to him myself?"

We stepped down on what felt and looked like polished marble, and the great golden gates swung wide. "In a few minutes only, Erik. I am to bring you before him at the very moment I arrive, and even now I see a runner going before us, telling Father that I am coming."

I wasn't sure I was quite ready for this. I didn't even know what to *expect* from this meeting. I was damn sure I wasn't what *he* was going to be expecting.

I tried to *not* look like I was gawking as I was led through the streets towards the Palace that lay ahead. The last thing I needed was to be overawed. I managed to achieve this, but only by doing something which — in retrospect — might have been more dangerous: looking almost entirely at Polychrome. And once more her beauty captured me so completely that I really, truly did not notice most of what we passed, did not become aware that we had entered the castle until a great thunderous clang echoed through my consciousness and I looked up, to see two massive portals swinging open before us.

"My Father!" Polychrome called eagerly. "I have returned!"

Seated at the far end of a pillared hall so immense that I was sure I could have flown the Goodyear Blimp down it without touching the pillars on either side, looking down from a throne that must itself have been twenty feet high, was the Lord of Rainbows. In the violet-stormy eyes and in something of the set of the jaw I could see that Polychrome was his true daughter, but the heroic frame, muscled like a Greek Titan, the iridescent armor, the white hair falling around a face chiseled and resolute and with a single scar across one cheek, these were entirely unlike the Daughter of the Rainbow. I knew I was looking at not merely a King, but some being of vast and dangerous power; I could *feel* it crackling in the air around us.

He rose and bowed. "Indeed you have, Polychrome, first of Daughters. And...this...is the Hero?"

She laughed. "So it must be, for every prophecy to now he has fulfilled."

54

He looked grave and — no surprise — doubtful. But he bowed again to me, and said, "Then I give you welcome. Iris Mirabilis, Lord of the Rainbow, Master of the Seven Hues, greets you."

I gave my own best bow. "I thank you for the welcome, Lord. I, Erik Medon, mortal man and little else, greet you."

A slight smile acknowledged my own lack of titles. "It is well. Daughter, leave us."

"But –"

He gave her a stern look, and Polychrome sighed and bowed. "As you will." As she turned, she whispered in my ear, "Don't let him scare you. He's really the kindest of fathers."

That's reassuring. We both waited until the massive throne-room doors had closed behind her. Then I turned back to Iris Mirabilis. "My Lord, I –"

The immense Lord of Rainbows had drawn himself to his full height — which was a lot larger than anything human-shaped had any business being — and a swirl of crackling blue-white electricity was forming about his hand.

"Whoa, now, hold on –"

"Stand fast, mortal! For now the truth shall be known — in life or in your death!"

And a blazing sphere of living thunderbolts smashed down on me.

Chapter 7.

Ugu looked up from the stone he was polishing as the Tempest swirled into the room. "You bring news?"

The bound storm-spirit bowed low before him, and in a thin shriek reported its observations. As he listened, Ugu felt his face tightening, lips thinning to a straight line. *And so it has begun.*

Once the Tempest had concluded, he nodded and waved it away. "Call the others back; I will have new orders for you soon enough."

Carefully he placed his tools back in their places; with the strength of a Herkus who had long since assimilated the strength of the mystical zosozo which was the sole province of that hidden group of people, he lifted the three-ton statue he was working on and carried it back to its sheltered niche. Assured that all was neat and clean in his workshop, he left, locking the door with a gesture.

"Lady Amanita," he said to apparently empty air, "we have something to discuss."

Her light and warm voice replied immediately. "But of course, my King. I will attend you in the throne room immediately."

Ugu mounted the steps to the great black throne — with its second green throne, slightly lower. He could not quite restrain an acid smile at that. Some would take that to indicate that he was the true ruler, and he suspected that Amanita intended him to view it that way as well. But he knew that despite his magic being pivotal to their recovery and success, her powers were at least the equal of his own, and she was in some ways far more dangerous.

As the beautiful green-haired woman, eyes sparkling and seeming warm and inviting, appeared on the throne — where a moment before had been fluttering a harmless-looking green butterfly — one aspect of that danger was reinforced. Ugu may have been a hermit in his first war against Oz, but that hadn't been because he was unaware of certain attractions; and when the former Mrs. Yoop had chosen her new appearance and name, she had made clear that she had very intimate ways to show her gratitude at finally

57

Ryk E. Spoor

being freed from her prior humiliating shape. Ugu had even allowed himself, for a short time, to believe that she might actually have fallen in love with him. But he had watched people as a sour-tempered Dove for... hundreds of years? He saw her glances in moments out of the corner of his eye, heard what his own spies reported of her behavior and words. Her enthusiasm was for power and control. Now that she had been forced from her comfortable self-contained retreat, the former desire for isolation had been replaced with a demand for mastery — one as matter-of-factly absolute as her prior assertion of dominance over her home.

So while he still occasionally enjoyed the pleasure of her company, he had to admit it also held the additional thrill of danger — because he was unsure, every time, whether she had some additional plans for his vulnerability. Which was why, in moments he could be assured of privacy, he made his own preparations. She had gathered an array of forces of her own, he knew — and while he had his own advantages, a Yookoohoo with the incredibly honed control that Amanita Verdant (*née* Yoop) wielded was a hideously dangerous opponent.

Which was, of course, why the first thing he had done upon acquiring access to his magical tools was to manufacture a charm that prevented any except himself from performing any transformation on him.

"My Lord." Amanita bowed her head prettily. "What news is this that has you looking so serious?"

"It is time you recalled your spies, my Lady Amanita," he said, gazing down at the map of Oz and the surrounding countries. "We need all that they have gathered, and we need it now."

Her green eyebrows quirked upwards. "Oh my. That sounds so...grim, Ugu dear. What has happened?"

"The Lord of Rainbows sent out his daughter but a day or so past."

"And? The dear girl travels far and wide, and has avoided our little realm." She knew, obviously, that only one of Iris Mirabilis' daughters would be referred to simply as "his daughter."

"And she traveled to the mortal world, *directly* to the mortal world, and left the Rainbow there."

All playfulness vanished and she shot to her feet, eyes narrow and cold. "Oh, she did, did she? And has she returned?"

"She has, my Queen. And bringing with her another — a mortal, I would presume." Ugu was pleased he had managed to surprise her. Often he would call her in with news, only to find that one of her own myriad of spies (in equally many forms) had already given it to her. "Given the reports that Polychrome had indeed rescued that accursed Pink Bear, and the rumors your spies had garnered of a Prophecy, I think we now need the full story. Immediately."

She nodded sharply. "It will be a loss; it took much to insert a spy undetected into the palace, which is why I have never contacted him before. But by now he must have at least some of the Prophecy, and with luck all of it. I will recall him and the others." She gave vent to a curse of such ancient power that one of the green plants she had set in the window nearby spontaneously blackened. "The fools! Did they think we would not know? They think to move against us, now, after we have had all this time to prepare — your marvelous armies, my own Faerie Bindings for power, and all Oz now resigned to our control? Better they had tried earlier — the result would have been the same, but at least they would have made a credible try of it."

Ugu shook his head. "Do not make the mistake of believing that the Lord of Seven Hues is a fool, Amanita. Even I may be a fool in my own way, but not all others are so stupid as you would make them. If he has chosen to wait, and to act only now, then I assure you he has waited for excellent reasons and has a plan."

At his quiet rebuke, she glanced at him with momentary fury in the poison-green eyes. But the fury vanished back under the cloak of her control, and she nodded unwillingly. "I... I suppose you are right."

"I *am* right, Amanita. We both made the same mistakes before. It would be very well for us *both* to remember that. We need each other's power, and we need each other to keep us both from *making* those mistakes again."

She stared at him unreadably for a moment, and then suddenly stepped up and kissed his cheek. "You *are* right, as you say. I should

59

remember that." For a moment, he thought she actually meant it. She certainly could not forget centuries as a Green Monkey. "Now I will go to the Great Binding and send out the call through the Spirits."

"Indeed. Go then, and tell me as soon as they return."

He watched her go, and shuddered as the door closed behind her. The Great Binding was the thing that most frightened him about Amanita Verdant; her greatest triumph, source of her power... and an abomination that even he found distasteful. When they had laid their plans, they knew they needed more power, to arrange certain events to occur in sequence very swiftly after they made their first detectable moves. Amanita had sought out certain other enemies of Oz, including the most powerful dark Faeries of all, the Phanfasms. Deprived of much of their memories in the climactic end of their attempt to invade Oz (and not so simply as the mortal books had depicted it), the Phanfasms had no real knowledge of who they had been, though they were no less powerful than before. They were mischievous, sometimes cruel children in their minds, and Amanita's beauty and words had captivated them. She had whispered pieces of the truth to them, awakened vague memories and rage, and they had sworn to assist her at the proper moment. She had even promised that this time they need not even march to battle.

And — as she always did — she had kept her promise. As Ugu cast the spell which was intended to bring down the Curse of Stone on their enemies, they had known great and powerful defenses would resist such a direct strike. Amanita called the Phanfasms in to "assist in the ritual," lending their power to the enchantment.

But the pentacle and runic circles she had inscribed had been a trap, something even Ugu had not fully recognized. With the First and Foremost, leader of the Phanfasms, in the center, and all the mass of his people gathered within focused on a task of malice and destruction, she had enacted a terrifying transformation – a combination of ritual magic and Yookoohoo power that bound the very essences of the dark Faeries into a swirling vortex of power, filled with hate and rage and dismay, that she could draw upon. So far, she had used scarcely any of that mass of power which, as far as

Ugu was concerned, was the closest thing in Faerie to the power of Hell.

He closed his eyes, then shrugged. As long as there was an external enemy, he needed her — and she would be focused outside, not inside.

And it was not as though he, Ugu the Unbowed, did not have his own reserves. When he no longer needed Amanita, there were ways to remove her. Perhaps even taking that tempting abomination for himself.

He smiled, and turned back towards the hall to his workshop.

First Vision:

Light.

She tried to turn away, but the light surrounded her. Not the bright and piercing warmth of the sun, the green-white of deep forest illuminance, the rosy color of castle lamps or pale white of the moon. It was the sick blazing actinic hue of daylight to one suffering a headache, the color of burning steel. There was nowhere to turn, no escape from the roiling unrelieved soundless conflagration of stabbing brilliance.

She tried to cry out, but she had no voice, she had no mouth, she had no *self*. There was only the terrible light and behind it the sense of loss, of failure. The pain of the people who counted on her, who looked to her in times of trouble, who needed her. Something monstrous had happened, but she was barely able to be aware of that fact, scarcely capable of realizing with molasses-slow thought that she, too, was caught in a trap, a web of deceit and diabolical purpose whose nature was all too clear, now that she could do nothing whatsoever.

And the light continued, searing into her. It was the light of prison, the light of torment, the light...

...the light of enslavement. Even as she thought it, she could feel it now, her own connection with the world being reversed, flowing from her, through her, at the will of another. She could not fight it; the binding was complete. Only something so utterly opposed to her enslavers that it lay completely beyond their knowledge or understanding could possibly break that binding... and it would then, of course, be something that could have no knowledge of how to do such a thing.

And the light burned on and on, wearing her away, ever thinner, yet never quite able to vanish, never able to die or be destroyed. She would have wept, had she tears or eyes to cry them. Despair was foreign to her kind, but she recognized that in the end even she would fall to it, with no help or hope remaining for her people, her land, and herself. Already she could feel it, an aching emptiness that, once fully opened, could never be filled again.

63

And then there was a single point of dark. So faint, so distant, but it was *there*, a negation of fever-brightness and hateful brilliance.

And without lips or face, still she smiled, because the name of the color of dark was Hope.

Chapter 8.

He gazed tensely at the smoke and dust before him. The detonation had been even greater than he had expected, a blast that had cracked the nearest columns and left a choking cloud obscuring the area of impact entirely. *Have I ended it even as it began? Or...*

A figure was becoming visible. The smoke suddenly cleared, and his gaze was caught and held by ice-blue eyes, filled with anger and shock, staring furiously from a salt-white face. The glare from those eyes was of startling intensity, and Iris Mirabilis found himself momentarily seized by an impulse to step back, even as a great tide of relief washed through him. He remembered how he had brought down the lightnings; fear had galvanized the smaller figure, but instead of fleeing, this Erik Medon had merely thrown up one hand to protect his face, the rest of his body poised in stubborn, unyielding resistance. *"Before destruction he will stand unbowed..."*

"Well done," he said as the last of the smoke dissipated. "Faced by danger, you do not turn your back upon it, showing that for you fear is weakness. You stand, you face that which would destroy you."

The mortal was breathing hard, but the glare — while slightly lessened — was not withdrawn. "You hit me with a goddamned *lightning ball* just to find out if I run or not? This was just some stupid special-effect test?" The man's voice, raised in anger, was surprisingly powerful; no match for the Rainbow Lord's own, but nonetheless sending resonant echoes of outrage chasing themselves around the throne room.

Iris shook his head. "Vastly more than that, mortal man, and vastly more important, important enough that I had no choice but to risk ending our hope in the moment it arrived. Look you down."

Now the anger in the face changed, yielding to astonishment and shock as the blond man realized that he stood on a narrow pinnacle of marble, barely wider than his own body, in the center of a still-smoldering crater sixty feet wide and reaching nearly ten feet in depth. "W-what the hell?"

The Rainbow Lord gestured; iridescent light coalesced in the hole, solidified to marble, leaving no trace of the devastation save the smell of scorched stone and the scarred columns on either side. "Come, Erik Medon. Sit with me, and I will explain. And in that explanation, I hope, you will come to understand that my actions were necessary."

He caused a chair to appear near the throne, and seated himself on the throne as his guest — still clearly shaky from the sudden attack — lowered himself into the newly-formed seat.

"Okay," Erik said finally. "Explain."

"I have no doubt my daughter explained to you that it was our expectation that the hero she sought must be a mortal. But there is mortal, and then there is *mortal.*"

The blond head, with its somewhat receding hair, nodded. "Yes. She mentioned that most of the so-called mortals in Oz had at least some small amount of fairy blood, which was why they could end up finding their way here."

Iris nodded. "Precisely. Moreover, those which appear mortal here in the realms of Faerie are themselves descended of such mixed blood. They are perhaps not possessed, for the most part, of any of the powers of the more pure of blood, but the key part is that the existence of that blood makes it possible for them to connect with the realms of Faerie...and for the power of Faerie to connect to them."

The mortal's understanding was swift; he saw the blue eyes flick back to the place where the crater had been, the brows draw close, then rise. "But one of truly pure mortal blood..." he began, slowly.

"I see you have the essence of it. Your mortal blood denies you any chance to have found Oz through the random events that brought others here. But it also denies Faerie power any chance to affect you without your direct and willing cooperation." Iris gazed outward as he continued. "Mortals live in the world of the physical, of the solid. The essence of your soul is there purely as the structure of life, the necessary spark that differentiates you from the base materials of which you are made. Contrariwise, the Faerie are beings of energy, of spirit, with a far slighter connection to the world of mundane matter."

66

"So what you're saying is that you Faerie types can't hurt me."

He laughed. "Do not make *that* mistake, my would-be hero. We cannot hurt you *with magic* — we cannot impress the pure will of our souls and powers on you. But I assure you, a hard-driven blade wielded by my hand, or that of any warrior of Oz or other Faerie realm, will kill you as surely as if it were wielded by mortal hands. You are not invulnerable, merely protected from certain forces in a way that no Faerie can be."

Erik Medon nodded. "I understand. Still, that's a pretty big advantage."

"A necessary one, in fact."

"Necessary?"

The Rainbow Lord leaned forward. "Understand me well, Erik Medon. You have passed the tests of prophecy, and now we step beyond the point where another might be chosen. If you cannot do what must be done, we shall fail, or at least be forced into a long and bitter war whose effects shall recoil upon the mortal world as well.

"Yet the prophecies of the Bear give neither you, nor I, certain paths to victory. Today I will tell you what I may — and what I must. But it will be still up to you to make the right choices. Some actions are clear. Some are not." He sighed, and for a moment he could not keep the worry from his face. "And the best of paths will still not be easy."

He looked down, to see the blue eyes meeting his with a surprising understanding. The mortal's mouth quirked upwards in a sad smile, and he spoke.

"I'm going to die, aren't I?"

Chapter 9.

For a minute I thought he wasn't going to answer me directly. His storm-violet eyes started to turn away; then they closed, reopened, looked back down at me.

"Erik Medon, this is one of the great uncertainties. Your precise fate..." He paused, face tense yet so controlled that I could not tell what lay behind the tension, then continued, "...your precise fate lies beyond any prophecy. The prophecy, in fact, ends at the moment you confront our true enemies. And as I have already told you, even the path to that confrontation is fraught with uncertainty. Die you may, and that well before we have reached even a chance for victory. Or you may fail in some less dramatic but no less final manner." He held up a hand as I was about to speak. "But I know that you mean to ask about the ultimate end of this adventure, and to that I can say: you may well die then."

He reached down beside his throne and lifted up a little pink stuffed bear with a crank protruding from its side. The crank began to turn of its own accord, and the little head turned jerkily and one paw came up. "Hail, Erik Medon!" the Pink Bear said in a high-pitched, semi-mechanical voice.

Now I understood; *The Lost Princess of Oz* had only shown the Bear to be a clairvoyant, but it made all too much sense that he was, in fact, a prophet as well.

"Hail, Pink Bear." I kept my expression grave, though I did have a momentary impulse to giggle; the poor thing looked so absurd. "My condolences on your losses." I saw the Rainbow Lord raise a startled eyebrow, and I continued, "For I see that your King is not here, and only his destruction would have allowed that."

"My thanks." The Pink Bear moved with clumsy dignity from the arm of the throne to the Rainbow Lord and took a seat on one massive knee, gazing down at me from button eyes that still, somehow, seemed alive. "My condolences on what you are to suffer."

"Don't," I said. "I've already had two lifelong dreams granted."

"Tell him of the ending," said Iris Mirabilis firmly. "He desires to know what will be, if past all the perils set between now and the end he has traveled."

"As the Lord desires," the Pink Bear said quietly. He then turned to me and spoke, in childish verse appropriate to a stuffed prophet:

> Now he comes to the end, few his friends, alone
> Held by words and chains before the Warlock's throne.
> Sorely wounded shall he be, and then his fate be known;
> If struck through the heart and silent,
> unable he to call
> then Ozma's power sealed forever
> and darkness shall rule all;
> Bathed in his heart's blood but still with voice
> Ozma's name he calls;
> Her power lifts him up, burns his soul away
> But in those final moments he may win the day.

It was silent in the throne room for several moments as I assimilated all of that. "Okay, that could have been better for me, I guess. I'm not sure what all of it means — par for the course with a prophecy, I guess. Either way, it sounds like I die." I tried to say it lightly. It was, after all, a set of verses, and I didn't have the capacity to see it as my final doom quite yet — though it might sink in later. "What's the bit about Ozma's power burning away my soul? Any idea?"

The Rainbow Lord gently set the Bear back down and stood; his pacing showed that he didn't find this discussion much more pleasant than I did. "More than an idea, Erik Medon. It is possible — if you permit it, given that you are a True Mortal — for a Faerie ruler such as Ozma, or myself for that matter, to place our power, our very essence of self, within you and allow you to use it.

"But since you are, in fact, mortal, and we are beings of spirit, your soul must be the channel and director of that spirit. It takes a tremendous effort of will to do this, for it will be very painful — although, at the same time, it would be as the Bear says uplifting, transcendent. The passage of such pure spiritual power through a mortal soul wears it away swiftly."

I nodded slowly. "Like...channeling hot water through a pipe of ice. The pipe can handle it, can even handle a *lot* of it...for a little while. But eventually it's going to go to pieces. So I die either way."

"Not necessarily." Iris stopped and dropped to one knee, gazing at me earnestly. "Princess Ozma's powers are vast, and if you can defeat your opponents swiftly enough, she may be able to return to her true self and heal you."

"But she's...sealed away. What's the bit about my calling her name?"

The Rainbow Lord looked even grimmer. "I have spent many years in this research — perilous research, for merely delving into certain things could have warned Ugu and Amanita of what I sought — and I believe that these verses speak of a dark ritual which takes advantage of a True Mortal's nature. Performed correctly, they would be able to simultaneously break the seal on Ozma while shattering her basic connection to Oz."

"And that would mean," I said, guessing, "that they would have permanent access to Oz's power — and she'd just be another sacrifice or slave for them at that point."

"Precisely so," he affirmed. "All such great rituals require some form of sacrifice — of a mortal or of a Faerie of some considerable power. No power is attained without price, no change in the Great Order permitted without great effort. A True Mortal's blood is of great significance, as you might guess, as significant in its own way as that of a Faerie such as Ozma. But all such rituals are also very delicate things."

"And so if I, the object of the sacrifice, call out to her, I'd... what? Bind her to me, in a way?"

"Give her the opportunity to escape *into* you, if you allowed it, and allow you to use her power against her enemies in ways she simply cannot, while still being defended in great part by the nature of your mortality."

Now *that* made sense, in this weird mystical way. I'd be sort of null-magic powered armor for her spirit to wear. "And if I finished it quickly enough, there might be enough of her left to be able to fix the damage done to me?"

"That is my belief, yes." His gaze was steady when he said that, so I thought he meant it; he wasn't just trying to give me a forlorn hope.

"But if I push it too much, I'd burn myself out — destroy my soul." A paraphrase of Disney's *Aladdin* zipped through my mind: "Phenomenal cosmic power...itty-bitty circuit breaker."

Iris Mirabilis looked at me sympathetically. "And along the way you will have to gain some idea of how you actually might wield this power. As you cannot wield magic in any other way, nor — in fact — allow yourself to be the subject of much significant magic without imperiling your protection, you will have to use her power with instinct and whatever insight you will have gained in your travels, for no one shall be able to train you."

Of course. I'll have to travel through numberless perils just to get to the point where someone stabs me through the heart, and then if I can manage to choke out the right word, use a Faerie Princess' power — that I don't know how to wield — to defeat two centuries-old, trained, super-powerful mages and all their minions, and do it really fast, but without burning myself up to a cinder. Piece of cake, really.

But I remembered Polychrome, and realized it didn't matter. I was, like they said in *Babylon 5*, their "last, best hope." I looked up. "Okay, Milord. But we're getting a long way ahead of ourselves. What's our actual next step? What can you tell me of the prophecies that come *before* that?"

"You accept all these risks?"

I chuckled, even though part of me did feel a cold touch of fear. "How the hell could I even explain it to you, Rainbow Lord? Maybe, being immortal, it's really hard for you to understand what it's like to know, every day, every week, every year, is bringing you closer and closer to the day you won't open up your eyes ever again. I don't believe – well, I *didn't* believe – in any gods or afterlife, though I might have to reconsider that now. But the cold fact is that most of us live out our lives of a few decades — seventy, eighty, maybe a hundred or so years, tops — and see almost none of our dreams come true. We make do. We settle for the best we can get. We dream and fantasize, and then go back to reality.

"So now Polychrome appears to me out of a rainbow, tells me I may be the key to rescuing Oz, takes me dancing through the clouds, and brings me here, to the Fortress of the Rainbow. And you say that I *might* die when it comes to the end, to a final throwdown with villains as black as any I've ever read about?" I couldn't help but laugh again. "I will die living a dream that most of us won't ever even conceive of. So yes, I accept them, happily and cheerfully and with a right will, sir!"

He stood and echoed my laugh with his own. "Well said, mortal. Well said. Very well, then, know that all the prophecy says for these moments is that the hero must be prepared to face the perils of his journey. How that preparation should proceed has been left to me." His smile now had a hard edge to it. "Unused I think you are to effort, a stranger to real discipline, and you will face many adversaries before the end. Time for you to be properly trained, I think."

It didn't take a genius to guess what he meant by *that*. "Oh, great. Boot camp."

"Your idiom is a bit obscure, but I believe you have grasped precisely my meaning. It is not seemly for the prophesied Hero to rely on my daughter for protection in his journey, and in fact she will not always be able to accompany you." He clapped his hands together, and the far doors opened instantly.

In strode a tall figure, perhaps seven feet high, armored in grey-blue steel like a metal lizard's scales. The warrior's frame was truly heroic, proportionately even more massive than the Rainbow Lord's, and over his shoulder I saw the hilt of a mighty two-handed blade. "My Lord?"

Iris Mirabilis looked slightly surprised, as though he had expected someone else. "Precisely who I was going to send for. Nimbus Thunderstroke, Captain of my Storm Legions, Erik Medon, mortal of the Prophecy. It is my wish that you make of him a warrior at least capable of defending himself in emergency."

Nimbus' face was hard and scarred, clearly a veteran of many battles. He looked me up and down, then grabbed one of my hands, looked at it, shook his head. "A tall order, my Lord."

Mirabilis laughed. "But not beyond your capacity, I think. He is a True Mortal, so remember this in your training."

"As my Lord wishes." He turned and bowed to the Rainbow Lord; I did the same. "Follow me, Erik Medon."

I did, suspecting that the Rainbow Lord was grinning behind my back as we left.

Chapter 10.

"So, Captain Thunderstroke — "

"Hah!" His laugh was as abrupt as his last name. "Nimbus, please. Or 'sir,' when I'm training you. But if the Rainbow Lord has decreed that I, personally, train you, we are equals. Say on, then."

I grinned back at him. I was probably going to hate this guy at times during our training, but I kinda liked him already. "How much do you know about the Prophecy? Is there anything I can't talk about with you?"

"Nothing is there so vital to our defense that the Rainbow Lord would have failed to tell me, and yet have told you, when you would be unable to fully comprehend it." He said this with a simple, matter-of-fact tone. While I could see he was a man very proud of his skill and position, there was no ego in that statement. And it made sense; if this guy was the head of his defenses, the Rainbow Lord had *better* trust him.

"Okay, got it." I said. "So when we were talking, he said my nature as a True Mortal wasn't just a neat advantage, but was *necessary.*" I associated the way Iris Mirabilis had said that word with the way that Mentor of Arisia would have used it. "What did he mean by that?"

"You cut to the heart of the matter. Let us hope you are so swift with weapons as well." Nimbus rubbed his hand through his already-wild (though short) dark-violet hair. "You are familiar with Oz through the distorted retellings in your world, yes?"

"Very familiar. And I'm quite aware that there were a lot of... liberties...taken with the reality."

He grunted. "Even so." We turned down a cross-corridor, and I was struck anew by the sheer *size* of the place. This palace couldn't be less than a mile, a mile and a half, across. Maybe a lot more. The translucent blue-prismatic crystal of the walls was like marble mined from some petrified ocean, and stretched on forever, it seemed. "The first and most obvious answer is that your adversaries are both mighty magicians indeed, and all of their greatest weapons are

75

things of fell enchantment and dark Faerie power. As a True Mortal, you can stand before them with a greater hope of victory than any others among us, perhaps even than the Rainbow Lord himself, perhaps even than the Above." At the last word he raised his head, nodding upward. "But there is a far more specific reason. Many things in the books were, as you say, not precisely what was written. The Deadly Desert was and is, however, quite real, as was the enchantment enacted by Glinda the High Sorceress to seal off Oz from the mortal world.

"The Usurpers Ugu and Amanita have taken control of that barrier and transformed it. The shield about Oz now excludes all but the most minute traces of Faerie power, save that which they permit to travel through; their spies and agents, in other words." I nodded to show that I understood. "A being such as yourself can pass through that barrier when none of us may do so."

"You are *not* telling me that I have to go charging into an enemy-occupied Oz *all by myself.*"

He laughed. I wasn't sure I liked the laugh. "We will leave *that* discussion for later, mortal. For here," he shoved open a huge portal, "we are."

The room inside was roughly the size of Iris' throne room, but instead of a dramatic seat of power, this was an indoor drilling field, a dojo on steroids. Hundreds of men with the same undefinably exotic air that surrounded Nimbus (and was much stronger around Polychrome and her father) were practicing — swinging swords, maces, blocking with shields, ducking, parrying, leaping in impossibly high arcs to evade and returning to ground to cut and jab and lunge.

"This is the palace guard?"

"A small number of them, yes. Understand that for a ruler such as Iris Mirabilis, the security of the castle and his people *is* the security of the entire realm. One could call us his army and be just as accurate. Ten thousand and more do I command...and," he fixed me with a heavy stare, "all ten thousand will I commit to the war if need be and if my Lord orders it. And no choice will we have in this, if you fail."

"Sure, sure, load me up with the responsibility." I tried to sound casual. At his sudden glare, I swallowed. "Sorry."

He sighed and looked regretful. "My apologies. Perhaps you do not realize just how long it has been that we have been preparing and waiting. It wears on us just as it would on you, my friend."

"I did get the idea that time went by a lot faster here than back home."

"As you measure time, it was nigh on fifty years ago that Oz fell. Here, it was three centuries and more agone."

Six to one time ratio. Well, that has some advantages for me. Still...! "You've been just waiting around for three hundred years for this prophecy to come due? They've had that long to lock it all down? Jesus, man, is it really that hopeless without *me?*"

He gave a bitter laugh as he led me into an alcove about as large as a ballroom. "It strikes me as improbable as well, Erik Medon, but yes, it is exactly that hopeless.

"Oz is the center, the very core of Faerie. That power is in the hands of beings who understand how to wield it and who have chosen to do so in a manner directly contrary to its normal nature. Not only does this affect all of us in one way or another, it is something virtually impossible for us, alone, to combat. As well lead your people's armies against the Sun. Assembled all together, the other Faerie realms might, possibly, equal the forces that the Warlock and the Yookoohoo command. But even leaving aside how difficult it would be to convince all of those squabbling little realms to unite against such a foe, the barrier they have made from Glinda's is an absolute and impenetrable defense, through which only one thing can pass."

"A True Mortal who is, by his nature, completely unaffected by magic, howsoever powerful," I finished.

"Exactly." He gestured to the left-hand wall; I saw, arranged in glittering, expectant ranks, dozens upon dozens of weapons: gladius-like shortswords, daggers, spears, clubs, staves, titanic two-handed swords, barbed nets, tridents, crescent-shaped blades like sickles, katana-like longswords, and more exotic offerings. "Choose a weapon, mortal. We'll test your instincts first before we begin the training in earnest."

"Just be careful not to kill me in your testing. As Iris pointed out, I'm not immune to sharp pointy things in my gut."

He gave another snort of laughter as I surveyed the wall of death-dealing implements, and drew his own weapon, something like a green-blue claymore; he leaned on it as he waited.

He's a lot bigger than me, clearly one hell of a lot stronger if he's using something that size. I'm never going to beat him, but I need to play to what strengths I've got. I finally selected a long, twin-edged rapier. *I've done a little swordwork with things like this, and it's fast. My only chance to even look halfway good is to use speed — stick and move and stick again, and not in any way, shape, or form try to match him one to one.*

I took a breath and turned to him. "I guess I'm as ready as I'll ever be."

A tiny smile curled one corner of his mouth. He brought his huge sword up in a salute and then stood there, waiting.

"Yeah, I figured you'd wait." I circled slowly, watching him turn easily in place. *A fast lunge in, then retreat immediately.*

I did several feints, trying to make it difficult to know when I was committing to the attack. He did unlimber his sword from the salute, watching my movements narrowly.

I gathered myself as if to commit, then pulled back, then did the *real* lunge forward. *Extend and –*

A baseball bat wielded by Hercules took me in the side of my head, spinning me sideways and sending me skidding prone on the floor, the useless rapier skittering away from my hand.

"Are you all right?" I looked up blearily to see Nimbus' huge hand extended.

I forced myself to grasp it and tried to grin. "Sure, never better."

"I saw your line of thinking. You noted our differential in height, my weapon choice, and so on. You elected to try to match my strength with speed and guile. A logical strategy."

Without warning, he suddenly bellowed, "*AND COMPLETELY WRONG!*"

Those words, shouted loudly enough to make my ears ring, certainly helped clear my head. "What? What other strategy *was* there, short of running away and hoping I could find a hole *you* wouldn't fit through?"

He grinned coldly. "Hit me, mortal."

"What?"

"Hit me. Here." He pointed to the center of his armored breastplate.

"You want me to break my hand? I –"

"I said *hit me*, you idiotic overweight soft-gutted pathetic excuse for a hero! Or aren't you able to follow even a simple command?"

I didn't see the point, but I set my jaw, drew my fist back, and punched.

There was a *crunch* and for an instant I was sure I'd broken my knuckles. But to my utter astonishment, Nimbus Thunderstroke literally *flew* backwards from the force of my blow, tumbling end over end as though he'd been hit by a truck, fetching up with an audible *thud* against the far wall. *What the hell...?*

He coughed, a pain-wracked sound, and slowly came to his hands and knees, then forced himself to stand. As he did, I saw that his grey-blue armor was *cracked* where I'd struck it, the metal scales crushed like eggshell. "Well... struck, Erik Medon. And yet I think you pulled that punch."

I did. A lot. I don't like hitting people, and even with practice, well... I didn't want to hurt my hand, either...

"What the hell's going on? I can't hit like that. *No one* can –" I suddenly stopped, mouth half-open, as understanding began to break through.

He smiled painfully. "I see you may begin to understand, Erik."

"It's... that difference in our basic natures again." I spoke slowly as the concept solidified. "I'm mostly material. Solid matter. You're a being of spirit, with just a moderate connection to the solid world. So if I'm resisting you instead of going along, it's like – what? I'm made of steel or something?"

He nodded. "Close enough, though not so alike that my swords will not cut you. And so — though your logic was perfectly reasonable — it led you to precisely the wrong conclusion." He pulled a vial from his belt and drank. I could see the color return to his face, and he straightened. "Alas that my mail will not be so easily mended. Now, can you tell me the other side of your new realization?"

I thought a moment. "Even someone your size will be faster than me. Less real mass but more mystical power, you'll be very quick. I didn't even see you move that sword."

"Partly that is your lack of training and mortal age. Some of that we can overcome with training and practice. But again you have the essence correct. So your proper strategy against us is –"

I suddenly burst out laughing. "To act as though I'm something more the size of Iris Mirabilis — you can outmove me, but all I need to do is hit most of you *once* and you don't get up."

"Exactly so." He smiled at my incredulity. "A man of your... condition obviously never would have expected to need to use such tactics." The smile suddenly turned predatory. "Which means that we will need to work *much* harder to make you able to properly take advantage of this."

Oh, boy.

Chapter 11.

Three blows hammered against my sword, trying to deflect it from its path, and just about succeeding; instead of smashing directly into the Storm Legionnaire currently trying to take my head off, the massive blade glanced off his scaled mail instead. Even so, the impact was enough to send him spinning away like a pinball.

Two more figures streaked in from both sides, which meant this guy had delayed me a split-second too long. I knew that dodging was out of the question, even with the practice I'd gotten in the past couple of weeks, so I whipped my blade around in a circular, flat arc; this forced the two Faerie warriors to pull up more than nine feet short, their own swords nowhere near long enough to reach me unless they wanted to try timing their rush.

I caught the sound of a third set of footsteps, but they were still a little farther off — and something slammed me between my shoulderblades, sending a spike of pain through my spine despite my thick padded armor. *Bastard's using a polearm! I have to remember they can make up for reach in a dozen ways!*

I tried to recover, but the jolt had distracted me, and the two swordsmen closed the distance. I was forced to drop my sword and surrender, or they'd have beaten me black and blue in seconds.

"Stop!" Nimbus commanded, and the others immediately brought their weapons to guard position. The massive commander strode forward, shaking his head. "Five exchanges, *five*, and you're already down? And only two of my men downed in the process? You may be facing a *legion* on your own, and *this* is the best you can do, with all your formidable capabilities? Do you *want* to fail?"

"It's been two goddamn *weeks*! What the hell do you expect?" I was standing despite the pain, which I happened to feel was something of an achievement. I wasn't used to people beating on me yet. "You've been training these people for years!"

He snorted. "Yes, years, but none of them are capable of picking up my other men and throwing them aside like dolls, or breaking weapons or armor in their bare hands. You have talent, mortal. I've seen you measure an opponent, judge an opening. You're not altogether terrible in your ability to learn the handling of a blade and you've become a passable swordsman for so short a time, so I'd expect you to be doing much better by now. I'm not sure what it is that's stopping you, but we'll have to find a way to get you past it." He shook his head dolefully. "If only Cirrus were here, perhaps he'd know where we're going wrong."

He'd mentioned that name before; Cirrus had been his right-hand man, second in command, tactical advisor, and — most importantly for our current issues — had been in charge of training new recruits for something like five hundred years. Cirrus had gone missing — on a patrol to watch the borders of the Rainbow Lord's domain — around the time I'd arrived. Not surprising with the stepped-up activity of the opposition, but a serious blow to Nimbus' ability to lead the Legion while also training a clueless mortal...not to mention the loss of his best friend, if the way he spoke about Cirrus was any clue.

I wanted to argue with Nimbus about his pretty harsh assessment of how well I was *not* doing, but I had to admit that in his position I'd probably be saying the same thing. If your recruit's effectively superhuman, he shouldn't *need* to be nearly as well-trained as the others to start kicking their asses. Besides, I was feeling a little ache in my chest and felt more inclined to save my breath for whatever he was about. Or maybe for buying time.

"Look, something's been bothering me about this super-strength of mine. It doesn't seem...well, consistent."

He looked at me sharply. "How do you mean?"

"Well... If I'm as much stronger than you as I seemed that one time, and as it seems when I hit these guys, well, I didn't even bark my knuckles on your armor. So...your swords and such shouldn't be able to cut me, and your swings should feel something like a toddler beating on me with a padded pole — that is, not even very noticeable. But that jab I just took *hurt* and it felt like someone pretty beefy hitting me, too. Okay, maybe not as beefy as I'd have

82

expected before, but it sure wasn't a toddler. And those weights you've had me lifting and walking around in don't seem to be much heavier than the ones your soldiers practice with — lighter, in a lot of cases. Plus if I was really that much stronger, Polychrome herself shouldn't have been able to lift much more than a teacup, but she seems strong enough to lift at least as much as I'd expect a girl her size to handle — maybe more. So none of this makes sense."

"Ha!" He grinned. "You are correct, Erik Medon. It is a more complex matter than simple increase of strength. In essence, your mortal nature reacts against the power of Faerie, or causes Faerie to react strongly against your presence — but this is driven by the focus of your soul.

"Now, when you strike against one of us, your soul is directing your blow, focusing the...anti-power, if you will, of your nature against your target, negating our strength and pushing us away from that which is the antithesis of our power. Except when you perform a powerful and conscious block of an attack, however, your nature is not so strongly directed in your defense, and thus you feel our blows much more as you would feel those of your own kind."

I nodded slowly. "Okay... so I could break a Faerie door down or something without much trouble, but if a Faerie roof fell on me without warning, it could squash me pretty much as easily as it would you?"

"A good general statement, yes." He straightened. "Enough talking, however. You've got a long way to go before you can be the Hero."

In his tone, I heard the unspoken *if.* Parts of the other pieces of the Prophecy that Iris Mirabilis had been slowly feeding to me passed through my mind...*struck through the heart and silent... Across the sky and sea, wisdom he shall seek; That which he sought shall he refuse, and by rejecting wisdom gains he strength...burns his soul away...*

It was always that last verse that kept coming back to haunt me. I picked up my sword again and began running through exercises, but I was still worrying at the dozens of lines of cryptic verse, and always returning to the endgame. Even though both the Lord of Rainbows and Nimbus Thunderstroke had agreed that it didn't necessarily mean I would have to die — that Ozma's power could save me — it was pretty clear that death was very much in the cards. And if using her power was going to burn my soul, that meant that there wouldn't be any of me left to go to the afterlife I was just now suspecting might really exist.

"*Enough*, you idiot!" Nimbus' voice broke through my reverie. "You've gone off again into your night-damned contemplations and your practice isn't even worth the sweat of my worst recruit's brow! Time for some real work! We'll do the dragging weights this time, all the way around the arena, five times!"

Oh, what I wouldn't give for the power of montage...

Chapter 12.

"A True Mortal! That little conniving snip of a Faerie and her father have brought over a *True Mortal!*" The sky darkened above the Grey Castle as Queen Amanita clenched her fist and muttered a phrase in a language so dark that even Ugu winced. He could understand Amanita's fear; as a Giantess in her origin, she was vastly more bound to Faerie than even he, for the Herkus were mostly mortal, merely using a magical supplement to gain their supernal strength.

But that was not the only thing driving her current anger. "And read this — *this*! A Prophecy of our defeat!" She whipped out a black blade and drew back her arm for a strike that would have taken the head from the armored figure cowering before her.

Ugu caught her wrist and held it effortlessly, concealing his own trepidation as Amanita's rage transferred itself to him. "Unhand me, you second-rate sorcerer, or –"

"Peace, Queen Amanita. You allow your anger and, yes, fear, to blind you to the advantages of our position."

Her other hand had been curling in preparation for casting a transformation — which would have revealed his own protections and possibly precipitated a final conflict that he was very loath to pursue — when his words penetrated. The icy green eyes thawed slightly and she tilted her head in curiosity; he slowly loosed his grip and watched as she sheathed the three-foot ebony blade. "Advantages, my lord? If you see any advantages to their gaining an ally who can ignore even the mightiest sorceries, I am astounded and filled with curiosity, for it seems to *me* that this is a disaster."

"Indeed, it could be. But first, let us not punish our best servants for bringing us news we would rather not hear. Instead let us reward Cirrus Dawnglory for his long and perilous service."

The bowed figure raised his head cautiously. "Thank you, your Majesty. Though I no longer have need of that name."

"As you will; yet you took his name and identity three centuries agone, and in many ways you have become him." Ugu had spent

85

many years studying his people — the enslaved of Oz, the collaborators, the elemental spirits forged from his magic and Amanita's and the souls of particular natives of the Four Countries and the City. He had gained much understanding of the thoughts and feelings behind their actions — enough that he would on occasion privately admit to himself that it was his lack of such understanding which had led to his original defeat, in an almost inevitable manner. Amanita, he suspected, was incapable of such understanding in any but the most superficial and mechanical manner. This might — he hoped — prove one of his advantages, in the end.

He applied this knowledge carefully now. "I am sure that it was not easy to return to us with all you have brought."

The eyes that met his were wary, fearful, and he could see the shift of glance towards the expectant green-haired Queen. "H...how do you mean, your Majesty?"

"It would be a great wonder, Cirrus, if you could pass centuries at the side of a man so capable and loyal, live in a realm of such beauty, speak words of comfort and advice and friendship, and not have part of the lie become truth. Indeed, I would doubt you could have succeeded in your mission if your entire time in Iris' realm were naught but pure deception."

Amanita's eyes narrowed and her hand twitched again towards her black sword, but his hand stilled her. *Part of her still remembers it was I who freed her. For now.*

After a moment, the false Cirrus nodded. "I... I did like him, Majesty. It...pained me to betray him in the end."

"I know it felt like a betrayal, Cirrus. Yet you entered there under our orders, following the imperatives of our kingdom. His own Cirrus did not betray him, but died fighting to the last — a noble death." He kept his face solemn and respectful; and, in truth, he felt respectful, even if Amanita did not. "You, then, have carried out a terrible and perilous mission for your true sovereigns, despite many temptations. Even Nimbus would understand this difference. You have done well. We will have much need of your counsel in the months ahead; go, rest. Refresh yourself. We shall send for you later."

Clearly amazed at his good fortune, the false Cirrus — once merely one of the twisted Tempests he had forged from a Gillikin soul — rose, bowed, and departed.

Once the doors had closed and they were alone, Amanita turned a slit-eyed gaze to him. "If you *ever* interfere with me like that again, I will seriously consider re-negotiating our bargain, *King* Ugu. Now explain to me these so-called advantages."

He prevented himself from either an acid retort or a too-condescending smile. He was coming to realize that Amanita was more volatile and possibly even less sane than he had previously believed. *I am tied to her, perhaps by destiny...and I had best be cautious until I have found a way to sever those ties.* "The advantages are three, my Queen. Of primary and most overwhelming importance is that — unless our plans have gone terribly awry — not even Iris Mirabilis himself suspects that Cirrus Dawnglory has been an impostor, a creature of ours since almost the day that Oz fell. Had any been suspicious of him, they would have acted long ere now. And the attack and destruction of his patrol was complete; none survived to report back that Cirrus had turned on them, and no other Faerie were within any possible range of perception.

"Thus, what we have learned from him is our secret and ours alone."

She nodded, slowly. "But a minor advantage unless there is much more to be gained from this knowledge."

"And there is." He smiled coldly. "We have the Prophecy — which prophesies our *possible* defeat, but also victory, *and they do not know this.* Can you not see how well this is for us?"

Whether as the isolated Mrs. Yoop or as Queen Amanita, the Yookoohoo had never been said to be stupid. She paused and considered, and her red-lipped smile was as a shard of poisoned ice. "Oh... Oh, my, yes, my King. My sincere apologies. We have here in our grasp the way to our defeat...and if we take care, we can guide our enemies to follow that course until it ends in *theirs.*"

"Precisely. We must take care that none recognize that we know how our end is foreseen. We must not interfere in any way that would reveal our foreknowledge. React, never act, but prepare, *here,* for the grand finale that will dash their hopes, shatter their belief in their protection from our powers and their futile hope that the Above shall one day rescue them." He slowly seated himself in the Grey Throne. "And this very Prophecy also shows that — by describing how it may be used against us — the final ritual we have often discussed would, in fact, give us final and total control over all the power of Oz."

She laughed, that delighted yet chilling *glissando* echoing through the throneroom. "And they will be delivering to us that vital ingredient which we were lacking!" She settled back in her own throne, looking much more relaxed, and then glanced back up at him. "You mentioned *three* advantages, your Majesty. What is the third?"

"The third, my Queen, is the major reason that I not only prevented you from killing Cirrus, but have rewarded him, and intend to continue doing so — and I hope you shall join me in this. Even if we succeed in this grand final ritual, you know full well that it is Iris Mirabilis and his Legions — and the connections that it is said he has to the Above — who will pose the final and greatest threat to our eternal power over Faerie and Mortal lands.

"And here, in Cirrus Dawnglory, we have one who knows every detail of that sky-fortress' defenses — every door, every wall, every passage obvious and hidden, the tactics and strategies discussed by the Lord of Rainbow and his Head of Hosts, every single aspect of their ways of offense and defense...and they suspect not a bit of this. With his help, we may find that we can send our own warriors into the Rainbow Fortress without even sounding an alarm."

Her laugh rang out again, and a moment later his chuckle joined hers.

Chapter 13.

Polychrome watched from the doorway as the group of Guards prepared for training combat. She knew that Nimbus and her father were deeply worried; Erik had the intellectual and, somewhat surprisingly, physical potential to be a good – perhaps even better than good – warrior. But when it came down to actual fighting, sparring with the men in the closest thing to real combat they could manage to give him...he just couldn't seem to use what he'd learned. He hesitated, he backed off, he was perhaps one-half or one-tenth as effective as he might be. That was why she had decided to watch today and see if she could figure out what was going wrong.

Erik stood at the center of the room, waiting. He was dressed in twilight-indigo crystal-metal armor and holding a shining silver sword, touched with a hint of emerald, that was about as long as he was tall. He held it in one hand, moving it absently as though it were a fishing rod instead of a huge blade of metal that, she knew, she could lift but would never be able to wield even with both hands even for a few seconds. His True Mortal nature rendered the mystical blade effectively massless for him — and not for his targets, making it terrifyingly effective if he was willing to actually use it properly.

Willing...is that it? No, I've been watching him these months. He was only telling the truth about his laziness — he doesn't like *working hard, but he's also told the truth about his dreams, and he's really been working hard for this dream, even though I've heard him complaining to himself a lot when he thinks no one's listening.*

Part of that work showed in his appearance. The armor he wore made his shoulders look very broad, but they *were* broader than they'd been when he first arrived, and the belt holding the mail now defined a true waist instead of something more rounded; his face had also become more defined, square and sharper with less rounding. She approved.

Unfortunately, appearance didn't mean much. It was performance that mattered, and he was consistently failing to perform. she'd heard the Guards whisper — and suspected he had, too — that he was already a failure. They would not speak unkindly to his face, they were too well disciplined and trained to do so to a guest of the Lord of Rainbows, but she knew that his failures were causing the Storm Legions to fear that already the Prophecy had failed and their cause was lost.

The Guards spread out, encircling Erik Medon; his eyes checked their positions carefully as he turned to watch their movements. Then he noticed her, and his eyes widened slightly.

"Ready, all..." Nimbus called, raising his hand.

The blond mortal gripped the sword now in both hands and seemed to gather himself.

The armored hand dropped. "Begin!"

The Guardsmen charged in a synchronized attack; Erik, recognizing that the last thing he needed was to get caught in the center of that mess, charged in the direction he was already facing, swinging the huge blade in front of him to clear a path.

One of the guards behind hurled a spear, but it glanced off the armor. Erik only winced slightly, bowling over one of the Guards in front and clearing him with an impressive leap that took him well out of the encircling group of Guards.

But he didn't do anything to make sure the one who went down doesn't get back up! Poly thought in despair.

Erik whirled, delivering a sweeping strike that shattered the shafts of two spears jabbing at him; she saw the sword actually bend slightly from the impact, springing straight but, she thought, possibly with a notch in one side. He caught a hard-swung mace in one hand and ripped it out of the Guard's hand like taking a toy away from a toddler, threw it over his shoulder, shoved the Guard away, and smacked another sideways with the flat of the sword.

But the Guards were faster. The ring was closing in around him again and they were matching his movements better, hemming him in. Half of them were disarmed by now but they grabbed his arms, his legs, and those with weapons remaining were starting to get in hits. She winced as she saw one point slip through the guards to prick Erik's leg; he cursed, then staggered as a pair of Guards struck the back of his knees. As he went down under a pile of Guards who were now systematically beating on him, she saw him raise his head, perhaps to see if she was still watching.

Her hand involuntarily went to her mouth in sympathy.

Then Erik vanished as the Guards *really* piled on. She saw Nimbus' eyes roll upward, his head shaking in frustration.

Then she heard a low, baritone snarl from under that pile, a pile that suddenly shuddered; she thought she heard a couple of nonsensical words in that sound that became a full-fledged roar as the entire mass of Guardsmen was heaved skyward, flung away from the figure at the center like straws in a hurricane.

Her jaw dropped at that display of furious power.

Erik's hand whipped out, grabbed a Guard and crushed the armor on his shoulder, before Erik hurled him through the mass of his fellows, bowling them aside, Faerie tenpins hit by a living bowling ball. Then his movements somehow sped up...a silver streak spun about in a complete circle, batting the still-recovering Guards away in a shower of metallic fragments.

They didn't move.

Erik Medon stood there alone, breathing heavily in triumph despite his breath's sharp, whistling undertone. His armor hung on him in fragments, there were trickles of blood from a dozen minor wounds and red welts of bruises which would undoubtedly become blue soon enough, and his mighty sword was a shattered, unrecognizable mess except for the hilt. He looked about with wide eyes showing anger fading to shock and concern.

Nimbus' expression, by contrast, had just changed from worry to savage delight. "Now by the Seven Hues *that* is what I was seeking, Erik Medon! *That* is the power, the strength, the skill I've been trying to get you to reach for these six months! Well done, well done *indeed!*"

Erik didn't seem to hear him. Instead, he ran over to the Guards, especially the one he'd used as a bowling ball. "Jesus, holy crap, Rain, you okay? Stratos? Mist? I'm sorry, guys, I—"

Rain winced. Red showed under the torn and crumpled armor, and he obviously was struggling to breathe, but even so, the

Guardsman managed a pained smile. "Think...nothing...of it, Lord Medon. I am...honored to have been...one of the first to learn that our hope is not gone." The others nodded, lines of restrained worry smoothing out despite pain.

"What? I could have *killed* you with that stupid –"

"*Peace*, Erik." Nimbus placed a hand on his shoulder. "None died, and the injured will be tended to." He shook his head with a wry smile, studying the mortal before him as another piece of Erik's armor — most of the breastplate — fell off. "Finding you equipment that will survive your use, however, may prove more problematic. Still, now that you have gotten past whatever had restrained you, let us continue."

Erik shook his head emphatically. "No way. I'm done for now. Maybe for good." He turned and walked away, slower now but with clear decision.

The Captain of the Legions went to stop him, but Polychrome shook her head, and went to follow.

She hung back, but caught up with him halfway back to his quarters when he slowed to a stop. "Erik—"

The whistling undertone had gotten louder, and she saw him suddenly grope under the remains of his armor, tearing it off and reaching into one of his pockets, pulling out the plastic-and-metal device he called an "inhaler."

It did not make quite the same sound as she remembered, and he triggered it twice more before she heard something more like the original quick, sharp *hiss*. He held his breath for a moment then let it out; slowly that undertone retreated, but it did not seem to be going away. "Sorry...I may be in trouble. That sucker's running out, and you don't seem to have a decent pharmacy around here."

"You need that...device...often?"

He grimaced and leaned against the wall. "If I exercise, yeah. You remember our little run, of course. Well, Nimbus has been driving me hard. I've tried to pace myself as much as I could, but it's not easy."

"Maybe Father could –" She broke off. "Oh."

"Yeah. There's all sorts of miracles your dad could do, I think. He *thinks* he can get away with fixing my vision; that's basically a one-time shot that just re-molds my lenses and softens them up, doesn't really change *me*. But fixing my asthma and allergies? That's a full-body biochemical change, maybe genetic, *or* it means I have to have magic running in my bod 24/7."

That would be self-defeating, she knew; the more magic that was made a part of him — even willingly — the greater the chance that it would compromise his True Mortal status, at which point the entire reason for his presence here would be in jeopardy. "Perhaps we can at least find a way to duplicate or re-fill your inhalers and your other medicines."

He nodded, clearly still recovering from his own body's attempt to suffocate him after that last huge exertion. "Yeah. I sure don't want to have to try to do this whole gig while having to guess when and how I'm going to keel over suddenly." He straightened. She noticed that he still kept his eyes focused exclusively on her face, or away from her entirely. "Poly, I'm sorry you had to see that mess."

"Mess? I got to see you succeed for the first –"

"I got *mad* for a minute and I almost killed the guys who are supposed to be teaching me!" he snapped, and there was a brittle edge to his voice. "It felt real good for a couple of seconds, until I realized I might really have *hurt* someone."

That explains a lot, she thought, and filed it away for her later discussion with Nimbus. "So why then? That can't be the first time you got...overwhelmed."

He looked away for a moment, a sheepish grin on his face. "*You* weren't there the other times. It's probably pretty stupid, but the last thing I saw as they hogpiled me was you looking at me as though I was so totally pathetic... and I just couldn't stand the thought of lying there being beat to a pulp while you watched. And with all of them punching and kicking...I just suddenly got really pissed and let it all out." He looked down at himself. "Er, look, I'm hardly in any condition to be talking to you right now, I hurt all over, I probably stink, and as soon as I get over my upset I'll probably just have to head back to training." He went to the door of his quarters.

She wanted to inquire more, but she thought she understood now. "All right, Erik. I'll...see you later?"

His face lit up. "If...if you want to, sure."

As he started to open the door, she said, "Wait. Just one little question before you go."

"Oh?"

"Well...it was something I heard when you finally acted..." She concentrated to make sure she remembered it right. "Um... 'Mortal smash?'"

He burst out laughing, and there was a touch of red on his cheeks. "Oh, that...um... Look, that'd take a while to explain. Later, all right?"

He is so hard *to understand sometimes,* she thought. "All right."

She retraced her steps to the training area and found Nimbus examining the shattered pieces of sword and armor. "Lady Polychrome," he said with a nod. "Did you learn anything of value?"

"I think so." She recounted most of the conversation. "So...I think the problem is that he really just doesn't want to *hurt* people."

"Um." Nimbus wrinkled his brow. "That's common for Faerie of a certain sort. You've got much of that in you, of course, though I've noticed you seem willing to overcome that. Most of your sisters. The Lady Ozma, of course. But he's talked about dreams of being a great warrior of various sorts, some I just can't quite understand. Does his dream, then, stand against his soul?"

She shook her head. "I don't know for sure, Nimbus. But I think that's the problem you've been seeing."

He sighed. "That could be fatal. Thinking along those lines, there's some things I can do to make him more effective, but in the end he has to be ready to hurt — or even kill — because sure as the Rainbow, our enemies will kill him if they get the chance."

"I know, Nimbus. But...is it not better that he be unwilling to kill than too willing?"

"I suppose," the Captain of Hosts said grudgingly, "but I just hope we won't pay for the luxury of a conscience."

Chapter 14.

I sat down at the small table; this time it was just me, Iris Mirabilis, Nimbus, and Polychrome. "So...what's on the agenda today?" I said after a pause.

"Nimbus tells me that you have made considerable progress." The Lord of Rainbows' tone showed that there were still reservations in that assessment. "While we have many concerns, it is clear now that you have the potential and the will needed, and that — for good or ill — we shall have to rely on you truly fulfilling the role of prophecy."

I really hate hearing that line. Too much on my shoulders. Yes, I know it's all there anyway, but whenever they say it, it just looms up that much more. "I don't think I'm done with my training yet."

"No, not quite," Nimbus agreed. "But we are nearing the point at which I will be unable to teach you much more without taking vastly more time. A few more months, at the most, and you will be ready for the final test. We cannot wait much longer."

"No," Polychrome said. "We evaded Tempests on the way here, so the enemy surely knows I went to the mortal world and did *something*. They probably even know I brought someone back with me. So they must guess we're planning to do something..."

"...and the longer we wait, the greater the chance that they will decide to act, rather than react." Iris Mirabilis finished. "So now we must begin the real planning of what you will do, how it will be done, and how we can best assure our victory in the end. You have heard the Prophecies of the Bear many times. Have they enlightened you at all? For I admit that often they remain opaque even to me, and I have spent many years indeed reading them."

I grinned. "In some ways, yes, I think they have. Though in most cases it might be best for me to keep things to myself, if you understand what I mean."

The Rainbow Lord's immense head tilted slightly, but his lips were touched with a smile. "I believe I may, Erik Medon. For your journey, your guesses and judgments must be your own." He turned to Nimbus. "Have you solved the riddle of his arms and armor?"

"I'm afraid not," the Captain of Hosts said reluctantly. "We do not generally work in mortal materials, and such materials would be too heavy and clumsy without proper modification. Our own materials, alas, simply cannot survive his use."

"Never mind," I said. "I already have my own answer for that problem. It's in the Prophecy."

The three looked at me in surprise. "In truth? I remember no lines that address your equipment. Not even thinking on them now," Iris said finally, "can I find a reasonable interpretation that would lead me to that conclusion."

Now it was *my* turn to chuckle. "Well, maybe it's not *in* the Prophecy literally, but it's sorta implied. Anyway, don't worry about it." I ran over the lines in my mind. "I'm more worried about the bit involving fighting a battle there when I happen to know that — as you've mentioned more than once — the Great Barrier around Oz prevents any Faerie from entering Oz. I'll admit I've managed to become a lot tougher than I would've thought, but I'm not an 'army of one,' so to speak."

Iris nodded slowly. "You are correct. This is a matter to which I have had to devote much thought.

"The Barrier cannot be broken from without. From within, however, it can be opened, and by careful examination of the magics used and what we have learned from the enemy's actions, I have devised a solution." From a pouch at his side he pulled a crystal — to him, the size of a large marble; to me, more like a golf ball — that flickered with the colors of his Rainbow. "Place this upon the soil of Oz and my Rainbow will bridge the gap, become a path from one side of the Deadly Desert to another."

That was a relief. "So — if you'll pardon me for trivializing something that's undoubtedly anything but trivial — all I have to do is get across the desert and I can bring through my reinforcements?"

The other three laughed. "Yes, indeed, that is all. An afternoon's work for one of your might, Erik," Nimbus said with a half-smile. "But there is more to concern us."

Poly nodded. "The lines that go:

Army faces army, fifty thousand strong
Both of Faerie, neither yielding
The battle will be long;

...yes?"

Nimbus grunted. "Any way I read that, I cannot come up with enough men. Even if I assume both armies *together* are fifty thousand strong, which would strike me as a most unlikely reading. I have ten thousand men, fifteen perhaps if I call for more volunteers. All of these I will commit, but that leaves us many short."

I nodded. "I know. What about the other Faerie kingdoms?"

Iris shook his head. "None of them will commit anything. They all see any attempt at attacking Oz as foredoomed, and any who attempt it will be destroyed. The only forces of warriors that might have been capable of being a significant factor in such an assault were taken by Amanita herself."

"The Phanfasms and some of the other nastier Faerie types."

"You speak truly. Not that they would have been inclined to aid us; though they were partially neutralized many years ago, still their nature was capricious and often cruel, and uninterested in aiding others."

Nimbus picked up the thread. "You of course represent a new factor...but we cannot discuss that factor with them. You are our secret until you leave here, and when you do so, you must be greatly cautious about those you contact, for any of them could be a spy or ally of our enemy."

I nodded. "I understand. I'm not planning on taking too many risks. But...I'll have to take some. Hell, the endgame means I'm going to be risking *everything*, so I think you — and I, for that matter — will have to trust my judgment on a lot of these things."

"Yes. We have little choice. But that 'endgame' is of grave concern. I am not even sure how to help you there. You would have to understand a great deal, especially about the basic nature of Oz and the Power of Faerie, before you could even begin to wield it. And you will have no time to practice...yet there really is no way to teach it to you except in theory. In the end, you will have to have clear in your mind the way in which you will wield the Power of

Faerie, and keep that clarity..." Iris frowned. "How to begin? The essence of Oz –"

"Is the Five Elements." I interrupted him. The startled, gratified look Polychrome gave me made my heart stop and restart.

"True enough," the Rainbow Lord said slowly. "But can you say what that means?"

"It's pretty clear after I thought about it a bit. Oz is divided into five areas — four quadrant countries and one central area linking all of them. Then you have the clue of the Tempests, which Polychrome once mentioned were derived from Gillikins, at least in part. So I guess this means that the Gillikin country represents Air, the Quadling country Fire, the Munchkin country Water, and naturally the Winkie country is Earth."

"And the Emerald City?"

"Emerald, the color of growing things, and the center of Faerie? Spirit, soul, the power of life itself. So if I'm right, Ugu and Amanita have not just storm-based Tempests but other twisted elemental spirits. Am I right?"

Nimbus looked pleased. "You are exactly right. There is much more to each element than their simple natures, though."

"Yes, I realize that. Together the five make up, well, everything, so things like, oh, intelligence have to be characteristic of some element or another. I'd guess fire, for that one in specific. Toughness is probably earth. And so on."

"Does this..." Polychrome began.

"...Help? Hell yeah. If you can give me a list of the associated properties for each element, I can get quite a bit of practice envisioning how I might be able to *use* them in an actual conflict. And with luck, it might even work the way I envision it, if the power combines with me as you say."

We all carefully avoided the issue of exactly what was going to be happening to me *while* I tried to use all that power.

"Polychrome? Please gather all this information for Erik. What he asks for, we indeed have." For the first time, I saw actual hope on Iris' face, and I was glad. The longer I'd been here, the more I'd started to understand what a terrible burden he lived under.

Just as long as it isn't false *hope*, the nagging part of me said. But it was right. I had come a long way, I had to admit. I had figured out several parts of the prophecy, and I was starting to see a path to the end of the journey... but any part of it could come unglued with just one wrong guess.

And boy, was I having to make a lot of guesses.

Chapter 15.

" . . . and these notes were written by the Wizard himself, not all that long before Oz fell." She placed the thick sheaf of parchment on top of the least-wobbly stack next to Erik.

The mortal could-be-Hero nodded absently, absorbed in sketching some sort of diagram or chart which, she could see, had already been re-sketched, modified, parts scribbled out and redrawn, with dozens of little notations that she couldn't really make out; his handwriting wasn't very readable to begin with, and he seemed to have a habit of using abbreviations or annotations which referred to things only he understood.

"Are... are you making progress?" she asked hesitantly.

He glanced up and looked contrite. "I'm sorry. Really, Poly, I didn't mean to seem like I wasn't paying attention."

It was strange how...formal, cautious, even apologetic he became around her. she'd watched him around other people and he didn't act at *all* like that around them — even her father. He wasn't *rude* normally, at least not intentionally, but he seemed almost impervious to the intimidation most mortals *or* Faerie would feel in the presence of the Rainbow Lord, and spoke to them apparently as he would to any reasonably respected adult. She couldn't understand why he was so oddly gentle and attentive with her.

But it *did* make these rather dull study sessions much more tolerable, so she smiled. "No apology needed, if you're getting anywhere."

He stretched, giving a prodigious yawn, and then smiled back, the smile that sometimes made him look years younger. "Oh, I'm getting somewhere. It's amazing what you can dig up when you know what you're looking for."

She couldn't keep her eyebrows from rising. "How could you possibly know what you're looking for, when none of us do, and you're not even a trained wizard?"

One of his eyebrows arched up and he raised a finger. "Because I know what I will need to be able to do, the Prophecy indicates it's

101

possible for me to do it, and this narrows down the approaches I can reasonably use to achieve it. More, because *I* was selected by the Prophecy rather than someone else, I have to assume that this, too, was no coincidence, but rather that it's what I am, personally, which will give me a chance to win this battle," he said in a professorial tone.

She shook her head. "Does that actually make sense, or are you just talking? Sometimes you are very hard to read, Erik."

"Oh, it makes perfect sense." He stood and pulled out a chair for her. "I'll take it apart for you. First, I know that I'm going to have to match — at least — both Ugu the Unbowed and Amanita Verdant up-close and in person, at the center of their power and with them probably by that point fully aware I'm a True Mortal. They've got all the power of Oz — minus whatever Ozma can give me, I suppose — to throw at me, plus servants or weapons wielding all the power they've managed to make use of in these three centuries. That means I have to face the full power of the Five Elements, and even if they can't *directly* affect me much, there's plenty of indirect effects any of these things could manage which would totally trash me. One of those Infernos setting the surroundings on fire, for instance.

"So I'll need to be able to equal, or better yet overpower, any manifestation of the Five Elements, and do it myself, with no time for formal training. The prophecy, by its existence, tells me I *can* win: '...but in those final moments he may win the day,' remember." He looked momentarily grave, as he always did when he heard that line.

She felt a small pang of guilt. *I brought him here to offer himself up for our sake. What must he think of me for that? Bringing a man to Faerie so he can die to protect us.*

She shook off the mood; he was continuing, and she wanted very much to understand.

"So, then, how can I possibly fight two masters of such wizardry without knowing any myself, *and* without destroying everything that I'm trying to protect? Ozma's power has to be directed and controlled by me. Maybe she can give me some pointers, but I have to assume it's really me doing the work." He glanced at the annotated diagram and smiled sharply. "So that means that I must be able to properly direct and control the powers pretty much by having a clear idea of what I want to accomplish, and the basic method of doing so using the Five Elements. In short, if I understand enough about *how* the powers work, then it's up to me to be able to visualize what I want them to do accurately and clearly and with enough...force, I guess, passion, will, to drive them. I'm the conduit for the force, or perhaps a lens to focus it."

She looked at the diagram. "And you think you're learning what you need?"

"I think I already *knew* a lot of what I needed. Oh, not the details, but I spent an awful lot of time — significant parts of my life since I was fourteen, actually — imagining things that aren't, powers that only existed as far as I knew in stories, figuring out how they worked under a dozen different sets of assumptions, visualizing these things...and here, in the notes from Glinda, the Wizard, others, are the keys.

"You mentioned before your father felt there was a connection between the Faerie and Mortal worlds; these papers prove it. Our dreams, our fantasies, our nightmares and visions, these cross through and touch the Faerie world, affect the fabric of your reality; and in turn, your actions, the changes and wars and triumphs of your world, echo back through the connection and affect our very souls. There are some terrible implications in this as well, ones we'll have to face later. But for now, it means that I already know *what* I want to visualize in many cases; I just needed the information on how I could make that work."

Now she could see that the diagram had symbols associated with particular groups of notations: a wave, a cloud, a flame, a mountain, and a star. "Oh! Water, air, fire, earth, and spirit?"

"Exactly! Each with the characteristics attributed to them by various researchers." He scratched his head. "Problem is that there isn't universal agreement here. In fact, there's a lot of overlap and confusion. You guys never quite got to the Industrial Revolution really and certainly haven't even knocked on the door of the Information Age. If I end up staying here, I may have to introduce the profession of research librarian."

103

He paused. "Where was I? Oh, yeah. Like I was saying, for Water we have of course the physical characteristics of water, plus wisdom — depth, you know — but also healing, self-knowledge, reflection, transformation in some ways. For Fire we get (besides heat, of course), speed, intelligence or cleverness, the symbolism of power; Air is truth and illusion — the clarity of a blue sky or the concealment of cloud, evasion, movement; Earth, toughness, solidity, defense, stability in all senses of the word, endurance; and Spirit is willpower, life, emotions, that which separates ordinary matter from the numinous."

"That makes sense," she said, appreciating his summary, "but how would you use it?"

He had the same slightly embarrassed look she remembered from earlier. "Well...rather than go into details on that, as a simple example it means that if he throws, say, an Inferno at me, I can counter with Water, a Tempest's lightning I can ground out with Earth, and so on. *These* people understand magic; *I* am a very devious and sneaky ba–" he broke off, continued, "er, guy, and I can think of things to do with magic that only an advanced technological civilization with our peculiar quirks would come up with."

He's a strange combination of diffidence, arrogance, confidence and uncertainty. "I'm sorry I got you into this," she said suddenly.

"I'm not." He looked at her directly and she noticed his cheeks looked flushed for a moment. "Yeah...I'm not all that excited about getting killed, which looks pretty likely...but then, a lot of people have died for things that were worth a lot less. You are...I mean, you know, you as in all of you," he stammered, speaking quickly, "you are...all of the dreams I had as a child, and aren't dreams worth dying for sometimes?"

Polychrome wondered at why she found those words so... frightening. "Well, Erik, let's try our best to avoid all the dying. In fact, I don't think I like this direction of conversation."

"Right. Too grim." He looked somehow relieved, yet tense. "Um...look, you know, I've hardly had much chance to talk to you or anyone about what you people do outside of the training and all.

I've been kept mostly a secret outside of the guards as far as I know, and so I haven't seen much since my original arrival. So...when there isn't some terrible emergency, what do you people do?"

She blinked. "Why, I..." She giggled. "That was a rather abrupt shift. I haven't thought about that sort of thing in a while. I do a lot of dancing, of course, and I've always spent more time around the Storm Guards than Father might like. But there's parties, and the Cloud Theatre, and sometimes magicians showing off their talents, or..."

"You go with people, I'd presume?"

"Well, yes, of course, any event's more fun with the right people. My sisters come to some events, though they haven't got my...well, what they call adventurous side, when they're being polite." *His gaze seems...so intense,* she thought as she continued, describing how she sometimes convinced some of the Guard to accompany her. *That's silly, though. It's not as if we're discussing anything of importance.*

But I...rather like the fact he pays attention so well.

Chapter 16.

"We're running out of time, I think."

Iris nodded, surveying the training area with eyes that seemed to look far beyond the walls of the castle. "You have come far, and your words have convinced me that you do have some plan. In a week or two, perhaps, no more. Have you decided on what you will do when you leave?"

"I'm pretty sure what I need to do. I have to cross the Deadly Desert alone, and even as a True Mortal that's not going to be easy. The Prophecy also says,

With one companion he sets out,
another he must win

But that could be I set out from here with one, or from wherever I'm supposed to seek wisdom." I glanced up at him.

The Rainbow Lord shook his head. "None from here. Polychrome will bring you into Faerie, but until you have found your way to Oz itself, I will not have her leaving again. She is marked by the enemy, and they watch her every move. A quick foray on the Rainbow to bring you down, yes, that she can do, but no more."

It didn't take a genius to see that Iris would rather she wasn't involved at all, but as I'd now lived there for nearly a year, it was also pretty obvious that no one had much chance at all in getting her to stay out of everything. "So what are you doing here now?"

"You could call this your final exam, Erik Medon." Nimbus leaned on his sword, a smile I didn't like at all on his face.

"I've been doing pretty good for someone who hardly ever *saw* a sword before, I think."

"And not one of us would disagree. As an older mortal — not *old*, true, but not in the bloom of youth — you seem to have gained some perspective which perhaps a younger man would not, giving you something to make up for the reflexes you might have lost." Nimbus effortlessly sheathed his sword, and paced around the room. "We have found a way to replicate the effect of your medicines, so your own body should not kill you if you are given enough time to use them, and you have become quite adept at judging exactly how far you can push your body."

I smiled wryly. "Learned a lot of that many years ago; pay attention to the signals your bod gives you, or it might never give you any again."

"Wisdom and truth, my friend. Still, all of your training has been with my warriors. Formidable they are, and very much like some of those you will have to face, and yet...not quite. We cannot give you a foretaste of the true power of the Tempests, Infernos, Temblors, and Torrents at the command of our enemies, but it is to be hoped that many of their advantages will find themselves useless against a True Mortal. However," he turned to face me again, "in the end you must face even more formidable opponents, and of *that* we can give you a sample."

I blinked. "Oh, I have a bad feeling about this." The old quote felt all too true.

Yes, that *was* a very evil grin on Nimbus' face. "All you have to do is take down both of your opponents. Not even, necessarily, show that you could finish them. Merely take them down."

I turned my head slowly, to see Iris Mirabilis, the Rainbow Lord, unlimbering a sword that would have been more appropriate as a helicopter rotor blade, twenty feet or more long and over a foot wide, double-edged. "Oh, you have *got* to be kidding me."

"Far from it, Erik Medon. You will be facing opponents as formidable as myself — perhaps, even, my size. For do not forget one of the new rulers of Oz was once a Giant, and may use other Giants against you."

"You said 'both' of my opponents," I said, still having a hard time taking my gaze from that monstrous blade, "who's the second? You, Nimbus?" That would be bad; with no false modesty I knew I'd gotten to be pretty damn good, but there was no way I would outmatch the immortal guard captain, especially with the Rainbow Lord ready to step on me like a bug.

"Oh, no, not me." The smile he wore was *still* evil. "Neither of your ultimate opponents are, after all, master warriors, though I would not underestimate their skills entirely. However, there is a much more appropriate choice in this case."

I glanced in the direction he indicated. Polychrome stood there, a crystal staff in her hand.

Oh, Jesus H. Particular Christ on a pogo stick. "I can't fight her!"

Iris' sword stabbed down inches in front of me, embedding itself in the smoky-blue floor, shattering the mystical stone like glass. "One of your opponents is a woman of beauty enough to perhaps even match my daughter, mortal," the Rainbow Lord said, looking grimly down at me as I recovered my balance from the sudden shock. "We do not require you to truly hurt or kill either of us, but you must be able to *fight* anything and anyone. Ugu the Unbowed is a master of illusion as well as of more direct magics, and properly cast, such illusions will fool even you until you actually touch their source. You must follow your convictions, fight your opponents, let nothing distract you."

Poly spun her staff around like a baton, showing that she wasn't at all unfamiliar with the weapon. "Erik, I appreciate that you don't want to hurt me...but if you don't at least *try*, I'm going to have to hurt *you*, and I really don't want to do that."

I stared at her for a moment, then swallowed. They were completely right. I couldn't be expected to fight the real thing if I couldn't win a sparring match against something roughly equivalent. "All right." I pulled out my latest sword and hitched my armor slightly; the armorers had gotten used to supplying me with replacements after every session, so at least now they fit me perfectly.

Nimbus backed off.

Even before he'd fully reached shelter, Iris Mirabilis charged, whirling his blade up and then down in a killing stroke.

He is actually large enough that I can dodge him...and I'd damn well better when possible. I tumblesaulted between his legs, trying to smack his ankle; I managed a glancing blow, but it didn't do much.

A blaze of clashing colors erupted around me, and I almost closed my eyes reflexively. Only my training in ignoring the actually-ineffectual magical attacks kept my eyes slitted open, which allowed me to see Polychrome streaking in through the dazzle. I swung the sword around, flat side to her. There was no chance for her to –

And she was gone.

A stinging *thwack* from behind. I whirled, saw Polychrome fading away again, but now I was dodging as that gigantic sword came down, carving a ditch in the mystical cloud-stone we fought on. I took advantage of that magical characteristic and jumped hard. The stone, as rigid and unyielding to Faeries as it appeared, bowed and rebounded like a mass of rubber under me; in effect, my anti-magic repelled the magical stone, sending me hurtling into the air where I took a cut at Iris' head. He ducked. I cut deep into his shoulder-guard, and he staggered with the impact.

One of his crackling balls of lightning thundered down at me as I landed, but I was more concerned with Polychrome. I remembered the scene in the Nome King's halls in...was it in *Tik-Tok of Oz*? ...where Ruggedo had tried to catch her and she'd simply humiliated him. Now I understood what Baum had tried to convey. The other Faerie were much faster than I was, but you could still *follow* them. Polychrome was like a flickering sunbeam off water, darting from one point to another. Part of me was getting frustrated, the other just fascinated, watching her move here, there, seeming almost everywhere at once. No single stroke of that staff was terribly damaging, but if I couldn't stop her –

And the Rainbow Lord was there again, slower by far than his daughter but still terrifyingly fast, the sword coming straight down, Poly disappearing to reappear — I was sure — behind me.

That gave me a minor inspiration. I brought my sword up in a focused parry and, at the same time, kicked out behind me.

I felt my foot connect at the same time Iris' massive sword slammed into my own. The impact jarred me from teeth to toes and I was hammered at least four inches into the stone as my sword shattered and Iris' was gouged deeply. He staggered back from the sheer force of the parry and I turned as fast as I could, seeing Polychrome just as she finished her tumble across the floor.

But she was getting up, though slowly; I shoved away my instinctual impulse to run to her and ask if she was okay. *I have to get both of them down!*

As fast as I was, it still wasn't enough. She dodged from me with a laugh. "That was well done, Erik! But you have to do better!" There was both encouragement and concern on her face.

And then I heard, too late, the *whoosh* of air behind me.

The flat of Iris' sword took me right across the back, sent me sailing up and across the room like a golf ball. I caromed off one wall, smacked into the next face first, and then skittered across the floor like an air-hockey puck. I woozily tried to roll, keeping the Rainbow Lord from getting another bead on me, but Polychrome was already there, bashing me about the head and body, beating me like a cheap drum. Every blow stung, and I could taste blood from where my front teeth had gouged my upper lip.

And this isn't a mob. It's just two very powerful people. Who don't even really want to kill me. And they're not going to hogpile me like the guards. They'll just keep bashing me piecemeal until I collapse or surrender.

And then I fail.

I forced myself to my feet, but that damn staff tripped me up again — and *just* as I hit the floor, Iris *stomped* on me.

The breath exploded from my lungs at the impact. *Thank whatever gods there are that the magical stone gives like rubber to me, or he'd be scraping me off his shoe.* I felt the stone rebound as he stepped back, and despite being almost totally disoriented managed to use that, flip upright, then tumble drunkenly away to buy just a little time.

Rebound...?

It was a crazy idea... but it fit with all the crazy things I could already do, and the way magic worked around me.

I rose to my full height, bringing both my arms up, seeing Iris already almost on me to the right, Poly streaking in from the left...

"Try *this!*"

I brought both my arms down, bending double, practically dropping to the ground, focusing my attack not on either of them,

111

but on the *floor*, the stone which was not real stone, but mystically-solidified cloud, the fabric of the Rainbow Lord's realm.

The impact bowed the floor under me by ten feet or more and rebounded in a shockwave that thundered outward like a tsunami, hurling Polychrome into the air and away like a toy and toppling Iris Mirabilis as though his legs had been cut out from under him. I was up in that moment, leaping through the air. I caught his impossible sword and laid it across his throat. "Down."

Polychrome had not yet risen; she stared from the floor in utter amazement, and her father's eyes were wide.

Nimbus emerged from the doorway, clapping, and his applause was echoed by the other warriors who surged into the room. "You pass, my friend!"

Polychrome launched herself from the floor and flung her arms around me, and then, laughing, danced around me. "Oh, that was *beautiful*, Erik!"

I couldn't take my eyes from her. *She* was beautiful. No, she *was* beauty itself. And strength, and joy.

And now I knew I was in real trouble. I'd fallen in love with Polychrome when I was a kid, reading the books... but that wasn't the same as this. I'd known her for a year. she'd been a support, an advisor, sometimes the only encouragement I had, and now I could see she was just as tough and strong as her father, and what I felt for her now was something I didn't dare even contemplate.

It's a good thing I'm leaving soon.

That was the right thought to have. But it made the whole adventure suddenly feel a tiny bit darker.

Chapter 17.

Iris Mirabilis looked down from the balcony at the very top of his castle, moonlight streaming down and turning the blue-grey skystone to silver. Far below, he watched a small blond-haired figure in a private courtyard, practicing cuts and jumps and rolls, sometimes stopping to indulge in strange sequences of movements that did not immediately make sense to him. Iris raised his gaze slightly, noticed another figure, slight and swathed in shifting rainbow hues, watching Erik from another balcony, lower than Iris' own but well above the mortal's line of sight.

Raising his gaze still higher, he could see the looming mountains of the Earthly Firmament encircling his city, with the greatest of them — Caelorum Sanctorum- towering steeply to a point far above his castle, one that even his eyes could not easily pierce, a shadowed eminence of indigo and black shading to a brilliant spark of light where the sun — many hours set — still touched.

"You sent for me, Majesty?"

"Yes, Nimbus." He glanced down at the Captain of his hosts, then back up. "Five days."

Nimbus grunted, then followed his gaze. "Five... " He stared, then turned directly to face Iris. "Your Majesty, are you certain? Few indeed even of our own people have attempted that. As I recall, even your own daughters were -"

"My daughters," Iris found himself saying with an unexpected vehemence, "are of my own blood and have duties that I would expect them to carry out for that reason, if no other. They are not men snatched from their own world to die for the sake of mine."

Nimbus was silent for a moment, and then — unexpectedly — chuckled. "My King may correct me if I am wrong, but it seems to me that when first you had heard the prophecies and come to the conclusions of what they demanded, you were not at all bothered by the fact that the hero of prophecy would likely not survive past the ending of the threat."

113

Iris restrained a glare. Instead he simply took a breath, held it, and released it with a sigh. "You were not wrong, Captain. Unlike Polychrome and my other daughters, I have had occasion to look upon the mortal world as time passed, and I was very much afraid of what sort of man I might get from that world, and especially how that sort of man would affect *us*." By "us," he suspected Nimbus knew, he meant Polychrome, but the Captain said nothing. "They are a world of machines, of dark and heartless countries and industries that seem almost themselves machines, while in his own country they are a people of light and empty and it would seem almost meaningless entertainments, oblivious to much of the world around them... not that the other countries are truly much different. The people of that country have become ever more oriented to pleasures, hedonistic, focused on the self. And when *he* came here, though he had a veneer of courtesy, I thought that might be all he was. But now... yes, he is brash in some ways, loud, he has little of the manners one might have hoped for..."

Nimbus nodded slowly. "... but he has a sense of wonder that carries him when his rude or odd manners might fail, and those 'light and empty' entertainments have given him the keys of imagination that he needs, it would appear. Still..."

The Rainbow Lord turned away and paced for a bit before looking back down. The mortal was now standing unarmed, hands and body going through gestures that seemed akin to, yet were not exactly, combat, muttering disjointed words Iris could not make out. Then Erik paused, and Iris could tell he had caught sight of the smaller figure above him; Polychrome waved down at him, and the mortal stood immobile, staring up at her.

But he realized he hadn't answered Nimbus's implied question yet. "...Still? Yes, Nimbus, still, there are many questions unanswered, but we simply cannot get those answers here. And there is the question of myself, of my responsibility to a man who has come here to serve the most extreme need of Faerie. Oh, indeed, I nearly did hate him for his presence, for what it would mean. But now..."

Nimbus was looking down as well. "Are... are you going to tell him, then?"

"I cannot. I *dare* not. The delicacy of following prophecy cannot be overestimated; with a single misspoken word, all may unravel and be lost, dispelled as the mist before the sun."

He could see in Nimbus' nod that the Captain of the Guard understood — perhaps all too well. "And so you can offer him this as a...salve to your conscience. Yes, I suppose so, although if he dies in the process -"

"—Then he is not truly what we thought." The Rainbow Lord frowned; Nimbus' straightforward phrasing was unfortunately accurate, and Iris did not like seeing in himself a King who would so cynically use those around him. But it would be worse to deny it. "He will be losing as much as even I in the end — even if he lives. At least this I can give him, and I think someone such as he will appreciate what he sees. Perhaps it will even be of use; the inspiration to do these things does not come entirely at random, you know." Both he and Nimbus looked to the sky for a moment and nodded.

"I will prepare him, then." Nimbus turned to leave.

"Wait." Below, Polychrome had danced her way down to the courtyard and was talking to the mortal; he could catch enough of the conversation to know she was taking him to the Evening Banquet at the Tower of Dawn, where many of the people of the Kingdom would be. In these last few days he was making the presence of the Hero known, raising the spirits of the Rainbow Kingdom by making it clear that they were now preparing to act, rather than merely survive. "Let him go for now. Tomorrow is soon enough."

Nimbus smiled sadly, and bowed. "As you will, Majesty."

Chapter 18.

I felt the chill of the morning deep in my bones as I awoke. *I never liked camping as a kid, and I don't like it any better now. Who was it who said that adventures were unpleasant things happening to people a long way away?*

I dragged myself out of the little tent and onto the remainder of the little shelf of rock I was on. I wasn't sure of the point of this little exercise, but you generally didn't argue with Iris Mirabilis. I got out the little folded picture of a campfire he'd given me and shook it four times as instructed — once to each of the four cardinal directions.

As I finished the fourth, the picture shimmered in front of me and suddenly there was a blazing little fire on the stone almost at my feet. I jumped a bit. *I'd pretty much expected that, but having it happen... Even after all the time I've been here, it's pretty startling, especially if it seems to be me doing it.*

I carefully didn't look very far around as I cooked a simple breakfast and ate. Then I washed up as best I could, and packed up everything. Pack settled, I took a deep breath and looked up.

Caelorum Sanctorum towered over me, a titanic mass of cliffs and ridges and slopes that seemed to go up forever. For a moment, the lazy, sour-faced part of me whined, because it didn't look as though I'd made *any* progress in the last few days.

I glanced behind me. I almost regretted that, because while it did demonstrate that I'd made progress, I damn near got dizzy enough to fall off. Below me the mountain dropped away and away and away, ten thousand, fifteen thousand, twenty thousand feet, more? I had no idea really how high I'd come, or how much farther I had to go. Iris apparently thought I could make it in five days, or maybe he just wanted to see how long it took me to give up.

Well, I'm not giving up. Not after all that training, and not after I've come this far.

I made sure everything was secure, and then stepped up to the rock face. I found a handhold, pulled myself up, set my foot on a little ridge of stone, reached out, pulled up.

Focus. I'd freeclimbed when I was much younger — a stupid, stupid hobby that I'd often looked back on with a combination of wistful memory and wincing recognition of how easily I could have died. I'd found anything I could climb and gone up it — alone. Without any equipment. Without help. Sometimes a few hundred feet in the air, alone, doing it for as far as I could tell just the sheer adrenaline thrill of *almost* getting killed.

And now I was doing it again... at least two orders of magnitude worse. Well, okay, this time someone else wanted me to do this stupid thing, and I *did* have a little equipment. I took one of the safety spikes from my pack and slammed it into the stone, tied my rope on carefully. *Hmm. No handholds here at all.*

I'd reached one of the sheer sections of the mountain, shining grey-white like polished cloud in the slanting sun of morning. It looked as smooth as a morning fog even close up. In fact, I realized with bemusement that it was smooth enough for me to see my own face dimly reflected in it.

"Well, not much longer." I reached up and focused, and the stone suddenly gave under my fingers like butter.

Too much. I took a handful of it away without thinking.

I tried again, this time remembering the exact procedure I'd perfected over the past couple of days. This time I ended with a scooped-out handhold with a perfect grip.

The entire mountain was, of course, an impossibility. It was also more than ever clear, now that I could look out over the entirety of the Rainbow Kingdom, that I wasn't exactly in the same world that I'd been born in. Here I was above the ground at what must be, by now, over 50,000 feet, but the sky was only a little darker blue, and while it was pretty brisk right now it was going to warm up later — and I could still breathe. This kind of thing would be pretty obvious on satellite view, so we had to be in the parallel, different universe of the Faerie for sure.

So here I was, climbing a mountain of solid cloud. One that I could scoop out like soft butter if I wanted, or walk on like it was stone. That wouldn't save me if I fell, though, not from this height. Oh, sure, if I focused it'd be like butter, or even water, instead of stone, maybe even cotton candy, but if you hit *anything* at terminal velocity... well, there's at least *two* reasons you call that "terminal."

So, I thought, *why the hell is Iris risking his hero doing this mountain-climbing stunt?*

I gave myself another handhold, pressed on. Iris Mirabilis was hard to figure. When I first met him he greeted me in a friendly-enough fashion — aside from that lightning-ball stunt — but I'd gotten the impression he didn't like me much. That had changed in the last few months, and I just didn't know *why*, which bothered me. I've always been used to some people not liking me, and other people liking me, but it's not often that someone changes his opinion without my understanding of what I'd done to manage it.

Still, that wasn't going to help me with the business at hand. I settled down and started climbing for real.

It was a few hours later that it happened. That's always the worst point — you've been going long enough that you've got a routine, you're starting to get really tired, you're thinking about maybe getting lunch, something like that and then –

I squeezed too hard, lunged up a bit too much, and suddenly both my handhold and foothold broke off under me.

I plummeted down like a rocket; gravity, at least, worked exactly the same here as it did back home, something for which I really was *not* grateful right now. I grabbed for my rope, held it in my gloved hands, tried to time it so I could slow myself gradually rather than –

I mistimed it; all my weight *slammed* onto the rope, and the safety spike *popped* out of the cliff like a rotten tooth. "Ohhh crap," I heard myself say in a sort of *Hellboy* tone.

After the momentary pause I was heading back down fast, and the recoiling rope caused the spike to bash me insultingly in the head. This did, at least, remind me I had other spikes. I pulled two from my belt harness, gripped them tight, and hammered down.

With my mortal will focused on the spikes, the metal tore into the stone easily. My arms screamed in protest at the impact, though, because it was like trying to hold a blunt knife straight as it tried to

119

cut through a moving couch. The noise was incredible, a screeching wail of stone and steel with sparks showering like a fountain from the point of impact. I saw the spikes wearing away, bending —

—I released those two, grabbed two more, slammed them in, and -

W H A M!

Slowly, I picked myself up. "Well... I'm alive. That's a good thing on my checklist, I think." I was in a ten-foot deep miniature crater, and by the way the wall on my left side was cracking, I suspected there wasn't much rock that way. I carefully stood up and pulled myself gingerly upward. As my eyes cleared the edge, I cursed.

I had just landed on — well, mostly *through* — the ledge I'd camped on.

Most of the morning had just gone to waste.

I took a few minutes to cool down, because my first impulse was to just tear my way up the mountain with bare hands as fast as I could go — something which would undoubtedly quickly end with me falling again without anything but the bottom to break my fall, and me.

But once I had my emotions under control, I began to climb with a calmly infuriated energy. I was sick and tired of climbing this apparently unending mountain, but I was *not* going to let it beat me. Grip, control, pull, step, grip, control, pull, step, up and up, every few hundred feet another spike, grip, control, pull, step...

I felt my stomach growl, paused, hung myself on a couple of spikes and ate a sort of compressed granola-type thing Poly had given me. I did smile at that, because a trace of her perfume lingered on it somehow, storms and flowers touching my nostrils.

Then I went back to climbing. Dig handhold, grip, control, pull, step...

Suddenly I reached up and there was nothing there. No, wait, there was, but *inward*...

I pulled myself up once more, shoulders and hands and neck screaming, and saw a much shallower slope, a ridge running straight to the peak of the mountain, and — standing precisely on the peak — the immense figure of Iris Mirabilis, looking somehow small against the vastness of the mountain. Despite my exhaustion — I realized now that it was evening, the sun setting and casting a rich rose over Caelorum Sanctorum — I rose to my feet and trotted the remaining few hundred feet to the peak.

It was cooler here, but still nothing like the sub-arctic unbreathable chill of near-space I'd have run into on Earth, that I'd almost died in the one time I lost contact with Poly on the way here.

Iris looked down and smiled as I reached him. "Well done. The evening of the fifth day, and you stand on the peak of the Mountain."

"You seem to have hitched a ride on a ski-lift or something. I didn't notice *you* climbing."

He laughed. "I climbed this mountain more than once in my youth, and in some wise it is a harder climb for me than you."

Looking at his heroic frame, I grinned back. "I suppose it might be, at that. So, no offense, but what the hell was the *point* of my spending five days clawing my way up this impossible mountain?"

He looked serious — not grim, as he had with other questions I'd posed on occasion, but grave. "There were many points, in fact, to this apparently purposeless challenge. The simplest, and most to the point in our ultimate purpose, was to see you alone, set a task that you were not forced to complete — that you *could* choose to abandon at any time, or could simply fail at without direct consequence, and a task which presented no little risk to you. It is in my mind that when first you came here — even had I been able to grant you in an instant the skill and strength you now have — you would have given up that climb long ere you reached the summit. Would you say I was wrong?"

I thought on that for a few moments, gazing back down towards the Rainbow Fortress, a tiny toy castle so far away that in the fading light it was hard to make out at all. Finally, I sighed. "No...no, I'd say you were right. I've had a lot of projects I started and gave up on after a while."

"But not this? You hold our fate in your mortal hands, Erik Medon. What guarantee have we that this is different for you?"

Despite the words, it wasn't an accusation, or even a demand. It was, to my surprise, simply a question.

I looked up at the Rainbow Lord; his face here was...well, *different* than in the Throne Room or other parts of the castle. He was no less impressive, no less powerful, but I saw lines of worry and care which I had never noticed before. "I wish I had a guarantee for you. All I can say is that..." *careful, Erik, careful...* "... the realm of Faerie, the land of Oz, and all these things are part of my soul in a way nothing else is. For years those were my favorite stories, and in some ways very *privately* so, because I never met anyone else who knew them all until I was much, much older. Baum's stories...they're one of the top five things that shaped my entire life, and finding out that they're *real*...there are no words, Iris Mirabilis. I've always prided myself on my ability to speak and write, but I have no words to say what this place and...and its people mean to me."

A faint smile touched his face, and I thought for a moment I saw a slight gleam in his eye that I couldn't quite read. Then he straightened up.

"Fairly spoken, and true. We are forced to rely on your heart and your head, Erik Medon; an unlikely hero you seemed when first you arrived, as you yourself admitted, yet much has become clearer to me since that day.

"Another reason I had you climb Caelorum Sanctorum is that here — and here alone — can I be absolutely certain that I speak to you with none other to hear. While I *believe* my castle is secure, while I have done all that can be done to maintain the secrets of my house, I know full well I am beset by enemies of surpassing cunning and power perhaps vaster than my own, who were able to fell the greatest of the kingdoms of Faerie."

"So while you're probably right, you're still not going to take more chances than you have to."

"You have the right of it. Truth be told, I would have had you brought and trained here, were it possible, that it be utterly impossible for any eyes save my own to know who and what you were."

I looked around the peak. The top was actually quite broad, with the literal peak — the highest point — a couple hundred yards away, a miniature mountain itself about sixty feet high and a few hundred wide. "Why couldn't you?"

"In a moment," he said, postponing that answer.

"Okay, then why did you want to have me up here where no one else can spy on us?"

"Because there are a few things I must say which cannot be said in my throne room, regardless of their truth." He dropped to one knee in front of me — which still left his head well above mine. "Erik Medon, I must apologize to you. I have committed — and must continue to commit — a grave wrong upon you."

"Er... how do you mean that?"

"In two ways, if I am to be honest. Firstly, even now — a year after you arrived — there are elements of the Prophecies which I have not told you, and cannot. Even though it is possible that they may have some vital key to your survival."

I'd known there were some things he was probably still holding back, but *that* was a new, unsettling wrinkle. "You're saying that the other material in the prophecy — the stuff you haven't told me yet — might be something that could save my life?"

He considered, then nodded slowly. "It is...possible. Not certain, not, perhaps, even probable, given what I now know about you and the other aspects of the Prophecy. And of course you and I are both aware of the terrible dangers of *acting* too overtly on Prophecy unless it is absolutely necessary."

Yeah, the classic Evil Overlord Mistake: someone makes a prophecy that a certain baby will be your downfall, so you run out and kill off all the babies that meet the spec, except naturally you miss just one of them, and she grows up being trained for vengeance upon the baby-killer. If you'd just left things alone, she'd have grown up to be a farmer. "Yeah. I know. But...that's still pretty hard to just ignore."

"And thus I must beg your forgiveness. For as I understand the Prophecy, I have no choice but to withhold this information."

And maybe get me killed in the end...but that's part of the risk of any hero-ing. I shook my head, then laughed a bit. "You're forgiven, I guess. You're the King, and you have to make the call as best you can."

123

"I thank you." He did not rise. "And in the second case, I wrong you in the simple fact of your presence. I — not Polychrome, though she was my agent and, she has said to me, blames herself for this — I called you forth from your world, brought you here to my castle, and I have had you forged into the best weapon that could be managed, all to protect my people. This is not your war. Even if there is, as you and I suspect, a connection between your world and mine, it is...unfair that you be drawn from your world in a single day, lacking time or knowledge, and set on this course. I feel it was necessary...but still I am ashamed that I, Iris Mirabilis, must hide myself behind a True Mortal and pin the hopes of my kingdom on one who owes me no such service...especially as we both know the probable end of that service."

No wonder he didn't want to say this in his throne room. He's implied some of this, but no King can afford to be caught doing this kind of abject apology.

But it occurred to me that he was also right. I *was* owed this apology. *But,* as I looked at his bent form, *not like this. If he's being honest, he deserves honesty.*

"Iris Mirabilis, stand up."

He saw the expression on my face, and stood, a questioning look on his own.

"Understand something, please, and perhaps it will remove your need for any apology." I took a deep breath. "I'm not doing this for you. I'm not doing it for your kingdom. I'm not even, entirely, doing it for Oz. I'm doing it for..."

He raised a brow at my hesitation. "Yes?"

In that moment, a part of my courage failed me. I finished the sentence, "...for myself. For my own dreams, for my own spirit." Which was true, as far as it went. But it did not quite go far enough, and perhaps I should have...but I could not bring myself to state the unvarnished truth facing Iris Mirabilis here, alone.

For a moment I was sure that he knew *exactly* what the real ending of that sentence would have been. His violet eyes seemed to burn through my own straight into my brain, and I was suddenly very aware that it would take very little effort from him to send me falling to my death, training or no.

Polychrome

But whatever he knew or suspected, he said nothing; instead he straightened. "Then...no apology is needed, I suppose. I have given you an honorable route to achieve your own goals. So be it." He turned towards the other side of the mountain, away from the Fortress. "To answer your other question, because this mountain is sacred to us."

Caelorum Sanctorum. No surprise there, at least not entirely. "So no training field on top of the Mountain of the Heavens."

He smiled very faintly. "No. That would be...unwise." He looked outward. "Erik Medon, you go to fight for all Faerie. I felt... it was only proper you stand here, where no mortal has in... millennia, at least. The Above watch us. Sometimes, rarely, they give us a sign. But even without a sign, this is a sacred place and one of great import for those who begin on such a journey."

"The Above and 'they'...so it's several gods." I was still unsure what to think of the whole god thing, but if even Iris took it seriously...

He gave a surprisingly open smile. "Several indeed. And hard to know the truth of them it is, as hard perhaps for us as knowing the truth of Faerie is for you. Yet –" he broke off. "Look! Mortal, look there. Do you *see?*"

The deep vault of the sky here was a deep cerulean blue, with only a few wisps of high cloud. But in one of those wisps, for a moment, something flashed. At first, it seemed to be just a sundog, the phantom rainbow glow from ice-crystals. But it bloomed and deepened, and for an instant of time that seemed as brief as the moment between life and death, and as long as eternity, I saw *into* that spectral realm, streets that glittered with gold and emerald, a mighty palace that seemed made of great beams of wood set in a pattern almost familiar, and – in a fraction of that timeless instant – figures of untold majesty.

Then it was gone. But I had no doubt what I had seen. "That... those buildings, the way the roofs angle..." I could barely bring myself to even try to say it; I felt a bone-deep chill of awe and disbelief, in some ways stronger than that I'd had when first I met Polychrome.

125

"And so I know you, Erik Medon, know your heart by what you have seen; not that you *have* seen it, but by what that sight is to you." He nodded slowly, seeming almost as affected by the sight as I. "Perhaps you *do* have a warrior's heart within. But whatever the meaning, they have given us a sign. They are watching. I shall hope this means we have their blessing as well."

"But...does that mean...are you...?"

"There are questions best left unanswered, Erik Medon," he said quietly. "Take that to be whatever answer you prefer. You saw...what you saw. It is a sight given to few enough of my people, and even less often to yours."

I nodded slowly. I wasn't going to get that answer. But as he summoned his Rainbow to take us, I could not help glancing back and thinking of the Rainbow that bridged heaven and earth, and the god who watched over it with a horn, seeing all upon which he fixed his gaze...and look up at the massive figure leading me to his palace, and wonder.

Chapter 19.

Polychrome danced lightly through the corridors of the Palace, out the gateway, and laughed. For there were gathered all the people of the Rainbow Kingdom, from the smallest child to the eldest of the wise old women, all gathered to see the Hero off. Far, far away, down the Way of Light that ran from the dawn to the sunset, she could see the tiny figures of Erik and Nimbus, and the much larger shape of her father against the brilliance of the rising sun.

The crowd saw her and gave a cheer; she blushed. *I don't know why I am so popular compared to my sisters. But for some reason I am. Thank the Above that the seven of them aren't too envious.* She gave a laugh and a spin, and then leapt up to dance lightly over the assembled people, feet touching as gently as a breath of morning mist on each of the upraised hands that rose to provide her a path to the beginning of the Way.

"A good morning to you, Princess," Nimbus said as she arrived.

"Bright sunshine and only clouds of glory, yes." She smiled back, then said with a touch of sadness, "I only wish Cirrus were here."

A shadow passed over Nimbus' face, and her father looked solemn. "Indeed. He knew on what errand you had gone, and it was his greatest wish to see this day. Well, possibly his second-greatest."

No need for this now. "Well, let us hope he watches us with the Above."

"So we shall," Iris Mirabilis said quietly, and then raised his voice so that it rolled sonorously over the entire crowd, "for today we begin the liberation of our brethren; today the Hero of Prophecy sets forth!"

There was a mighty cheer.

We have all waited for this day, Polychrome thought, *waited for long enough that even we wondered if this would ever come.* She turned to Erik, whose cheeks had flamed red in embarrassment, but who stood tall and straight and faced the crowd, and she laughed suddenly. "And you look every bit the part!" she cried with delight, clapping her hands.

"What? Don't joke with me about that, Poly." He was trying to maintain a properly respectful and determined expression, but his voice was that of someone being presented an award for someone else's work.

"Joke? Have you never *looked* at yourself?" She gestured and danced, the Music of the Spheres chiming about her in happy laughter, and called the air and warmth and light to do her bidding, formed a mirage-mirror in front of the mortal.

It was fortunate that from behind the mirage blurred his form, because the expression of disbelief would have been a comical and perhaps inappropriate sight for this particular day.

For this day Erik was dressed in the final and finest armor the artisans could create, a creation of cloud-metals and crystals of blue and gold with touches of sunset crimson. The helm was light, almost a circlet or crown rather than a helmet, but it did the older mortal a service in hiding the retreat of his hairline. His shoulders were wide, waist narrow, dark brows emphasizing the glint of blue eyes, and over his shoulder the tall hilt of a mighty sword projected. A small pack, a few other small pouches or containers about his waist, but little else to mar the clean lines of the armored figure.

He's very different than he was when I first brought him here, she thought, remembering the oddly-dressed, somehow soft-looking man who had searched for some Earthly beauty amidst the clutter of his lonely rooms. *And yet,* she mused, seeing how he looked at himself with wonder and then at *her* as though *she* had wrought the change, *maybe he hasn't changed much at all. Maybe he — and we — are only seeing the man who could have been there all along.*

The Little Pink Bear was there as well, almost invisible in a carrying pouch at Iris' side. Now the tiny stuffed creature climbed stiffly out and marched to Erik, who knelt down to view the Pink Bear eye to eye. "I wish you good luck," the Bear said in his high-pitched childish voice. "I cannot see the end of your road, Hero."

"It's okay," he said, so quietly that none in the crowd could have heard him. "I won't let you down. I'll beat them, somehow.

And as long as I do that, what happens at the end... I'm okay with it."

The little Bear bowed stiffly, and Iris picked him back up. "All of our good wishes and our prayers go with you, Erik Medon." The Rainbow Lord stretched out his hand, and from the very end of the Way a brilliant Rainbow stretched, out and down and down and down, its end coming to rest somewhere in Faerie. Only Iris and Erik knew exactly where that was, although since she was guiding him down the Rainbow she thought she'd probably figure it out, if he didn't tell her. "Go, and may the Above guide and protect you, your courage uphold you, and your strength never fail you."

Erik simply bowed, apparently feeling that he had no words to say. But then he turned to the crowd and in a single movement unsheathed the great sword, holding it over his head in a single hand, the immense blade blazing in the morning sun. "For Faerie!"

The roar of the crowd was as deafening as summer thunder, as powerful and joyous as a downpour after a drought, and Polychrome felt a tiny sting of tears at the corners of her eyes. *He does understand the power of his symbols.*

As dramatically as he had unsheathed the blade, he returned it to its sheath with a theatrical spinning flourish and then bowed low to her. "Lady Polychrome, would you lead the way?"

"With pleasure, Lord Erik." She waved gaily to the people, who gave another cheer, and began to dance her way along the Rainbow. Erik gave a last wave of his own and then strode after her, keeping pace with her light-footed dance with a straight-forward, almost military rhythm that lent purpose and power to even his simple exit.

It was many minutes before the cheers faded behind them, but slowly they did, and after an hour there was nothing but the gently-curving Rainbow beneath them and sky and clouds around them, with the dim mass of Earth below.

"You have the Jewel of the Bridge?"

He grinned and pulled from his belt the glittering crystal that her father had made to bring his Rainbow Bridge through the Great Barrier that separated Oz from the rest of Faerie. "Never left my side since he gave it to me."

"Good." She wondered if she should tell him that her father said that as long as he carried it, they could also watch him, using her father's powers. Probably not; after all, they wouldn't be able to *do* anything, only watch. "My father says that the Jewel will also serve as a Letter of Introduction to any of the true rulers of any of the Faerie kingdoms," she said instead.

"I admit that's a relief. I have a suspicion that despite the nice open way Faerie was depicted by Baum, some random guy walking into a king's throne room and saying 'Hi, the Rainbow Lord sent me down, would you care to give me some help defeating the conquerors of Oz' might not get a completely positive reception."

She giggled, and the Music chimed around her. "No, I think you're right about that." She saw him tilt his head and grin. "What?"

"Oh, the music. It's just so neat how you Faerie have sort of a living soundtrack. Though I notice that it's not all of your people that have it."

She shook her head. "Only those of us with a lot of true Faerie blood. It gets fainter and fainter as one becomes more mortal."

"Still, it's pretty neat." They walked along in the near-perfect silence of the sky for some moments. "Hey, Poly — something I'm curious about. You guys mentioned Cirrus, Nimbus' second in command. If this was his *second*-greatest wish, what was his first?"

He would *pick up on that.* She found herself unaccountably hesitant. "Well..."

"If it's something you can't talk about –"

"No, no... well, it's just that..." She took a deep breath. *It's just a simple question and answer, why do you have a* problem *with this?* "We were betrothed, and Nimbus was just saying that our wedding day might have been Cirrus' greatest wish." It hurt to talk about it. But not exactly the way she had thought it might.

He blinked, looking both startled and shocked. "You were engaged to be married? I didn't... Holy crap, I'm sorry, Poly, you never told me this guy was someone you were in love with! I mean, you never showed how upset you must've been..."

Now she felt *really* uncomfortable. "No, no, Erik, it's...not quite like that. I liked Cirrus, really, I did. And I'm sad he's gone, he was very sweet. Very kind, and a very good warrior and a good friend, and I've said a lot of prayers for him over the past year. But...I wasn't *in love* with him. Father simply felt that it was time for the next generation to begin."

"Hmph. I didn't think of Iris as a sexist pig."

"A what?" For a moment she couldn't even understand what he was saying, then she managed to dredge sense out of it in the context of some of her other conversations with Erik over the last year. "No, no. It's policy, Erik. If I was a boy, he'd have chosen one of the court ladies. Nimbus was his first choice, actually, but Nimbus refused — and by the morning *mist* did that make things uncomfortable for a while."

Erik's expression was unreadable, though he had an odd smile for a moment. "I would think it would. That's a real 'offer you can't refuse.'" Again, as with so many things, it was clear he was referencing something she had no background for. "Nimbus doesn't *look* crazy, so what was his reason for refusing?"

"He said that his responsibility was to serve the Rainbow Lord, and that if he married anyone he'd have two people to serve." Privately, Polychrome thought that the reason was simpler: he didn't want to marry anyone for anything but love, and not being a prince or princess, he didn't have to.

"So you don't get to choose?"

She shook her head. "It's not common."

He was silent for a while, occasionally glancing at her with that same hooded look. The glances did give her another subject to talk about, though. "You know, you were right. You do look *much* better without those glasses. I'm glad Father was able to do that for you."

"Oh, you have no *idea* what that means to me!" he said with a clearly relieved expression. "I'd tried to have them fixed back home, but the treatments we had...well, they told me my eyes didn't qualify. Which reminds me..."

He withdrew the thick-lensed glasses from the pack he carried and stared at them. "I've wanted to do this for forty years."

With a sudden violent motion, he hurled the glasses into space; they disappeared into a nearby cloud, a tiny speck plummeting to an unknown doom. Erik gave a whoop and leap of joy. "HA! *Abayo*, you stupid pieces of glass!"

She laughed at his joy. "You really disliked them that much?"

"As I said, you have *no idea*." He grinned. "When I was a kid, people made fun of my just *having* them. And in practical terms, they were just a *pain*." He strode on, still smiling. "And for *this* sort of situation...they were kind of a symbol."

She danced along, an answering smile on her face. "I'm glad."

Erik looked at her face for a moment, his smile brighter.

She became aware that for some moments they had simply continued moving, looking at each other in silence. *That's dangerous,* she thought, and wondered what in the name of the Above she meant by that. Still, she felt it was terribly important she say something. "So for once a mortal knew where the Rainbow would end before the Rainbow Lord, I understand?"

"What?" He seemed distracted for a moment, then nodded. "Oh, yes. Yeah, I had to decide where I was going to start. So much time, so little to do — wait a minute. Strike that. Reverse it." That slightly-lopsided grin again. "Fortunately, the Prophecy clearly tells me where to go. 'Across the sky and sea, wisdom he will seek.' Follow that path, and I'll also get the companions and the means to cross the Deadly Desert."

She paused in the dance to stare at him. "From that line, you know where you're going?"

He laughed. "From that one and the ones following? Most certainly." He looked down. "And it looks like we're almost there."

Below were bare, rocky hills, mountains rising to the south and west; she seemed to recall seeing the ocean as they were descending, off to the East, which would mean the great Nonestic Ocean. *One of the coastal countries. Can't be sure yet — I'll look more carefully when I go back up.* "Be careful. The last part of the bow is...tricky for a mortal."

"You forget who you're talking to." He grinned, and she noticed that he was simply setting his feet down a little harder and creating miniature steps, notches in the normally impervious mystical substance of the Rainbow. In a few more moments, he

132

stepped to the ground, the stones crunching faintly under his feet. "Well...I guess...this is goodbye."

"Yes." She found herself unable to say anything else, yet not quite able to just start dancing back up the Rainbow. "Will you...do you think you'll be all right? Will you be able to find your way...get across the Desert?"

Oddly, he did not answer right away. Instead, he asked, "Poly...I know I have to cross the Desert on my own, even without these companions I'm supposed to find. And I might not live through that. But...if I do... If I get to Oz..." He took a deep breath. "Will I see you again on that side, before the battle that...well, will probably be my last?"

She laughed, but for some reason his words, spoken so low and earnestly, seemed to cause an ache inside for a moment. "Father wanted me to stay safely at home. But I told him that if he didn't *let* me go with Nimbus and the others, I'd find my *own* way there without him. I saw everything fall, Erik. I'm not going to stand back and not even *be* there when everyone else is fighting. I'm going to be there. You'll see me there." She laid her hand on his. "I promise."

His eyes lit up as his gaze locked on hers, and she felt a strange shiver go down her back as he gently put his other hand on her own. "In that case, Lady Polychrome...there is *nothing* I cannot do."

With an extravagant bow over her hand, he turned and walked to the East.

Chapter 20.

Ugu the Unbowed stood on the balcony overlooking the petrified Emerald City; halfway to the horizon the pure dead grey ended, in a line as sharply drawn as if by a knife, and the green of the surrounding lands began. "And so it begins."

"Sire?" Cirrus Dawnglory — or, at least, the being who now wore his name and face — said, clearly unsure of what his King meant.

"Ah, you are here. Excellent. Walk with me, Cirrus." Ugu turned from the balcony and began a slow, deliberate walk into the depths of the Grey Castle. "Our spies — the finest and most subtle of the transformed spirits of Air which the Queen could craft — have reported back, and today — precisely one year and five days after his arrival — the mortal has left the Rainbow Kingdom and landed somewhere in Faerie."

Cirrus drew a deep breath. "I see. So the forces are now moving and the war cannot be far away."

Ugu nodded. "Indeed, and this is why I have called for you. Cirrus, you — and you alone — are truly suited to prepare our defenses against the forces of the Rainbow Kingdom and — potentially — the other kingdoms of Faerie. We must discuss this now, at some length, as we have no way of knowing exactly when the assault will come, or in what form, and you may have extensive preparations to make."

Cirrus' head, crowned with hair as fine and white as his namesake, nodded sharply. "I understand, Sire. I have many thoughts on this." They passed from the South Wing to the West, walking now through the area of the Castle reserved for Ugu's use.

Ugu smiled thinly. "I am sure you do — and you will write them all down later."

Cirrus glanced at him, puzzled.

"We have far more important matters to discuss. Matters involving Her Majesty."

Cirrus went several shades paler. "M... my King, I..."

"You wonder that even I would speak of her? Remember, Cirrus, it was I who helped her regain her form. I whose recipes and apparatus removed first my form, and then gave to her the shape she now wears. I, Ugu the Unbowed, am a master of many magics indeed. I studied the lore of Glinda, and the Wizard, and many others, those in my line and those beyond, sorcerers, witches, warlocks, Faerie, alchemists, even the secrets of the Yookoohoo herself."

"She has spies –" Cirrus burst out in warning before he could catch himself.

"Do you think I do not know this? She can transform nearly anything or anyone as she will, and place her own will upon many such things. Yet here, in my portion of the Castle, she is still unaware that I have complete control. Her spies still see us talking, and report to her that we are discussing strategies and tactics. Which I will, at the end, command you to prepare a detailed report on, including annotations indicating what useful additions I may have suggested."

Cirrus stared at him, both hopeful and apprehensive. "She cannot...?"

"She hears precisely what I wish her to hear, sees only what I wish her to see. Only within this part of the castle, true — I cannot safely extend my powers outside of this area without her potentially discovering it. Now," he continued, pausing and looking down coldly at the young man, "we must talk.

"You see, I am quite aware of the Queen's nature. She has... given you much incentive to focus your loyalty, has she not?"

Abruptly the lightly tanned face flamed red, then went pure white. Cirrus stared up, immobile with fear.

"I see." Ugu chuckled. "Draw breath, and fear no more. I am hardly unaware of those temptations, General Dawnglory. And even less am I held by them. You, of course, must follow whom you choose. But here you may speak freely, and so may I. And I say to you that she is a viper, a serpent of great beauty and skill and yet deadly to the touch, one who in the end will destroy all she encounters until she is finally eradicated by one who understands her for what she is."

136

Cirrus' face was slowly regaining its color as he realized that the King had not brought him here to suffer a painful and permanent accident. His expression shifted to puzzlement. "But... Sire, if you know of the... favor shown to me, and her promises... are you not –"

"—taking considerable risk in revealing these things to you?" Ugu nodded. "Oh, certainly. And yet, I think, not so much risk as others might believe, for you — though not born a warrior of the Rainbow Kingdom — have become such a warrior, and one of such skill and courage that for a hundred years you were the right hand man of the General of Hosts. Such a man is the sort to see where his true interests lie, no matter what silken promises may be made by others."

Cirrus seemed thoughtful, trying to decide how to reply. As he opened his mouth, a tremor ran through the castle, and Ugu held up his hand sharply. Another tremor. Another, and it was clear that these were footsteps, the massive tread of something so immense that even the tremendous stone edifice of the Castle had to respond to its movement. Both stood frozen as the titanic figure drew closer and closer. Suddenly, for a moment, the nearby tall windows were blacked out, the entirety of the third floor thrown momentarily into shadow by the hulking armored form of something so huge that even here, forty-five feet in the air, the head was still too far up to be visible through the windows.

Ugu only lowered his hand once the footsteps had faded away. "The Yoop has sharp ears, and is entirely her creature — one I cannot influence."

Cirrus shuddered. Ugu could not entirely blame him; what Amanita Verdant (*née* Yoop) had done to her erstwhile husband was a thing of horror, transforming an ordinary giant into a monstrous and twisted juggernaut of destruction which lived only to serve her will.

On the other hand, I have heard enough from her in the dark of night to know how little sympathy the Yoop deserves from anyone, for it was he who made her what she is, in truth. A part of him was, honestly, somewhat sorry for Amanita; the torment she had suffered at Yoop's hands — and other parts — indicated that the Yookoohoo's vengeance had not only been richly deserved but had, perhaps, merely brought to the surface the monster which had always been there.

Still, it was also another proof of her own vicious and heartless nature.

"As I said, Cirrus; I believe you understand your position well. I know what sort of a creature the Queen is. I was allied to her from convenience, and she to me, and both of us know that sooner or later one will betray the other. We both make preparations.

"But she believes that this is in the end a war of magicians, of sorceries, and that her powers will exceed mine. She may be right in the latter; but I believe this is also a game of alliances, of powers within the people. I made many mistakes in my first attempt to conquer Oz, and I will *not* repeat them. I had no allies, nor did I attempt to gain any, believing myself sufficient unto all things. I paid for that. I paid *dearly* for that." He restrained the snarl that always came to him when he remembered his centuries as a nearly-helpless Dove. "I believe that having a loyal General commanding thousands of troops is a very powerful weapon. I believe, in fact, that a General who will have to examine all of his resources and describe to me their deployment – and how they might serve in small tactical areas as well as large, strategic ones – may be the most powerful weapon I could ask for. More than sufficient, perhaps, to balance out whatever small advantage in power the Queen may possess."

The widened eyes showed that Cirrus understood exactly what he was saying. "I am no fool, Cirrus Dawnglory. Unlike her, I have learned. I will reward loyalty well – loyalty and honest effort, Cirrus, not merely success. I understand – none better – that failure is a possible consequence of trying. If you give me your best effort, I will not punish you for failure. You will not find the Queen so tolerant."

"No, Sire... I agree with you." Cirrus said finally. He had, after all, seen much of Amanita's temper. "But when –"

"We need not speak of that now. You need neither write nor say anything of *that* matter until I say otherwise." He smiled with a sharp and cold expression in his eyes. "But *think* much upon it, and how best it can be accomplished when the time comes – perhaps just after the True Mortal has been captured and the final sealing ritual performed. I need her for that — but afterwards, she will be no longer necessary."

He sighed. "And to tell the truth, Cirrus, she is far too dangerous to live much longer. You have seen her...volatility. As she tampers more and more with the darkest forces...I am afraid she will only become worse. She will be a danger, not just to me, but to our entire realm." Ugu looked straight into Cirrus' eyes. "What say you then, Cirrus Dawnglory? Are you with your King?"

For answer, Cirrus dropped to one knee. He drew his sword and held it up, presenting it to the King. "I swear to you, my King. My loyalty and my strength and my will are yours to command."

Ugu smiled and took the sword, reversed it, and placed it back in Cirrus Dawnglory's hands. "It is well, Cirrus. I accept your pledge with gladness. Rise, and let us continue our walk."

They walked for a moment together, the tension in Cirrus clearly draining somewhat away... to be replaced by the tension of new realization.

The nature of that realization was writ clearly upon Cirrus' face. "Yes, that will be a problem, my friend. You must continue to play your part with her." He gave a sudden laugh. "Ahh, perhaps I will show some jealousy over this favor of hers, giving her both the belief that she can still control me in that fashion and that I have no clear hold over you. How sits that with you, Cirrus? Could you manage to carry out such a deception?"

Now it was Cirrus' turn to laugh. "My King, my apologies for reminding you of what you doubtless recall... yet you speak to one who walked the Rainbow Fortress for three centuries and more and never once was suspected."

"Ha! No, my apologies to you instead. Of course such a simple task you can manage. Amanita is far less subtle than Iris Mirabilis or his General, I think." He nodded, noting where they were. "We are close to the area where her spies will begin to hear us again. So I will begin to speak of another important matter, one connected to strategy, which follows logically from what she will have seen." He took another deep breath. "General, I have one other command for you, and I suspect you will not like it."

Realizing he was once more potentially under the watchful eye of the Queen, Cirrus looked suspicious. "And what is that, Sire?"

"While you may have to journey the country for a short time in the next few weeks, you are to return here *immediately* if any sign of enemy forces is seen. Moreover, you are *not* to allow yourself to be seen outside of our most loyal troops. Your name will not be mentioned; you must choose another name for your persona as the general of our forces. As soon as it seems even *possible* that an agent of the enemy could be in Oz, you will return to the Castle and remain there, never emerging until and unless I give permission."

"What? Why, Sire? A general cannot command his troops nearly as well when he must remain hidden!"

"Because," Ugu answered levelly, "your very *existence* is one of our greatest weapons, and under no circumstances do I wish this revealed until we have the Mortal in hand and under control. You are welcome — encouraged, even — to devise all of the stratagems, plots, and tactics that you wish, and we will make all manner of use of them, but you will take absolutely no risks that may betray your identity." He looked down at Cirrus, face forbidding and grim. "Is that understood, General?"

Cirrus' look of resigned frustration was picture-perfect; Ugu could not tell how much of it was honest annoyance and how much was merely following a script that the younger man clearly understood very well. "As my King commands."

"So I do." He glanced at the sun in the sky. "I have other duties to attend to for now. General, I want you to write up a report on all we discussed this day and submit it to me — with your recommendations — before three days have passed."

General Dawnglory bowed. "It will be done."

"Then that is all. Dismissed."

He watched the argent-haired warrior depart and allowed himself a small smile. Let Amanita make of *that* what she would. He now knew he had a powerful ally which the Yookoohoo would underestimate...and he knew how best to use him.

In a few months, there would be only a King in Oz.

Chapter 21.

I walked straight to the East, not looking back. Not *daring* to look back for a while. It had been almost impossible not to just blurt it all out, looking at Polychrome then, when I knew I might die before reaching Oz - that this might be the last time I saw her. But she didn't need that burden, even if it was something she wanted to hear, which I really didn't think she did. I was pretty sure she did like me as a friend, now; we'd worked together a lot and she'd gotten used to me. But that was just more reason I needed to avoid that subject. I *really* didn't want to get the "I think of you as a friend!" knife in the gut, and our recent conversation had shown that it wouldn't matter much anyway; her father and politics would be choosing her dating regime as much as she would.

Finally I glanced back; the Rainbow, and Polychrome, were gone. I walked on, just a bit heavier of foot for a while until the job at hand focused my attention. I'd picked this location at the border of the Nome King's domain very carefully; Eastward, where I was heading, lay the kingdom of Gilgad (which Baum had whimsically chosen to re-name "Rinkitink"), and its similarly-named capital city. Iris *could*, of course, have dropped his Rainbow right into the city itself, even on top of the royal castle, or possibly right at my first destination. And in some ways, that would've been a good idea.

On the other hand, there was absolutely no reason to give any spies a blazing flare-lit tipoff, complete with rainbow-colored arrows pointing to my destination, as to what I was doing first. And I could use a little bit of time walking through the countryside and getting accustomed to the larger world of Faerie outside of the Rainbow Fortress.

There was a faint path visible here, which appeared to head in the right general direction. I strode along easily, something I found amusing as hell; me, the quintessential nerd, now making my way in (admittedly very light) armor along steep mountain pathways and not even really breathing hard. A year of heavy training sure makes a difference.

As I crested a hill, I saw the trail getting clearer below... and grasses and trees carpeting the slopes farther along. I was now past the Nome King's domain, which as described was almost lifeless barren rock, and entering Gilgad. Scents of earth and forest reached me, startlingly appealing and nostalgic; I realized that I hadn't smelled anything like them in the Rainbow Kingdom. I'd known, of course, that they'd had to do some considerable work to keep me fed (either summoning the food, creating it, or maybe even having to occasionally send some Faeries on a food run), but until now it hadn't really registered just how *alien* a world that was in some ways. Iris Mirabilis' kingdom was entirely a place of sky and wind and rain and light. There was no true stone or steel or grass or any other ordinary living thing to be found there.

This was much more like home, and I felt suddenly steadier in a way. *This* was the sort of land I understood, even if there were a lot of strange things to be found. I moved under the canopy of a light forest, enjoying the sparkle of sunlight and the green-tinted light in the shadows.

Glancing around, I noted signs of habitation; hewn stumps of harvested trees, tracks of indeterminate nature in the leaves and soil. Good. I needed to find people, get a good route to follow to the port city and capital of Gilgad, and get things rolling.

As I rounded a corner, however, I realized things might not be quite that simple.

About a hundred yards ahead, the path opened up into a clearing, in which was a small house with some cultivated fields around it, a small stream flowing through, clearly inhabited by a woodsman and his family. I say "clearly" because I could see the man, his wife, and two children in front of the house. They were not having a good day, as evinced by the fact that the man himself was being held dangling above the ground by the hand of a seven foot tall tailed monstrosity while a similar beast held an axe poised to strike the cowering children.

I took a step sideways into the forest and moved forward as quietly as I could; it looked to me like this was an interrogation, and I wanted to get some idea of what was going on before I busted in. As I got closer, I could make out what was being said, beginning with the grinding-gravel tones of the first creature:

"...ast time, mortal rat, where is it?"

I could see the man more clearly now; as you'd expect from a man living in the woods without near neighbors, he was strong-looking, weathered, the sort who would probably face down a wolf without a second thought; the futility of his struggles against the indigo-skinned hand gripping his throat showed just how strong the monster was. Supporting his weight partially by gripping the thing's wrist, he managed to choke out an answer. "If... I tell... you let my family go..."

"I might *think* about letting them go." The deep chuckle from the other made me — and from his pale face, the poor woodsman — suspect that there wouldn't be much sincerity in the thinking.

Time to get to work. "Oooh, good. Then *I* might think about letting *you* go, too." I said, stepping out from the forest.

The things whirled, the one tossing away the woodsman like a rag doll, and snarled.

I froze for a moment, unable to move or answer. All my training had been against human or very humanlike people. These things were nothing of the sort. Indigo-grey skin, like some sort of shadowed basalt, covered their bodies. The eyes glittered yellow crystal in the sun above wide mouths that had the jagged-fang look of a rock crusher combined with a steam shovel, but the mobility of flesh in the cruel curve of their smiles as they saw me go white; they wore grey-white stone armor and carried thick bronze axes, while their hands and feet sported sharp black claws.

Gut-deep fear shot in a chill through me, and for an instant I felt myself starting to take a step back. I'd seen thousands of monsters on TV and movie screens, but that's nothing at all like seeing them in the flesh, any more than watching a dozen shark specials on television compares to the first time you meet one in the surf, all white teeth and grey sandpaper skin and black, dead eyes, as I had once as a child.

The leader laughed. "Oh, loud of mouth but not so brave when facing the opponent, are we? Too bad for you, worm. This is Oz business."

143

Oz business? The part of my brain that never stops thinking grabbed that, shoved it forward, and dumped a bucketload of shame over me. *You want to save Oz, hero, and you're too scared to face a couple of Ugu's bullies a thousand miles from his stronghold? Run back to your little house now, then; let Poly see just what a loser she's picked.*

I swallowed, but got my limbs back under control. "This isn't Oz, monster. If you know what's good for you, you'll go back right now."

The creature — which I now guessed was a Temblor, one of the twisted Earth spirits under Ugu and Amanita's control — sneered. "From one human shaking in his boots with a sword too big for him to swing?"

The other moved forward slowly, swinging its axe lazily. "Should I kill it, Morg?"

Morg nodded. "Why not, Gron? Might finish convincing these others to talk. Make it messy."

Gron grinned widely, showing interlocking teeth like razor-sharp crystals, and lunged forward.

I'd had enough time to get a grip and prepare. Gron moved fast, but Earth spirits weren't *anything* like the Faeries of the air that inhabited the Rainbow Kingdom. The massive Temblor was actually no faster than me, not even as quick as Iris Mirabilis, and I first leapt aside as he charged, letting Gron thunder past.

He recovered and spun to face me. "Duck and run all you like, little man, you will tire, and I will not. Better to die with courage. Draw your blade."

Time to learn if what works in training works in the real world. I straightened, and gave my own sneer in return. "And get it dirty? Come on, then."

Gron gave a snort of disbelief mixed with amusement. "So be it." He raised the axe and charged.

Bracing myself for an agonizing impact, I gritted my teeth, stepped forward just inside of the axe, and swung my fist with every ounce of force I could muster.

Stone armor, rocky skin, and mineral bone broke, split, and shattered at the impact, that felt to me no more than a hard punch into a sandbag. Gron flew backwards at a terrible speed, struck a tree, broke it off like a twig, continued on through two more before smashing into the mountainside with a sound like doom.

I stared in awe and felt a hell-bent grin spreading across my face as I turned towards Morg, who was staring in utter disbelief. "Your turn."

Morg brought up his axe, but I could see there was no smile on his face now. "Wh... whatever trick this is, you are still a fool! Do you not know that this will bring Mombi's vengeance upon you? And if that does not suffice, then the power of the King and Queen itself?"

Now I moved forward, and *he* was the one starting to back away. "Mombi, eh? I *thought* she'd be one of the ones they'd choose as a viceroy. Of course I know that. If, of course, you get your chance to report home."

He was backing away in earnest now. "No! You mortal idiot! Whatever magic you're using, it cannot equal theirs! Don't you realize this?" As I closed in, he swung. Not without a chill of fear that it would end with my hand being chopped off, I reached out to catch the blade.

It was like catching a styrofoam prop; the thing stopped with barely a jolt and I could see the blade crumple a little on impact. "Here's a surprise for you, Morg." I ripped the weapon out of his hand and broke it, then caught him and held him up by the throat, just the way he'd been holding the poor woodsman. I brought his face close to mine and whispered, "I'm not *using* any magic."

Then I threw him as hard as I could. That might have been something of a mistake, because he flew *over* the nearer ridge; I never saw him hit the ground, and given how he was basically made of stone, he might well survive. But...I really didn't want to kill anyone, now that I thought of it. At least some of these twisted elementals were Winkies and other natives of Oz, warped by enchantment. I couldn't go around killing randomly. I would've pulled my first punch, if I'd thought about it and been sure I had the power to spare.

Now I knew. My True Mortal abilities were even more formidable than I'd thought, at least against the foot soldiers.

But enough of that. I turned to the woodsman and his family, who were staring with eyes so wide I thought they might pop out of their sockets. "Are you all right?"

After a speechless moment, the father recovered. "Y... yes, sir. You... you have rescued us before they could truly harm any of my family."

"What were they after?"

The woodsman grimaced, rubbing his throat. "Stoneseeds. Grow just at the border between the Nome King's lands and Gilgad and a few other lands. Dark magic has many uses for them."

"And you know where to find them? Or you gather them yourself?"

"Both, milord." He straightened and bowed proudly. "Amrin Stoneseed am I, and such has been my family's name for generations."

"Then I'd guess there are not-dark uses for the stoneseeds?"

"Oh, many. A stoneseed picked at full ripeness may be grown into many things — stone walls, stone houses even — under the right conditions by a skilled wizard. Unlike those growing on this border, such a seed will produce only sterile stone, not stoneflowers and new seeds, so there is always a need for new stoneseed crops."

That made sense in the usual Faerie context. And undoubtedly, since such things couldn't grow except on the borders of the Nome King's territories, it was worth it to Oz to send out collection agents. "Well, I'm glad I was able to help. I hope it will not cause you worse trouble later, though."

Amrin looked glum. "They will try again sometime, I am sure."

"Well," I said with a grin, "if they'll hold off for a bit, they just might never get a chance."

He looked up sharply. "Do you mean...?"

"I mean that all is not lost. Can I ask your help?"

He looked at me, eyes showing a flicker of hope. "After what you have done, of course."

"Tell me how I can reach Gilgad, the city."

Amrin looked at his wife and children. "I will do more than that. I will take you there."

146

Erik Medon

Chapter 22.

"And so I will be sending several Hands of Temblors, perhaps even of Infernos, to teach a lesson to -"

"*SILENCE!*" roared the King.

Mombi stared at Ugu in confusion. "Y... Your Majesty?"

He pointed his finger down at her and muttered two ancient words. The old witch, dressed in finery terribly unbecoming to her, suddenly hopped as though standing on red-hot coals. "Ow! Aaaaah, have mercy, Majesty, mercy on an old woman who does not understand!"

He withdrew his hand, and Mombi stopped, shivering with fear. "Then I will explain. Perhaps you are fortunate that the Queen is busy with her own work, for if she were of my current state of mind, I doubt not that you would be leaving here in a different form than that which you now wear." He leaned slowly back in the Throne and glowered down at the Witch and the battered form of Morg. "We are currently at peace with the other Faerie realms. This has been long arranged. Apparently, you have interpreted the word *peace* in a fashion I find quite enlightening; it means that we simply don't let anyone *talk* about the little invasions we're carrying out, is that it?"

Mombi looked up, fear mingled with defiance. "We all have done this. What makes my actions so terrible, Majesty?"

Idiots. I am completely surrounded by idiots, except for my Queen who is planning to kill me and my General, who may be my best chance. Ugu stood up, causing all around the room to step back a pace. "Make no mistake, Mombi; I have been busy with affairs of policy deep enough that perhaps I have been remiss in watching the actions of my Viceroys. That is ended as of this moment. I assure you, the same message will be conveyed to all the others.

"We have kept here to our borders. We have assured them we mean them no harm so long as they do nothing against us. We all know, of course, that one day we will change that truth to another,

149

but that change will happen when *I* say, when the *Queen* says, and not one second sooner! By these raids you give them reason to remain afraid, reason to be prepared, reason, in short, to ready themselves for war. To seek ever and ever for ways to destroy us, to harry us, to weaken us."

Mombi nodded slowly. "I... I suppose. But there is much that they have which is not to be found in Oz, and –"

"—and we shall trade for it, *fairly* trade for it, do you understand? Until the time comes that my armies and my spells and the Queen's are readied and all is decided, until that time we shall be the very model of good neighbors." He bent lower. "And if you or your compatriots do not understand this," he hissed, "*you* shall be once more stripped of your powers and sent to be washerwoman to the Nome King's armies, Lady Coo-Ee-Oh shall be again a brainless swan," his voice rose higher, to a thunder that echoed throughout the Throne Room, "I'll fry that plotting Dictator of the Flatheads to ash along with his entire miserable court of sycophants, and I shall level such a curse of shrinking on Blinkara of Jinxland that not even all the microscopes of the mortal world could find her with a thousand years to search!"

By the end of the speech, Mombi was cowering on the floor along with the Temblor Morg, begging for mercy. He stared down in distaste. *We chose people who had no reason to care for the way Oz was, but of course they had little reason to care for anything at all. If we learn nothing on how to rule carefully, we shall soon have nothing at all to rule.* "Get up."

The old witch scrambled to her feet, bowing all the while.

"Enough. Now, Morg. Tell me exactly what happened. Not the account Mombi gave. I want your words, your memories, exactly as it occurred."

He listened carefully, nodding. Finally, when Morg was finished, he sat back down and gestured, muttering a few more ancient words; Morg looked down at himself in amazement, his injuries now entirely gone. "Well enough done. In this case — and I say, in this case *only* — it was well you were there. This information is of use to me. So I shall let the issue of your abuse of power drop. For now. Remember you well my words, Mombi. Now leave us."

Once she had left, he looked back; from his concealed area behind the thrones, Cirrus emerged. "You heard, General?"

"Indeed. So he was landed at the border of the Nome King's lands."

"Yes." Ugu frowned. "Certainly a wise choice if one seeks allies of any credibility. Yet King Kaliko has also been wise, and seeks no war with us; he balances his natural dislike and fear with caution and policy. Unless this Mortal has something quite extraordinary to offer, I doubt he will get much from the Nomes."

Cirrus nodded. "But there are few other choices, as I can see them. Aside from the darker spirits which our Lady the Queen bound, the Nomes were the only Faeries who maintained a great army at all."

"Assume he can gain some trust. What then?"

The former officer of the Rainbow Kingdom wrinkled his brow, trying to take into account all of the factors he knew. "Well, certainly the Nomes have a vast army. None of their warriors individually can match ours, of course. Yet... they must find a way *into* Oz. The barrier you have arranged is proof above the ground and below, so the prior tactic of digging a tunnel is no longer an option." His head came up. "There is *one* way..."

Ugu was startled. "There is? I would have staked my life that no way through that barrier exists for any Faerie or of Faerie born — and while a True Mortal may pass, he does not eliminate the barrier and his allies would remain behind."

"All true, your Majesty," Cirrus agreed. "Yet any of us may pass through unstopped, and allow others to return under certain circumstances."

"Ahh..." Ugu said softly. "What if they have a traitor within our own ranks? Is that your meaning?"

"It is, Sire."

Ugu thought on that possibility. The ordinary warriors of course could not do that trick. Equally obviously, any of the Viceroys or their immediate entourage could. Yet he and Amanita had quite carefully picked those people for their inability to tolerate the earlier regime, and — quite deliberately — inability to work well with others except out of fear. There were of course drawbacks to this, but...

"I find myself drawn to a single rather inescapable conclusion on that subject, General," he said finally. "None of our Viceroys or their people are at *all* likely to be traitors. Not that they love our royal persons so much, you understand," he smiled grimly, "but they fear us greatly, and none outside of Oz would trust any of them. They would see a trap in any offer of assistance."

"But in that case, Sire..."

"... in that case, General Cirrus, there would be only one person who could possibly let in an enemy army, and who might be trusted enough to do so. You."

Cirrus looked thoughtful. "I do see your point, Majesty. Yet I brought up the point itself, which you had not thought of at all. Meaning no disrespect, Sire."

"I take none. Yet one with sufficient subtlety to conceal his presence for three centuries in an enemy stronghold might count on the subtle misdirection involved in revealing the weakness to make himself appear innocent."

"Do you truly suspect me, Sire?"

Ugu looked at him wordlessly for some moments, considering. "In all honesty? No, not at all, Cirrus. Had you wished to betray us, it would have been better for you to do so before you came here, or do it immediately, rather than bringing to us the Prophecy and so much other information as you have given us. You have done marvels in preparing our forces.

"But because of this, I conclude that they are very unlikely to have any traitor of high standing here, and without that, they cannot breach the barrier directly."

"And yet they shall, if the Prophecy is to be believed at all."

Ugu chuckled. "Oh, now, that is a different matter of policy, my friend. It is quite possible that they will enter without any need whatsoever of treacherous assistance. After all...if I believe they will be easier to defeat here, I can *let* them in, can I not?"

Cirrus nodded slowly. "Indeed you can, Sire."

"What of Gilgad? Can you see anything he could gain from there?"

"Not really, Sire. The country *does* border on the Nonestic Ocean..." A thought seemed to occur to him, and for a few moments he stood silently before he shook his head. "...but no. Yes, the Sea Faeries have considerable forces of their own, but they will hardly be very effective on land, even if a single Mortal could manage to convince them to ally in force with him. Note that we are aware that Iris Mirabilis did seek to build a grand alliance early on, and failed, and — despite the minor depredations of Mombi and her ilk — our keeping our word to stay out of other countries' business has convinced many of them that their best course of action is to stay out of ours."

"Then send a few spies to watch the Nome King's lands. He may try a different route, now that he has encountered some of our people."

"It is already being attended to, Highness."

"Excellent, Cirrus." He nodded, giving leave for his General to go.

Everything seemed to be progressing well. He glanced in the direction of Amanita's throne. *And that, too, will be dealt with. Once he is here.*

Chapter 23.

The gates of the city of Gilgad stood wide before us, a full fifty feet high in a wall of white and black marble. The wide street continued on, with houses and larger buildings visible, street vendors, and hundreds of people bustling about on the city's business. "You should be safe here, Amrin. At least as long as anyone is, and I hope that will turn out to be a long, long time." I shook his hand.

"Many, many thanks, Lord Erik," Amrin said, and his family — Ralla, his wife, and Amril and Rallin, their son and daughter — added their own thanks with an enthusiasm which I found to be acutely embarrassing. After all, I'd just happened to be in the right place in the right time, and I was getting an awful lot out of them from that happy accident. I could have spent a long time wandering around before finding my way to the port city, and by walking with Amrin and his family I'd gotten a clear and detailed picture of the situation in Gilgad and surrounding areas.

"Well, you're welcome again," I said aloud. "But please, stop with all the 'Lord Erik' stuff already. I've got no titles yet. Just a sword and pretty armor."

"And the strength of a mountain!" Amril piped up enthusiastically.

"Ha! Not that simple, Amril. Not that simple at all. Why, your father could probably out-wrestle me."

He laughed at that and of course denied the possibility; after what he'd seen, naturally, that wouldn't seem possible, and I wasn't going to try to explain the True Mortal business. No need, and good reason not to. "You won't have trouble living here?"

"No, L... Erik. I have a few stoneseeds already harvested and some savings we brought. It will keep us for quite some time." His tone of voice reassured me that I hadn't just brought them here to hide in genteel poverty.

After a few more farewells, we finally parted. My destination wasn't hard to spot; the great square-cut castle dominated the center of Gilgad, with outbuildings ranging eastward towards the sea.

Now for the next step... and thanks to Amrin, I even know what I'm doing after this little sequence of events.

The stoneseed farmer almost certainly hadn't guessed the significance of various things he — and his children — had told me. The most important being something little Rallin had said shortly after we'd set out: "At first I thought you were the Penitent, but then I realized you were much too tall."

The Penitent... a local folk hero. No one knew where he came from or who he was, a mysterious grey-cloaked figure who appeared from out of the mountains, striking down raiders, leaving food for the hungry, jewels for the robbed, never staying long enough to accept thanks, almost never speaking... but that told me all I needed to know. *I know who you are, Penitent, and when the time comes, we will definitely be talking.*

But that wouldn't be for a while yet. First things first. I strode up the center of the street, conscious of the stares of numerous residents of Gilgad. *Wish I could be subtle... but I'd stand out here anyway. Most of these people are shorter than me, even the men, dark-haired, tanned... No, I'd have about as much chance of sneaking in to see the King here as I would in Japan.*

To my surprise, the King of Gilgad was, according to Amrin, the same man as the one described in the books, though his name was Rin Ki-Tin — making it obvious where Baum had gotten the name Rinkitink, given Baum's love of wordplay. But Amrin's description — given with affectionate smiles from all his family — depicted the same personality, a man of immense appetite, vast girth, and even vaster mirth, who nonetheless hid shrewd statesmanship behind the guise of a rollicking buffoon. He was old, very old now, but as far as Amrin knew he was still as sharp-witted as ever.

Lucky for me if that's true. Old King Rinki... Rin Ki-Tin was just the man I needed to talk to.

The guards at the gate were leaning up against the walls, looking rather bored, but they straightened up as I approached. One

156

held out his spear, barring my path. "Hold, stranger. What business have you here?"

"I'd very much like an audience with the King, if I might, sir." I'd found that being respectful to guards, police, and soldiers was always the best policy. They often got to deal with people who didn't respect them in the worst possible conditions, so giving them their due gave you the best reaction. Usually.

"Well, now, nothing wrong with wanting an audience, but the King isn't receiving visitors right now. Seeing as he's not here right now."

Damn. "Is he expected back soon, then?"

The guards exchanged glances and chuckled. "Whenever Chancellor Inkarbleu despairs of being summoned by the King and goes to find him of his own accord. Which will earn the Chancellor another three days of awaiting his terrible execution and then a stay of execution, and another three weeks of rewards for his invaluable service to the Crown."

Well, now I knew where the King was and who I needed to see instead. "Then would it be possible for me to speak with the Chancellor? I have travelled a very, very long way."

The two had been studying my armor, and I was rather gratified to see that they were clearly recognizing something unique to the design. "One moment."

The two guards withdrew, conferred for a moment, and then turned back to me. "Please step inside."

Once inside the entryway of the castle — a large, arched tunnel through impressively thick walls — the guards motioned me to a side room which was obviously a guard office. "Now, sir, your name — and if you can, your business?"

I smiled. *Smart guards. Someone chose well.* "My name is Erik Medon. And you're right, I'd rather not state my business to anyone except the Chancellor. But I think you've probably guessed part of it. And you are...?"

They looked startled; I guess that people didn't ask their names very often, treating them like speedbumps or door-openers. "First Sergeant Huru Ro-Van and Second Sergeant Zammu Rin-Aro, sir!"

157

"Glad to meet you both, Huru, Zammu." I shook hands. "Now could one of you let the Chancellor know I would like to see him at his earliest convenience?"

Huru nodded at Zammu, who saluted and set off at a near-run. "Is it... happening, sir?"

I looked at him for a moment, considering. Then I said "It might be. But a lot could still go wrong, so I don't want it getting out, understand?"

Huru straightened, and nodded. "Understood, sir!" But I noticed the gleam in his eye.

I felt both glad and a little guilty. Glad that I could bring some hope to these people, and guilty that I was using him, Zammu, and Amrin's family. All of them would quietly spread the word. There'd be a whispering of hope, getting stronger, no clear source, hard to trace — but rising up, building support for what we needed to do. *Sorry for being a manipulative bastard, Poly. I hope you don't think* too *badly of me for it.*

Zammu came running back. "Sir! Chancellor Inkarbleu says he will see you immediately."

I followed Zammu and Huru through the main courtyard, up wide white marble steps with polished black rails, into a vast entryway. *Impressive for something built basically by hand, even if the whole castle would have fit inside of Nimbus' training hall.* At the end of the entryway, twin doors were thrown open, and Zammu announced, "Erik Medon, traveller, to see the Chancellor!"

I stepped through and looked up, the doors shutting behind me and leaving me alone with the Chancellor. Chancellor Inkarbleu was seated in a secondary throne, mounted three steps down from the high dais where the King's throne sat. Inkarbleu stood, and I met his gaze, sharp black eyes in a seamed, narrow face atop a very spare frame in simple formal black robes trimmed with silver. "Erik Medon. An unusual name, indeed."

"Not terribly common where I come from, either," I admitted.

"What brings you here, traveller, and what do you seek from Gilgad?"

"From Gilgad directly, I merely seek passage on one of your vessels to a destination only your captains know."

"That... destination is a closely guarded secret," Inkarbleu said, tone carefully neutral. "I need something more than the word of an unknown traveller to even consider your request."

"Of course." I reached into my armor, and brought out the Jewel.

Immediately the huge gem flared with polychromatic radiance, and a brilliant arch stretched outward, filling the room from one side to the other. Inkarbleu staggered back, knees striking his throne's edge so he sat down hard, staring. The Rainbow hung there for a moment, and I could hear the Music of the Spheres, chiming and singing, a Faerie fanfare. Then it faded, and I returned the Jewel to its hidden location.

Inkarbleu's face was white beneath its tan. "The Rainbow Lord moves against the Usurpers?"

"He does. We are asking little of Gilgad, but that little is absolutely vital."

Inkarbleu shook his head slowly — not a refusal, but a sign of disbelief and the need to think. "If they suspect we are assisting an actual attempt to overthrow them, Ugu and Amanita will *level* this land, Lord Medon."

I didn't contest the assignment of nobility here. "Yes, they will. If it's worth their time. But if the bid against them fails, they are more likely to use the actual participants as an example. I won't pretend you won't get more pressure brought against you. There would be costs, and they would be ugly.

"But if no one will help, they'll come for you anyway, someday. All of you know that, every single land in Faerie *has* to know. This temporary peace lasts exactly so long as they're not quite sure they can take you all."

Inkarbleu sat, looking down, for a long time. I didn't dare interrupt his thoughts; I was asking him to make a decision which really was the King's to make, one that could affect every living person in his country, and I could pressure him no more than he was clearly pressuring himself.

But then his head came up, and with a rising heart I saw that he was *smiling*.

159

"My Lord Medon, these are weighty matters of State indeed. Matters of deep policy and terrible consequence," he said, rising slowly, still smiling. "And I am afraid that I simply cannot make this decision myself. To involve this country in these affairs? No, no, it would not do, it would be an inexcusable over-stepping of my authority."

The words were not encouraging, but the smile was broadening, so I simply smiled back. "And so...?"

"And so, my Lord, I must insist that you ask the King yourself, directly." The smile became a grin, and mine answered as I understood how Inkarbleu had found the perfect solution to the problem. "And as the King has already been too long absent from his throne, and as your business is most urgent, I will myself go to fetch him hither. And," he said, with an elaborately careless air as though it were an afterthought, "you may accompany me on that errand, if you will, and thus ask your question somewhat earlier than otherwise."

I could not help but laugh. By taking this approach, Inkarbleu could quite honestly say he had made no decision to assist me in anything, had committed Gilgad to no sides. And at the same time, by inviting me along, he would be bringing me exactly where I wanted to go, giving me exactly the assistance I needed while on an errand which, as Huru and Zammu's conversation had shown, was an expected and oft-repeated one, one which would draw no undue attention and which thus might not even be immediately connected with what I was doing.

I bowed deeply to the Chancellor. "I would be honored beyond words, sir, if you would be so kind as to allow me aboard your vessel so that I might put my case directly to the King."

"Very well, then," he said. "You may stay here in the Castle until we depart — which will be early on the morrow, if I have any say in it, and I believe I shall. *Zammu! Huru!*"

The doors popped open. "Yes, Lord Chancellor?"

"Show Lord Medon to the First Guest Chambers, and then tell the Master of Ships to ready the Royal Galley. I have decided it is time our aged and reckless monarch returned to his seat for a time." As the two began to lead me out, he called out, "And have old Keys clean out my favorite cell. I'm sure the King will have me prepared for execution as soon as we return and I want everything ready!"

Chapter 24.

"He *is* clever! And lucky! Oh, Father, this might work, it might really work after all!" Polychrome was dancing around the viewing pool, the perfectly circular bowl of mist and rainbow through which Iris and those in the throne room could, when he willed it, see that which passed in the area of the Jewel of the Bridge.

Iris watched her closely, a faint smile on his lips but a chill in his heart. He glanced over at Nimbus, whose gaze met his grimly. *It has begun.*

There were so many things his instincts told him to do, to try and avert that which seemed more and more inevitable. But he dared try none of them. Any attempt to interfere could — almost certainly *would* — recoil upon him and his entire realm.

And instead I must take the hardest path of all. "It may indeed, daughter. A long road ahead of him, but thus far he has taken steps straight and true."

She nodded, watching as Erik Medon left the Throneroom of Gilgad, then turned back to him as he continued to speak. "But there are more pressing matters today, Polychrome Glory."

That gained her undivided attention. "Yes, Father?"

Carefully. Carefully. "Did you mean what you told me — and him — some time ago? That it was your will that you be present, even at the final battle?"

The delicate face hardened, the chin came up in the stubborn way he knew all too well. "You are *not* about to argue me out of it, Father!"

He raised his hand. "Speak not to me in such a tone, Polychrome. Yet know that I have no intention of arguing with you; long since have I given up any hope of persuading you to do anything save that which is already in your mind."

A brief flash of a smile like the sun itself, and she bowed. "My apologies, my Royal Father."

"Accepted as always, errant yet beloved." He sighed. "Polychrome, if the field of war you would take, then prepared you must be, as prepared as any of my warriors — as prepared, indeed, as the finest of them, for you shall lead them."

So shocked was she that the ever-dancing feet halted in mid-step and she stumbled. "What?" She glanced in confusion at Nimbus, then back to him. "Lead them?"

"Not in the details of war and strategy, My Lady." Nimbus said. "What Lord Iris Mirabilis means is that you shall be the High Commander and his representative, though I shall of course continue to direct military matters."

Polychrome looked suddenly uncertain. "Father?"

The lordly smile he wore was one of the hardest expressions he had ever had to maintain, against the twin fears he had. "Polychrome, I must remain here. Well you know the power of our enemies, and I will — as the Prophecy requires — be in essence emptying all of the Rainbow Land of its warriors. In case Ugu and Amanita attempt, in that time, a strike to the rear, an assault on my kingdom, then only one force remains to me that might defend this castle, this city, this land and all my people: myself. I must remain here, vigilant, ready for any and all threats and assaults that may come while my General and his armies are assaulting the Grey Castle and its legions.

"But still, someone of the blood must be present, so my hand will be shown as clearly as though I myself were there upon the field of battle. Daughters only have I ever had, and of all of them, one, and one alone, has the courage, the will, the strength, and the heart to be my right hand and my sword." He reached down, and took his daughter's hand. "You, Polychrome."

Her eyes were wide, and her grip spasmed tight on his hand as she came to understand. "I..."

"Lady Polychrome," Nimbus said quietly, "this is simple truth as well as grim and necessary policy. If the assault upon Oz fails, Faerie cannot afford to lose Iris Mirabilis; he remains the sole and only hope the lands have. Yet if the Rainbow Land falls, we cannot afford to lose hope, and the armies I command must return to take it; but retaking the Rainbow Castle will be of no use if there be none to take the Rainbow Throne. And only one other lives who could rally our people, one other that the other children of Iris Mirabilis will follow, one other whose face is known and loved throughout Faerie, even more so than our King himself."

It seemed to sink in, finally. And as the lovely face became just a tiny bit older, the shoulders sagged beneath an intangible burden and then straightened as though bearing up that weight, Iris Mirabilis thought his heart would simultaneously break for the loss of one more drop of her innocence, and burst with the swell of pride as she accepted the royal burdens.

"I... I understand, Father, Nimbus," she said after a long pause.

He embraced her then, allowing him a few moments to clear the unshed tears from his eyes. "It is well, daughter. Very well." He rose and returned to the throne. "So you must train now, and train well, and train hard. As hard, perhaps, as the mortal Erik Medon did, and in some ways harder; for though he is surprisingly kind of heart, and unwilling to do injury, still he has the savagery of his ancestors locked within, and none of a Faerie's inborn hesitance in warfare, that normally only those of dark and twisted nature may overcome." He signaled to Nimbus, who bowed and hurried away.

Polychrome grew thoughtful. "I think I see. You can carry the battle to the enemy yourself, Father, and if I am to represent you or..." she hesitated, then forced out the words, "...or succeed you, then I must be fully as formidable as you."

"As much as may be possible... and much is possible, my daughter." The tall figure of Nimbus re-entered, carrying the polished silver box, four feet long and two square, that carried the seal of rainbow, spear, and hammer. Iris took the beautiful yet simple case from his General and laid it before Polychrome. "This was a gift to your mother from... your great-aunt, I suppose would be the best term. She never had need of it, for which I was always grateful; but now it has passed to you, her first child, and the time has come."

Polychrome slowly reached out and touched the box; the seal reacted instantly to her touch, unlocking, the top springing open with a martial chime like a trumpeting bell. From inside, his daughter drew out armor, plate with mail permitting ease of

165

movement, carven with ornate grace to be both elegant protection and shining symbol. "This... was mother's?"

"In name, yes, although as I said, never did she wear it. I am unsure if she ever opened it, in fact." He touched the mail, which rippled like water in sunlight. "Forged in the fires of the Above and passed to us. But armor is of little use to one who has not learned to make use of it."

"Oh, Father... I will. I *will* learn, Father! I promise!"

Seeing her shining face, imagining herself taking the battlefield in the Armor of the Gods, Iris felt his heart sink once more. *Yes, you will. Oh, Father and Mother help me, you will learn.*

Chapter 25.

"Chancellor, we have stormclouds ahead."

Inkarbleu glanced up from the small dining table we were sharing. "That is... unusual, is it not?"

"Very, sir. Weather indications for this time of year are usually clear — for weeks or months at a time." The Captain looked grim.

I rose and ran up the steps to the forward deck.

Black stormclouds loomed up in a narrow front, focused on the *Pearl of Gilgad*, our ship, and her escorts. I narrowed my eyes, trying to see better, as I heard the others coming up behind me. "Captain, can I borrow your spyglass?"

The tiny telescope brought the roiling clouds several times closer. Just enough for me to make out what I was afraid I'd see.

Three tiny dots moving within and about the clouds, guiding and shaping them. Three dots of a sickly black-green-yellow that I had seen once before. *Tempests*.

"We're in trouble, Captain." I handed him back the telescope, a sinking feeling in my gut. Given the situation — on a ship in mid-ocean — "sinking" was not a word I even liked using to describe my gut feelings, but it seemed all too appropriate. "That's a Faerie storm. Tell your people to batten down the hatches and everything else. This is going to be very, very rough."

Inkarbleu gazed up. "A storm? How odd. Why in the world would they not simply send a Torrent or three, raise a wave that would crush us like matchwood or drag us through a great whirlpool to the very bottom of the sea? This may actually afford us some small chance to survive."

I watched as the storm moved rapidly closer, thinking. "My guess? These waters are probably the territory of the Sea Fairies, and King Ugu isn't ready to piss them off by trying to send his own emissaries straight through their own country." Given what I knew about Pingaree, that seemed a pretty good bet. "I dunno if that makes things much better, though. They can raise waves on the surface just fine, maybe even cause a whirlpool, certainly hit us with enough wind, rain, and lightning..."

"Lightning is not a terrible danger; we have long since forged steel and copper into our vessels to disperse much of its power," Inkarbleu said. "Waves and wind, however, remain the boon and bane of all ships."

The sea began to heave, waves slowly building in height, as the winds started to pick up. "Chancellor, you'd better get below. I don't know if there's anything I can do... but I doubt there's anything *you* can, and neither I nor the Captain need to be worrying about you while we try to survive this."

Inkarbleu had already shown he was a man of great practicality; with a simple nod, he headed below.

I took one of the lines available and bound myself to the forward observation post; I had no intention of being stupidly swept overboard. The armor of the Rainbow Kingdom, fortunately, was ludicrously light — I suspected it was actually lighter than water by a good amount — and would probably *help* rather than hinder me if I ended up in the drink, but I sure wouldn't be able to swim the rest of the way to Pingaree. We were about halfway to our destination, which made sense; if Ugu and Amanita wanted to stop us, do it at the point farthest from any possible help.

It bothered me they'd caught on this fast. I'd hoped the distraction at the border of the Nome King's lands would actually lead them to look at Kaliko's domains first, but it seemed that hadn't worked too well.

Now I could make out the Tempests without the spyglass, swirling dots the color of twisters and destruction. *Damn. They're nothing but pure magic bound up in a tiny bit of matter. If I could reach them, they'd probably pop like evil little balloons, but there's no way I can think of to manage it. Despite a couple of cheap comic-book imitations I've done, I can't pull off flight, or even leaping over tall buildings. Maybe a medium-sized building, if I'm in a really high-magic area, but this ship is mostly mundane. I'm not feeling much resilience from the deck.*

The *Pearl of Gilgad* heaved as a twenty-five foot crest hit the hundred-fifty foot vessel, and I wavered in my balance.

The ship and its escorts turned into the wind, not letting the waves hit them broadside. They slid up and down smoothly, and it was clear that it would take vastly larger waves to threaten them.

I saw the Tempests spiral downward. *They've reached the same conclusion.* The rain was now sheeting down and a spark of lightning split the sky with an echoing blast, but the ships sailed on. *They need to amp up the storm quite a bit, and they can't do that way up there.*

I frowned. The rain made it harder to see. A *lot* harder now as it pounded down, mixed with hail, the wind screaming through the rigging, waves reaching crests of nearly fifty or sixty feet. Despite the roller-coaster rises and dips, I still felt the deck startlingly solid beneath me. *They build good ships, Gilgad does.*

Then I felt it. A slight roll.

"Wind's shifted!" I heard the Captain bellow over the howl of the storm. "Seas shifting ... Bring them around, ten points!"

The fleet began to turn, following the signals barely visible in the storm-gloom. But the rolling continued.

"Shifting again, Captain!" shouted one of the crewmen. "Eight... Ten more points!"

The cresting waves were clashing now, making it harder to judge the angle of attack. I tried to cover my face, get a feel for things. I noticed, oddly, that the wind and rain seemed not quite as intense near me.

Of course. The Tempests are driving this as hard as they can. Their magic drops off near me. Has to.

But then, feeling how the wind was shifting, I realized I had something a lot more important to worry about. "Captain!" I called, but by now the screaming wind was ripping away any sound. I grabbed a nearby deckpin and pulled it up, waving it back and forth to get his attention as the rolling increased.

Dammit, look *at me!*

The glittering of my armor moving apparently caught his eye at last; he made his way over with careful steps. "What is it, Lord Medon?" he shouted.

"*Whirlwind*, Captain! They're making a tornado!"

169

He cursed. "Of course! That's why the wind keeps shifting! But not a tornado, boy, they'd have to do that personal-like!

"They're making a whirlpool, turning the winds, turning the sea!"

Now I could see it, shadowy movement around us, cresting waves higher in a sinister circle, flattening inward, turning, turning...

"Oh, crap. Now what?"

To my surprise, the Captain grinned, a savage smile that would have looked at home on Nimbus. "Now what? Now we sail right out of their trap, Lord Medon! Use the speed of the currents and the winds to whip us up and over! Thanks to you, we've seen it in time!"

He raised his arm and signaled his crew, who sent up lights and flags. The ships turned. Then turned again, sails belling out in the storm, and I felt the *Pearl of Gilgad* lunge forward as it caught the power of the storm. It slid down the forming curve of flowing might that was the developing maelstrom, gathering speed, accelerating at a tremendous rate, turning again with the whirling wind. The masts creaked, inaudible through the storm but something I could *feel* through the deck, bending with the centripetal force, like a car careening around a too-tight curve. Before us loomed a clashing barrier of black-green waves, nearly invisible against the green-black sky.

"HOLD ON!"

The *Pearl* hit the waves with a shock that stretched my mooring lines almost to the breaking point, forced me to catch the Captain as he fell. The ship was momentarily in freefall, literally having jumped the crest, and then it came down with a mighty splash, running before the wind.

"Ha!" the Captain said, still grinning. "Let them try that trick again, we'll head right back out! See, see, my lord! All of the fleet, still with us!"

I looked up.

Three miniature stormclouds were descending, trailing more storm behind them. "I think they realize that didn't work."

The Captain followed my gaze. "Blast. *Now* you'll have your waterspout, Lord Erik, and I'm not sure we have anything for that."

170

The wind was now whirling tighter, the storm contracting, more and more intensely upon the *Pearl of Gilgad*. It was clear that this was their target.

The sails guttered, flapped, and the ship stalled. I saw the banners hang limp, then lift... starting to point up. Spray whipped around the ship, rising higher, more intensely.

A funnel cloud was forming above, following the descending Tempests, narrowing, dropping towards us as the spray rose to meet it.

Rose to meet it...

The Captain gaped as I suddenly released the ropes holding me. "What are –"

"Tie yourself down, Captain!" I said. "And if this doesn't work... well, you may still get out of this alive."

I threw myself into the rigging and began climbing as fast as I could, trying to ignore the swaying of the ship and the increasingly distant deck. *Got to get as high as I can...*

The Tempests were getting closer, much closer now. I could make out their spinning, roiling forms, living clouds the color of bruises and agony, glints of lightning-blue for eyes, and the howl of the twister was growing, the entire ship starting to turn despite the efforts of the men at the rudder. The whirling funnel was dropping with terrifying speed. *A few more seconds... Got to get higher...*

With a final lunge I popped out into the crow's nest, weaving dangerously, catching the mast with one hand as I yanked my sword out. *Wait... wait... judge it...*

Just as the funnel cloud was about to drop upon me, I saw a deckpin go flying up. *NOW!*

I judged the jump through sheer gut instinct, seeing the Tempests almost to my level, spinning in a perfect triple circle around the tornado. I hit the updraft and was carried up, moving outward with the whirling winds, sword extended.

There! For a moment I thought I'd misjudged it too badly, even angling my body, turning –

– but it saw me. I don't know if it recognized me, and thought it could finish the job on its own, or just thought it had found a new and temporary plaything. For whatever reason, the Tempest slowed, turned, and our courses were bent together. Too late it saw the sword, too late it realized there was no terror, only a grim smile, coming through the wind and mist to greet it.

"I've got you, my pretty — and your little fog, too!"

The sword cut through the Tempest like a hurricane through a wheat field, causing the twisted elemental to burst into disintegrating fragments of vapor. I continued on, sword and my True Mortal body ripping through the side of the mystically-controlled tornado. The whirlwind seemed to stagger and waver, coming apart at my passage.

Then the second Tempest was suddenly in front of me, trying to somehow regain control of the storm, realizing a fraction of a second later that it had made just the wrong move as I reached out and plunged my hand into its icy center, causing it to explode into nothingness.

The mighty upwelling winds broke apart as the last Tempest retreated, understanding that there was no longer any chance of this plan working.

I looked down. "Oh, boy. Now I know how the Coyote feels."

Five hundred feet below, the wind-tossed sea began a lunge up at me.

I closed my eyes, gritted my teeth, and tried to align my body into a spike. *Armored feet will hit first. Rest of the armor will brace me to some extent. Might survive if I hit just right — a wave just dropping away below me. Keep the Eustachian tubes open, you'll be going way, way down... open your damn eyes a crack, you have to know when you're going to hit so you can hold your breath -*

The ocean was rushing closer, reminding me of my prior fall from a great height. This time I was in better shape, I was armored, I was falling into water, not onto land... but there was no Faerie princess to rescue me this time, either. *Almost there... Hold—*

IMPACT!

A drifting pattern of darkness... a spark of tormented light, far away, calling in green... I reached out, but the light went dark, as did everything else.

An immeasurable time later, blackness lifted to dim grey and I heard a voice speaking to me.

"Lord Medon?"

I opened my eyes, becoming aware of aches in almost every part of my body. The Chancellor was looking down at me.

"...Wow," I managed. "I'm... alive."

"Just barely, it would seem, but you should make a full recovery by the time we reach Pingaree." Relief was written clearly on Inkarbleu's face. "Your armor and luck appear to have saved you." He raised his voice. "Tell the Captain he has awakened and appears to be himself."

"How... how long was I out?"

Inkarbleu smiled faintly. "Hard to say precisely, sir. You were floating unconscious when we found you." So I'd been right about the buoyancy of the armor... fortunately. "But it has been about two days."

"Two days we have waited in fear that we could not thank you." The Captain stood in the doorway. "Lord Medon, you took a fearful risk to save my ship and crew, and we cannot easily express our gratitude."

I tried to wave that away, but my arms were not cooperating. *Any* movement made me wince. "Forget it, Captain." I said, feeling the ache in my jaw as I spoke. Even my *tongue* hurt. "You wouldn't have been in any danger except for me being there, so it was the least I could do. I don't think they'll try that again, though."

"I would hope not. But ah, what a song this adventure will make!" The Captain bowed to me, and then strode out on deck, presumably to tell everyone the news.

I turned my eyes towards Inkarbleu. "I... think I need some water and food. Soup. Chewing would hurt. And then real sleep."

"It is good," Inkarbleu said as he rose, with a thin smile, "to see that some heroes can actually be sensible... once they've regained their senses."

Chapter 26.

Ugu found Queen Amanita in the Third Garden, one of the few spots of green in the Grey Capital. She was apparently experimenting with transformations, morphing a butterfly into a sort of winged centipede with a dozen sets of brilliant wings, then into a bird with butterfly wings, and other variations on flying pretty creatures. *She has an excellent eye and appreciation for beauty, but her art is as cold as her smile, alas.*

As he waited for her to acknowledge his presence, he reflected that the latter thought seemed somewhat odd. *How has this changed me, I wonder? I have found myself spending much time contemplating the best way to keep this realm for my own... and it seems that the best path has led to understanding those around me...*

The train of thought made him uncomfortable, and it was almost a relief when Amanita Verdant turned her brilliant smile in his direction. "Oh, my apologies, Majesty. I was so involved in my work I did not see you there. What brings the King of Oz to visit me here in my humble garden?"

Ah, the charming and harmless flower approach. A shame none of your disguises, of body or of speech, work any more upon me. It was sometimes better, then. "Merely... curiosity, my Queen, as to some differences in policy which you appear to have directed without informing me. I would, you understand, prefer to know if any changes in Our directives are to be undertaken, that we appear to speak with one voice to the people."

Her eyes widened and she gave her most innocent gaze. "To what differences do you refer, King Ugu?"

Play the ingénue as you will, then. "I am certain that you heard — if not with your own ears, then by proxy — my directives to the Viceroys, that assaults on the others of Faerie were forbidden. And now it appears that an assault was made on the flagship of Gilgad, one which nearly sank the object of *our own plans*, mind you, and which seems to have been directed by none other than yourself,

175

Queen Amanita. Might you be willing to clarify these actions, which seem to me ... a bit difficult to reconcile?"

"Oh, *that!*" Amanita laughed, then covered her mouth with a show of contrition. "My apologies, Majesty. I had thought you more clever than... that is, I had thought my reasoning entirely transparent."

As transparent as your attempts to goad me. But we shall play the game. "Take care, Amanita. What is this obvious explanation which I am too stupid to understand?"

Her green eyes flashed for an instant with amused malevolence, but immediately returned to the wide-eyed harmless girl-queen. "Well, my King, we are agreed that our great advantage is in knowing the Prophecy, while our adversaries believe we know nothing — save, possibly, that a Prophecy exists, but nothing of its specifics, yes?"

Ugu nodded. "Iris Mirabilis has wisely treated the details as a state secret, and while we could ascertain that there is some 'prophesied Hero,' no more than that would be available to us were Cirrus not one of us."

"Exactly! So we should keep that advantage, I am sure you agree." She scattered a dusting of sparkling powder with a gesture and the ground itself formed seats for the two of them. "Well, if we knew only that there was some prophesied Hero and he was moving against us, would we not, in turn, move against him?"

Ugu grunted, as though he began to understand her point.

"I see you agree. Of *course* we would. For us to *not* attack him and his allies, at least on occasions when they seemed vulnerable, would possibly reveal that we know more than we ought, don't you think?" She smiled prettily up at him. "So I had Cirrus direct a small but credible assault on that annoying little ship. We also have learned something of our opponent this way. Is this not a wise thing I have done?"

Ugu's mouth tightened. His expression made clear that he did not like being so simply out-maneuvered. "I... I commend you on your strategy, my Queen. You are, of course, completely correct. Yet I would point out that General Dawnglory has been under my command, as you seemed more interested in your researches for the mystical defense of the realm, and I would prefer you not simply insert your commands into the military structure. Had you revealed these thoughts to me, I would certainly have given those directives, and this confusion would have been avoided."

She smiled and ran her fingers sensuously through her silky hair. "Why, Ugu, I'm so terribly sorry. It wasn't at all like that, it was just a personal request to Cirrus –" She put her hand delicately over her mouth again, the very picture of a woman who has accidentally revealed too much.

So that *is the point she wishes to make.* "Personal indeed, *My Queen*," he said, with a hardness to his voice which – to his surprise – was not entirely an act. *She is beautiful and talented and skilled, and helped bring me from my accursed bondage of centuries to rulership of Oz, and a part of me still wishes she was... what I once thought she could be.* "Think you that I am entirely blind, or so old that I cannot see, or unable to watch as things pass within my own realm? I am aware that General Cirrus has been seen leaving your quarters at most inappropriate times. That will stop, Amanita, and it will stop *now*."

All the gentleness vanished, and now there was just poison-candy venom in her smile. "You think you can order *me* in that fashion, Ugu? Order my personal life? Oh, I understand you may miss certain... aspects of interaction, but let us be clear that you have long since had all of your rewards in that area. Cirrus is a far more... compliant and entertaining companion." She leaned forward and her voice carried the silken hiss of a cobra. "I will see whosoever I like, *your Majesty*, and unless you wish to show yourself as foolish as other men, you will not risk your life or your current *shape* by trying to tell me otherwise."

Ugu's face was white and his voice, when he spoke, showed the strain of iron control. "I would not dream of interfering in whom you show the favor of your bedchamber, *Queen* Amanita. But for *your* sake, as well as that of my own image as the Ruler of Oz – an image you find useful, I remind you – what *will* stop is the clumsiness of these assignations. You may see whom you will, but you will no longer allow witnesses. The respect of the realm will *not* be tarnished by such sordid conduct."

Her eyes narrowed, but the smile slowly returned; apparently she was willing to accept the practical directive with the knowledge that she had truly won the battle. "Oh, of *course*, my King. So we shall speak no more on that subject."

Ugu nodded ungraciously. *A change of subject.* "Then allow me to ask how your researches have progressed, my Queen."

Her expression lightened. "Oh, *very* well, King Ugu! In fact, since we are here, allow me to describe this to you — in privacy ensured by my magics, even better than your own."

And so she tells me subtly that she has realized I have assured myself of security in my own chambers. But I doubt she realizes how carefully or subtly that security has been managed. "I would be most pleased to hear anything you would be willing to tell me."

She turned and gestured; a small table grew from the ground between them, and the pebbles and grass upon it flickered and became an afternoon tea, with a number of dainty dishes on crystal and china. "Well spoken, my King.

"You understand that our greatest concern is that — despite all of our advantages and preparations — the mortal somehow achieves his power, the fusion of the power of Oz embodied in the Princess and the strength of a mortal being. I have dug deep and searched wide — often with the inestimable aid of your elemental servants," she bowed in his direction with only a hint of mockery, "who have brought me much information from the other lands of Faerie. Such incidents have only happened a very few times in all our known history, but the past months have permitted me to assemble perhaps the most complete collection of accounts of all of these." The smile widened. "And it turns out that even in that extremity, we have a good chance to triumph."

Ugu leaned forward. "You fascinate me greatly, my Queen. How is this so?"

"His time is limited not merely by the nature of the fusion — by the fact that his body and soul will be overstrained by the alien power within him — but by something else." Her smile grew even wider, a predator's grin.

And as she continued her explanation, his own smile joined hers. *Ahh. So very clear, even inevitable. So as soon as he gains the power, his very triumph is burning towards its own defeat. We need only survive long enough!*

Ugu stood. "It is well, my Queen. Though, of course, we hope that this knowledge shall not be needed, as he will serve far better as a sacrifice than as a failed Hero."

"Of course, King Ugu. Though," and her smile was even more cold, "the failure of such a Hero would also do much to secure for all time our hold on this land."

"As you say."

Ugu bowed and left Amanita, and strode away, deep in thought, for some time. Finally he reached his own section of the Grey Castle.

"My lord?"

He smiled and nodded to Cirrus. "All is well. *Very* well indeed."

"So she suspects nothing?"

Ugu's smile was wry. "She suspects *many* things, my friend. But she does not give you credit for the strategy, and thus obviously suspects not at all that you passed to her the hints of action against the Hero, or the way in which I might be ... missing critical aspects of the situation."

Cirrus bowed. "Then all proceeds as planned."

Ugu looked at him. "No... second thoughts?"

Cirrus did not pretend to misunderstand. "Majesty... she is quite beautiful. And...talented in certain areas. But... she is intending to use me as well. And she is even more mad than I had thought." He shivered. "I will be well pleased when this is over, no matter how... entertaining some of the nights may be."

Many are the men who would still be unable to think so clearly. A unique and precious find you are, Cirrus Dawnglory. "Soon, my friend. A few more months, I believe... and it will all be finished."

Second Vision:

A gony of boiling light, cruel radiance tearing her slowly apart, pieces of her own self taken away, forged with hammers of blazing selfish will and cruel luminant ambition.

But the tiny comfort of the point of darkness remained, and she clung to that. Over days and weeks and untold passage of time, when her eyes and soul felt tormented beyond endurance, she could seek it out, so small, but still there, the one still and solid hope in all the light of the terrible world of ceaseless burning cold mystic fire.

Sometimes — for a moment or an eternity — she thought she saw something else, a flicker of different light, almost familiar, not terrible or destroying but laughing, and it danced around the dark point, then away, as though it did not know why it was drawn to the darkness and fled, heedless, to the realms of killing brightness that lay hidden behind all.

She could scream, but there were none to hear, save those who might be taking the strength from her, and they would not care.

And then, one day, like all other infinite days, but it was not. For on *that day*, when she awakened from the unsleeping rest she found within the unending baking light of all deserts distilled, she opened her never-closed eyes, and looked, and the darkness was no longer a point, but something else, a shape she could not see, but closer, and she knew and laughed, a laugh soundless and tired and agonized, but a laugh.

For Hope now walked towards her, and a Mortal had set foot on Faerie.

Chapter 27.

I couldn't help but grin as *Pearl of Gilgad* pulled up to the docks of Pingaree. In some ways it was exactly as I had pictured it; in others, it was far better.

The pearl-fishing kingdom lay on an island, but one considerably larger and grander than Baum had depicted. Still, it was mostly low, with a sea of green palm trees running to the edge of brilliant white sand beaches, surrounded by a magnificent reef breached only in three places, where three small, swift rivers ran down to the sea. Dozens of ships and boats, ranging from sleek little rowboats or sailboats to dual-hulled catamarans and many others, were moored at the docks, or casting off for another voyage even as we entered.

The major difference was one I'd always suspected — and, in fact, was one of the few areas I'd envisioned differently even when I was a very young man. Despite Neill's illustrations, the description of Pingaree, its tropical climate, the primary occupation of its people, and its surrounding countries had led me to expect what I now saw: a civilization of more Polynesian than European style, with dark-haired, dark-skinned people vastly predominating.

But this was no simple desert island paradise. I could see on a rise a mile and a half from the port a great marble palace, somehow combining many architectural styles from around my old world — classical lines of Greece, the light, airy colors of the American Southwest, the graceful curves of India, symmetries and carvings that evoked both Mesoamerican and Egyptian civilizations — without seeming a hodgepodge. The city before me wasn't a collection of palm-roofed huts, but proud houses of light stonework, open courtyards, white stone streets running straight and true through the city. Gilgad had been impressive, but I wasn't sure if Pindaras (the name of the capital city of Pingaree) wasn't even more so.

The *Pearl* had of course been recognized far out at sea, and so I accompanied Inkarbleu and his party as they were immediately

183

escorted to the Palace. My odd armor, light skin, and blond hair naturally drew notice, but mostly they seemed to accept me as just a member of Inkarbleu's guard.

Pearls were everywhere in evidence, even in the ornamentation of the houses and on all the people, young and old. In truth, pearls were what brought me here — three Pearls in particular, gifted to the rulers of Pingaree by the Sea Fairies: the Pearl of Strength, the Pearl of Protection, and the Pearl of Wisdom. If I had interpreted the Prophecy correctly...

Our party was led through the main gates and straight into the castle. I heard both the tinkling of many fountains and, as we continued, an increasing background of music and many people talking. A set of immense double-doors, appearing to be marble-faced with steel interiors, were thrown open before us. "Lord Inkarbleu and party!" our escorts announced.

Inside was a huge, long table, apparently carven from a single gargantuan tree and supported by fanciful Polynesian-style figures, with room for well over a hundred guests; most of the spaces were in fact full, and we had quite an audience for our entrance. Musicians spaced around the polished white and black hall paused as we walked forward, lowering or straightening up from a surprising array of instruments; while some of them were the woodwinds and simple percussion instruments I might have expected in the setting, there was everything else up to and including a baby grand piano. *Not surprising; they can trade through Gilgad with any other country in Faerie.*

At the far end, I could see seven very distinct figures sitting at a raised section of the long table. A slender old man, white hair contrasting splendidly with dark-teak skin, sat next to an equally old woman; both had slender circlets of gold on their heads. Similar circlets of gold adorned the heads of two much younger people, a girl and a boy seated opposite each other. Both were dark-haired and dark of skin, the girl appearing to be about seventeen or eighteen, possibly taller than anyone else at the table — about six feet, I'd guess, though she was sitting down — while the boy was tiny.

They sat to the right and left hand of the pair of seats at the very head of the table, which were occupied by a tall, handsome man with black hair, wearing a larger crown; next to him was a beautiful woman of the same age but with lighter skin, almost an Italian cast to her face.

Seated across from the older couple, in a chair so wide both of them could have easily fit in it at once, was an immense man, not terribly short and very much terribly wide, with a great bushy mane of white hair, rosy cheeks and a red nose, who was apparently in the midst of an animated conversation with the others when we had so rudely interrupted.

The latter heaved himself to his feet and glared down the table at us. "*INKARBLEU!*" he bellowed, in a voice both deep and resonant and with higher overtones that helped it cut across all other speech. "Inkarbleu, you faithless dried-up scurvy dog of a Chancellor, have you deserted your post *again*? What have I *told* you about that? Eh?"

"That I will be executed for such flagrant and terrible abandonment of my post, Your Highness," Inkarbleu replied with equanimity. "But I hope perhaps you will forgive me, or at least wait to carry out my execution until such time as your Highness has finished your dinner."

King Rin Ki-Tin dropped back into his chair, threw back his head, and gave vent to a long series of laughs. "Ho, ho, ho, hee-hee-hee! When I am... Ha, ha... finished with my dinner! Ahhh, ha! Ha! Finished! With my dinner!" He laughed longer. "Seeking a stay of execution... ha, ha, heeee! ... a stay of execution long enough to outlive me, I see! Finished with my dinner? I am never finished with my dinner until it is finished with me, and eventually it's become breakfast, I think!"

"King Rin Ki-Tin," the tall man at the far end said, with a fond smile on his face, "Perhaps we should let the doomed Inkarbleu at least tell us what dire errand has brought him here."

"Oh, indeed, indeed. No executions at dinner, I agree!" the fat King said cheerfully. "Inkarbleu! Justify your conduct, then, to my good friend King Inga!"

I thought so. King Inga. I guess Kitticut retired and handed his son the throne. Which would make the woman with him Zella, I'd bet, if the subtext I got was right.

Ryk E. Spoor

"A matter of deep policy, your Majesty," Inkarbleu said. "And one best discussed in more privacy."

The look Rin Ki-Tin shot Inkarbleu was sharp and shrewd, greatly at variance with his clownish exterior, and the way his gaze shifted to me showed he might have already guessed some of the essence of my mission. "Policy is so tiring. You know, I believe I once made a song about –" he broke off at a glance from Inga, "– but enough for now. Ah, well, I suppose we could retire to the inner chambers long enough for the extra dishes to be tidied up and the next course laid."

He moved with surprising ease for a man so fat and old, following King Inga who gestured for us to follow; the tall girl started to rise, but a glance from the King — *her father,* I guessed — dropped her back into her seat. Inkarbleu motioned for me to accompany him but left the rest of our entourage behind.

The next room would have looked quite large had we not just come from the immense dining hall. King Inga, Queen Zella (if my guess was right), and King Rin Ki-Tin seated themselves on one side of a wide conference table and indicated that we should sit as well. *I see. The former King and Queen will remain with the festivities.*

Inga turned immediately to me and bowed. "Sir, it is clear that faithful Inkarbleu has risked much to bring you here. I am King Inga, and this is my Queen, Zella. You now have the advantage of us."

"Erik Medon," I said, returning the bow.

"An emissary of Iris Mirabilis himself," Inkarbleu finished.

All trace of the clown vanished as Rin Ki-Tin sat up. "Now indeed I forgive you, Inkarbleu. Though undoubtedly I shall threaten you with execution later, just for form's sake. Deep policy and dangerous, dangerous. So the Rainbow Lord moves at last, does he? HA!" The jolly face was, for a moment, transformed to grim savagery. "Long have I thought my days would end before that day came; you have already brought me great joy, just to hear that hope has not abandoned us."

"Rin Ki-Tin speaks of hope," Zella said cautiously, "but we know well the power of our adversaries. What hope is there, truly, Erik Medon?"

I turned to her. "Enough. A prophecy from a source well-trusted by the Rainbow Lord. I may not look precisely as a hero of legend, but I have... certain advantages over others."

At this range, I could see that the royalty of Pingaree wore — as one might expect — many jewels, especially pearls of all sizes and colors. The King himself wore two earrings with magnificent matched pure-white pearls of extraordinary size. Now, I saw him tilt his head slightly, as though listening to something. He nodded his head and sat a bit straighter. "A True Mortal?"

Excellent. "You see clearly, King Inga."

"So what can Gilgad do for the Rainbow Lord and yourself?" Rin Ki-Tin demanded.

I grinned. "Already done, and cleverly by your Lord Inkarbleu. What I really needed was to get here. What *he* needed was to do that without actually committing Gilgad to such a radical cause." Quickly I explained Inkarbleu's decision.

The three monarchs looked at Inkarbleu with such approval I saw a faint blush on the old cheeks. "So clever a statesman should have been King himself," Rin Ki-Tin said, with a gentle laugh.

"Such a clever statesman knows far better than to want the post, your Majesty," Inkarbleu responded, garnering a gale of laughter from his ruler.

"Hooo, hooo, hoo! Too true, too true! As I know, from trying in my manful way to flee from the dread and terrible responsibilities."

Ignoring the byplay with the same fond smile, Inga leaned forward. "So it was to Pingaree you wished to come. What do you seek here? We have no formidable army, in truth, and while something of a naval force we have acquired, that would do you no good against the Usurpers of Oz."

"Nothing so obvious or direct, your Majesty," I said. "Here, I seek only two things — besides of course a trip back to the mainland. First, I need your people to build me a ship, a boat of a very particular design. Nothing too terribly large," I hastened to assure him, "indeed, just something suitable for a long journey for one person. And to have it transported to a particular spot."

"And that is all?"

"Well, no, that was really one thing — I mean, getting the ship won't do me any good if I can't use it where I want to. The second thing I seek... is the wisdom of Pingaree."

The King and Queen both straightened and looked sharply at me — as did King Rin Ki-Tin. "How exactly do you mean that?" the King of Pingaree said finally.

I grinned.

Inga looked at me for a moment, and then stood. "Excuse me for a moment." He stepped to the side and through a door which, it appeared, led to a small side alcove.

Zella studied me curiously. "Do you know what you are asking?"

"I think I know *exactly* what I am asking."

The door opened again and King Inga resumed his seat. He reached up and — as I had expected — removed the righthand earring. Not without reluctance, he placed the earring with its magnificent white pearl into my hand. "If wisdom there be in Pingaree, you now hold it in your hand," he said slowly. "No other has ever carried that which I give to you, save only those of my family."

The Pearl of Wisdom. "I know of this... and I can guess how difficult my request is for you." I raised the Pearl to my ear. "You advised him to offer yourself to me, didn't you?"

From the Pearl came a clear, though distant, voice. "*You are correct, Erik Medon.*"

I grinned, and then tossed the Pearl back. Inga was so startled he almost failed to catch it. "What...?"

"King Inga, these are perilous times indeed. I will not deprive you of what is undoubtedly your greatest resource, especially when — if I fail — you will need wisdom more desperately than ever. I only have a couple questions to ask the Pearl, and that is all."

The relief on his face, and that of Queen Zella, matched his surprise. "You are a man of some depth, I see," Inga said after a moment, with a smile. "Ask, then."

I had thought about this for quite a while. Really what I needed here was validation. I had thought everything I could through, but there was so much I might not know. I couldn't ask for things of too great detail — that pesky question of over-working the Prophecy and making it backfire on me was always looming above me.

"Pearl," I said, "First, tell me: are my guesses about... a certain individual... correct?"

Inga listened, then nodded. "The Pearl says 'yes.'"

Good. "Then... The course of action I have planned... is it a good one?"

"Yes."

I sagged back in my seat. "Then that's all I needed. That plus the boat, which I'll sketch out tomorrow."

King Inga looked at me with a curious expression. "So... you needed only verification of a particular course of action and this boat? You need nothing more from Pingaree?"

"Nothing." I said. *Well, nothing I could ask.*

"And you will travel alone... where?"

"After I get back to the mainland? Well, eventually to Oz, of course... but the Nome King's domain is my next destination."

For a moment, everyone was silent. Finally, Rin Ki-Tin said, gently, yet with a puzzled air, "Lord Medon... You do realize that the Nome King will help no one, even for the Rainbow Lord?"

"Maybe," I conceded. "Yet I have no choice. There is no other force sufficient to even have a credible chance against what Ugu and Amanita have to throw at us. Combined with the Rainbow Kingdom's, it might be enough." *I can't tell them the whole thing. Partly because the whole thing, in the end, comes down to a big throw of the dice, and whether I'm tough enough to survive the pain and take action at just the right time.*

"And do you have... any plan to *find* the Nome King, let alone convince him to involve himself in this war?"

I grinned. "Oh yes. And that's what I was asking your Pearl."

"If the Pearl says it will work, then it'll work!" a new voice broke in. "So, Father, I'm going with him!"

I turned, startled.

The tall girl from the end of the table stood in the doorway, grinning confidently at us all.

King Inga glared at her. "Zenga, have you been *eavesdropping?*"

189

"You said I should take more interest in the running of the kingdom, Father."

"Not by spying on secret councils!" Inga sighed. "You have no idea what you are saying, anyway. You are far too young to be getting involved in –"

"*You* were younger than I am when you saved Pingaree, liberated Regos and Coregos, and faced the Nome King yourself!"

"That was entirely –" Inga broke off. I was working very hard to keep a smile off my face, because I was pretty sure grinning at a royal family spat would be very impolitic. "No. I will not play this debate game with you, Zenga."

Queen Zella spoke up. "Let her go."

Inga stared at his wife. "I beg your pardon, my love – did I just hear you correctly?"

"Let her go with him." She rose smoothly and bowed to us. "But this is a discussion for more privacy. My lords – dear Rin Ki-Tin, Inkarbleu, and Lord Medon – please, return to the dining hall. The King of Gilgad never refuses a meal, and I am sure that after weeks at sea both of you would be pleased with a feast. We shall resolve this discussion anon."

I bowed back. "Of course, Queen Zella."

We filed out of the conference room and returned to the dining hall, where two seats were placed for us near King Rin Ki-Tin. Inkarbleu glanced at me, shaking his head with a smile. "An interesting development, that. How do you think it will go... and will you take her with you, if that is the decision?"

"I," I said, reaching out and grabbing a piece of bread, "have gotten about as far ahead of myself as I want to right now, so I'll leave *that* decision for when it happens."

Inwardly, I grinned. *I admit I didn't exactly foresee these details... but even so... all that has transpired here has done so according to my design.*

Chapter 28.

"So, Lord Erik, we head for the Nome King's domain once we have landed?"

I turned and smiled at Zenga. She was easy to smile at, having the dark-coffee skin of most of Pingaree's people combined with the sharper-cut features of her mother to produce a girl of striking beauty. "Yes and no, Princess."

"You are far too young to speak in riddles," she retorted, leaning on the rail next to me. "That is the province of wizened old wizards and priests."

She was dressed in an outfit that I, being totally unversed in the ways of clothing, couldn't give a name to, but it was some sort of protective clothing that was meant to allow someone free movement... and apparently to still be properly stylish as well. As she came from and was used to a very warm climate, it also wasn't particularly modest, which did put some slight demands on my eyeball control. Fortunately, I'd had a great deal of practice with that around Poly.

"Old as your father looks, at least. Old enough so that I could have had daughters of my own who had children by now." I couldn't use the line that first occurred to me, which was "old enough to be your father," since the way time flowed and the slightly-Faerie humanity of these realms aged, she was still probably as old or older than me in actual years. "Still, it's not exactly a riddle. Eventually I have to get to the Nome King, but first I have to find the key that unlocks his door."

"And you know where to find this... key?" She studied me curiously. "I have no doubt there are a number of people that would like to find such a thing."

I don't doubt it. "I know, I think, how to go about finding it, even though I don't know exactly where it is."

She nodded, though undoubtedly that didn't really explain much to her. "So first we are heading...?"

191

"... to the border between Gilgad and the Nome King's lands. That's the best region to search." I glanced into the sky, noting that this time there wasn't a sign of cloud; so far it seemed that our adversaries weren't going to attempt another ambush at sea. "I don't think I'll say anything more until we're on our way there."

She blinked, then looked around the ship. "You ... suspect a spy on the *Pearl of Gilgad*?"

"Oh, no, not at all," I answered with a chuckle. "However, even an overheard word can turn out to be a danger under some circumstances, and in this case since you're going to be following me regardless — you made *that* clear enough — I have no reason to take *any* risks in that area until we're somewhere that makes it necessary that you understand what's going on."

Her head tilted and she gazed at me speculatively, curiously. "And yet certain things you have made no secret of. I'm not sure how to read you, Lord Erik."

"Good," I said, in a voice deliberately deeper with a slight higher-pitched secondary tone which I was pleased to note came out well; my Vorlon imitation was always a tough one.

Zenga blinked in confusion, and I laughed. "The point being that if people traveling with me can't figure me out easily, then hopefully neither can my adversaries."

"That makes sense." She bit her lip — in what was I thought a clearly deliberate affectation that made her look younger and more innocent. "Could... I ask you another question, Lord Erik?"

"As I always say, you can ask any time; whether you get any answers, that's a different matter."

She made a very disrespectful face, which of course just made me grin wider. "Why *did* you let me come along? It was clear to me that you could have said no, and my father would in many ways have preferred it so."

"Yes, that was fairly clear." King Inga's face had shown how worried he was, even if somehow his wife and daughter had argued him into it, and when it had become clear that she was, in fact, going, he'd taken Zenga aside and had a talk with her well out of earshot and mostly out of sight of everyone else.

Some of my reasons I wasn't going to tell her yet, but there were others I could. "Well, the Prophecy said I had to pick up companions on my way, so I was expecting actually to get one at Pingaree. I suppose I'd originally expected Prince Inga — the books kinda get stuck in your head when you've read them so many times as a kid, and I hadn't thought much about him growing up. Your brother didn't seem at *all* interested in coming, either."

"Nikki?" she said, using the diminutive of Prince Nikkikut's name. "No, Nikki's into the books and studies. It's all that Father can do to get him out of the library and into the sunlight most of the time. Except for fishing — he's one of the best pearl-fishers his age."

"And it was pretty clear to me that you weren't unable to take care of yourself."

She patted the hilts of the twin swords that hung near her hips, somehow staying in the inverted sheaths that crossed her back, the tips projecting over her shoulders. "My swordmasters say I'm one of the best. Father did have me trained from the time I was little; I think he was still remembering the time he had to survive the attack on his own."

"So," I continued, "I figured that I had good reason to have you along based on the Prophecy. Second, you're a Princess of Pingaree; even though Pingaree is known to have only a small navy and no army to speak of, its defeat and eventual consolidation of Regos and Coregos gives your country a powerful reputation. King Inga, by sending his eldest child, is sending a message that he has chosen to cast his lot with me and the Rainbow Lord. This is a very significant political signal, and one that I hope will be useful."

She glanced over my shoulder; I reached up, curious as to what she was looking at, and my fingers found the empty scabbard that was just visible to her. "You didn't feel you needed protection?"

I laughed. "Not in that sense, Princess –"

"–please, call me Zenga."

"Okay. Not in that sense, Zenga. Truth be told, I'd forgotten I lost the sword." I'd lost it, of course, when I'd fallen five hundred feet into the sea. "And honestly speaking, it wasn't that big of a deal. I keep breaking the swords. I'm surprised I haven't broken my armor yet."

She looked at me with an expression of wary suspicion, clearly trying to figure out if I was putting her on. "You do not look so... mighty as that makes you sound, if you will forgive me for saying so, Lord –"

"–Erik, if you're insisting on 'Zenga'."

"Thank you. Then, if you'll forgive me for saying so, you don't appear so mighty as to have to worry about shattering your weapons and armor, Erik."

That got a grin. "No doubt. And I'm not so much mighty as just different. But that's one of the reasons I need to find the Nome King. *He* can almost certainly make weapons and armor that will survive my use."

That was one aspect I'd thought about quite a bit. The Sky Fairies like those in the Rainbow Kingdom hardly ever touched mundane materials. The Nomes, on the other hand, had to tunnel through rock, work iron and brass and stone and so on. Even though a lot of what they dealt with was, of course, also magical, I was pretty sure that if they understood what I needed they could probably make me stuff that I couldn't break no matter how hard I used it.

I could see she wasn't quite clear on why I found my current material so fragile — obviously *she* wouldn't be able to break my armor if I handed it to her and let her beat on it all day — but my matter-of-fact delivery seemed to convince her that I wasn't just bragging. "And you think you can convince King Kaliko to help you, when he's refused to take sides at all for centuries?"

I shrugged, but then nodded. "I can't be sure... but yes, if I can find my key and get in front of him, I think I've got a good shot at it. He has to know that — like everyone else — in the end Ugu and Amanita are going to come for him. They'll have to, to secure their realm permanently. He's too powerful to take a chance on."

"And you're not telling me any more."

"Nope. Not right now. Once we're alone in the wilds, yes."

"Well, then, I look forward to being alone with you."

What? Was that a wink? I found myself staring, momentarily very discomfited, as Zenga swayed across the deck to where a practice area had been set up, drew her swords, and began warming up.

Inkarbleu came up next to me as I watched her practicing. "A man of deep policy is King Inga... or perhaps his Queen."

"Huh?" I admit this wasn't perhaps the most witty rejoinder. "How so?"

"A Queen is unlikely to encourage, nor a King agree to, the sending of their only daughter on such a dangerous expedition unless they foresee a potential for vast benefit in it."

"Well, yeah. They want Ugu defeated and they understand I have to have political backing besides just the Rainbow Lord."

Inkarbleu looked at me with an expression that made me feel like an idiot. "Hmmm... perhaps you are as naïve as you sound. How ... refreshing, in a way. That political backing could have been achieved in a number of other ways, none of which would require risking his eldest and most beloved child."

"I... suppose. But then what's the point of sending her?"

Inkarbleu blinked, then smiled. "Perhaps... perhaps none at all, my Lord Erik." He walked away, shaking his head and chuckling.

What the hell was so funny?

Chapter 29.

"Ha! You'll need to be faster than that, Erik!"

Yeah, no kidding. Zenga was dodging most of the blows I sent at her, and I couldn't do nearly so well dodging hers. My armor did make up some of the difference, though.

This was worthwhile practice, I had to admit. My workouts in the Rainbow Kingdom had been against Sky Fairies, and mostly near-pure blood, which meant that my True Mortal advantage was tremendously pronounced against them. Zenga, on the other hand, was more human than Faerie, and in sparring with her I almost had to invert what I'd learned in the Rainbow Kingdom. She was quicker than me, but only in a human sense; she had the reflexes of a seventeen- or eighteen-year-old girl, while mine were those of a late forties man. On the other hand, since I'd spent a year working out under the Master at Arms of the entire Kingdom, I was now in superlative shape for a late-forties former geek, which meant that even though Zenga was young and in top shape, I was undoubtedly much stronger than she was.

Still, it was basically an even match, and she'd hit me hard. I still did have a little edge with my Mortal nature, but nothing like I was used to.

We were sparring mostly hand-to-hand, since I was missing my sword — there being no point in trying to replace it with the ordinary weapons available, as those Gilgad could offer were either so mundane that they'd never survive conflict with major magic, or magical enough that I'd shatter them the first time I swung. Also, sparring with edged steel in the wilderness just didn't strike me as a good idea anyway.

As I parried a flurry of attacks, I noted that I didn't have any advantage in range, either. She was just about exactly my height, maybe an inch or so taller, and with her long arms and legs she probably had a slight edge on me in that area.

I ducked and covered, then bulled my way forward, taking a clip on my jaw that sent pain rocketing through my ear, but didn't stop me from barreling into her with a crude but pretty much unblockable body-check. She cushioned the blow and tried to roll off, but I caught her arm, went with her attempt to throw me and grabbed the long braid that ran down her back, pulling her off-balance and slamming her to the ground. Without armor to cushion the impact, I could hear the breath *whoosh* out of her, and I rolled and came up, arm drawn back, hand in blade formation. "Yield."

She laughed. "Yield!" she agreed, bounding upright. "That's one fall each, Erik; best of three?"

I smiled back, breathing hard, then held up my hand. "Give me a few moments first." I pulled out my inhaler and took a couple of puffs a minute apart. The building tightness slowly retreated.

Zenga regarded me curiously. "What is that?"

"One of my Achilles' heels," I answered. "My own body has it in for me if I expend too much effort too fast."

She stared. "In truth? You run or fight for too long –"

"—and I stop being able to breathe, yes. Been that way all my life."

We started the next match, but she seemed more tentative until I kicked her in the shin. "Don't you *dare* baby me, Zenga! None of our enemies will!"

With a yelp of pain, she stared at me, at first angrily and then with a devilish smile.

She won that match, too, managing to get my arm twisted up behind my back and me pinned in a way that didn't allow me the leverage to get her off me without giving her the chance to break it. "Yield!"

"Ouch! I yield!" I smiled at her as I got up. "That's more like it. Now let's get some dinner; that sure worked up an appetite."

The sun was now down past the mountains and the light starting to fade. We returned to the little fire we'd built before starting our sparring match, and I got out a round-bottomed pan something like a wok and the bottle of oil. Quick-frying or roasting was pretty much the rule on the road, unless you just ate jerky or waybread. We were carrying enough stuff to live on for a while, and if we ducked in and out of Gilgad territory we could probably catch some game or maybe buy something from farmers or woodcutters along the way.

Zenga watched with approval as I stir-fried a mix of vegetables, some dried, some reasonably fresh, some dried meat, and a couple of sliced potatoes, then added just enough water to let it cook for a bit, moistening the meat and dried veggies. I'd also made sure to bring along a few packets of dried spices; I like flavor in my food. "I'd heard that many countries consider cooking to be women's work," she said finally.

"Used to be the case where I came from. That actually mostly changed in my lifetime. But I've been cooking for most of my life; my parents always said that if I didn't like what was for dinner, I'd better cook it myself."

I served up the stir-fry, which hadn't turned out badly at all given the improvisation I'd had to try with the mix of ingredients, and we ate in silence for a few minutes.

This was the first night we were truly in the wilderness; up until now we'd always been able to find a family, a cabin, somewhere to stay for the night. Without anyone else to distract me, I found myself looking at Zenga more. Which made me distinctly uncomfortable. There was no denying she was very much worth looking at, but she also appeared to be considerably less than half my age, which was definitely putting me into dirty old man territory. Yeah, Polychrome didn't look much (if any) older, but after spending a year around her I knew that it would be entirely wrong to view her as being anything like an ordinary girl her apparent age. Zenga, on the other hand, *did* still strike me as a teenager, or at best a very, very young woman, albeit with some considerable hardheaded common sense and discipline.

"So now we are undoubtedly alone, Lord Erik," Zenga said, breaking me out of this uncomfortable reverie, hopefully not because I'd been staring at her too hard. "Can you tell me anything new? About this key, or about the advantages you've talked about having in this enterprise?"

Ah, a reasonably safe topic of conversation. "I can certainly tell you some things. As your father mentioned, I am a True Mortal — not even just a distant descendant, as you are or as were those other

199

outsiders who came to Oz and surrounding lands over the years, but someone with, as far as any can ascertain, not a single drop of Faerie blood in him." I summarized how I'd come to Faerie — how Polychrome had come to me, tested me, and how I had learned that I was a True Mortal, and the advantages this gave me, with Zenga asking a few questions that showed she actually grasped the ideas quite well.

When I was done, she was looking at me with new respect — and an almost appraising look that brought back that uncomfortable feeling. "Now I do indeed understand why a single man can be so important, Erik." She moved slightly over around the fire, closer to where I sat. A part of me had the impulse to scoot around and keep my distance, but I rejected that as just plain stupid. "What does this Prophecy say about what you are to do, though? For you have — I think quite rightly — kept much of that to yourself, but if I am to travel with you to the end, as I intend to, I would think I should know what to expect."

She has a definite point. Well, I don't have to tell her everything, but I can summarize that, too. I tried to soft-pedal my own potential downfall, but I couldn't avoid the concept entirely. I'm generally a *terrible* liar.

She looked at me with wide eyes. "But... how can you possibly hope to win, sir? Ugu and Amanita have spent centuries mastering their powers, and you — as a True Mortal — can't even *try* to use magic until... that one crucial moment. At least if I understand you correctly."

"You're correct," I said, smiling slightly.

"Then... I don't understand. Any warrior knows that sufficient skill can overcome even a vast disadvantage in strength, and even if you claim the power of Ozma herself and her connection to Faerie, still will they have great powers of their own, and hundreds of years of skill to pit against you."

I grinned. "Imagination is the key, Princess Zenga. And of all the things I have brought from my world — of all the knowledge and skills I have ever had — that one is the greatest I have." I remembered having a similar conversation with Poly, months ago, and for a moment I felt a terrible pang of loneliness despite Zenga being nearby. I wanted nothing more than to see spun-gold hair and violet blue eyes laughing, talking to me, even for a moment, even though I would never dare tell her the truth. "The Prophecy promises that I have a chance to win, and so the essence of it comes down to my being able to envision ways of using that power that is given to me. You're perfectly right; if I just try a sledgehammer without any control against them, it's almost certain that they'll have more than enough finesse to beat me. But... where I come from, leisure time has gone far beyond anything you know. It's become an artform, many artforms, all devoted to entertainment. Some of these... involve a lot of imagination. And I was and always have been darn good at imaginative games. Plus..." I patted my pocket where my inhaler sat. "That kept me pretty much housebound as a child. I did very little other than read, and I read a lot of books of imagination, including of course the books of my world that dealt with Oz. So I not only have my own imagination; I have the accumulated imagination of a thousand others, and more." I looked up into the sky, seeing the patterns watched by a hundred cultures; the might of the Zodiac as seen through a dozen sets of eyes. "And that is a weapon that none of them have ever seen."

Zenga frowned, brows drawn down in concentration. "But how can that work? That is, surely we are not all unimaginative here."

"Not at all," I assured her, "but you've never *codified* it, so to speak, to the point that it was as valuable a commodity as food or weapons; it damn near is, where I come from. And when... it happens, I won't be learning to *do* magic, I will *become* magic. Magic held in a case of mortal essence, but basically pure magic to be directed by thought and will. That's the only answer that really makes sense of the Prophecy, you see."

Her eyes lit up. "Oh! That *does* make sense." I noticed that somehow she seemed to have moved a bit closer without my noticing. "And what exactly are we doing *here*? Where is the 'key?'"

I looked at the mountains, which were now just pure black silhouettes against the dark sky. "Somewhere out there. We need to find him."

She blinked, something I could see clearly because she was quite nearby. "*Him*? Your key is a person?"

"Yes." I looked back out into the darkness, and it struck me suddenly how isolated we were. *If we're attacked here, it'll be just me and Zenga, and I don't have much experience protecting anyone else.* Part of me very much wished I could have left her behind. Sure, the Prophecy had led me to believe I'd find a companion there, but it didn't state that outright. Maybe I should have considered asking someone else — say Huru, he'd have been overjoyed — to accompany me and sent Zenga back.

I glanced back at Zenga, who was waiting to see if I'd say anything else. The fact she was leaning slightly forward did not help me stay focused on the matter at hand. *Why the hell did Inga send her out with me, when –*

And then I remembered Polychrome, and her story of Cirrus, and Inkarbleu's laugh, and it suddenly all made a terribly comedic sort of sense. "Oh, Jesus H. Particular Christ on a pogo stick. He did *not* do that."

"I ... beg your pardon, Erik?"

Whoops. Mr. Evil Overlord, Sir, you're monologuing out loud again! I shook my head. "I... have suddenly had a rather disconcerting thought as to why your father and mother might have allowed you to come with me on this mission, when it could easily get you killed." I looked up, and suddenly she was quite close. Very close.

"Disconcerting?"

"Um..." *Dammit, I am* not *very good with words in this kind of thing, not that this kind of thing has ever really happened to me, but I know what I mean!* "That, well, you're a Princess, and if I manage to keep from dying in this mission, I'd be... well, a most eligible bachelor, so to speak."

"And that's disconcerting?"

I took a deep breath, which might have been a mistake, because it brought her scent to me — some sweat, but mixed with a coconut sweetness and something warmer, spicier. "Dammit. It's disconcerting that a girl might be sent out to basically possibly get married to me because it would be a political advantage!"

She pulled back slightly. "Lord Erik, do you have an objection to women?"

"No, no, not at all." *Far from it.* "But I think they should be entirely able to choose who they marry, or even just who they want to spend time with, not be ordered into it."

She leaned back towards me. "Lord... Erik, you are correct that my mother and father partially agreed to this because of careful consideration of what our position could be if the Usurpers are defeated. But I am not a child, no matter what you may think, and the decision is entirely mine to make. And in the few weeks we have travelled, I have decided that there are many far worse choices I might make."

She was very, *very* close now, and her eyes were firelit pools of ebony, like the hair that tumbled over smooth chocolate shoulders and trailed down towards shadowed curves...

Chapter 30.

Polychrome stood with a jerky haste uncharacteristic of her, and Iris looked at his daughter with a raised eyebrow.

"Well!" she said, a bright and brittle smile on her face. "I... don't think we should be prying into any private life of our Hero!" She gestured to close the viewing pool as she walked quickly away. "I... I really should be practicing. Nimbus says I need more training!" The doors of the Rainbow Throneroom closed behind her.

I do not know whether to be relieved, or worried. Or furious. It was not usual for the Lord of the Rainbow to be indecisive. He turned back to the Pool, which despite Polychrome's gesture had remained open; Iris Mirabilis intended to see the truth for himself. *Did I misread the Prophecy? Is he something other than I thought? Less constant, or weaker, or simply with a weakness all too common for Men?*

The beautiful Princess of Pingaree was leaning close to Erik Medon, and one of his hands was slowly reaching out, touching the night-blackness of her hair, so different from the golden sunshine of Iris' daughter.

And in that moment the hand pulled back, Erik rolled to his feet, and backed off, muttering a curse from his own land.

Zenga looked shocked, and not a little disappointed, even hurt. "Lord Erik –"

"Sorry. Sorry, Zenga. And believe me, part of me will be and already is telling me how stupid stupid stupid I'm being... but I can't. I just... can't. I... you're beautiful. There's nothing wrong with you at all, I mean, you're like any fantasy a guy like me might have..." he trailed off. "Damn, that doesn't sound good either. I..."

Iris felt a chill stealing back over his heart. *No relief. No reprieve.*

Zenga rose slowly and looked at him, hurt and disappointment giving way to real concern. She could see that whatever was bothering the older man was not some random impulse or anything having to do with her. "Are you all right?"

Erik laughed hollowly. "No, I'm stupid, that's what I am. I'm here in the wilds of Faerie with a talented, smart, beautiful princess who can match me stride-for-stride and who's just told me that she likes me enough to make a play for me that even *I* can't miss, and I go throw it in her face for... for what? Some fantasy that's impossible even here?"

Gradually, Zenga's expression changed from concern to a sort of tragic amusement. She giggled and then clapped both her hands over her mouth, but that still didn't stop the giggles.

Iris watched as Erik's face registered hurt puzzlement. "Hey, come on, this isn't all that funny to me!"

"I... I'm sorry, Lord Erik, but..." another unladylike guffaw came from her, "... oh, by the Pearls themselves, you *poor man.* You've fallen in love with the Daughter of the Rainbow!"

Erik stood frozen in position for several seconds before he finally bowed his head. "It's that obvious."

"With what you said — and didn't say — in your description of how you came here and learned of your power... yes." The Pingarese Princess brushed strands out of hair from her eyes, pearl-and-gold bracelets chiming slightly.

"I don't see what's so funny about it, though."

"It's *not* really..." Zenga seemed to be struggling to figure out a way to explain it. "It's just that... Erik, a Faerie Princess like her, a *true* Faerie, they can't fall in love with a Mortal."

"What? Then how is it there's so many mostly-Mortal, part-Faerie types out there?"

"All right... it's only *almost* impossible. It's happened, oh, three or four times. But love among the true Faeries... it's almost instinct. Usually they don't meet anyone they love, though they can have lots of friends — I've heard Polychrome herself does. When they find the right person, if there *is* a right person, they'll be drawn to them by a... resonance, a tie between them. And it's almost always another Faerie. Even that doesn't always work out," she continued. "One of the stories in the library is about Infiernos and Undine — a Fire Faerie who fell in love with a Water Faerie."

Iris saw that penetrate despite Erik's personal upset. "Oh, ouch. Neither one's realm or even personal essence compatible."

Zenga nodded. "It's a tragedy. I don't like reading those much."

Erik gazed up into the night sky. It seemed for a moment that he was looking straight at Iris, and the Rainbow Lord felt a pang of guilt. "Yeah. A tragedy. I wish I could be sensible about this... but I can't. I was with her for a year, Zenga. She saw me as I came here, and she brought me to Faerie, and she never said a single word to let me know how disappointed she must have been at first. And she spent I don't know how long helping me. And..." he shook his head. "I dunno. I just know I can't accept even a marriage of convenience with someone if every time I see them or touch them I see someone else. If all I can see is her."

Zenga was looking at him sympathetically, but he turned away. "That's the truth, you see. I tried to tell her father... but I chickened out. The truth? I'm not going to go out there and get myself killed just because of Oz, even because of my childhood dreams. I'm going to do it for *her*, because *Polychrome* is all of my dreams in a single one, and dying to protect her is worth it all, every bit of it, and maybe it's better that way because I don't know how I'd live after I go back to my life without her."

Iris *did* close the pool that time, because he had truly seen enough. *A part of me hoped, indeed, that he was untrue. That he could be swayed, and many men would have been. But I was told differently, and truly here is my proof.*

And no one but myself to blame in any case. Who gave her tasks that kept her in close contact with the Mortal? Who encouraged her and advised her in her work with him? No, King of the Rainbows, this is as much your doing as that of any prophecy...

...because you knew, full well, what kind of motive your daughter would be for such a man. You have turned him into a fell and dangerous weapon, one that is driven by the sole purpose of preserving your daughter's life.

And that, of course, was the key. She *would* insist on being present at the battle, and risking her life against forces more than capable of killing her. No better protection could he give her than people whose motive to save her life was even greater than his own, and who were — in the cold light of policy and reason — far more dispensable than either his daughter or himself.

He was not sure how long he sat there brooding when the door opened. "My lord King," Nimbus said quietly. "Might I speak with you?"

"What is it, Captain?"

"I am wondering exactly what has possessed your daughter, sir, that has caused her to injure seven of my men in practice so severely that they have all gone to the healers?"

"What?"

At his startled expression, Nimbus gave a small, wry smile. "I would presume it has *something* to do with the Hero because she was muttering various disjointed things under her breath. But for whatever reason, she became quite the menace this afternoon."

"Hmm. Yes." *As I had feared. There is no escaping the ending.* "She witnessed the Princess of Pingaree make an... offer of close alliance to Erik Medon."

Nimbus' eyebrows vanished into his helmet. "So. And by her reaction we know her heart. I would have hoped Lord Medon be more constant, or at least more considered."

"He was. Polychrome left at a poorly-timed moment."

"Ah. The comedy does write itself, I suppose." Nimbus was silent for a time. "So what do you intend to do about this, Sire?"

Iris sighed and shook his head slowly. "I am afraid... nothing." He glanced, with a combination of resentment and pity, at the Pink Bear. "I have attempted all the resistance that I dare. The Prophecy seems unaffected.

"So it must play out as it was foretold... and if the best happens and Oz is freed, still will I be mourning in that hour."

Chapter 31.

"What are we –"

"*Shh!*" I gave a quick gesture. She was speaking too loudly for this area; the high, steep walls of the valley — almost a canyon — with its nearly bare, scrubby walls and tumbled rock would channel sound all too well.

Zenga's mouth tightened, and for a minute I thought she might continue speaking. Despite her apparent easy acceptance of my embarrassing predicament, things hadn't been entirely comfortable between us since I'd turned her down.

But she gave a barely audible sigh and tried again, very quietly this time. "What are we doing *here?*"

"You mean, as compared with other possible locations?" She nodded. "This area is right near the border of the Nome Kingdom, Gilgad, and the land of Ev. The Wheelers and a couple of other groups squabble over control of part of the area, even though it's really part of the Kingdom of Ev.

"The Wheelers and their allies make ocean shipping possible but a nuisance, so most of the commerce between Gilgad and Ev comes along the border of the Nome Kingdom — but doesn't actually cross over, because the Nomes have a notorious dislike for uninvited intruders." I gestured at the high rock walls surrounding us. "This particular valley happens to be one of three which end up funneling a large portion of trade directly through them... and this one is nearest the Nome Kingdom, and so avoided as much as possible. But it's also the most *direct*, and thus used by people in a hurry."

Zenga nodded her understanding, and her reply was *almost* too loud, but she quieted herself without reminder. "Ah! And so the most desperate... or those with the most valuable cargoes — are the ones to use this route."

"And thus are exactly the targets that certain forces are going to be going after."

"And you think –"

209

"I'm *sure*."

Okay, that was a bit of an exaggeration. But I had a good feeling that if I was going to find what I was looking for, it would be here.

He would be here.

We waited quietly, patiently. With Zenga's help and the memory of Nimbus' training — and some of what I could dredge up from camping with my father ... was it over 30 years ago? ... we'd put up an entirely mundane shelter and blind, concealing us from sight and sense in a manner that I hoped would be "under the radar," so to speak, for beings that played in a more mystical realm. Zenga being mostly mortal and physically close by should minimize the chance of her being sensed.

Time passed. I knew that this was a waiting game; even if I was right, our passage would have been noted, though the details of that passage would — hopefully — not. Good guys and bad guys both would be waiting to make sure no one else was around.

The waiting was not easy on either of us, I suspect. It certainly wasn't easy on me, being that close to Zenga and, ironically, far more aware of her presence now than I'd allowed myself to be before. And yes, that one part of me was regularly kicking me for being a blind romantic idiot. But what I'd told her was still true.

"Hst! Lord Erik!"

Her eyes were sharper than mine — no surprise that, given age differences, even with Iris Mirabilis' thoughtful rejuvenation of my inborn lenses. A tiny movement was visible at the northwest end of the valley, the Ev end. "Looks like a small caravan — ten wagons, maybe."

She nodded. "So we wait a bit longer?"

"See how things go. Yes."

The little group of wagons trundled slowly closer, moving along a narrow trail that was well-defined by the passage of countless prior travellers. I could see outriders in front and on either side, watching, scanning. So far they had seen no sign of opposition, but their movements showed that they were nervous — quick movements, a little too quick and jerky.

Even the best eyes would not have helped them in this situation; we'd been here for days, but even we were taken completely unawares when innocuous boulders suddenly flickered and transformed into two dozen bowmen, with another dozen men carefully spaced around the perimeter, three on either side front and back, who — with very nasty grins — pulled out the logs that held back carefully-engineered artificial landslides.

Even the outriders had been taken utterly by surprise; the front and rear went down under the masses of granite, and the others froze, realizing they were in a perfect crossfire.

"What?" Zenga whispered. "Not any of the Temblors or Tempests?"

I shook my head, watching. "For the most part, Oz has kept its word not to interfere; I ran into a sort of independent operation, I think. No, this is more home-grown banditry, but bolder, knowing there's no power around that can afford the effort to wipe them out."

"Shame about those two!" a cheerful voice called out. We could now see, stepping into view atop the front roadblock, a flamboyantly dressed man in a red and gold cloak, a slender circlet of gold in his black hair. "Doing their jobs a bit too well, or not well enough... that's the problem, you see, over-eager and undertrained. Unlike *my* men, I think you'll agree."

The man on the lead wagon stood slowly. "Very well, you've caught us. And killed two good men while you were at it. I'd prefer to avoid bloodshed."

The cheerful man's laugh was somehow sinister. "I'm sure you would, I'm sure you would. So you'll be turning over your cargo to me, then?"

"I do not see how I can prevent you. We could fight, and perhaps kill some of you, but..." he gave an expansive, futile gesture.

"A man of reason! How excellent. Then you and your people will move away from the wagons — leaving your weapons, of course. And any valuables."

The leader of the caravan waved downward to the others. The outriders began to move in, tossing their spears and bows to the ground, but one rode near to the leader, who stiffened and turned. "Pardon me, sir, but might we know your name?"

"How... courteous of you. Though a shame you needed a reminder in courtesy from your own outriders." The crowned man gave a deep, elaborate bow. "I am known simply as the King of the Road, and these are my kindly Highwaymen."

Oh, crap. There were of course a lot of brigands working these routes, but even in that group of bastards, this one stood out. The few who'd survived meeting him and gotten to Gilgad had described scenes of slaughter and depravity as terrible as any I'd heard of from the mortal world — which made this guy even worse from a Faerie perspective. Something like him couldn't have *existed* years ago, and I had a grim suspicion as to why he could now.

"We have to help them!" Zenga hissed.

I hated to give up our concealment, but if — as it appeared — the leader of the caravan was about to change his mind, he'd need as much help as he could get, now that over half his people were already disarmed.

"ENOUGH!"

The new voice was deep, sending rumbling echoes chasing themselves around the valley, and yanking everyone's attention upward, gazing at a point in the valley directly across from where Zenga and I sat in our blind.

A single figure stood atop a tall spire of stone, grey cloak streaming out in the wind, a polished staff of stone gripped in one hand, head concealed within a deep cowl. "These people are under *my* protection now, O King. Stand aside and let them pass."

The King of the Road shook his head in an exaggerated double-take, shading his eyes and gazing about in a dramatic pantomime of disbelief. "Truly, your men conceal themselves marvelously, for even now I cannot descry their positions; yet surely you must have many men indeed to contest my rulership of the road, for only a madman would dare do so alone." Then it was his turn to stiffen, momentarily, and he continued, "Only a madman... or the Penitent."

The grey-cloaked figure gave an ironic bow.

All humor and civilized veneer vanished in that instant. *"Kill him! Kill him now!"*

Now I held Zenga back. I had to see. I had to be *sure*.

The Penitent vanished from the stone in the instant the King shouted, vanished as though he had never been there as a storm of arrows screamed through the space his figure had occupied. The caravan took advantage of this distraction, grabbing up their weapons.

The grey-cloaked form materialized — there was no other word for it — from the dusty greyness of the ground, near to one of the archers, and struck with his staff, shattering the bowman's weapon and then laying him flat on the ground. He leapt and rolled aside as though the cloak enclosed not a man but a ball, tumbling nimbly down the slope with an erratic, almost impossible-to-follow motion that confounded the efforts of the other highwaymen to strike with bow or catch with desperate sprints.

The King of the Road flung out his hand, muttering something too faint to catch, but I could see a poisonously green powder fly forward. Virulent emerald leaves sprouted from the dusty ground, transforming into spiky vines that reached and grasped, slowing the Penitent, pulling at his cloak. The same vines avoided the King as he leapt down among them, drawing a black, serrated sword and striding with a cold, cruel grin towards the Penitent, who brought up his stone staff and prepared to meet the bandit leader — despite the still-growing thicket of vicious vines.

"That is our cue," I said.

We burst from our concealment and charged down on two Highwaymen who had engaged one of the outriders; he barely had time to curse before Zenga's double-bladed cut took off his head. The others raised the alarm, and the King of the Road's eyes narrowed as he took in my glittering crystal armor and Zenga's terrible dancing blades. "More uninvited guests! What a bothersome day. But at least it shall end with a considerable nuisance dispatched."

The Penitent was not cooperative, however; though the vines hampered his every move, still he managed to parry the strokes of the black blade. He was unable to strike back, though, and it seemed clear that eventually the King would find an opening.

We were in better condition, however, as the combination of the Penitent's distraction and our sudden appearance had allowed the caravan to start fighting back in earnest. The attackers were no longer in an overwhelmingly powerful position; if the archers on our side turned to focus on the caravan, they were open to our assault, and if they focused on us, the caravan's archers could target them. Most of the caravan's people were now on our side of the wagons, making the other archers essentially useless; they'd have to come down and engage hand-to-hand.

One of the bigger bruisers came at me; I ducked aside, took a blow on the armor that stung, and did a leaping kick that took him right in the temple; I winced inwardly as I felt the impact, and though I knew this guy must've done things that would earn him the death penalty, I still hoped I hadn't killed him.

But that left me an open path towards the still-widening sea of twining greenery. "Zenga! Keep it up!" I called, and sprinted downward.

"Lord Erik! Look out! You'll –" she was forced to stop her warnings as two more of the King's Highwaymen engaged her.

But I focused my will and strode forward. As they reached towards me, the vines abruptly stiffened, then fell limp, shriveling at the merest touch. A massive, thorn-covered tentacle lashed out; I slapped it aside, hard, and it broke and shattered like an ancient, dried-up branch. The King whirled in disbelief, seeing me coming through his deadly tangle as though walking through a harmless garden. "Wh–what..."

The stone staff lashed out and cracked with bone-breaking force on the brigand's left arm. The King restrained a shriek of agony and struck back, forcing the Penitent back on the defensive, and then leaping away, sheathing his sword. With his good hand he pulled forth a black sphere, an oversized marble that seemed to have a faint red glow at its heart, and drew back his arm. "I do not know... who *you* are..." he said, in a pain-wracked voice far different from his prior false urbanity, "but perhaps I will learn from your corpse!"

The sphere bulleted forward, and instinctively I put up my hand. It smacked solidly into my palm and my fingers curled around it as though catching a tennis ball. I held it up and studied the now-greying sphere, the light within fading away. "Oh, I don't *think* so."

The expression of disbelief on the King's face was almost comical. I smiled back. "Here, catch." I pitched the sphere back at him.

Reflexively he raised his own hand, realizing too late that it had become the same red-tinged black as soon as it left my hand. On contact the glassy sphere detonated in a flare of searing red flame and dead-black smoke.

That was more than enough for the Highwaymen; seeing nothing but a greasy column of fire where their leader had been, they broke and ran. The singing bows of the caravan made sure that few of them completed their escape.

On the self-proclaimed King's death, the vines too had died. The Penitent emerged from the collapsing thicket and nodded. "My thanks to you, stranger. And strange indeed you are. Still, it was good fortune you passed by."

"No fortune — as I suspect you already guess," I answered, seeing Zenga coming down towards us. "I was in search of you, and knew from the stories that this was the sort of place you must be found." Up close, it was clear that the Penitent was very short, little more than half my height, though his movements and actions had shown great strength and considerable length of arm.

The caravan's people were now tending to each other; they would surely come to us shortly, but for now we were alone. The Penitent glanced in their direction, and then back to me, face still concealed within his cloak's hood. "And for what purpose do you seek me, stranger?"

"I need you to guide me where no other can lead, Penitent. I need you to show me the way to the Nome King's door, give me entry to his kingdom."

He gave a laugh, one I thought might be tinged with bitterness. "He welcomes few to his lands at all, stranger, and even fewer who seek his door uninvited. What makes you believe I could even do as you ask?"

"I believe so because I know who you are, Penitent, and why you bear that name and do these deeds. Because you were once much as those who rule Oz now are, and you have come to regret that." He had frozen and stood still, now, still as stone. "Because you were driven from that kingdom and now walk its borders, alone, homeless, friendless save for those you protect, yet never one of them, because you seek to make up for sins they cannot know." Zenga's eyes widened as she realized what I was saying. "Because you are Ruggedo, once Roquat, the Red, who once was King of the Nomes."

Chapter 32.

For several moments – that seemed to be an eternity – the Penitent stood stock still, gazing at me from within his shadowed cowl. Then, very slowly, he raised his hands and pulled the hood back.

Fierce, proud onyx eyes under wide, snowy brows met mine, from a face as seamed and lined as the earth around us, and much the same grey-brown color, the shade of rock and stone and dust, yet with an undertone of flesh and a hint of pink on the cheeks. Wild white hair framed his face and a great beard flowed down from his chin, vanishing within the folds of a robe clearly cut to conceal these features. "You have named me, stranger, by both the name I chose and the name I once bore. How, then, are you named?"

"I am Erik Medon."

He nodded slowly. "An unusual name...and your appearance, even more so. From what realm do you hail?"

"From the city of Albany, in the State of New York, of the United States of America in what you call the Mortal World."

The brows raised. "So. The world from whence came the Girl." I had no doubt who he meant by that. "Yet you are not Her. Different, I think, much different." He glanced up and saw that the caravan survivors were beginning to approach; he pulled the hood over his face again. "Follow me, then, and we shall speak more. I promise you nothing beyond that."

Good enough. "As you wish," I answered, and saw Zenga fall in behind us.

I focused on following Ruggedo and tried to minimize my disruptive Mortal nature; I suspected that he was using some native Nome magic to essentially disappear into the rocks, and as I followed him this was confirmed. Pathways appeared just ahead of him and closed behind, leaving no trace of our passage, going straight where normal men would go around, climbing at impossible angles yet seeming flat and level. By the time he stopped, in a shallow cave set in a mountainside overlooking the forests of

217

Ryk E. Spoor

Gilgad, I had lost track of where we were. Zenga was staring around in awe, realizing that somehow we had crossed mountains in minutes.

Ruggedo threw back his hood and let his beard hang free as he took a seat on a rude stone chair. "From the Mortal World you may have come once, Erik Medon, but the armor you wear is of no mortal make; its substance cries out its Faerie nature. So you have been here for some time, and won some favor in the eyes of powerful forces.

"But there are few powerful forces in Faerie these days. You seek the Nome King, so he is not your patron. Gilgad, strong though she is, has no true Faerie power. This is not the work of the Sea Faeries. Most of the other kingdoms have no power, or else none of the will, for this work. That leaves but two possibilities: that you are from Oz, an emissary of the... new regime, or that you have come from the Rainbow Lord Iris himself. Truly does your armor have the mark of a Sky Faerie's work, but Ugu and Amanita have such bound to their service. With whom are you aligned, and what proof have you of your allegiance?"

I drew forth the Jewel and once more it painted rainbow glory and song through the air. The former Nome King's head bowed slowly, almost unwillingly, as though he had both hoped for and feared that answer. "So, indeed. And by this I know you have been sent as his first move against the Usurpers themselves. What ..." his eyes narrowed, and then he smiled, and laughed, a startling deep, jolly sound that recalled the original description, likening him to Santa Claus. "Ho, ho! A True Mortal, I'll bet my golden buckles on it! Thus you walked through that enchantment of the self-styled King of the Road, cast his spellsphere aside as though it were the merest pebble! I am right, am I not?"

I bowed, unable to restrain a grin. "You are no less clever than I hoped, Ruggedo."

"Flattery, always a good start." He turned to Zenga. "But I have been terribly remiss in my manners. You know my name; might I be honored with yours, my dear?"

Zenga glanced at me; I nodded. "I am Zenga, daughter of Inga and Zella of Pingaree."

"*Princess* Zenga!" Ruggedo might be living in the wilds, but it seemed that didn't keep him from keeping up on the news. "What an honor, my dear, and I must apologize for the state of my quarters. So you have made one... no, two other alliances, for I know well the work of Gilgad and your other equipage is clearly of royal make. Gilgad and Pingaree stand with you and Iris. Well, well, well." He studied us both. "A momentous quest you are on, my friend. Is there truth in rumors I have heard, that a Prophecy was made that may lead to liberation?"

"It is possible." Keeping some rumor of the Prophecy's existence from spreading would have been impossible, even though Iris had managed to keep its actual contents secret.

"Hmm-mmm-mmm! Well, then, I must consider carefully. You have had, no doubt, several tiring days waiting, for your blind was unknown to me or to the King's Highwaymen; retire into my cave, therefore, and rest. You shall find a small side cavern to the left which holds something of mortal food and pallets suitable for your resting."

The words were a clear dismissal, and Zenga and I bowed and moved off to find the indicated cave. It turned out to be a clean little stone room with a floor of swept white sand, illuminated by veins of gently glowing crystals. "What do you think, Lord Erik?" Zenga asked as we set down our packs.

"I think it's a good start. He's interested — cautious, but that's only reasonable — and he knows that Iris Mirabilis is the only credible threat to Ugu and Amanita. At the same time, he has to know that the Nome King's forces are some of the few remaining question marks in the strategic equation, and if I can convince him to join up, I'll have seriously improved my position."

"Do you think he'll help?" She spread her own blanket over a pallet.

"I can only hope."

We ate something and then got ready for sleep. I lay awake for some time, listening to Zenga's slow and steady breathing (with an occasional almost ladylike snore). Finally, somewhere in the middle of the deep quiet, I drifted off.

I jerked awake as something poked me. Blinking, I could just make out the figure of Ruggedo standing over me in the now-dim light of the cavern. He gestured for me to follow and walked out. I took a moment to get my mental bearings, and then followed him to the cave mouth, where the brilliant stars shone down with just enough light to outline the old Nome in silver.

"Sit down, Erik Medon," he said quietly. "I have been thinking, and trying to make decisions, and I find that I need to know more of what passes in your mind." He took out a long pipe and filled it, lighting it with what appeared to be a live coal that he took from his pocket. For several moments he sat, quietly puffing out clouds of aromatic smoke (which, I noted with gratitude, fortunately drifted mostly away from me; I didn't need an asthma attack right now).

Finally he spoke. "Let us suppose that I aid you, and that I can, in fact, find the way into my ancient homeland. You know that I am an exile. The best I can expect is to be quickly escorted out, or — if Kaliko wishes to indulge you — allowed to stay for exactly as long as you."

I nodded. "Yes, I understand."

"Hmmm. Well, then, understand that while Kaliko is not a bad Nome — a good one in many ways, far better than ever I was, and I'll make no bones about it — he is still King, and not a king ruled by sentiment. Backing by Iris Mirabilis, that is a good argument, and if you get close enough to present that part of your case, I think old Kaliko would listen. But it won't be enough. Your friend from Pingaree –"

"If you bring us, I won't introduce her that way. I'll say she came with me from Gilgad."

He raised one of the silvered brows. "Indeed?" He studied my face. "I see you must have some plan already. Well enough. For I suspect even if he favors you, Kaliko will wish to test you, and exactly how even I cannot guess. And some of his tests can be painful. Even lethal."

I shrugged. "I have to take the chance."

"But *I* do not, you see. You ask a great deal. A very great deal. While — as I suspect you know — the stories of the Mortal World distorted much, I am an exile in truth, by the hand of Oz itself. You ask me to risk my life for the sake of the country that took away my kingdom."

I laughed quietly.

"You find that amusing?"

"You are testing me, Ruggedo. Or perhaps yourself."

He tilted his head, a shadow against the night, and in the silence I could hear a deep, distant music, a sad yet proud march of rolling gongs and deep cello resonance and rumbling organ pipes. "Am I? Speak your insight, then, mortal man."

"Today I saw you risk your own life in battle for the sake of mortals you had never before met. You left, with us, without even accepting their thanks. You have been doing this for... a long time. Hundreds of years, perhaps even longer than the Usurpers have been around. The Penitent is a legend, a symbol of hope. I suspect even Ugu and Amanita, or their Viceroys, have on occasion sent people to see if they could find you, root you out.

"You've admitted yourself what you were once like. You aren't like that any more, and I don't think you bear Dorothy and Ozma much ill-will for their intervention. Not now."

He was silent, save for the Music of the Spheres that was at once so unlike, yet very much like, that of Polychrome, and then he gave a low laugh, echoed by a rippling rise of horns and drums. "True, true enough, my friend. I was a spoiled, selfish tyrant, and I gave them little choice, especially when even temporary loss of my memory did little to cure my habits of personality. Oh, I cursed them mightily at first... but exile has a way of wearing on a man, or Nome, and quiet isolation without pomp or servant or other amusement to distract you...well, thinking may occur without warning. The next thing you know, you're musing on the past. And one day I suddenly, honestly found myself considering what they must have been thinking, and for a moment — just a moment, mind you — I felt rather guilty."

He refilled his pipe. "But that sort of thing is rather like a pebble on a rocky slope. It can start an avalanche. And...well, you have seen and yourself described the results. No, I don't resent their actions. Indeed, I owe them an apology, and thanks; alas that it is far too late now."

"But it's not. Not if you help me."

He pursed his lips, blew out an impressive smoke ring that ascended towards the heavens. "Well, yes, so you *say*. And, I suppose, you mean it. But prophecies have a way of being misleading, and sometimes they can be simply wrong. Also...I am, after all, a Nome. We work for others when it is wise to do so. What do you offer *me* for the double risk of escorting you? Double in that not only might I anger the current Nome King, but that in helping you I name myself your ally in the eyes of the Usurpers — and they are mighty and fell opponents, as well you must know."

"I offer you redemption, Penitent." My tone was deliberately hard. "You have been seeking to redeem your actions by doing charity, by rescuing others, and that's all well and good. But your actions for centuries were selfish and injurious, and on a grand scale. You tried to conquer other nations, and nearly succeeded. You had to be forcibly ejected from your throne to come as far as you have.

"Now you have a chance to *truly* make up for your sins. Help to restore the throne you would have taken to its rightful rulers; rescue those who have — as you admit — saved your own soul from a bitter and dark prison of your own making. That's what I offer you."

He looked up at me, eyes glittering thoughtfully. "You have a gift of speech, mortal. And your words have a ring of truth, indeed they do. Yet... I have much reason to fear, and more: though Kaliko is King, still the Nomes are my people. If your mission succeeds, you intend to bring them into this war, to pit their arms and the might of that which was my kingdom against the even greater might of Oz. Even with the aid of the Rainbow Lord and whatever powers you yourself wield, the ending is far from certain. What is your offer that would make this risk worth it?"

I studied him myself in silence, until I saw that even he began to fidget uncomfortably. "Ruggedo the Red, are you *truly* penitent? Would you protect the people of Gilgad, *and* the Nomes your native people, *and* of Oz, and all of Faerie?"

He opened his mouth, then closed it, and I could see he recognized the deadly serious tone in my voice, and that I was speaking not an idle question but something more on the lines of an oath. He nodded, slowly. "I have learned the lesson that solitude had to teach, and the truth of the stone and wind. I am a part of the world, and my bitterness was a poison to it, and to me. Yes, I would protect them all, if it were in my power."

"Do you mean that? If it were in your power? For here you have little power, save the native magic of the Nomes and the strength of your arm. Had you the power, would you return to that which you once were?"

His eyes glared into mine. "No!" Then his gaze fell. "But ... you have no reason to believe that. No one does. And truly they would be fools to do so."

"I may be a fool, then." His gaze snapped back up to me. "I believe ... I *have* to believe... that a man, or Nome, can change. As good men have gone bad, bad men can be redeemed. And the worst sin would be to refuse the redeemed the chance at the rewards of redemption."

"What... what are you saying?"

"That I will offer you one more thing. If you will help me — if you will stand beside me, whether I win the support of the Nomes or no, whether any allies follow me otherwise or whether I am alone at the last — if you will do this, then if the Usurpers are thrown down, to you will be returned that which in the end lost you your throne, and made your kingdom less than it was. The Magic Belt, that which held your power and protected yourself and your realm, taken from you by Dorothy Gale."

He stared in disbelief. "Do you believe you can even *make* such a promise?"

I nodded. "Yes, I do. Ozma has always been one to favor redemption. More, if I have freed Oz, I do not think they would deny me any boon; and if I am dead, they would not dishonor my memory by making me a liar in death."

"You..." His voice was low, and I thought I caught a trace of roughness in it that was not the sound of his stone-born heritage;

crystal chimes echoed behind the bass and drums. "You would trust me with that power? That I would not fall back into darkness?"

"Someone must trust to allow another to be worthy of it. And I always rather liked you, even in the distorted pictures I was given. There was something more than a simple villain there, and what I have seen here is something much greater."

He bowed so low his face nearly touched the stone. "Then I promise you, Erik Medon. I shall walk with you, yea, even to the Grey Palace that stands where once was the Emerald City, even if you and I be alone when that time comes. And if you win through, then... then I shall leave the payment of that debt to Princess Ozma. You have offered me your trust; I shall repay that with my own."

We shook hands, and I could feel the strength of stone in that long-fingered grip. It was a solemn moment.

And then his face stretched in a devilish grin. "But before any of that matters more than foolish words, my mortal friend, you'll have to get past Kaliko — and that, mark my words, will be a pretty task indeed!"

Chapter 33.

The grey-brown stone rose high above our heads as we traversed the barren canyon, only the unnatural flatness of the surface under our feet hinting that this was a pathway and not one of a thousand other arroyos in the rugged, almost lifeless mountains of the Nome territory. "So, are we going to run into a giant with a hammer?" I asked.

Ruggedo chuckled. "Nay, Lord Erik. Even though the guardian machines I had were somewhat more fearsome than your writer portrayed, still eventually it was decided that they were more the cause of trouble than its solution. I suspect you can guess why."

I hadn't thought about it before, but with that hint... I laughed, the sound echoing down the dead canyon. "Two reasons, I'd say."

Zenga's laugh echoed after my own. "Oh, of course! Such a wonder would draw many to see it, to think of how it worked, perhaps to try to pass so they could seek out its creators to build more for their own cities."

"And," I continued, "it would also be a challenge, like a gauntlet thrown down, a dare. And you'd have a lot of people — young and stupid, or simply the sort that like to take on any challenge — coming here just to prove they *could* get past your sleepless mechanical guards."

"You know your people's foibles well," Ruggedo agreed, a faint smile tugging at his beard, which I could just make out under the hood; he hadn't pulled it up quite so far as he did for his standard "Penitent" disguise. I suppose he figured it didn't matter.

Something caught my eye; I glanced in that direction, but saw nothing. But something seemed to move now on the other side. Yet there was nothing there. Zenga stopped, looking around, uneasy, yet not able to spot anything.

I concentrated, pretending I was looking through a telescope. I used to do that a lot when I was young, an amateur astronomer, and I'd learned a technique all naked-eye astronomers learn: averted-eye vision. The center of your field of view isn't quite as sensitive to certain details, especially low-light, texture, and movement, as the area just a little bit off the center. Avert your eye, just that tiniest bit, and concentrate, and you could suddenly see a tiny bit of detail you missed — banding on Jupiter, a bit of structure in a nebula.

And now I saw it: faint, impossible movement, vague outlines so blurred as to be like the shimmer of heatwaves above pavement, like the ghostly shapes you might see, "floaters" inside your own eye. "I think we've been noticed."

Zenga still clearly couldn't follow them, but something was making her uneasy. Ruggedo glanced up at me, following my eye movements. "You have spotted them? You follow their motions, even within the rocks which are theirs to traverse as though air? Your perceptions are excellent, for a mortal." He continued to walk forward, unconcerned. "Yes, indeed, we have. This is far the preferable way of guarding our lands. It is difficult to traverse these mountains; harder still to find the few canyons out of thousands that conceal one of the entrances to the kingdom. And if a mortal finds his way that far, they travel through a deserted land, with nothing they can see, and yet somehow they feel as though they are watched, followed, endangered. They return home, with tales of the terrible dead land of the Nomes, a place haunted by ghosts or worse."

"And if they actually keep going?"

"They will not find an entrance unless we choose to show it to them. And if they bring sufficient men and tools to try to force the issue...well, you have not come here without the knowledge that we can indeed fight. Here, in our homeland, none would be foolish enough to challenge the Nome King."

Zenga gasped, and I whirled.

Behind us were twelve or more figures, no taller than Ruggedo, in stone and metal armor, with glittering spears and sharp swords already out. Zenga had her weapons out as well, but I touched her shoulder gently. "No. We are intruders. They have every right to be cautious."

More had appeared in front of us. Ruggedo threw back his hood. "A good day to you, Krystallos."

The lead Nome, in armor edged with gold and silver, spat contemptuously. "Exile. And now, I see, a traitor. Leading these mortals by the secret ways?"

"I seek –" I began.

"Be *silent,* mortal!" Krystallos snapped, and I saw the weapons raised higher. "What you seek is of no interest to us whatsoever, and if you do not die in the next few moments it will be only because we are in a merciful mood — a mood which will not be improved if you argue. This is a matter of the Nomes alone."

"Tsk, Krystallos," the once-King of the Nomes said with a cheery smile, as though weapons were not aimed at us all, "you are so unwelcoming to one long away from the homeland. And to accuse me of *treachery,* now, that's a harsh and cruel term." His tone abruptly shifted. "And one that I might answer with stone and steel, if you insist on using it again!"

"You? YOU would dare a challenge of *combat?*" The disbelief on Krystallos' face was plain, and it shifted to pure humor as he laughed. "Oh, now, my former King, it seems your exile has, at the least, made you able to appreciate a jest or two."

Ruggedo chuckled with him. "Oh, there are many jests I have learned to appreciate, my old friend. But if you do not withdraw that most unfortunate characterization, I will show you a jest too grim for laughter."

Whatever position Krystallos held — guard captain, I guessed, or at least some officer fairly high in their ranks — it was certainly not given to the stupid. His laugh cut off abruptly and he glared — slightly up — into Ruggedo's eyes. "Grim, yes, for one who spent his ages on the throne in indolence and tyranny." He studied his former ruler for a moment. "Yet...exile has at the least hardened your hands and you carry a warstaff. Perhaps you would not embarrass yourself. Very well, I withdraw — with reservations — that characterization. Explain yourself, then, exile."

Ruggedo gestured to us. "These mortals seek an audience with the King. They do so not for crass reasons of business, nor from idle impulse, but for reasons good and sufficient, I think, to justify the risk. I have come here to guide them, through the maze, past the enchantments that would mislead or conceal. Think you I do not know what I risk? A tyrant, yes, a bully, a loud and arbitrary monarch, yes, all of these I was, but not an utter fool, nor one easily swayed. Would I come here, perhaps to my death, for reasons inadequate to the risk?"

Krystallos turned his spear idly between his fingers, obviously thinking. He glanced at me finally. "Very well, mortal. What is it you seek?"

"As he says, an audience with King Kaliko. My reasons... are ones I hope he will find compelling. I think he will."

The gaze switched to Zenga. "And you?"

"I travel with Lord Erik to assist him, and support him."

"Do you." The tone was neutral, but I noticed his eyes shifting their gaze across her clothing, armor, weapons, and I suspected he recognized the origin of some of our equipment.

Finally he shrugged. "So be it, then. The King has had little entertainment of late, and whatever your fate will be, it is sure to keep him — and possibly us — amused. We shall leave the decision of whether it will be something *you* find amusing to him."

Decision made, Krystallos turned and had his men march with us, ahead and behind. Now we didn't have much choice but to follow him, as the ones behind made clear. We marched nearly another mile over an increasingly steep path, and abruptly Krystallos' men took a right-angle turn and walked straight into the rock wall.

I supposed they *could* be setting up a crude practical joke — to have me try to follow them and end up smacking into solid rock — but I figured I didn't have all that much dignity to lose and I'd gain some by not flinching, if it *wasn't* a joke. I turned and walked towards the cliff at the same point they had.

It wasn't a joke. The rock gave before me like a curtain of rippling mist, and abruptly I was in a high-vaulted corridor, with walls of polished stone, lit by blazing gems set in the walls, a sparkle of every color imaginable flickering from the walls with every step. "Whoa," I said in my best Keanu voice.

"An impressive piece of work, yes," Ruggedo said from beside me.

Zenga's mouth was half-open. "It's...beautiful!"

"Did you expect rough rocky caverns and smoky torches?" Krystallos' voice was edged with faint scorn.

"Torches perhaps not, given the rocklight we have seen, but it was always said the Nomes lived with rock in its native state."

"In many areas, yes. Yet this is close to the Heart of the Mountains, the castle beneath the ground," Ruggedo said, "and here we show the extent of our artistry to any who may come. Even Queen Ozma herself could boast no more magnificent a home than our ruler, and this is nothing but simple truth."

As we were led inward, through cavern after increasingly-dazzling cavern, I was forced to agree. The Emerald City, no matter how great, would be hard-pressed to beat the awesome yet Faerie-delicate constructions of crystal and gems and gold that were a part of every wall, worked through the very floors and ceilings, of the Heart of the Mountains.

Finally we reached an immense set of doors, of hand-beaten gold and platinum and inlaid with a thousand gems — only half of which I thought I could name. The guards at either side of the doors started a bit as they caught sight of our little party, but bowed and opened the doors at Krystallos' gesture.

I took a deep breath as we stepped forward. *Here I go again.*

The Thronehall of the Nome King was a perfectly circular room, startlingly simple in many ways compared to the increasingly fanciful and ornate caverns that had preceded it. The roof rose to a perfect polished dome of flawless agate, rippled, dendritic patterns making a natural ornamentation that no artisan could have enhanced. The walls were carved from the living rock, columns supporting the perimeter. Eight sets of doors led into, or out of, the Thronehall, and in the very center was the Throne. Cast or forged of solid gold and set with every gem known, it drew and held the eye, and shone with a light of its own, a light that limned and made darker and more mysterious and impressive the figure seated there.

That figure suddenly leaned forward. "Ruggedo?"

Krystallos and his men stepped aside, leaving an open aisle towards the throne. Ruggedo moved forward, stopping near the base of the throne. "It has been a long time, Kaliko."

"Not nearly forever, which was the term of your exile, Ruggedo," answered King Kaliko. But his tone was more curious than angry, and a slight smile was visible on his wrinkled, beardless face. "How fare you these days?"

"Aside from my current precarious position, well enough, well enough, old friend." He turned and gestured us forward. "It is really to these mortals you should be speaking, however; my defense from being given the Death of Cuts, or thrown into the Pit, or whatever your favored punishment may be in these times, rests on their mission being sufficiently interesting."

"Indeed." Kaliko transferred his attention to me, eyes grey as granite studying me carefully. "Then tell us, mortal, of your mission."

I said nothing; I simply drew forth the Jewel, and once more it painted in ethereal, transcendent color the shining glory of the Rainbow across the room in which I stood. Its celestial beauty momentarily made even the Nome King's throne look cheap and tawdry, a dimestore toy next to the painting of a master.

Kaliko sat frozen, still as the stone of his realm, for a long moment. Then he gestured imperiously, and the guards — Krystallos, his men, and all the others which had been stationed around the room — left, emptying the room and leaving the three of us alone with the King.

Then Kaliko chuckled. "Now you most certainly have my undivided attention, mortal. The Rainbow Lord begins his move, as all have hoped and feared for centuries. But the Usurpers are hardly unaware that he has intended to act against them, and may have already realized he has begun. Who are you, and what is it you seek, and why should I grant it?"

"I am Erik Medon, of what you call the mortal world. This is Zenga, who has accompanied me from Gilgad to support me as well as to assist in protecting me."

Kaliko raised one snowy eyebrow. "So *Gilgad* has aligned itself with you? I confess to some surprise. So you come to me not merely as the emissary of the Rainbow Kingdom, but another more earthly land. And you have convinced my old King to assist you. These, I admit, speak well to who you are and that you may have something of interest to my kingdom. Speak on, then: what do you seek of us?"

"Two things, Your Highness. First, I am not merely from the mortal world. I am, in your terms, a True Mortal."

Kaliko sucked in his breath. "Indeed? A True Mortal... That in itself explains many things. But continue."

"Unfortunately, while this gives me many advantages, my allies of the Rainbow were and are Faeries of the sky. Their armor –"

Kaliko laughed, a tenor laugh which, I was glad to hear, had real humor and little malice in it. "–is forged of moonbeams and fantasy, material mighty against spells and magic-forged weapons... and likely to shatter like glass when you extend yourself. Oh, now I see your first request, and it is a wise thought that brings you to us. Indeed, we could forge for you armor and weapons that would let you wield your strength to the fullest without breaking, and yet would still ward off many spells and weapons mundane and enchanted both. It is possible we would do this for you, perhaps merely for the asking, perhaps not. And second? What else do you ask of us?"

"Your lives, your fortunes, and your sacred honor," I answered with a challenging grin.

Kaliko set his jaw, the way someone would when confronting something they've long been expecting...and dreading. "You mean an alliance of arms."

"I quoted from some of the founders of my own country, King Kaliko, and I did not do it idly. Here, today, you are free. I do not think you expect that the Usurpers will stay always on the other side of that desert. Perhaps you have told yourself you can remain neutral, safe here in your fortress because they would not risk challenging you here. Maybe you are right...but they have Faerie of the Earth in their own service, and they would not leave so mighty a potential foe unmolested, if the rest of Faerie were in their power. You may be the last to fall, but fall you will, I think."

"Perhaps." He leaned back in his throne, considering. "But perhaps not. I have many legions of warriors – perhaps more than if they converted all of Oz to their armies, and this they would not do, for they wish to rule a fruitful country, not a barren wasteland.

And my artisans have not been idle in these centuries. Engines of destruction we have designed and built such as have never been seen in all of Faerie."

"And still these would be far better employed at a time of your choosing, with a powerful ally, or more than one."

A nod, acknowledging my point. "As you say. But perhaps better employed as a threat suspected and too dangerous to discover, leaving us entirely free." He shook his head, then looked to Ruggedo. "You have escorted them here, and I agree your actions were justified, Ruggedo. You may leave freely. I even give you leave to renew your supplies before you go."

Ruggedo bowed. "You are kind and generous as always behind your prickly exterior, Kaliko. Yet I cannot leave, for I have taken an oath to stand by this man's side even to the very end of his quest."

That got Kaliko's attention, possibly even more than everything that had gone before. Finally, after staring at us for several seconds, he spoke. "So you come having forged, not one alliance, but two. The second of which I would not have believed...but I hear the truth in your voice, my old King. Little power there may be, in the end analysis, in that alliance...but to have accomplished it at all is astonishing, given the Ruggedo I knew."

Kaliko rose from the throne and walked down the steps, carrying the huge scepter with the single fist-sized ruby that was the symbol of the Nome King. "I agree that — if your position is as strong as it *could* be — it may be in my interest to support you now rather than wait to the end. But I could also simply bide my time, perhaps strike *afterward* when both sides have weakened each other. I need to think on this...and, I believe, I need to see exactly what sort of a man you are, Erik Medon." He clapped his hands, and several guards entered instantly. "Take our guests to the Crystal Suite, and house them there." He turned back to me. "I will think on what you have said...and you, Erik Medon, I shall test, in my own way, in my own time. How you deal with these tests will do much to make my decision."

I bowed — it was clear this was not an offer, it was an order, really. "As you will, King Kaliko."

We were led through a maze of corridors to finally arrive at the "Crystal Suite", a quite comfortable set of six generally-round rooms ornamented with natural crystals of quartz, tourmaline, and beryl. The largest was a central room that could serve as a living or meeting room and a dining area; the other rooms branched off from that central room; if you were standing looking in from the main entrance, there were two doors on your left, two on your right, and one straight ahead. The latter was basically the bathroom, and the two on each side were bedrooms. Zenga took one of the ones on the right, and Ruggedo and I took those on the left.

After putting our meager gear in our chosen rooms, we returned to the central area, to find the table already laden with food for all three of us — odd mineralized concoctions for Ruggedo for the most part, while an assortment of more normal human food was available for Zenga and me.

Ruggedo nodded to me as we sat down. "Well enough done, Lord Erik. But you realize he does mean to test you, and test you as hard as though you were a weapon whose temper was not known."

"Yes, and I suspect I know part of how this is going to go down, too."

"Go down? Ah, you mean, you have a guess as to exactly how the tests will proceed?"

"Exactly...well, maybe not, but I have a guess as to the general form. What about Zenga?"

Ruggedo shrugged. "He seemed exclusively focused on you, accepting her as a political representative and a protector from more mundane threats. You are the key. I doubt he will be testing her directly. He would not bother with me, of course; he knows — or *thinks* he knows — my capabilities very well."

Zenga shook her head. "I don't like the idea of him doing some kind of unspecified and possibly lethal tests on you, Lord Erik. Perhaps I should stay in your room just in case –"

"No!" That sounded too hasty. "No, Zenga, I think we have to follow this through by their rules." I didn't know why a mental red *danger* flag popped up at her suggestion; we'd been sleeping within an arm's length or two every night out in the wilderness. But this was a bedroom — with, as I had noted, a very large and comfortable

233

bed in each room — not the outdoors, not roughing it, and the idea of *Zenga* combined with *bedroom* somehow seemed like a very bad idea, because it also sounded like a terribly *good* idea. *You know, I'm not a teenager any more, so why the hell haven't my hormonal issues gone away?*

She still looked dubious, but acquiesced after realizing I was serious. This caused me to give an internal sigh of relief, not unmixed with another bit of instinctive *what's wrong with you?* kicking.

It had been a long day, and after a few more exchanges we agreed it was time to get some rest. I made sure to lock my door, then lay down on the first real bed I'd slept in since we left Gilgad.

Sometime in the middle of the night, I came half-awake with a slight dizzy sensation. There was a faint scraping noise and the feeling that things were shifting, but it stopped almost before I really registered it.

Nonetheless, I grinned. *One more guess confirmed.* The grin faded. *Now I just have to live through it...*

Chapter 34.

"We have lost track of the mortal."

Ugu nodded calmly. He had already heard the same news. "It is of no great import, Cirrus. We will find him again, and while we know not exactly what he sought out at sea, we know — from where you have lost him — what he seeks on land."

"Yes," Cirrus said, a grim note in his voice. "An alliance with the Nome King."

Cirrus followed Ugu as the King of Oz strode through the grey halls which had once been the colorful and open castle of Ozma, near the center of his own Grey Castle. In truth, Ugu regretted the absolute nature of that spell; he was not insensitive to beauty of color as well as symmetry. But it had been effective.

"You sound concerned, General."

Cirrus' smile was wry. "I would hardly be a General worthy of the name if I was not concerned over the possible reinforcement of my enemy by the largest army Faerie has ever seen."

Ugu raised an eyebrow.

"Yes, Majesty, perhaps even larger than yours and Queen Amanita's. No," he corrected himself, "*certainly* larger."

The sorcerer realized that his General was deadly serious. "How is that possible?"

Cirrus looked slightly relieved that Ugu was giving him his full attention. "Simply put, because old Ruggedo was a suspicious and hostile sort, who trusted none of his neighbors and they, with good reason, never trusted him. He spent *ages* amassing and equipping his army, and it was never deployed in full force save for once — and in that one attempt, he actually lost no men, only their memories. And soldiers can be easily re-trained. Kaliko, while not being inclined to either conquest nor overly fearful, has seen absolutely no reason to weaken himself, and — with no disrespect meant — the actions of your Majesties have certainly given him every reason to increase rather than decrease his military might."

Yes, I suppose they have. Were I in his position, I would certainly be building up my own forces. "How, then, do you evaluate the threat?"

Cirrus gave a slightly apologetic smile. "In all honesty, not terribly great. Firstly, I have yet to determine how any great force can be brought across the barrier spell, and without that, all the force they can assemble is, in the end, pointless posturing.

"However, even if they do have some nigh-miraculous way of bringing across their forces to confront mine..." Cirrus stiffened, a look of caution on his face, "...pardon, *yours*..."

Ugu chuckled. "Fear not. In warfare they shall indeed be yours, in the end, though working for our goals."

"So. Even if they can reach us, individually their warriors are on average even less formidable than those of my former home. Oh, they have some quite dangerous individuals, and my agents have given us some intelligence indicating that the Nome King may have constructed some impressive war machines; still, while his forces may outnumber ours, even combined with those of Iris Mirabilis I do not believe it will be enough...even," Cirrus added with a sharp smile, "if they knew that I was to direct the defense of Oz."

"Which," Ugu said, returning the smile, "they almost certainly do not." He was happy to see that smile — and that very feeling, the warmth of knowing that a...friend...was recovering from a justifiably deep and conflicted period of gloom, startled him. *How strange this is. Never did I think of any man or woman as a true friend, and few indeed have been the chances I had, since once I set myself apart from my fellow Herkus.*

"No," agreed Cirrus, oblivious to the startled state of Ugu's mind. "I think that –" He broke off abruptly, as they came around the corner to see the one remaining spot of color in all the Castle of Ozma.

The huge, broad, thick strip of leather and gold and silver and gems sparkled like a piece of Iris' rainbow brought to earth and carved by the greatest sculptors imaginable. Cirrus approached, his steps slowing as he studied the girdle-like Belt, gripped in the hands of a grey statue, and then turned with stunned disbelief to Ugu. "Is that –"

"–The Belt of the Nome King? Yes, indeed. The very source of my original undoing."

"Why have you not taken it to use?" There was an unspoken implication there, which they both understood and neither verbalized: that such a powerful talisman might well provide the final key to safe victory over the volatile Queen Amanita, when the time came.

Ugu's lips curved in a thin smile. "Take it for yourself...if you can."

Cirrus stepped forward and grasped the Belt in both hands; his hands were far larger than the delicate fingers that had been tight on the Belt when the change came on her, and Ugu winced to see the sharp, strong pull; instinctively he expected to see those slender digits of stone break, as even far larger pieces of stonework would have broken under the strength of a Faerie warrior such as Cirrus Dawnglory.

Yet the Belt remained fast; the stone fingers did not so much as bend the width of a hair. After several increasingly violent attempts, Cirrus gave up and looked with complete confusion at his King. "How...?"

Ugu laughed. "Ah, it is really quite ironic. A matter of a few seconds either way, and the Belt would have been mine. But Princess Dorothy was in the very act of seizing the Belt and putting it on; as you can see, there is no way of removing the belt without breaking at least a few of her fingers.

"The clasp, however, was partially engaged. It was on its owner, and the Belt protects its wearer from all harm. Apparently," he continued, "being turned to stone is not sufficient to disqualify you from ownership."

Cirrus' laugh echoed Ugu's. "Ha! So one of the greatest treasures of all Faerie is removed from any possibility of use...by the sheer working of chance."

Perhaps...perhaps it is just as well, Ugu thought. *That power might have fallen into Amanita's hands.* He shuddered inwardly.

"You have deployed your armies?"

"Yes. The majority of them are in the northwest of the Winkie country; I would expect that if any invasion is to happen, it will be there. I have given Coo-Ee-Oh clear instructions on the contingencies for action. There are pickets set along the entire border, with patrols — mainly Tempests, with some Infernos — moving in irregular patterns across the land, to prevent any observers from predicting them." Cirrus looked at him. "You, Majesty, have been extremely busy of late — as has Her Majesty, as well." His expression said that the latter was something of a relief. Despite Cirrus' virtuosity in his role, it had to be wearing to maintain the deception in the presence of a sorceress so volatile and suspicious. At least in the Rainbow Kingdom there had been no real reason for him to be suspected. "Are you...preparing, as well?"

"It is indeed as you say," Ugu agreed. "Realize that much wizardry, many rituals and spells, normally require careful preparation, rare ingredients, burning of unique herbs and papers filled with powders volatile and dangerous. Yet," he continued walking slowly, "if the worst does happen and either the Mortal succeeds against all odds in gaining the power of Oz, or somehow your armies are routed and we stand against the united forces of the Nomes and the Rainbow Lord, time will be what we are most short of."

Cirrus gave a nod, showing he understood. "And so now..."

"Now Amanita and I are preparing the enchantments ahead of time, compressing them and arranging them in gem and staff and crystal, that they may be called forth by a gesture, a short phrase, even a particular event. Dozens, hundreds of spells, even, all at our fingertips for that ultimate eventuality." He gave a sardonic smile. "Not wasted in the end, of course, even if all goes according to plan. Such convenience will be its own reward, whatever comes."

Cirrus looked relieved. "I must confess, Majesty, I had been somewhat concerned about that...limitation of your Majesties' powers, but I was unsure how to broach that subject safely. A man in my position making such queries..."

"...might be seen as a man trying to divine the weaknesses in those who sit upon the throne...perhaps all the better to remove them from the throne himself. Yes, of course." Ugu gave Cirrus a quick, reassuring pat on the shoulder. "Amanita may be sharp of temper, but rest assured, General, I will assume you mean the best for our realm. You have sworn to me, and I believe your words. If you have any concerns — any at all — I want you to voice them to me, whenever — such as now — we have privacy."

The former warrior of the Rainbow Kingdom drew himself up in gratified pride. Ugu looked on him and for a moment he saw the original Cirrus, staring into his eyes with agonized, defeated resistance that clung to nothing but a burning pride in his own existence. Somehow he kept his expression calm, but in that instant he felt a jab of phantom pain in his heart, a pain so rare and unfamiliar that it took a moment to place it; regret, not for his own failures, but for this success. This man before him was part-Tempest, but also part Cirrus Dawnglory, and there was tragedy in that.

To distract himself from these thoughts — *which are useless, for there is no going back, nor any apology that would mean anything, even if I would* — he returned to earlier conversation. "You have positioned your troops reasonably. Have you any particular strategies?"

Cirrus shrugged. "Many, but none that really will matter unless and until I see the nature, size, composition, and leadership of the opposing forces. I would expect to have at least one engagement which I don't care if we win or lose, simply to gauge the mettle of our opposition. We will have all the advantages of home ground here, and I will exploit that to the fullest."

"And the Mortal?"

Cirrus bowed. "I assure you, all the instructions are given...and with Your and Her Majesty's forceful backing, I believe they are *completely* understood."

Ugu smiled. "Excellent." He looked out one of the windows, where he could see the walls of the greater Grey Castle. *We do not know whether your current mission will succeed, Mortal Man...but succeed or fail, your fate is already decided.*

Chapter 35.

I rose from the bed, stretched, and looked around. The bedroom *looked* pretty much the same as it had when I went to sleep. One exception was a small table and chair with, as Baum often described it, a smoking hot breakfast laid out. I went to the little attached washroom and freshened up, then came back and ate.

It was when I went to get dressed that one change became evident. The closet where I'd put my cleaner clothes — and my armor and sword — was empty. Looking very carefully now at the floor and roof areas, I could *just* make out seams that showed what had happened; there was a trick wall, like those seen in many movies, and they'd rotated the full closet out and left me with the empty.

I grinned and pulled down the covers. My gauntlets and greaves were still there; I'd slipped them under the covers while I was undressing in a deliberately disorganized way. It would've been nice to have all of it — especially the sword — but this was a hell of a lot better than nothing.

My old clothes, slung over the nearby chair, would have to do. I don't mind re-using pants, but the other articles offended my Twenty-First Century sensibilities. Unfortunately, unless I wanted to try to launder them in the tiny washroom and then wait hours for them to dry, I didn't have much choice. And I'd dealt with worse things in the last year or so.

Clothed, I put the usual remaining mortal possessions in my pockets — my keychain with mini-pointer, Swiss Army knife, recharged inhaler — and slung my small bag of vital possessions (such as my medications) over my shoulder. Finally, I put on my remaining pieces of armor, took a deep breath, and opened the door that should have led to the common room.

I'd expected the dimly-lit, rough-hewn tunnel; that didn't prevent a little feeling of shock at actually *seeing* it. Just like the closet, the entire room sat on a pivot, and now the doorway led into Kaliko's Gantlet.

"Ah! Time for a refreshing morning exploration!" I called to the dead silence, hearing my voice echo faintly down the corridor before dying away. As there was enough light to see by, I began walking down the corridor. I tried not to jump when the door slammed and locked behind me; after all, this was all according to the script.

Now I had to be cautious, though. I *suspected* that some of the traps and tricks Baum had described might still be here, but there was no reason new and different ones could not be added. Not that it necessarily made much difference; my abilities and those of Inga were drastically different and things he could, in effect, walk through could kill me easily.

I continued down the corridor, finally emerging into a room about forty feet across with three other corridors. I *did* jump this time as a steel door slammed down inches from my back with a thunderous *clang* that resounded through the caverns. Apparently I wouldn't even have the option to retreat back into the corridor near my room.

"*Ichi, ni, san...* which of you should I choose, *ne?*" I muttered. My gut told me it probably didn't matter which, but I still liked to make a decision. Finally I chose the one directly in front of me, continuing my walk straight ahead.

I got about fifty feet down that tunnel when the lights went out and a rumbling *boom* told me that another door had blocked off my retreat. I waited a moment, but heard and saw nothing in the impenetrable gloom; then I chuckled. "Ah, quite a problem this could be. Blind and having to move forward down an unknown corridor." I reached into my pocket. "But for now, I think I'll level this playing field."

Cool white light shimmered into being from the LED flashlight built into my keychain. I began moving forward, and almost immediately saw a huge black void; the floor I'd seen in front of me before the lights went out had disappeared, withdrawn or collapsed probably when the door behind me had come down. I moved cautiously to the edge and shone the light downward; nearly at the limit of vision, an array of sharp points glinted darkly.

"Traditionalists indeed. The old spike-at-the-bottom-of-the-pit ploy," I said in my best Don Adams voice.

This *did* present something of a problem. I could barely make out the other side of the pit, thirty or forty feet away, and though — when I stamped deliberately — I could feel some springy "give" to the stone that showed I was in a magical land, there wasn't nearly enough to allow me the trampoline-like leaps I was able to get away with back in Iris' castle.

There was a little ledge left around the edge of the pit, which otherwise filled the corridor side-to-side, but way too little to walk on. It looked like I was going to have to cross by using my rock-climbing skills to work my way across.

In the dark, because I was going to need both hands for this one.

"Okay, round two." I moved over to the lefthand side of the pit and reached out, getting a good idea what the remaining ledge felt like and where it was. Then I clicked off the light and reached down.

The rock was solid, but only an inch or two remained. The interior wall had some rough spots, but I couldn't rely on it to provide much of a foothold. As I slowly lowered myself and felt the strain on my hands, I felt my heart starting to hammer. I had to cross forty feet using mostly my hands.

A year before, I don't think I'd have had the ability to make five feet without my hands giving out; back then, it'd been almost twenty-five years since I'd tried the idiotic trick of freeclimbing solo. But as I felt my fingers grip, slid my right hand out, got a good hold, then slid my left over, it began to sink in just how much I'd changed. It wasn't easy — no way! — but I was moving along pretty well, and it felt like my hands could actually take it. Five feet. Ten. Fifteen. Twenty. *Hey, this isn't so bad...*

Overconfidence can kill you, and as I went to make the next move, I slid my hand out a little too casually, gripped but hadn't finished when I started to move my left, and the shift in weight suddenly pulled my right hand free.

With an inarticulate cry, I found myself dangling over the black void, hungry spikes an invisibly lethal distance below, hanging on by three fingers. *Shit!*

243

I didn't dare move for a moment, just tried to make sure my left hand kept its grip. Then slowly, slowly, I brought up my right, feeling the movement threatening to pull my fingers free. And the sweat of fear wasn't improving things. I could feel the second finger starting to slide the tiniest bit...

And then my right hand clamped down on the ledge.

I hung by both hands and tried to get the rest of me to relax a little. I couldn't take much time, though, because now my hands *were* really starting to scream with the strain, but I was not taking any chances now. Focus. Move with very careful coordination. Right hand slide. Clamp. Left hand slide. Clamp. Right hand. Twenty-five feet. Thirty. Got to be getting near the edge. Thirty-five, at least near as I could guess in the dark. Forty, and now I could sense that faint deadening in the air that you get from approaching a wall. I slid my right hand over and found the edge of the pit, got my hand on it, moved until both hands were on, then heaved up with a last protest from my abused fingers, rolling onto the flat surface of the corridor.

I lay there for some time, regaining my breath and massaging my hands. I was probably going to need them again. I had to hope I wouldn't have to do *that* trick again, though, because I wasn't sure I could manage it.

Still, I felt pretty good about pulling off that Lara Croft, and sat up finally, shining the light in front of me. More corridor, ending in what looked like a dead end.

"Well, it *could* be, I suppose," I said as I walked up to it. "But Kaliko said *test*, and testing indicates there's ways to survive."

Hidden doors were the *trick du jour* for Nomes, so I began tapping away at the wall. Sure enough, off to the righthand side I found an area that didn't sound quite like the others. Using the magnifier from my Swiss Army knife, I found the crack. *Not large enough for a person to fit through. Not a person my size, anyway.*

Poking and pulling at various projections eventually located one that slid, causing the little door to pop open.

"So *that's* the reason." Inside was a lever which, I guessed, would open the door at the far end and let me out. I reached in and turned it.

Dim light returned, and I could see the door opening and the pit being covered by a rock surface. The solid *click* of a shackle locking around my wrist, however, put something of a damper on my relief.

"Traps within traps," I muttered, looking down at the broad, steel shackle attached to a thick chain. "Like I expected. And at least *this* time," I grinned, and with a tug pulled my hand free of the gauntlet, "I out-thought you." I reached in and pulled my crystal gauntlet the rest of the way through. "And I'll take this back, too."

I walked back to the doorway, but I slowed. It was different... something was in that room...

Baum had described a "giant." Me, I'd call what I was looking at more like an ogre or a troll, massive, huge, inhuman yet very humanoid, with grey stony skin, black eyes without a trace of white that reminded me of a shark's, and the teeth weren't far from that, either. The chain it was attached to wouldn't quite let it get to any of the exits, fortunately for me. Unfortunately, it *could* reach any part of the room, and as it stood something like fourteen feet high, I was not at all comfortable with that thought.

It had already seen me. "Good morning, little man," it said with a humorless grin, showing off tiger-shark teeth with grinding back molars. I became aware of a low, discordant humming, a faint tune that had become stronger as I approached. "You seek to pass; I seek my breakfast." It chuckled as the light dimmed farther, leaving me unable to clearly distinguish the creature except by a faint phosphorescent glow of the eyes. "One of us will gain our desire, I think."

This sucks. The thing wasn't quite as huge as Iris, but I had almost no armor and no sword. It had an immense reach advantage, could see me in the dark — with those eyes, it could probably see perfectly in light that was nearly pitch-black to me — and while I might well be able to hurt it if I got close enough, the getting close would probably end up fatal. Or crippling, *then* fatal.

See in the dark.

I could not restrain a pretty evil chuckle. "Oh, my friend, you are so very right."

245

That's when I let the thing have the mini-laser pointer right into the eyes, five milliwatts of coherent light blasting away the darkness and hammering into eyes vastly more sensitive than mine.

It shrieked, staggering backward, tripping over the post that held it chained, and I charged forward. It whipped its claws out blindly, but I ducked under, leapt up, and and slammed my right fist down onto it with everything I had.

The Music of the Spheres had told me the creature was a nearly-pure Faerie; it was no more prepared for that strike than the Temblors had been. Pinned between True Mortal and unyielding stone, I heard it *break*, a sickening sound like a small animal run over by a truck, magnified a hundredfold; the impact resounded through the rock as though it had been struck by a wrecking ball. The scream cut off in a gurgle; the light in its eyes went out and the light of the room came up.

I moved away, feeling nauseated for several moments. I didn't regret killing the thing as such — it was clearly about as Not Nice as anything I'd yet met — but I just kept feeling that crunching sensation and it made me shudder. I hadn't really wanted to kill anything. Even things like that. And that had been a pretty gruesome death.

After I'd slightly recovered, I chose one of the other passages and headed down it. *Good thing I had a big breakfast. I've been doing a lot of work this morning.*

As I continued, the light seemed to be getting brighter, with a slight orangish tinge, and my lips tightened. *I have a suspicion...*

Coming around a bend in the corridor, I could see my suspicions were correct. A broad bed of glowing, nearly white-hot coals nearly filled the room ahead. The room itself was getting uncomfortably warm, and getting closer to the coals felt like approaching an oven. The giant barbeque pit was about sixty feet across, maybe seventy. I could just make out, through the light and wavering heat, an exit on the far side.

I backed off and thought. This was a much stickier problem. Glancing around the room gave me no immediate ideas; the walls were much smoother here, so there wasn't much chance I could somehow climb over and around the coals, even assuming it wasn't impossibly hot above them. Unfortunately, it felt *very* hot indeed — about as hot as my dad's forge used to get when he'd set it up for a bit of blacksmithing.

After sitting there for a few minutes, I thought I noticed something about the coals, so I sat up and paid a bit more attention. After a few more minutes I was sure. The coals weren't shrinking. That meant the fire was magical.

Momentary elation was replaced with self-annoyance. *Yeah, sure, Einstein, the fire itself may be magical, but the heat it gives off isn't. Otherwise you wouldn't feel it much.* Secondary effects weren't covered by my True Mortality; a landslide of rocks started with a magical crowbar would kill me just as dead as if it had been a mundane crowbar starting the slide.

I went back to the corridor and tested the stone. While it *did* give under my fingers, I wasn't sure if I could even reasonably *try* Inga's solution; my Mortal nature didn't give me super-strength, just something that *looked* like it under certain circumstances. Lifting, carrying, and throwing large chunks of rock weren't some of those circumstances. Magical rock, yes, if I punched it right it'd fly away — or break in a thousand pieces — but I couldn't lift and carry it any more than I could the mundane stuff.

It was even worse than that anyway, now that I thought about it. Inga was a healthy boy. I was an asthmatic middle-aged man, even if I was in a lot better shape than I used to be. If I got a whiff of that superheated air, I might go down like a pole-axed steer. I sure wouldn't be very functional. Even if I did somehow get a bunch of stepping stones set up across the fire, I might never get across.

Still, there *had* to be some way to solve this. I wondered if I could use the body of the ogre some way, but I didn't see how. He wasn't nearly large enough to do much more than make a grease spot in that inferno.

Something about that nagged at me, though. I replayed that quick, brutal fight in my mind again, wincing once more at the finale...but that was the point my subconscious was nagging about. What was it...?

The shockwave.

My anti-magical nature could be extended and directed to some degree; I'd demonstrated that in my battle against Poly and Iris, and other practice I'd done confirmed it. If I was right about the fire's essence, I just might have a solution. That just might also end up killing me, but in what would at least be a more interesting fashion.

I backed up in the corridor and hyperventilated. I wanted to be able to hold my breath and take no chances when I got near that pit of flame. After a few moments, I took a deep breath and held it, then advanced.

The heat struck almost like a physical thing. I wavered at the edge, nerving myself up for the test. If I was wrong, I might cripple myself. Gritting my teeth, I shot my hand out and grabbed one of the coals.

Instantly the coal went black — as had much of the hair on the back of my arm, from rising heat. My breath *whooshed* out in relief, and I just *barely* caught myself in time, before I breathed in a whole lungful of that incredible heat. I backed away fast, returning to the corridor.

The fire *was* magical — almost purely magical — in nature. That gave me one chance... if I could pull it off.

I hyperventilated again and took a deep breath. This time, as I approached the edge, I focused on myself opposing magic, directing my will and force in a very specific way. As I reached the pit, I drew back my fist and then punched down and outward as hard as I could.

The punch slammed into the mass of coals like a heavy boot stamping down into a few inches of new-fallen snow. A shockwave of True Mortal antimagic kicked the coals aside like dust in a hurricane, rippling outward, shoving other coals backward, leaving a twelve-foot clear oval extending from my slightly-scorched fist.

I kept enough presence of mind to back off before I gave vent to a triumphant whoop. "*That's* the way you do it!"

This process was going to take a while; I had to wait for the stone to cool at least *some* before I could move farther out and clear another area. But there was no sign of anything trying to undo what I'd done, so I was determined to take the time and do it right.

It took three hours, near as I could guess, before I had a wide path cleared through the three-foot-deep bed of magical coals, and there were some scorchmarks on my boots before it was done. But finally, after waiting another half-hour, I took a deep breath and sprinted the seventy-five feet across, not risking another breath until I was well into the far cavern.

I walked a short distance and this time found that the corridor ended in a plain, ordinary door. I shrugged and opened it.

Before me was the Nome King's throne room; King Kaliko glanced up from a chessboard as the door opened, and his eyes widened. Ruggedo, seated across from his former Chamberlain, chuckled. "Ho, Erik Medon, you have kept us waiting. But perhaps you would care to join us for lunch?"

Chapter 36.

I grinned at Ruggedo. "Don't mind if I do. But," I became aware of a tightness on my face and arms, and of other sensations previously ignored, "I think I need to freshen up a bit. Your Majesty, do you...?"

Kaliko, surveying me with a tactician's appraising gaze, nodded and gestured with his scepter; one of the many doors about the room opened. Crossing to it, I found a short corridor ending in a quite large bathroom. I closed the door and went first to the sink; a polished sheet of silver or platinum served as an excellent mirror. In it, I saw myself; reddened skin, some small scorches and blisters, black soot covering much of my face as well as my hands and arms, smudges all over my clothes — as well as traces of green-black blood from the ogre and cuts and scrapes from my rock-climbing escapade.

I washed up carefully, trying to blot the worst of the mess from my clothes as well as clean my skin. I winced as the water and soap hit the burns. This might stay with me for a bit. I noticed there was a small tub of something that looked like Vaseline; I sniffed at it, touched it; it wasn't quite the same but there was a similarity. For all I knew, it was the Nome equivalent of hair conditioner or skin softener and I hate oily sensations anyway. I decided to tough it out. After using the other facilities, I felt more human, and *very* hungry (and so thirsty I'd also taken a drink from the sink faucet while I was washing up).

Emerging back into the throne room, I saw a third chair had been placed and the table was significantly larger, with a large luncheon and a huge pitcher of water in front of the place set for me. I went over and sat down, pouring myself a glass right away as I surveyed the food. "I've had a busy morning."

"You take it with good humor," Kaliko observed. "You could have been killed."

I shrugged. "You wouldn't have gotten anything out of your tests if there wasn't either actual urgency, or a convincing sense of urgency, in them. I knew what I was getting into when I came here."

Kaliko nodded slowly. "I suppose you did. Iris Mirabilis chose you well."

I chuckled. "Between us, your Majesty, Iris did not do the choosing; that was done by the Prophecy."

"Hm!" He considered that, as I bit into a sandwich I'd assembled from the assorted materials in front of me — sort of a roast beef sub, though I wasn't sure the meat was roast beef. "If true, that constitutes an additional point in your favor; a specified Hero has great weight of the Above behind him, even if the Prophecy is not entirely guaranteed."

"It's quite true." I quoted the relevant pieces of the Prophecy to him; the parts of the Prophecy which were long past should be pretty much harmless, and he wasn't likely to communicate anything to Ugu and Amanita anyway.

Kaliko contemplated that, and answered a move by Ruggedo, who had been waiting for several minutes. He then looked sour as Ruggedo moved instantly. "Check, old friend."

"And you fulfilled all of those conditions? Impressive, especially showing the Daughter of the Rainbow a beauty that would strike her heart." Kaliko surveyed the chessboard again, looking suspiciously at Ruggedo, who was smiling with perhaps a bit too much self-satisfied complacency.

I shrugged. "More a matter of realizing that Polychrome had certain limits that told me that there were some things she almost certainly could *never* have seen."

"I see." Kaliko brought his queen across the board, blocking the check. Ruggedo began to reach out, then gave a surprised snort of his own as he realized the move had produced a situation where moving the piece he wanted to would put *his* king in check. "You are a man of quick thought and ready improvisation, I see."

"That's probably a good way to put it. I do sort of long-term general plans, but," I gestured at the board, "I'm terrible at detailed long-term strategy like that. I play by instinct, so I'd probably lose fast to you guys in that kind of thing." I poured myself a glass of what seemed to be fresh orange juice; I wondered how *that* was being managed here in the middle of the almost-sterile wasteland of the Nome Kingdom.

"Still, not a poor choice of emissary. Long-term plans against the Usurpers would require in-depth knowledge of their capabilities, which you lack and even I do not have to any great extent, and you will undoubtedly have to determine your actions at least partially in an *ad hoc* fashion." Kaliko's brows came together as Ruggedo finally made a move. "I trust you *do* have some general plan or method for defeating the Usurpers?"

"I do. Though I'm giving no one any details who doesn't need to know and — no offense — you don't need to know, especially since I have yet to hear whether you're going to help us or not."

"Hmmm. Fair enough, and true, I have not yet spoken on that matter." He glared across the board at his old King. "Ruggedo, I distinctly recall that I used to have to *let* you win most of our old games!"

The jolly laugh that emphasized the old Nome's resemblance to Santa Claus rolled out, echoing through the throne room. "I have no doubt of it, no doubt of it at all, old friend. But I have had quite some centuries of time to learn many things, and not all of it was spent swinging a weapon."

"So it would seem." Kaliko sighed, smiled, and knocked over his king, ceding the game. "To my surprise, I am quite enjoying your visit, Ruggedo; perhaps I might relax your exile."

"That would be *most* generous of you, old friend."

He turned back to me. "As to the matter of assisting you...You ran the gantlet quite handily, solving the challenges with — I will acknowledge — an excellent combination of foresight, inspiration, and clear, controlled force. I have no objection, therefore, to fulfilling your first request. I have in fact already given the orders, and I believe you will find your new armor and weapons to be far superior in all ways — save, perhaps, in beauty, for though my people are masters of the forge we admit that in the creation of beauty we cannot surpass the Rainbow Kingdom.

"Your second, and far more weighty request, however," he continued, "I still find myself reluctant to grant. Aside from the one

253

ill-conceived adventure of my predecessor," he glanced at Ruggedo, who gave a rueful grin, "the Nome Army has never been truly at war, only a standing and impressive threat against any who would seek to take our homeland. You ask for me to send much, perhaps most, of our forces to another land into a battle against tremendous powers." He looked up. "Assuming indeed that you *can* bring them thence at all."

My answering grin held challenge in it. "I assure you, we can. Iris Mirabilis and I already have the answer to the Desert and the Barrier."

"So. Even granting that, I am not naïve nor uninformed; the powers the Usurpers have assembled are tremendously greater individually than my Nomes, and even with my war engines and Iris Mirabilis' own forces, I am unconvinced that the battle can be made an even one."

He had a point. Part of the problem was that — in the end analysis — it didn't *matter* if his and Iris' forces couldn't, by themselves, defeat Ugu and Amanita's army. I was going to be the key to that, and in fact at least some level of defeat was going to be necessary to get me put in the position to trigger the rest of the Prophecy. However, his forces would be needed to make the invasion a really credible one, and — if I failed — to give at least some hope of victory against the Usurpers.

And I didn't really want to tell him that, because the fact that I was going to basically end up a sacrificial lamb was the key secret of our entire attack. "Maybe it can't. But King Kaliko, you've watched them, as best you can. I really don't think you can look me in the eye and tell me you believe that they'll just leave you alone. They may leave you to the last, but they'll come for you in the end. And by that point, even if you've spent a few more centuries building up your army against them, there'll be no one else to help you, and they'll grind you into dust eventually by sheer weight of numbers — assuming neither of them comes up with some equivalent of a doomsday machine to blow your whole kingdom to hell." I didn't doubt that Ugu and/or Amanita could eventually invent a magical equivalent of a nuke if they had to. "You're never going to get a better chance than you'll have right now, with me and the Prophecy and, maybe more importantly, the forces of the Rainbow Kingdom to work with you and back you up."

Kaliko stood, pacing for a few moments, before he finally ascended the steps and sat in his throne. "Your words hold considerable truth, and I have thought on these very facts — for most of the last night, in fact.

"And you passed my tests, and argue your case persuasively. Still, I am aware that some version, garbled though it may have been, of my little testing gantlet must have made it through to the Mortal World, and unless I miss my guess you have quite some knowledge of those writings. So in at least some wise you may have benefited from significant foreknowledge." He held up his hand to prevent me from speaking. "This is not meant to belittle your success. It was clear that whether you had foreknowledge or not, you faced and resolved the challenges in an efficient manner and without using anything which I could rightfully categorize as 'cheating.'" He turned his throne, which appeared to be mounted on a concealed pivot like my erstwhile room, to face a different wall. "Still, the true mettle of an adversary is to be seen when they are confronted by unforeseen challenges and choices." He gestured with his staff at the wall.

A large section of the stone became transparent as glass, showing that it was actually a set of double doors, now allowing us to look into a circular room with an enclosed, sealed cylindrical chamber within. And inside that chamber was Zenga.

The Princess of Pingaree was seated on the stone floor, chains on her ankles and wrists. She didn't appear harmed, and seemed both bored and annoyed.

Apparently the transparency was two-way, because she suddenly glanced up. "Lord Erik!"

"Zenga!" I turned to Kaliko. "What the hell are you up to?"

"As I told your friend," Kaliko answered, "This is a test for you. Though I have not told her the exact nature of the test until now."

The King of the Nomes touched a jewel on his throne, and with a low, throbbing hum that vibrated the floor, the ceiling of the chamber Zenga was in slowly began to descend. "Here I present you with both a test and a choice. If you simply agree to leave with your armor and weapons, but ask no more of me, I shall stop this device and release her, and after a week or so of pleasant relaxation here you will leave, with the equipment you sought, thus better off than when you came.

"Or you may attempt to rescue her. But make no mistake, Erik Medon; that is what you might call a hydraulic ram. While materials in its construction have been made by magic, little magic is in the actual device itself. It is more powerful than any such device your people have ever made; thousands upon thousands of tons of force can be exerted on whatever lies within that room.

"And if you choose to rescue her, the die will be cast. You must either succeed... or watch her be crushed into nothingness."

Ruggedo looked darkly at Kaliko. "You have become hard indeed, old friend."

Kaliko met Ruggedo's gaze impassively. "These are perilous times, Ruggedo. I dare risk no more without a test equally perilous."

I stared at Zenga, who stared back at me, then glanced up, looking at the polished metal descending towards her. I turned to Kaliko. "I cannot leave without your backing, your Majesty."

He sighed. "So be it." He turned another gem. "The trap is set, the process cannot be reversed or stopped now. The cycle must complete...or *you* must stop it. So, Erik Medon, Hero of Prophecy, what will you do to rescue your companion in the — perhaps — ten minutes that remain to her?"

I grinned slowly, broadly. "Nothing," I said casually.

I saw both Ruggedo's and Kaliko's jaws drop. "What?" Kaliko managed finally. "You will sacrifice her to...to what? Make some point to me about ruthlessness? What —"

"I will do nothing because I *need* to do nothing." I looked at Zenga, smiling confidently. "She doesn't need *my* help to save her."

She stared at me, eyes wide in understanding. "You...you *knew?*"

"Of *course* I knew, Zenga. For it was said: in rejecting wisdom, he will gain strength." I smiled even more broadly as she started to stand. "Now show them what a Princess of Pingaree can do."

Kaliko whirled. "*PINGAREE?*" Realization was written in shock across his face. "Oh, no."

"Oh, *yes.*"

Zenga stood up and placed both hands above her on the polished steel...and pushed.

The subliminal hum turned to a groan of strained levers, valves suddenly finding themselves feeding a pressure that mounted, ever higher. My eyes went to the bracelets on her arms, found one, the one I'd noted when she first joined me, with a centerpiece of a huge smoky-blue Pearl.

It was a battle of two Faerie realms now, the power of the Nome engineers and their magical machines against the supernal might of the Blue Pearl of Strength, the second of the Three Pearls the Sea Faeries had gifted to the rulers of Pingaree.

Now the smile was on *Zenga's* face, a sharp and savage grin. Her arms went taut, her whole body rigid, and I could see the muscles standing out on her shoulders, her biceps, her legs, muscles smooth and perfectly sculpted from a warrior's training, her eyes shining with the elation of this single moment. The descent of the huge ceiling slowed, stopped, as delicate veins began to stand out on her temples, and she bared her teeth wider in a smile that was half-snarl. Then she gave a low growl and *shoved.*

That hydraulic ram — built to crush anything ever made with millions of pounds of force — *backed up.* Underfoot there was a screaming and the floor rocked, distant echoes of thunder rumbling down the corridors and through the Kingdom of the Nomes as — somewhere below — steam and water engines, magically powered, overloaded, exploded with backpressures never imagined even by their engineers. A warrior's joy at the power in her hands transfigured Zenga, and for a moment I couldn't take my eyes off her; she was for that instant nearly as beautiful as Polychrome, but in a wild and untamed way that made the breath catch in my throat.

The ram suddenly split in the center and jammed, motive force fading and material no longer up to the impossible stress. Zenga dropped her arms and stepped forward, shackles snapping as though made of cobweb, drew back her fist and shattered the transparent enclosure with a single punch, scarcely pausing in her stride to the huge doors that were the only thing now separating her from the Throne Room. Her delicate coffee-colored fingers found the seam of the doors, jammed themselves in, and both arms *pulled...* and with a

257

screaming moan of tortured metal, the doors flew open, half torn from their hinges.

I turned back to Kaliko. "Well, your Majesty? Admittedly, I didn't follow your script. But I prefer to write my own."

Kaliko finally stopped staring at Zenga and looked at me. Gradually, his expression shifted from shock to chagrin, and suddenly he burst out laughing. "You give yourself far too little credit, mortal, for you played that game twenty moves ahead. You hid an ally, hid her power, right in front of my nose! So not two, but *three* allies you have made, and one of them powerful enough to have outdone me in these very caverns many centuries agone."

His smile was filled with his own joy now. "You have won, Erik Medon. And a part of me is glad indeed of it, as I have hated sitting here, waiting, wondering what the end of this would be. Perhaps — even if we fail — it is better to fail this way than mine."

He nodded emphatically. "Find a way into Oz, Erik Medon; give me the path you have promised, and my armies will march side-by-side with those of the Rainbow, and we shall see how fares Prophecy and your cunning against the power of Oz and its Usurpers!"

Chapter 37.

Polychrome stood to the rear of the balcony and tried to slow her heart. *I've spoken to crowds before. I've never cared before about speaking in front of them. What's wrong with me now?*

She saw Nimbus and her father in front of her, giving their own speeches, but the words did not register. Only the rhythm of the words, slowly building to the point that *she* would be expected to step forward. To step forward and –

And take command.

That was it. *My whole life...I've danced through life without worry, without fear, without care...*

Without responsibility, without the duties...not even the ones my sisters had. She glanced with sudden guilt and shame at her sisters — Azure Radiance, Crimson Glow, Golden Dawn, all of them — and wondered: *Why do they still love me so, when I have always left them, when Father has always allowed me so much?* And she wondered, too, about these thoughts, so new and different.

It's not just that, she realized with a shiver. *It's Father. I will be doing this because Father will be here nearly alone, in case the Usurpers press their attack to the Rainbow Kingdom. It will be Father's power against theirs...and I must be far, far away in case he falls.*

The very *thought* of Iris Mirabilis, the eternal Rainbow Lord, *falling* was almost ludicrous, but she had seen all too clearly in his eyes that he knew it could happen. That it *would* happen.

And then I will be the ruler of the Rainbow Kingdom. It struck her, now, with a thrill of horror, that her father had *always* intended she be the one to replace him, and thus her name, Polychrome, no single color, not like those of her sisters... Polychrome, many colors, ruler of the hues of the Rainbow. The only one of her sisters to be encouraged in her mingling with all the peoples, allowed to be seen and known throughout all Faerie...

...The only one with armor and weapons waiting for her. She felt the light, silvery plate suddenly weighing on her shoulders as though the very towers were balanced on that Above-forged steel, the argent sword dragged at her hip like an anchor. *Armor and weapons my mother had, but never wielded. Oh, Father, was even this something foreseen by the Above? Did they tell you, one day, that your firstborn daughter would sit on your throne?*

Cheers from below, and she knew Father and Nimbus were nearing the moment she must step forward.

How can I? All the training...it has taught me to fight, I've gained some smattering of strategy, but I'm no leader! I need so much more time...

And in that moment she saw Erik's face, pale, disbelieving, as he grasped what was being asked of him, and the pain of it went straight to her heart...and brought a momentary laugh to her lips. *So this was what he was feeling, all those months, as we tried to teach him all of the things that his life had never given him.*

And he took those lessons, inadequate and limited as they were, and accepted what we asked of him. She had watched him run Kaliko's terrible gantlet and seen his triumph of mind and will.

I'm just being asked to lead. By the Colors, even if I want to fight I'll bet Father's told Nimbus to make sure someone's always watching me. If poor Erik can be out there...ready to die *for...*

A part of her stopped, pulled back, and evaded some monstrous, half-seen precipice. She knew not exactly what fearful thought lay on the other side of that half-finished phrase, but she dared not look at it. *...for Oz and all of Faerie...I can't be afraid.*

I won't *be afraid. I won't fail Father. I won't fail Nimbus.*

I won't fail him.

And now the noise rose to a roar, and the two men had stepped aside, and even as she stepped forward, Iris Mirabilis said, "Warriors of Faerie, Army of the Rainbow, I give you Princess Polychrome Glory, High Commander of the Hosts, Heir to the Rainbow Throne, Blessed of the Above!"

She reached the edge of the balcony of the Rainbow Castle and looked down.

Ranged in perfect array before the Castle stood rank upon rank of the Warriors of the Rainbow, hundreds, thousands, ten thousand strong, all assembled, and as she looked upon them they gave a mighty cheer, a shout of gladness and welcome that brought a sting of tears to her eyes. *I don't deserve this...but I must try. I must.*

"Highest of all the Armies of Faerie, I thank you!" she called out, and to her astonishment her voice did not tremble, did not waver, but rang out clear and strong, echoed across the immense plaza with confidence and certainty. She had no idea what she could say next, but their answering roar gave her another moment or two. "It is nearly time, the time we have awaited three centuries and more! The Hero has gained his allies, and we shall not march alone!"

They fell silent at that, a tense, expectant, hopeful silence, and she felt a savage smile on her face as she gave them what they hoped for. "The greatest of the Armies of Faerie, solid and true as stone, the forces of the Nome King shall march beside us! Earth and Sky shall move as one!"

And they took the line and repeated it, and in that moment she knew she had said *exactly* the right thing. "Earth and Sky shall move as one!"

"Earth and Sky shall move as one!"

Chapter 38.

Grasses and tough brush grew here, at the border between the northern edge of the Nome Kingdom and the Land of Ev. I watched as a small contingent of Nomes assisted the Pingarese workmen in opening the crates they had brought here a few weeks ago, according to my instructions to King Inga.

Kaliko and Zenga watched with some bemusement. "What is this that you have my men assembling, Lord Erik?" Kaliko said finally.

"My ticket across the Deadly Desert," I answered. "The barrier makes it impossible for the Nomes to tunnel across. I can't fly by myself, and no Faerie magic would get me across and through the barrier. As it's about two hundred miles of desert, walking is out of the question; it's not all that bad here, a few hundred yards out, but the magic that makes the Deadly Desert so deadly intensifies everything. It's like the Sahara with toxic sand. The magic part of the destroying sands won't hurt me, but some of the toxins are mundane.

"So I needed a mundane way across the desert. Fast, low-tech enough that I could get it built here, *and* it had to be something I could use. So I took a cue both from Clive Cussler and from Baum himself." I grinned as I saw the mast being raised, making the nature of my "solution" clear.

Zenga clapped her hands in understanding. "A *sand-boat!*"

Kaliko and Ruggedo grunted with surprise and appreciation. "An elegant solution in some ways. But have you any idea how to handle such a craft? Your world is filled with automated metal conveyances."

"Ask Zenga," I said, "or old Inkarbleu; I learned to handle a small sailing boat when I was much younger, and the seamen of Gilgad gave me quite a refresher course."

"Good enough, then," Ruggedo said, "but tell me, why from here? The prevailing winds, as you know, are due East from here. If you began a hundred miles or so farther south, you could run straight before the wind and arrive in Oz as swiftly and surely as any might hope." He gave a nostalgic grin. "That was, after all, the course my tunnel took. If you run straight with the wind from here, you will miss Oz entirely. You will need to tack somewhat southerly to strike land."

"You're entirely correct, Ruggedo. But the Usurpers know these things as well, and while they haven't had tremendously good luck following me, they certainly know I'm coming for them. So where, exactly, are Ugu and Amanita going to deploy most of their watchmen and troops?"

Understanding dawned on both Nomes' faces. "Along the border of the Winkie country. Most concentrated at Oogaboo and points immediately south, where the domain of the Nomes and Oz are at their closest."

"Exactly. As I have no intention of charging straight into their most heavily-armed troops, I am going to sail along the northern border and then cut south, landing in the *Gillikin* country instead. This should be less heavily guarded – their magic cannot, after all, track me directly, so they will have no idea, even if they guess my intent, of knowing *exactly* where along that border I will land – and it is rougher country overall, so they'll have a harder time redeploying. Once I'm there –"

"–all you need do," Kaliko finished, "is drop that Gem upon the soil of Oz, and the Rainbow will span the distance from here to there; my Nomes will cross and they will be joined at the top by Iris Mirabilis' forces. Within a few minutes, an hour at the most, our armies will be assembling in Oz." He turned to Ruggedo. "Well, Ruggedo, you have told me of your adventures since exile, and they're quite impressive...Penitent. I, on the other hand, have become an able administrator, but am not so experienced in the outside world. I am therefore appointing *you* commander of our armies."

Ruggedo's jaw dropped and he stared at Kaliko for a long time. "But...I am..."

"An exile no longer. I exiled a petty tyrant and a selfish, short-sighted man who had imperiled the entire realm. I do not see much of that man in you, and I have spent – quite deliberately – most of the past few weeks in your company. For you, exile has served to bring you to the maturity your kinghood had denied you. Not like General Guph, alas."

Ruggedo's eyes were suspiciously bright; I thought I saw a trace of a tear at the corner of one. To preserve a bit of the old Nome's pride, I asked, "What *did* happen to Guph, then?"

"I exiled him shortly after Ruggedo when I discovered he was actually trying to arrange a coup against me. This did not have the salutary effect on him that it appears to have had on my old King. He cultivated his grudge against me assiduously, assisted many attempts to invade or exploit our lands, and eventually offered his services and knowledge to the Usurpers."

"Hm-m-m! That's bad. That's very bad," Ruggedo said gravely, only a hint of roughness in his voice indicating that he had been very near tears at Kaliko's sudden lifting of exile. "Guph was an ambitious and prideful Nome, no doubt of it, but he was an excellent strategist and tactician, not to mention a cunning negotiator. I suppose his ultimate goal was to become one of the Usurpers' Viceroys, taking over the Nome Kingdom when they finally moved against our people."

Zenga snorted. "If half the stories I've heard are true, his *ultimate* goal would be to turn the Usurpers against each other and take Oz itself from them."

"Good luck with that," I said. "Still, that probably means that they've got themselves a good general to coordinate things. Another reason for me to make sure that we get to assemble and move as an organized unit far away from where they've got the bulk of their forces. With luck, we might be able to cut a swath straight south through the Gillikin country and hit the former Emerald City before enough of their armies can redeploy to stop us. Take out Ugu and Amanita at the capital, and the whole thing may be finished."

"A fine thought that is," agreed Ruggedo. "But I doubt we should plan on it."

"No. But we should, at least, have surprise and position on our side when it starts."

The assembly of the little craft was nearly complete. It was about thirty feet long and had a beam of about eight feet, with a long outrigger on either side to balance it. The boat was designed with an aerodynamic shape that should minimize resistance; instead of wheels, which would have been my first choice, the Pingarese had built narrow skids coated with something shiny that Zenga said was called "Sea Fairies' Kiss"; it made the areas it was coated with extremely smooth, very hard and resistant to wear and in water repelled things like barnacles. I ran my finger along the skids and was astonished; the stuff felt so slick it was like moving an air-hockey puck over the table. There were a few bare areas at intervals on that and the rudder and hull, to provide good contact for control and steering. The boat was longer and somewhat higher than it would have been in normal circumstances, but I had to make sure it kept me reasonably high off the sands, out of the concentrated level of toxins. As it was, I was taking with me several masks crafted by the Nomes which should filter out incidental poisons and stray sand grains, but they would be for emergencies, not constant wear in the hundred-degree-plus heat.

Now the Nome soldiers that had accompanied us began the quick loading of supplies into the sand-boat. I had no idea how long it would take; with luck I might average twenty miles an hour while moving, given a brisk wind, which would mean it would take probably thirty to thirty-five hours of sailing to reach my destination. Unlike a water craft on the ocean, though, I couldn't afford to just lash the rudder and take naps when I got tired; there were potential outcroppings of rock, the small vessel would likely be temperamental...and there were rumors that *something* lived in the Desert, where nothing should live. So I'd have to sail only when I was awake and alert, stopping whenever I couldn't pay attention. "Figure it'll take me a week to get there," I said, finally. "Eight hours of concentrated sailing a day will be more than enough in that heat."

"A week is a good time," Kaliko said. "That will allow me to assemble the armies underground here, ready to emerge at a moment's notice, and prepare all the supplies they must bring with them. The war engines, especially, will take some time to bring up."

The last jug of water was placed onboard and the last Nome jumped off. I walked to the bow of the little ship and took up the pot of paint that I'd requested. Zenga looked momentarily puzzled, then brightened. "Of course! No ship must go un-named!"

"Bad luck, at least that's what I've always been told," I agreed. I looked up in the sky, where — far off in the distance over Ev — the massive white and grey anvil of a cumulonimbus drifted; for a moment I allowed myself to imagine I could see a faint glitter, as of the towers of a mighty castle in the sky. *And now I take a single ship to throw back the invaders of the greatest of the lands of Faerie.*

I painted the name carefully; the paint dried unnaturally swiftly, as I wasn't allowing my True Mortal nature to interfere. *Yes. It's the right name. May this one fare better than the first.*

"Zenga? Would the Princess of Pingaree do me the honor of christening my ship?" I found it amusing that the word "christen" was used here, even though there were hardly any Christians in evidence in the Faerie realms.

"With great pleasure, Lord Erik." Zenga took a bottle of wine from Kaliko, who apparently had arranged to carry just about everything he might want with him, and drew back her arm, reading the name inscribed on the bow before speaking. "May the spirits of air guide you; may the strength of earth uphold you; and may the Will of the Above protect you; in the name of Faerie and the Above, I christen thee — *Thunder Child!*"

The wine bottle shattered perfectly, spraying sparkling shards far and wide, and — for just a moment — I thought I heard, from the far-off cloud, a low rumble. *I will believe I did, anyway. Perhaps he's watching, somehow. Here I go, Iris.*

Zenga put her foot on the boarding step, and I caught her arm. "No, Zenga."

She blinked. "But, Lord Erik, I am -"

"—more than enough a resident of Faerie so that you cannot pass the Barrier," I said firmly. "You might just be blocked — in which case neither you nor I would enter — or the barrier might kill you. Either way, you have to stay." I looked out at the grey-brown, desolate expanse. "I have to do this alone."

Slowly she stepped back down. Then, before I could react, she darted forward and kissed my cheek. "Good luck, Erik Medon," she said, and stepped back quickly.

I was momentarily thrown completely off. Then I took a deep breath. "Thank you, Zenga."

I swung myself up to the little deck and prepared to unlash the sail. The Nomes braced themselves against the stern and pushed; *Thunder Child* slid smoothly across the grass and gravel and onto the level, lethal sands.

I stood up and waved; a cheer went up from the twenty or so gathered there, and Ruggedo raised his staff in salute. I bowed, and then let out the sail.

The wind caught the light, strong material instantly, with a pull so strong that even with the tackle assisting me I was almost pulled along with it. The boom swung outward and *Thunder Child* began moving, picked up speed. I reached back, adjusted the rudder; a gust of wind at angles to the main breeze momentarily tilted the little sand-boat, and I shifted my heading a few points.

Thunder Child was a good little craft, but it still took me some time to get used to her handling; I kept some of the sail reefed in until I could feel confident that I knew what I was doing, and what I *should* do if certain emergencies were to happen. Eventually, though, I felt sure I could handle her well enough, and looked back.

The dark ridges of Ev and the Nome Kingdom were still visible, but the low border between the sand and safe land had already vanished. I was alone on the Deadly Desert.

"Well," I said after a moment, "raise the curtain for the final act."

I settled the goggles I'd gotten from the Nomes onto my face, turned back to the bow and let out all the sail. *Thunder Child* lunged forward, hissing over the deadly sands. Traces of acrid fumes tickled my nostrils, made me squint even more. This was the most dangerous part of the entire journey — at least up until that part where I had to let myself get stabbed, anyway. If the toxins and irritants triggered the wrong reaction, I might end up a victim of the Deadly Desert, my True Mortal nature useless before my own body's asthmatic fury.

But there was no other choice. I was the only one who had a chance to pass the Barrier.

Aware more than ever of the threatening tightness in my chest, I turned *Thunder Child* fractionally Northward, keeping myself heading due East.

Together we flew towards the sun, trailing a lethal cloud behind.

Chapter 39.

Brilliant sunlight burning into my face. The sting and grating of acrid wisps of toxic vapor, scraping my throat raw, reddening my skin, making my breath catch in a sometimes frighteningly familiar way. The hiss of runners over endless gold-grey sand, the whip-rattle of taut canvas and lines. This was the entirety of the day, for as long as I could focus. I'd put on one of the masks when I could, but once the sun mounted beyond the lowest angle, the brutal heat became so great that I could hardly stand to keep the mask on for more than a few moments.

A pause near mid-day to take a lunch, hunkered down behind whatever part of the deck might afford the most cover from the wind. Then back to the burning light, the acid rasp of poison air, the hissing scrape of runners on sand. Even the goggles couldn't entirely relieve the glare, but they were crucial to keep bits of sand from getting in my eyes.

When night fell, it was blessed relief — for a little while. But like many deserts, the Deadly Desert became cold indeed after dark, and I had to wrap myself up well to sleep. On the positive side, I could wear the mask all night, which gave me a desperately needed respite from the low but unmistakable poisoning of day; by the end of each day I would grow disoriented, sick and weak from the constant exposure. I dared not over-use the medicine Polychrome and Iris had given me; magically improved or not, I had to be worried that it might cause a paradoxical bronchospasm, and even if not, there was only so much of it.

Overall, I'd have much rather have travelled at night, but that simply wasn't an option. Without even a primitive village for uncounted miles, the nights here were as dark as anything imaginable, lovely blazing stars overhead just barely painting the dunes with a dusting of ghostly silver that could lure the unwary into believing they could see. I needed to maintain a heading, stay far enough from land that none of Ugu's scouts might spot me in the Desert, and avoid the occasional outcroppings of rock which could loom up almost without warning from the infinite sand.

And, I thought as I steered a touch more northward, *avoid maybe other things as well.* Several times, both day and night, I had thought I'd seen something else moving on or under the sands, something that wasn't shifting sand or the terrifying threat of a poisonous dust devil that I'd had to outmaneuver a day or two ago. I couldn't restrain a shudder at the thought of being caught in a whirlwind of that lethal sand, but I was even more concerned with the idea that there were some sorts of living creatures out here. That hadn't been depicted in the books, and there was no way such things lived here naturally.

Which meant, almost certainly, that the things were the creations and possibly spies of the Usurpers. Double the reason for me to avoid them.

I squinted ahead, trying to judge my speed and heading again. It had been about a week, and I was now seriously considering that it was time to "cut south" and make landfall. Oz being so broad, I had considerable latitude (pun intended) to decide where exactly to land, but obviously I couldn't wait *too* long.

Wait. What was that...?

Something about the sand ahead...that ridge. It seemed to curve...

I hauled sharply on the rudder and *Thunder Child* heeled over hard on her left outrigger. Even as I made the turn, we reached the ridge I'd seen, cresting it to see — exactly as I had feared — that it was part of a perfectly circular funnel-shaped hole, a hole whose edge began to crumble beneath us, causing *Thunder Child* to slew sideways. I kept the rudder hard over and tried to catch more wind in the sail as we skidded sideways.

"SHIT!" A pair of fanged jaws eight, no, *ten* feet long erupted from the center of that sandy maelstrom, snatching and slashing at the ship that was *almost* within reach. *Ant-lion from hell!*

But the ever-blowing winds caught at the sail again, sending us skimming forward just the tiniest bit faster, and we were past the monstrous insect, riding up the sandy wall, up, up, and then over, airborne for a moment off the crest like a skier taking a jump.

Thunder Child came down with a jarring *thud* but her outriggers kept her steady, and we continued, running before the wind.

That was too close. I held a mask over my face, ignoring the heat until my heavy breathing slowed; no need to breathe more of this crap than I had to. *Okay, that does it. I've come far enough and I don't need to keep tempting fate.*

I laid the rudder over and turned us southward, glancing at the sun. *We're about eighty miles from Oz right now, I think. Given the time of day, I won't quite make it before nightfall. But by this time tomorrow, I'll be out of this poison-sanded nightmare!*

I kept going as long as I could that evening, until I realized that the fading light was just about gone. A quarter-moon was up, but that wouldn't be enough for safe travel. I put on my mask, got out my dinner, ate, and made sure I drank enough; the last thing I needed was getting dehydrated out here. Finally, I tucked myself in for a good night's rest — hopefully the last one I'd need out here. It didn't take long at all for me to fall asleep.

Creak.

I snapped instantly awake. *That didn't sound like any of the normal ship sounds.* I looked up at the sail, which was partially open, taut, keeping tension on my anchor lines. If I had to move, I didn't want to have to spend extra time running out the sail; there were ways to instantly release the anchors from this ship.

Scrape.

That time I felt a faint vibration. Through the hull. *Something's moving under me!*

I stood up, very slowly, carefully, and reached over my shoulder. Grasping my sword — one of the Nomes' gifts — I slid the big blade slowly from its sheath.

Even as I did that, *Thunder Child* rocked as a huge something rose up from beneath the sands, looming like a cloud of darkness against the stars, two yellow-green eyes glowing out of the black. The misty silver edging of the moon and stars outlined the head and neck of a colossal serpent, something that seemed the size of one of Frank Herbert's sandworms. Well, maybe a bit smaller, but at least the length of a tandem tractor-trailer, if not quite as wide.

Spine-sharp teeth glinted in a savage smile. "Why, what have we here, moving across Our sands? A little Man in a little boat, I see." The voice was wind, sand rattling over dead rock, the scrape of scales on dust.

"Good evening," I said. If it was inclined to talk, I'd take all the time I could get. The problem with fighting this thing was the same as the one with fighting the troll back in the Nome caverns, only about ten times worse. Anything alive in this hellish desert would be so bloody magical that if I could just stick it *once* I was pretty sure I'd kill it, but if it struck when I wasn't ready, just being *brushed* by it would probably squish me like a bug.

"And a good evening to you as well, little Man." It was on the other side of the *Thunder Child* from me, not that this would stop it. I took note of the exact position of the mast and sail; if I had to duck and dodge, I'd need all the advantages I could get. "We are Chiindemon, little Man; who are you?" It moved its head fractionally closer, nearly touching the far side rail.

"I'm Erik Medon, Chiindemon. How kind of you to ask."

"Kind?" Its laugh was a hiss of water on a dying fire. "We are not kind; We only seek the names of those who are Our meals, for few are the meals We are given in the Desert, and worthy of remembrance and repetition, in the long days between."

"I really don't feel like being eaten." *Angle... he's moving like this...* I edged just slightly sideways.

"We are not giving you a choice, Erik Medon," Chiindemon said, with cold malicious humor. Eyeing my sword, it sidled cautiously forward, looking for an opening.

"Since you're so fond of names, do you know what this part of a boat is called?" I asked, pointing. The snake-monster's gaze flicked sideways in the direction I pointed, allowing me to reach out and grab the rope.

It glanced back at me, slight puzzlement in its hungry eyes. "No, We do not. What is it?"

I yanked the rope, releasing the knot. "Boom," I answered.

The power of the wind whipped the boom around, across the deck with the speed and strength of a club swung by a giant. Chiindemon saw the movement and tried to draw back, but a fraction of a second too late; instead of evading the strike, Chiindemon put its head in the precise path of the boom's tip.

Iron-bound boom met scale-armored head with a shattering impact that shivered throughout *Thunder Child*. I was already in motion, charging, leaping from the deck as Chiindemon reared back in agony, one eyesocket crushed, black blood streaming down. My sword, driven by my full weight behind it, sliced almost effortlessly through the mystic creature's scaly armor and I slid down, gripping the hilt of the sword and gutting Chiindemon along a fifteen-foot length.

The steam-whistle shriek almost broke my eardrums and I was flung fifty feet through the air to tumble across cold-searing sands. I forced myself groggily to my feet, away from the lethal dust, and looked back.

Chiindemon coiled and looped in juddering, twitching death-throes, slowly, slowly settling into stillness. That much, at least, was well and good. I wasn't going to be anyone's evening snack.

Unfortunately, the monstrous corpse lay half-on, half-off the broken hulk of *Thunder Child*.

Chapter 40.

"Impressive, my Queen," Ugu said.

Inwardly, he decided he would by preference have said *horrifying*.

"You think so?" Amanita's voice was light and cheerful, the voice of a girl showing off her latest dress, or perhaps a lovely sampler she'd just finished stitching. "I *do* think they are some of my best work. And I've thought through their names *very* carefully."

Before them stood four huge figures, bowing before their creator and mistress. One was a huge yet indistinct shape, yellow eyes glinting venomously, sometimes manlike, at others spreading insubstantial icy wings and screaming like a bird of prey; the second a massive, blazing figure of fire, eyes rimmed with coal black and a fanged, smiling mouth, horns, and cruel, clawed hands; the third a bloated, jellylike *thing* with glowing green eyes and a slavering maw that smelled of death and decay, at moments coiling into a shape like a decaying serpent; and the last a grim, angular, reptilian shape of stony blocks, a glowering, dull countenance with eyes like the flicker of light off crystal and a hungry, hateful expression.

"I have heard rumor of these names, my Queen, and – if you will excuse me for saying so – I am concerned that there may be a bit of hubris in them." *I have become something of a master of understatement in these centuries, when dealing with Amanita.*

"Why, you're *concerned*, Ugu dear. How kind of you. But really, now, it's merely sending a little message. We *do* intend to take it all, now, don't we?"

Even after all he had seen, all the dangerous games he had played with this more than half-mad Yookoohoo, very nearly that simple question undid him. It was a matter of desperate control to answer with any semblance of his usual aplomb. "I...would say these are things to be decided as the time comes. You know me, my Queen; take things in their order, all things in their time. Let us finish the matter of the Mortal, and we shall see what the next steps shall be."

277

She frowned, but prettily, clearly not truly annoyed. "Oh, Majesty, you are such a *cautious* man. But there, now, that is your job, I suppose, as you have been so kind as to assume the drudgery of managing much of Oz while I do my...research." She gestured, and the four monstrous figures rose. "Go now, Surtur, Jormungandr, Nidhogg, Hræsvelgr. Go and ready yourselves for when you are needed."

Ugu bowed and excused himself as well. "I have many duties to attend to, my Queen, and I see your work here is...well in hand, indeed."

Once clear of Amanita's range, once within his own section of castle, Ugu sank into a chair. *Mad. Utterly mad. It matters not that I see where the madness came from; truly our success...and perhaps the stress of knowing that a war is coming...has finished loosing the chains of reason that were strained to breaking long ago. She believes that we shall challenge the Above and Below once we have won Faerie.*

For a moment, he allowed himself to wonder if perhaps she was not mad — if the Great Binding would even give her that much power.

The thought filled him with even more fear than the belief that she was well and truly insane. He set his jaw. *I must make sure all of my plans are laid, all things arranged precisely. There must be no possible route to failure.*

"Majesty?"

Startled, he looked up to see Cirrus Dawnglory standing over him with concern on his face. Quickly he stood up. "General."

Cirrus still looked worried, but asked no questions as to why his King sat silent and alone. "The Wardens of the Sand have spoken. Something moves across the Desert."

"Indeed? How far, and where?"

"I have a hard time crediting the reports, Sire. The sound of moving, they say, is like a whispering wind, and moves as swiftly as the wind across the sand."

"I see." Ugu frowned. *Moving across the sand like the wind. Minimal magic. Now, if I were a Mortal, what...*

Suddenly he laughed. "Ingenious! Most ingenious, my Mortal enemy. And if you are as worthy an adversary as you have appeared... Cirrus, tell me; it does not cross at the narrow place, but is passing to the North, yes?"

The flash of startlement and increased respect warmed Ugu momentarily. He was pleased when he could see something before his General, who was — truth be told — uncommonly sharp and well-versed in his strategies. "It is even so, Sire. Yet...how do you know?"

"He rides the winds themselves, my friend, on a vessel like those used to cross the waves. *That* was his goal in travelling to Pingaree, artisans of the highest skill to build him a ship that might cross even the deadliest sands with speed and surety. And he lands not at the places you have fortified, but seeks to bring himself to land in the North, the Gillikin country, where it will be hard indeed to bring our forces to bear. A clever and dangerous man they have chosen, one who has been thinking several steps ahead. Bring in all your forces from the Winkie country, they are not needed. Pickets along the North, one side to the other, immediately!"

"At *once*, Majesty!"

As Cirrus strode off, Ugu nodded. *The end of the game is nearly in sight. A few more preparations to make. It must be perfect. There will be no route to salvation for the Mortal, no possible direction that will not end with his final sacrifice in Amanita's great array.*

And then – as soon as the sacrifice is complete, in that very moment — then Amanita must die — for the sake of Oz, and all the world.

He wondered at himself, for even that thought — as true and necessary as ever a thought was — left him feeling grim and sad.

This killing and plotting...when will it end? When can I stop?

Chapter 41.

The sun came up like a bolt of flaming lightning – except lightning stops, and the sun didn't. I wasn't sure how far I had to come; my best guess was twenty miles.

Twenty miles. Hardly anything. I biked forty when I was a wussy little kid. I can walk at six miles per hour, I could do this in four hours.

But the grey-brown-white sands slipped under my boots, and I didn't dare fall if I could possibly avoid it. I was a couple of feet closer to the sand now than I'd been even on *Thunder Child's* low deck, and not protected by wood and space from the savage gnawing power of the Deadly Desert.

If I hadn't been a True Mortal, I'd have been dead long since, maybe from the moment Chiindemon threw me to the ground. As it was, my legs itched in that tight, hot way that warned me that the itches would become pain in time. I had the Nome mask firmly fastened across my face; I might have to loosen it from time to time, but I had to balance the need for cooling with the need to keep from breathing poison. The goggles weren't comfortable either, but they sure beat having poison sand in my eyes.

And I was going to need cooling, that was certain. Already I could feel myself warming up on my left side, and the coolness of the night was fading, fading fast.

At least it is *my left side,* I thought. That meant I had taken the right direction last night. I'd been *pretty* sure I was heading south, but it had been a terrible, lingering doubt that somehow I'd gotten turned around and ended up going the wrong way. But going south meant the rising sun on the left.

My muscles weren't protesting *too* much yet, but I'd only been going for a couple of hours. I'd spent some of the evening right after Chiindemon's fall collecting up what I'd be able to carry — mostly water, of course, as I had a relatively short distance to go, or so I hoped, and with water and some salty foods to keep the electrolytes balanced I should be functionally all right.

The problem was the damn *featurelessness* of the desert. It had dunes and valleys and blowing sand, but all of it looked pretty much the same, and the wind erased traces of passage so it was really hard to know where you'd come from. I had to keep re-checking my bearings using the sky, and once the sun started getting high up, that might be a problem.

The white-hot disc of the sun bombarded me with light that seemed, impossibly, twice as hot as it had been on *Thunder Child*. Or maybe not impossibly; my sand-boat had done most of the work, and now I was doing all of the work — a lot of work to go short distances on dunes like this. The sand slid backwards, mocking the very idea of forward motion, flowing out from under my feet like an escalator going the wrong way. Sweat trickled down my neck, more of it down my face. My mouth and nose felt like they were breathing inside a saturated oven. I slipped, caught myself, kept going.

I had to keep making choices about how to deal with each obstacle. That dune lay right across my path — I pretty much had to go over it. But the next one ended not all that far off to the left, I could go around it. But that lengthened the route. If I did that, I'd be walking more like thirty miles. Of course, climbing up a dune slowed me up, and took energy, and I couldn't charge heedlessly down the other side to try and make up the time. *Better face it; you're doing the equivalent of thirty miles or more either way you try it. Take the route that takes the least effort.*

I reached the top of the next dune and stopped, breathing heavily, fighting the urge to rip the mask off. *No! Do not let yourself do that! Finish catching your breath! The Nomes made these things just fine, you're not suffocating no matter what it feels like!*

I drew on years of self-control over my breathing, my heart rate, my body, and forced relaxation, acceptance, slow, slow, slower... Finally, I could tell my breathing was normal. I yanked the mask off and hung it off the pack, then took out a cloth, wiped the inside, and wiped my face. *Time for a drink and a bite.*

I'd chosen this spot deliberately. There were hardly any shadows left by now, so the main point wasn't to avoid the sun, it was to avoid the slow-lethal fumes which rose from the sand. The highest point available kept me out of the worst of it — although there wasn't any true refuge outside of the mask. And the mask itself was not an unalloyed blessing.

I had to take my time drinking and even eating. Absorbing the water was vital, and I couldn't just gulp it all down, much as I wanted to. I took out another mask, putting the first away; this would give the first one more time to dry out. I yanked the mask on and continued walking.

Now my shins inside the boots were hurting, a raw, nasty feeling like I'd ripped them bleeding on pavement and then put rough canvas around them. *Sand working its way into the boots. Feeling stuff like that all over now.*

Even though I was in better shape than I'd ever been, I was starting to feel this... I was feeling it a *lot*. My legs were aching inside, too much climbing up and cautious sliding down.

It occurred to me that there might be a better way. *This is some of the most magical real estate in all of Faerie. Got to be. So...*

I stopped in one of the valleys, regained my bearings... though the sun was nearing its peak, which meant I had to also check with the wind. *All right...*

As I had when fighting Iris and Poly... months ago? Seemed like years... I raised both arms above my head and brought them down, channeling my anti-magic into the blow and visualizing it as a shockwave moving out from me.

A cataclysmic wavefront exploded outwards, smashing the dunes before me like sand castles before a tsunami, rolling onward; there was a squalling screech and I saw one of the gargantuan ant-lion creatures hurled skyward; it landed in a cloud of dust and I saw more sand ripple as it fled.

But as I surveyed the results, and tried a few cautious steps, I realized to my chagrin that I'd made things *worse*. Along the widening path of the shockwave the sand had been roiled and shaken to the point that it was of an almost unbelievably loose consistency; I'd sink to my knees, maybe just *keep* sinking, if I tried

283

walking through that. *Well THAT was brilliant, Hero. Now you've got a quarter-mile detour to make.*

I made it past my ill-considered experiment, forced my way onwards. One good aspect of it was that undoubtedly the local unnatural wildlife had just been given an unmistakable lesson as to how very, *very* bad an idea it would be to mess with me — which meant I would hopefully *not* have to actually fight anything.

I realized I had been trudging along for close to half an hour mostly staring at my feet, one foot in front of another. *Get your bearings. Sun on your left. You need to –*

I froze, my heart hammering, as I realized what I'd almost done. The sun had crested and begun to *set* while I was walking, but my tired brain had tried to just keep the same set of rules. I'd almost turned around and started walking *North.*

Concentrate. You have to keep going. Stop every so often and drink. Eat something. I wondered, with my mind now becoming slower as I became more exhausted, how fast I'd been going. *Three miles an hour? Two? If it's two, I have to keep moving for fifteen hours... if my guess was right as to how far I was.*

Fifteen hours on my feet, moving constantly. I managed a dry chuckle for a moment, the smell of my sweat momentarily overwhelming me in the mask. Before Nimbus had beaten me into shape I probably couldn't have managed to keep moving for *five* hours without resting. Here, of course, I had a...unique problem. I *couldn't* rest here, not real rest. I could pause for a few moments, yes, but I couldn't even sit down, let alone lie down and camp, get a night's sleep. I hadn't *brought* camping gear, and if someone had suggested it back in the Nomes' territory I would've laughed at them. There wasn't any place in the Deadly Desert to camp, and — if I got across safe — all the gear I could want would be arriving shortly. But until I got there, I had to stay upright. I had to keep moving. I couldn't stop. I couldn't sit. I had to stay up, or I'd die in this venomous wasteland.

I drilled myself into a monotonous routine: three dunes forward, stop, regain bearings — checking off the indicators and making sure they agreed with each other. Every ten stops, drink something.

Shadows stretched out far to the left now as the sun dropped swiftly towards the horizon. I slid numbly down the face of a dune, began the next. Part of me realized that the setting sun meant I'd been going for close to fourteen or fifteen hours already... but I hadn't seen Oz yet, not from the top of the highest dunes.

Either I was going a lot slower than I thought, or I had been way off in my calculations. If I couldn't spot Oz from the dune tops, it was at least eight or ten miles farther off, maybe more.

No choice. And while I wanted to argue that inner voice, I couldn't. I didn't have a choice. There was no other direction left for me to go, nor was there anyone else to help me.

Night fell, and sweat dried, replaced by the ache of cold that failed to dull the burning, acid pain of the sand-sores that were forming all over me. *Move. Feet forward. Three dunes. Check heading... stars... wind direction... turn slightly this way.... Move.*

The stars turned slowly overhead as I moved. It was strange, I thought as I kept walking. Light and wind and shadow made it look as though there were other things there.

A ghostly shimmer danced from dune to dune, and I started. *Polychrome!*

But she danced by and suddenly I saw it was just a tiny dust devil. *Oh, crap. I'm starting to lose it. I can't afford this!*

But there wasn't too much I could do. I was eating and drinking from my fast-shrinking supplies, but there wasn't anything in the pack to replace sleep, and it was sleep I really needed. Chiindemon had interrupted last night's sleep; I'd taken a little nap before starting out, but that wasn't the same.

My knees gave way and I tumbled down the next dune, burning cold sands stinging exposed skin, a surge of poison going up around me. I gave a tired curse and somehow levered myself up, feeling my head spinning as I did so. *Can't do that. Can't. One or two more like that and I'll never get up.*

"Never?" Zenga said to me with a pout on her face. "A hero always gets up."

"Not...a hero." I protested honestly, forcing myself to walk since she wasn't stopping. I felt it was rather unfair that she was able to walk on the sand without sinking ankle deep or more. "Just... lucky, I guess."

"Walking aimlessly in the Deadly Desert? This you call luck?"

I laughed, but it was funny how it sounded more like a cough. "I've gotten to do...a lot of traveling. Besides," I pointed down, "you're just...a delusion. No footprints, no feet." I felt very proud of that deduction, and apparently she agreed with me because she wasn't there the next time I looked up.

That was a shame though, because the black desert was terribly lonely. I wondered if the ant-lions got lonely out here. It must be a terribly boring existence. I stood still, wondering what I was doing on top of this sand dune. The sand looked very soft. I reached down — *ouch!*

"Rest is for the winners, not those who haven't proven themselves, mortal!"

I shook my hand, trying to get the pain out of it, and glared at Nimbus. "You didn't have to hit me that hard."

"You hit yourself. Take your bearings, Erik Medon."

Oh, *that* was what I was up here for. I blinked and focused. It seemed to take a long time to run through the sequence. In fact I got confused and had to start again. "Okay...this way." I started sliding down the dune. It was hard. My body wanted to just fall, but I knew I couldn't.

The next stop I was puzzled. I kept tipping the canteen up and nothing was coming out. Finally Ruggedo made me drop it. "It's empty, boy. You have to move on."

"I've got another," I protested.

The old Nome was walking ahead of me. Oddly he looked a lot more like the Neill drawings, a round ball of a body on bandy legs, with a wide jewelled belt around his nonexistent waist. "You need to save that for the day, friend."

I wish he hadn't walked back into that dune. Christ, I'm having a hard time telling reality from these half-waking dreams! I made myself check bearings quickly this time; the last thing I needed was to *dream* I'd checked them right. But it seemed I'd drilled that habit in well enough to stick.

I could see the dunes a lot better now. Maybe I was finally getting used to the night. The silvery color of the light seemed a bit warmer, too.

Light flared across the sand and I suddenly woke up a bit more with the realization I'd kept moving through the *entire night*. I almost collapsed. *I've been going more than twenty-four hours, dammit. Have I gotten turned around? Am I just going insanely slow?*

The wind hissed and chuckled around me, and the acid burning scent of the sands rose up, redoubled. My eyes hurt so badly I could barely squint ahead. A light laugh floated across the dunes.

I yanked my head up. Poly was there, dancing at the top of the next dune. She glanced back, laughed again, and danced down the other side.

"Poly!" I called, before I realized it was another dream. Nothing of Faerie could be here, and certainly not anyone on my side. Trembling legs moved slowly, I staggered more than once, but I reached the top.

And for the first time in an age and a half I felt a glimmer of hope, because far ahead I could see something else, something dark and tinged with purple-green and other colors, stretching from one horizon to the other.

That's Oz!

The realization that I could *see* the greatest of the lands of Faerie, that I was that close, gave me a spurt of energy that lasted for several dunes. Now I didn't have to check direction except by an occasional glance forward.

But it was still a long way off; miles. I drank most of the last canteen in what seemed like one long pull, gnawed some salted meat, then finished the water and tossed the canteen aside.

I'm almost there. Keep moving! Keep moving! I'll be damned *if I'm going to collapse in* sight *of Oz!*

I slipped and tumbled, shielding my eyes against the explosion of lethal sand. *I'm too weak. I can't get up!*

"Yes, you can."

I couldn't believe it. I knew that voice. I looked up at the speaker, a man with white hair and a face whose lines were so very much like my own. "Dad?"

"Erik, get *up*. I know you're tired. It's just a little farther."

"I'm sorry. I never did finish anything I started."

"Don't apologize." I somehow got up. He was helping me, I just couldn't quite see how. "Just finish *this*. You're not going to disappoint her, are you?"

"You...never met her."

He shook his head. "Wish I could have."

It was then I remembered he was dead — lung cancer — and I reached out as he faded away into the next dune. I felt a tear on my face. *I'm not going to disappoint her, Dad.*

I drove myself on somehow. I fell, I got up, each time sure there was just no way I could manage it, but remembering Poly, remembering her promise to me. I had to make it.

Finally, after what seemed an endless time of burning heat and corrosive fumes and sickness dragging like weights, I looked up and realized that I was going to fail.

Oz loomed up before me, a low plateau rising up out of the lethal sandy sea, and — for as far as I could look in either direction — there was not a single path up. A fifty-foot cliff barred any entry.

I screamed out my denial, but my throat made it a pained whisper: "No."

Had I reached here in *Thunder Child*, I'd have been able to climb that like a mountain goat. Hell, if you'd dropped my untrained overweight self here, I might still have made it up. But I could barely force one foot in front of the other, lift them enough to climb the last small dunes between me and that final barrier. I couldn't possibly climb it.

Part of me wanted to laugh, the other to cry. It was unbearably ironic that I had managed to make it through every threat I'd encountered, on sea and under rock, walking through the Deadly Desert itself, killing self-proclaimed demons and monsters of the Usurpers and here, now, I was helpless against a tiny wall of rock. *Goddamn it, I climbed up a thirty thousand foot mountain. Now fifty feet of rock beats me?*

But I knew with certainty it was true. I didn't have the strength left, not even enough to try some True Mortal stunt. I was only standing because I knew, with the same certainty, that if I fell again I really would never get up again.

I looked up, seeing a hint of grassy movement, a flutter of a few purple tinted leaves. A bird flew a few inches over the edge, turned back, never looking down; of course, there never was anything to see. I wondered if I could get its attention somehow.

And then it hit me. One last chance.

I reached inside my armor — which had been at least as cool as any clothing could have been — and grasped the Jewel of the Bridge. "One chance, Poly."

The *Jewel* had to reach the land of Oz, lie on its soil.

I pulled off the mask, let it drop, let the goggles follow. I needed to be as unencumbered as possible. I looked carefully, judged the angles... and then wound up and *threw* the Jewel as hard as I could, the very last ounce of strength going into the throw, sending me backward, down, hitting the sand heavily.

The glittering Jewel arced up, tumbling end over end, rising up, getting closer — *oh no, it's going to hit the cliff!*

But just as it seemed the multicolored gem would bounce off the dark stone, it reached the apex of its arc and — just barely — cleared the edge, brushing aside a few blades of grass and disappearing.

My hands were burning where they lay in the sand; I tried to lift them but they were too heavy. *Maybe if I just rest a minute...* I wanted to keep my eyes open, but they *hurt* so much and the sun was so bright and maybe I was wrong, maybe I had to be there to place the gem...

Voices.

"... almost dead..."

"Can't use much magic on him..."

"... do us no good dead!"

I was in terrible pain, but it was also so *distant*. I felt that all I had to do was let go.

Something cool touching my lips. "Please, Erik, drink, please..."

289

I couldn't even place the voice, but something about it... I had to do what that voice wanted... I opened cracked lips, swallowed, but the act of swallowing caused splintering pain.

But the moment the first swallow passed through, the pain began to ease. I took another swallow, and another, and suddenly everything seemed to be growing clearer as my pains started to fade away. I opened my eyes.

A radiant vision of golden hair and violet-storm eyes hovered above me, perfect cheeks startlingly marred by two tears trickling down. "Poly...?"

"Erik!" Her face lit up, now so beautiful that I couldn't have spoken even if I had to, and she grasped my hands between hers for a moment, that single contact sending a surge of strength through me that had nothing to do with the healing potion. "I... I'm so glad."

"Believe me," I said, wishing I had the courage to reach out and take her hands again, "not nearly as glad as I am."

Third Vision:

Т he burning light still surrounded her, and at times she wanted to scream, and tried, but the bodilessness of her nonexistence prevented it. Sometimes, in the depths of the terrible radiance, she heard voices, but she did not know if they were delusion or reality. Insanity danced around her like a taunting insect and a blessed promise of relief in one, and it was so *hard* not to welcome it.

But Hope remained, a single point of darkness in a world of blasting white and searing green, burning red and screaming violet, incinerating blue and corrosive yellow. She followed it, tried to cup it in her hands, but she had no hands, no voice to call to it, no body to run with. Only the sight without eyes, the vision of the magic of Faerie burning, burning her away.

The blessed cooling darkness was tiny, but no longer a single point. It moved, now here, now there, but slowly approaching her through the tracklessness of the blank realm of Faerie-fire. The screaming of her mind was — sometimes — less when it seemed a bit closer.

Now, she thought within the thoughtless blankness of pain, it appeared to be moving closer still, with swift purpose. Almost, almost she could descry a shape within, a shape she desperately longed to know.

But now it was still! It moved no longer!

Wait…it did, now, but slowly, so much more slowly, as though wounded. She shook a head that was not there, biting back another cry of fear and loss. The darkness was fading. Trailing strands of dark shadow rose, lightened, faded like steam, like ice melting and sending evanescent vapor into the air, to disappear forever. *No. No.*

But it shrank more, still moving towards her, but fading, like a cloud promising rain but passing over the desert, shrinking to nothingness. Now it had faded to a single point of darkness, so close, yet as small as it had been when first she had known Hope,

291

and she would have closed her eyes in fear and denial, but there were no eyes to close as even that tiny point of blessed blackness began to disappear.

She knew then that Hope was gone, and madness was the best she might hope for; that perhaps she could reach out to that taunting insect and escape knowledge of torment. Yet she was not quite ready.

And then the Darkness flared up, a point, a dot, a spot growing, rising, *towering*, shoving aside blazing fire-white, consuming the all-consuming radiance, becoming a figure, a man's figure, standing against the light as though he stood before her, not fifty yards distant, and she laughed, with delight that denied the possibility of madness, for the screaming of her soul faded even as the darkness grew and filled her with comfort; she could *hear* the voices around her now, slow, voices of dreamlike distance, but voices that were *alive*. A young woman murmuring of the distant Nome Kingdom, a clever old man whispering spells he wished he had completed; inanimate straw thinking of ways out of deadlock, a mighty cat holding to courage in his heart...

Her friends were *not* dead, and a True Mortal had set foot on the land of Oz itself, and now it was not the light, but Hope, that was the brightest flame of all.

Chapter 42.

"They are coming, Princess."

She turned, heart beating faster. "You're sure, Nimbus?"

Nimbus nodded. "The birds of Oz have, for the most part, been unaffected by the Usurpers' actions, but still they have been aware of the change. Many of them now serve us as scouts, and they have sighted the Army of the Usurpers on the other side of this part of the Twilight Forest."

She said nothing as she tested the buckles and straps of her armor, then took up her sword-belt and put it on. "How many?"

"The Doves will have that information for us soon. From the first report, I would guess no more than thirty thousand. They are holding back much of their force; this is a test. They do not intend to stop us here, I think, unless we turn out to be much weaker than they expect. Their commander wishes to see what forces we have at our command, observe our strategies, decide on what tactics will be most effective in the final battle."

She frowned, trying to look as serious and confident as her father would. *I can't help but feel this is all just some terrible stage-play. If only someone would bring down a curtain.* "Should we hold back our own most important resources, then? Hide our advantages?"

"It's a difficult question indeed, Princess," Ruggedo said. "Nimbus and I have been considering that very issue for the past two days."

"On the one hand," Nimbus said with a nod, "holding some of our most unusual and significant powers in reserve means that we leave unknowns in our adversaries' ability to guess what we can do, and how we might do it. This is not an insignificant advantage."

"On the other," Ruggedo took up the discussion, "there is a great deal to be said for a direct and full confrontation, especially against a smaller force. A swift and final victory against their forces would very much reduce our casualties, in all likelihood, and has very significant benefits in terms of morale."

Polychrome nodded slowly. *What a tragic joke. They are looking at me, waiting for the Princess of the Rainbow to make the decision.*

"The three of us — and Lord Erik, of course — know what the real purpose of this invasion is, gentlemen." She felt cold and distant, speaking that way, but it was the only way she dared speak about the subject. "The fact is that it is on his shoulders — and his alone — that final victory rests. We must of course be prepared to fight as well as may be if, by terrible chance, he fails, but the real focus of our attack is to present a credible threat *and* to place ourselves, and Erik Medon, in a position where he can be captured in some manner, while not *looking* as though this is an outcome we expected or desired."

The two nodded. "Clearly stated, and understood, Princess. How do you see this applying to the decision?"

She tried to smile lightly, as though pointing out something of entertaining consequences. "Well, they can hardly scheme to capture and use our True Mortal in their nefarious plans if they don't know what he is, can they?"

Ruggedo gave a snort of surprise. "Boulders and brace-beams! I hadn't thought of that, but you're entirely right, my dear. He has to be seen *now*. They need time to see his actions, realize what they mean, and *then* formulate some plan to take him from us, or force us to give him up."

Nimbus looked at her with respect. "Well thought, Princess. And that *does* make the decision obvious."

"We can't unleash *him* without throwing all of our major forces at them as well," concurred Ruggedo. "Doing so would indicate there was some reason we wanted that weapon — one which, one would expect, would be *most* effective if kept secret up until confrontation with Ugu and Amanita directly — called to their attention."

"But if we simply do an all-out assault, the assumption will be that we are doing it to maximize the speed of our victory, minimize the cost, and hopefully break the morale of the opposition, as well as allow us to make it to the Grey City as quickly as possible," Polychrome finished. It was a hard decision to make, but this one made sense; it *felt* right, even though the reasons behind it made a part of her feel like it was dying. "So we will hold no reserves; we will do our best to crush this first force utterly." She wondered that yet *another* part of her seemed almost...*eager.*

"Agreed." Nimbus and Ruggedo looked at her again. Finally, the old Nome said, "Your father...chose well, Princess." He tilted his head, as though listening. "They are nearly ready, I think. Come." He led the way out of her command tent and to the crest of the ridge.

Erik and Zenga were already there, the two close but like companions and friends, no more; Polychrome still didn't know what to make of the fact that this thought somehow cheered her. It wasn't at all fair to either of them, and why they *weren't* close she didn't understand; something must have happened when she hadn't been watching, but she was afraid to ask what. She knew Erik was easily embarrassed, and from occasional glances she didn't think that Zenga had changed her mind.

Polychrome looked down from the hill of broken stone; on the purple-tinged plain, stretching out before her like a field of bladed wheat, the Armies of Faerie were assembled. At the front-and-center, the sparkling forces of the Rainbow Kingdom, armor of diamond and pearl and sapphire, swords and spears like bitter icy blades, siege engines sculpted from mist and crystal and crackling with the power of the storm and light.

Surrounding them, backing and reinforcing them, the immense army of the Nomes, stony grey and obsidian-black and earthy brown, with startling blazes of gems here and there amidst the rank-and-file, with the officers' corps arrayed in gold and silver, with swords of cold iron. Here and there, immense engines of steam-power and gears moved with earthshaking deliberation, unstoppable-seeming weapons of war that had the shapes of men or monsters.

The latter had caused Erik to give vent to another of his incomprehensible exclamations of joy: "*Sugoi*! Steampunk mecha! I wonder if they have Sparks among the Nomes?"

She found herself looking at him again with relief swelling in her heart. *We did not dare use more magic to heal him; for a few hours, we thought it might already have been too much, but his Mortal nature strengthened.* And he had recovered with impressive speed; in the two days they had been here, he seemed to have come fully back to himself.

Erik turned from his appreciation of the view and caught her looking, and she saw his face...change, somehow, soften, yet seem for a moment more intense than ever, an intensity that made her shiver even though the sun was warm. But before she could think of what that meant, or what she ought to say, he spoke.

"You did this."

"What?" She laughed uncomfortably. *How can he say that? I just...did what Father asked.* "Father gave me the forces of the Rainbow. You were the one who brought the Nomes. I'm..." She trailed off as he shook his head, smiling.

"You are the one *they* will follow, Poly. Nimbus told me how a few simple words from you brought his soldiers — men he'd trained and led all his life — to their feet with a cheer that shook the very castle, that brought them down to join with the Nomes as though they had been brothers all along; how that unstinting openness warmed the Nomes' own hearts and caused them to take up the same cry — a battle cry *you* invented, a cry that sends *chills* down my spine from its pure rightness. And you did *this.*"

He swept his arm out across the field, where the last groups of their forces were falling into formation — a small contingent of the Sea Fairies, a band of the Noble Pirates of the Nonestic, the Royal Guard of Ev, not many, not many at all...

Erik seemed to hear her thoughts, for he answered her as though he did: "...no, not many, but enough, enough for those watching to know that not one of the lands of Faerie will stand idly by, that all of them know the Usurpers are their enemies and no longer will they pretend to be friends or allies or even neutral."

She saw his eyes shining as he looked out over the sea of warriors, seventy-five thousand strong and more, and suddenly he raised his voice, a baritone that somehow echoed out across the plain. "No, Polychrome; *you* let it be known, even as I set out across the desert, that the Rainbow Lord and the Nome Kingdom were making their stand, and that you, Polychrome Glory, called upon them to show where they stood...and they *came*, Polychrome, they came because *you* called, because through all of Faerie there is no one else left that is so known or so loved as the First Daughter of the Rainbow."

Her eyes stung and she dared not blink or look away — or look too closely at him, and looked out at the arrayed armies, who were looking up, listening, and she realized that Nimbus and Ruggedo stood near them, and Ruggedo had raised the Scepter of Command that Kaliko had given him; that was receiving Erik's words, casting them outward across the entirety of the Armies of Faerie.

The Mortal turned and suddenly shouted out, his voice thundering across the Gillikin Plain below. "What say you, warriors of Faerie? Will you follow Polychrome Glory against the armies of the Usurpers? Will you risk the pain of war and the oblivion of death for the sake of Oz and all your lands? Will you risk it for *her?*"

And seventy-five thousand voices answered with a roar that shook sand from the hill and swayed the trees in the great forest beyond, "*WE WILL!*"

The tears did come, then. *I don't deserve this! The carefree Faerie girl who never stayed, never listened, never* hurt *as they, how could they follow* me?

But in that moment, Erik spoke, this time in a voice only those on the hilltop could hear, low and earnest. "I will."

Ruggedo's craggy face glanced at the mortal man and at her, and she saw a smile send a ray of whiter white past the snowy beard and mustache. "As will I."

Zenga studied her for a moment, and she, too, seemed to see something that made her smile, though hers looked almost like a challenge. "And I."

"All of us will, Princess," Nimbus said.

She took the Scepter then and spoke. "Armies of Faerie..." Her voice almost broke — *did* break, a little — and she swallowed.

Chuckles rippled out across the assembled armies, and she suddenly smiled, tears still in her eyes, and let those tears be heard in the tone of her voice. *Why shouldn't they know the truth?* "Armies of Faerie...I am as frightened as many of you, as appalled as

297

all of you that we have come to this. But what you have heard is true. There *is* a Prophecy."

The Armies came to complete and still attention, listening. "There *is* a Prophecy, one that tells us that we have a chance of victory, no matter what the power of the Usurpers, no matter what their strategies or all the forces they can muster. And we have fulfilled a part of that prophecy even now, just by coming here, through the Great Barrier, where none of Faerie have passed without their will in three centuries and more. We face the Usurpers on their own stolen ground, and with a force such as Faerie has never seen."

A Dove fluttered down and landed on her shoulder, and spoke in her ear. She listened, blinked away the tears, and then let the rising silver song of the Spheres that answered the fear and anticipation in her heart bring a brilliant smile to her lips. "And now they come, their army is sighted — and we outnumber them better than three to one!"

There were some cheers, but murmurs as well. *I have to keep their belief, even if I don't trust myself as well. Father has faith in me. Nimbus does. I have to have faith that I will not fail them.* "What's that? You say that this is but a tithe of their strength? That they hold back their might to test us? That they have fell warriors of the Usurpers' magic, their engines of dark power, their Tempests and Infernos, their Temblors and Torrents?" She heard, in her own voice, an echo of the power and certainty of her Father, of Iris Mirabilis' absolute conviction. "True enough; yet what of it? We have our weapons as well, Armies of Faerie. We have the Thunder of Dawn and Sunset, the Nomes' Engines of Destruction. We have Princess Zenga of Pingaree. We have Lord Erik Medon, who — alone, unaided — crossed the Deadly Desert, who comes to us — like the Princess Dorothy, like the mighty Wizard — from the Outside World, the Mortal World, in our moment of need, as they always have — as they always will, for the sake of the touch of Faerie in their hearts that endures even in the mortal world.

"But we have more than that!" she shouted, and now they *were* all watching her again. "We have ourselves, our companions, and the Above. We have unity. We are not here to grasp power for ourselves, but freedom. We fight for our homes, our friends...our souls, in truth.

"And we will *show* them that truth." She looked at the mass before her, the Nomes, the Sky Faeries, the small but precious additions. "And I will lead you, though I feel smaller than the task demands." Now she drew her sword, feeling a chill run down her own spine at the thought of what that meant.

She turned and pointed to the forest before them. "Beyond that our enemies lie in wait. They have enslaved our brothers and sisters, and those we will have to face before we reach their masters. But they will not stop us. They *cannot* stop us. What is your cry?"

"Earth and Sky shall move as one!"

"Yes!" she shouted, "that and more, I say, for more have come. Earth and Sky and *Sea* shall move as one!"

"Earth and Sky and Sea!" they answered, and took a step forward, and the earth shook. "Earth and Sky and Sea!" Another step, and birds fled from the trees before them. "Earth and Sky and Sea!" And the thunder of their march rolled out like a storm on a promontory.

She turned and leapt down the hillside, lightly in her armor, coming to the head of the great formation, and the others came with her. Her smile stayed, brilliant and almost savage, but inside she felt terror and elation in a nauseating, incomprehensible mixture. *I'm leading so many of them to die...and we may all be just a distraction. We are just a distraction, a ploy, to get Erik to where he has to go.*

The thought made the smile falter, because she knew where the mortal man needed to go, and what awaited him at the Grey Castle, and something in her seemed to go cold. But she forced her thoughts away from that.

"Well done indeed, Princess," Nimbus said, as they marched through the forest, trees moving aside, making room for the columns to pass. "But you left out one of our greatest weapons of all."

She blinked. "I did?"

"Yourself, Princess."

She wanted to laugh. "Compared to the others? I have some skill—"

"We can afford no false modesty — nor honest underestimation, either," the Commander of the Storm Guards said bluntly. "You are your father's daughter. You are his chosen successor. Within you runs the strength of the Above, if only you have the will to use it. We have a mighty army — and as you say, not just from your actions, but because our Hero has proven to be equal, thus far, to every task set before him. But it will not be our army that will break that of the Usurpers. If — and I admit, I say only if — that can be done, it will be because of the four great forces we command: the presence of a True Mortal, the Strength of the Princess of the Sea, the Will of the Penitent, and," he touched her arm, "the Power of the Rainbow's Daughter."

Chapter 43.

I stood at the forefront of the Armies of Faerie and stared at our opposition. Less than a mile distant, thousands of forms — some mere dots, others visible as twisted shapes that hinted at their immense size and power, others clearly engines of destruction such as those of the Nomes and the Rainbow Kingdom — sat motionless, awaiting some signal to move forward. They sat directly in front of a narrow valley, the only pass through the low range of mountains that lay across our path; if we had to go *around* that, we'd add nearly two hundred miles to our march and lose days of time, so getting through that pass was a major objective.

My heart hammered and my hands, when I reached back and grabbed my sword hilt for its faint reassurance, were clammy, slick with sweat. It was one thing to confront individual monsters, however terrifying. This, though...this was war, and before us were almost uncountable numbers of monsters, any of which were willing and perhaps able to kill me...or my allies.

I glanced to Polychrome, something I was doing far too often to be safe. But she was beautiful — even more beautiful than I remembered, which seemed impossible. But in that silvery armor, sword at her side, she looked less Daughter of the Rainbow and more a slender goddess of war, a Valkyrie whose courage was the equal of her beauty.

I tore my gaze away and faced forward. "What are we waiting for?"

"These things must be done properly," Nimbus responded. "We have brought our armies to face one another. Now one or the other will send out messengers under truce — most likely they will, as they hold this ground — and we shall formally introduce ourselves and present our demands, and they theirs. When we reject their terms, the battle will begin."

I shook my head. "Where I come from, they'd have started the attack by now. Probably by a rearward assault, aerial bombardment, or simply by having mined the area we're going to walk over."

Ryk E. Spoor

"Then allow me to say I prefer this way; war is terrible enough without it being something without restraint or honor."

I wasn't going to argue with Nimbus. To be honest, I was of two minds on the matter. This was a...prettier and more ceremonious way to wage war, perhaps, and seemed somehow more civilized, an echo of ancient traditions which probably had never really been adhered to in the real world, but in the end it was going to come down to sheer ugliness nonetheless. And the ceremony might simply be covering that up, allowing people to pretend that war was something more glorious and noble than it was.

Five figures advanced across the waving grasses, the foremost carrying a white flag. I glanced at the others; Polychrome nodded, and the five of us — Polychrome, myself, Nimbus, Ruggedo, and Zenga — moved forward to meet them.

As they got closer, we could see that it was one humanoid figure — no, too short, a Nome, almost certainly — with four others: one flowing, coiling Torrent; a glowing-eyed Temblor; a dancing flame of Inferno; and one of the green-black crackling Tempests.

Ruggedo was the first to speak. "Guph, my old friend. So we meet once more."

General Guph did a double-take as Ruggedo pulled back his hood. "Ruggedo? You cowardly old tyrant, you petulant little child, how do *you* come into this?"

Only the narrowing of Ruggedo's eyes showed his annoyance at the insults. "Oh, here and there, *old friend*. I see you've found someone else to hold your leash while I've been gone."

Before Guph could do more than begin a snarling retort (rather, I thought, like the dog Ruggedo implied he was), Polychrome held up her hand. "Enough. General Guph, you represent the Armies of the Usurpers?"

He looked proudly back at her. "I represent the Armies of Ugu the Unbowed and Amanita Verdant, King and Queen of all Oz. They call upon you, who have intruded unwanted upon their domains, to surrender immediately or be destroyed; if you surrender, you shall be brought before them to experience their judgment and mercy." His smile did not engender confidence in the

302

nature of that mercy. "And who are you, who speaks for these invaders?"

"I am Polychrome Glory, Princess of the Rainbow Kingdom," she responded.

The note I heard in her voice was that of steel being unsheathed; I felt a chill go down my spine. *How can that make me find her even more gorgeous? I guess I like them badass as well as beautiful.*

That reminded me of Zenga in her triumph, and I looked at her on my other side. She had a smile like a tiger baring its teeth. *Oh yeah, that is definitely it.*

"I am Polychrome Glory," she repeated, "and I lead the Armies of Faerie, the Storm Legions and the Nomes and many others, and I say to you and your masters that it is *you* who must surrender or be destroyed."

Guph began to laugh.

"*Silence!*" she snapped. The Nome General's laughter cut off instantly, to his astonishment, and maybe — judging by the momentary blinking of her eyes — to Polychrome's as well. But she did not pause. "You laugh at your peril, Nome, traitor to Faerie. Here assembled is a force never seen between the Above and Below, and though I be no warrior," the glittering of her armor making that seem an ironic and dangerous lie, "I have threescore and fifteen thousand at my command, and other powers besides. Consider well, General Guph, for this chance will not be given you again. Surrender, or, if you will, stand aside and let us pass. Hinder us not, and you and your people will live past this day."

Guph had recovered from the shock of her command, and was studying us with a military precision. He nodded, a tiny show of respect. "Your...courteous offer is noted. But I and my...associates," the four twisted elementals chuckled in tortured sounds, "feel you overstate your case, and overestimate your powers. Perhaps — perhaps, I say — you may gain victory over these forces, but many more await...and at the end, you must face Amanita Verdant and Ugu the Unbowed, and none of you are their equal. So your offer, too, is rejected."

"Then, General, the battle must begin. My pity to your forces."

"Save that for your own."

Both groups withdrew speedily then, and I could feel tense sweat under my armor, cool though it usually kept me. *And I am supposed to be one of their super-weapons. I wonder how the regular warriors can stand it.*

"General," Polychrome said, still with the steel in her tone, "I give command over to you. As you will, direct our forces, including myself."

And then suddenly she turned to me, stepping away from Nimbus as he began signaling the troops. "Erik...I wish we were back in the Rainbow Kingdom, studying," she said, in a voice that was shaky, low, unsure.

At that moment, I wanted nothing more than to reach out and take her in my arms. But even if she had allowed it, it would have been a terrible mistake; she might speak to me like this, but no one else could see that she was any less than she had allowed herself to appear just a few moments ago.

"So do I, Poly," I said, remembering the year I had spent with her... Now, I realized, it had been the happiest year I had ever lived, though I'd been driven by Nimbus to efforts I could never have imagined. Though I hadn't ever had the courage – or more likely the stupidity – to speak to her about what I felt. "So do I. But this is the beginning of the end. One way or another, we'll finish this."

"And after –" She stopped suddenly.

Could it be? I didn't dare think on that. "If there *is* an after for me," I reminded her, emphasizing what had obviously stopped her there. "If there is... Well, we'll talk about that then."

"Lord Erik, it begins," Ruggedo said quietly.

The Usurpers' Army was on the move, a large contingent moving forward, a smaller group remaining concentrated before the pass through the mountains. At the same time, trumpets sounded and now our army began to move, splitting into three sections, twenty-five thousand to the left, twenty-five thousand to the right, and the last twenty-five thousand straight forward. "No subtlety of strategy this time," Nimbus said as we marched forward slightly slower than the main body, letting them come between us and the initial forces of the enemy. "I will keep my skills in reserve; the

304

point of this battle, as we decided, is to hammer home to them our utter superiority. For that we use no special tactics save one, and that one after the first clash, when we have a chance to evaluate their forces."

Half a mile separated the forces, and suddenly, almost as though signaled by the same impulse, the great war machines on both sides cut loose. Red-blue bolts of lightning screamed out into the Usurpers' Army from Thunder of Dawn and Sunset, while black fireballs hurtled down upon our forces from a monstrous trebuchet seemingly carven of dark bones. One globe of ebony was dropping towards us; I gathered myself, but Polychrome held up her hand and shouted something in which I heard the name of her father; multicolored light caught the ball, crushed it into a shadow, into nothing.

Other great weapons were firing, blasts of light and dark, cold and fire, stone missiles and concussions of air battering at each other. The two armies were *moving* now, charging, a hundred and fifty yards apart, weapons cleared, spells being woven, shields of bright and dark materializing, Nomes in hard stone armor backing glittering-crystal Storm Guards while Infernos and Tempests bore down upon them. A hundred yards, fifty, twenty –

The clash of two armies was an echoing, shattering sound that shook the plains, thousands of throats shouting orders, screaming in rage or pain, swords meeting in bell-ringing opposition as spell rebounded from spell-shield or tore through with terrible effect.

Our fears were true; one to one, our men and women were no match for most of the Usurpers' enchanted warriors, not even with the armor and arms of two Faerie kingdoms to draw upon. Tempests swirled through the ranks, controlled and hungry tornadoes, while the Temblors bashed through their opposition like walking landslides, Infernos turned our soldiers to ash, Torrents battered shields and bodies aside like a remorseless flood.

But there were far more of ours than theirs, and the monstrous creations of Ugu and Amanita had a fatal flaw; they *were* monsters, not very bright ones either, and were driven as much by hatred and a lust for destruction as they were by orders. Nomes and Storm Legions reformed, organized, focused, and by blade and spear and spell began to methodically, mercilessly, and inexorably whittle away at the berserk elementals, withdrawing, striking, distracting, using the maddened hatred to blunt the charge, divert them to something just out of reach and then strike from behind, causing the creatures to reverse, hitting them again.

The human forces — drafted from the Four Countries, Munchkin, Gillikin, Quadling, Winkie — may have been enhanced, modified, or controlled, or merely intimidated into serving; but in no way could they match this trained and coordinated force, not even directed by a General such as Guph. I realized that even with the superior powers of the Dark Elementals, our army would triumph.

But the goal here was not just triumph, but, as the game might say, "flawless victory." Nimbus was watching, and I saw him straighten and gesture to us.

"There. Ahead of us. We need to break their hold on the pass. They have their most powerful forces there," he said. "Princess, Lord Erik, Princess Zenga...Penitent," he continued, "*That* is your goal. I want you to go and break them, cut through their forces from here to there as swiftly as you may, destroying what you can of their resources on the way, and then shatter their blockade. Lord Erik, you will lead the way, the others will follow and strike as they see best."

My mouth felt like sandpaper and I almost couldn't speak. *There's at least four or five thousand warriors between here and there, and gods alone know what else!* I thought, but didn't say. Instead, I swallowed, and pasted a smile on my face. "No problem," I said.

His smile showed he saw through to my heart. He raised his hand, and the trumpeters blew a fanfare — one of those, I realized, they'd blown when I left the Rainbow Kingdom, and I glanced at Polychrome. She remembered too, and for just an instant she grasped my hand, squeezed, and I squeezed back. I had no doubts at all.

Seize your dreams. Be the Hero, if only for a few moments.

I charged forward, and the three others followed, as the mass of the Usurpers' Army loomed before us.

Chapter 44.

Father and those Above, grant us the fortune to survive this, she thought, offering a rare prayer to the Powers which she knew existed, but almost never saw. *Because it would be so terribly ironic for us to die here before we reach the end of the Prophecy, while trying to draw attention to ourselves.*

The Armies of Faerie parted before them, and the four crashed into the main line of the enemy. But before the forces of the Usurpers could recognize the change, she saw Erik leap up, twenty, thirty, forty feet up, a jump that told her just how magical the entire Land of Oz must be, and come down, drawing his arm back to deliver a strike to the very ground itself.

She braced herself, remembering the first time he'd used that trick in the battle against Iris Mirabilis and herself; even so, the concussion staggered her, caused the front ten ranks of their own armies to stumble and fall to one knee; but that was the merest remnant, the backwash that the True Mortal couldn't quite control. In front of him, fanning outward like floodwaters across the plains, the earth *rippled*, heaved itself up and flung hundreds, thousands of the opposing army flat, sent them spinning helpless through the air, toppled siege engines like toys. At the point of impact the ground was shattered; Erik stood alone in a dust-smoking crater, a blue-indigo-crystal-armored figure whose terrible power now, for a moment, had caused the entire battle to pause, all eyes staring at the inexplicable.

Of all the opposing creatures caught in the earthshock, only those that flew had been unaffected. After that moment of stunned immobility, the Tempests and Infernos screamed towards Erik Medon.

But Polychrome found herself already in motion. Springing from the edge of the crater, she leapt into the air, dancing on spectral light to meet the first Tempest with her sword. Its dark-crackling blade parried her strike, and then shattered to pieces. She watched, feeling almost outside herself, as Nimbus' training sent her arm on a swift and sure course through the creature's center; it burst in a whirl of dark energy and the body fell, looking now more like a human than a monster.

I... I killed *him!* The thought brought nausea to her gut, even as she turned towards an Inferno's blazing brightness, and she wavered for a moment, blocking the fiery blows of its weapon but unable to bring herself to strike.

At the same time, she felt that strange, alien excitement rising. Below her, Erik struck twice and two of the Usurper's monsters collapsed, puppets whose strings of power had been severed. The Penitent whirled his battlestaff and his blows struck fast and hard; she wondered, for Ruggedo seemed even more powerful, more swift and deadly, than he had when first they met.

Movement caught her eye, one of the stone-throwing siege engines slewing around, coming to bear on Erik, and her uncertainty evaporated. Two more blows and the fire before her blew out, ended in smoke; the nausea was still there, but fainter, and the excitement rose, a cold and thrilling feeling of certainty that terrified her even as it lifted her up in elation. "Erik! To your right!" she called.

His head turned, but it might be too late, the siege engine was loaded, almost aligned –

"Now *that* shall never happen!" The clear, confident voice was Zenga's.

From the other side of the crater, the Princess of Pingaree picked up and hurled one of the other, toppled siege engines, throwing the multi-ton mystical cannon as though it were a child's toy. It collided with one about to fire on Erik, and the two shattered in a black explosion that cast soldiers aside like burning chaff.

"Well struck!" Ruggedo shouted.

Erik's grateful grin to Zenga was echoed in the dark-skinned girl's own brilliant smile. Just as Polychrome registered the odd fact that something about that exchange of glances bothered her, Erik looked at her, and that was gone from her mind. Somehow, she knew what he was thinking.

"Follow me!" he shouted to the others before catching Polychrome as she dropped towards him. Then he *flung* her up and outwards, hurtling forward at a speed her dancing couldn't have matched. Another concussion, focused, clearing the way, as she landed ahead, atop one of the dark magical engines hurling destruction at her army. She found herself laughing as she danced aside, around the defenders, striking down Temblor and Torrent, Inferno and Tempest, as though they were the least of Nimbus' soldiers. The weapon itself shattered as Erik reached it.

It was not the Mortal's strike, but Zenga's, that cleared the next path, with a boulder the size of a house. She glanced behind, and saw that the Penitent was methodically and unstoppably guarding their backs, his blows as solid as the foundations of the earth, his defenses as impenetrable as a mountain.

From one mobile fortress to the next they moved, and it was like a dance, a wonderful, terrifying, perfect dance. Erik would catch her, toss her, then return, be carried by her upwards, then down; it was as though she knew his moves, and he hers, before either of them spoke a word. He merely looked, and she knew where they went and what they were doing.

A mob of fiery abominations swept down upon her, scorching her cheeks, pain of heat through even the silver Armor of the Above, but the pain meant nothing. She called out the name of her father and the Rainbow Kingdom as her sword flickered back and forth like her enemies' flames, her shield caught their fire and quenched it with cold, mist-born light. And then the mob broke and fled, screaming, many of their number already fallen before her and the others now running in terror from the terrible True Mortal whose merest touch was enough to put their fires out and still their movements, perhaps forever.

That seemed almost to be a signal. The enemy army withdrew before them in ragged order, trumpets braying *retreat, regroup, fall back!*

Breathing hard, a chill of victory down her spine that made her want to cheer or cry and she knew not why, she glanced around. Erik had a few scratches, but no real injuries. Ruggedo's smile from under his hood showed no pain, and the only injury Zenga seemed to have suffered was a small cut on her upper arm.

Before them was the pass. Only a few siege engines, mostly abandoned now, blocked their way. In a few minutes, she thought, they would have finished!

But now she became aware of something else. The enemy's army had withdrawn, but now formed up into lines, leaving a wide space through which they walked; but now the enemy soldiers were saying something. Just a few at first, but then more and more, until the indistinct, rhythmic sound became louder, more forceful, and finally became a single word, repeated over and over:

"Yoop. Yoop! *Yoop!* **YOOP!**"

Erik looked over at them. "I'm not sure I like the sound of this."

From ahead, there came a booming noise, a faint shudder through the ground. Another, slightly closer, and then another, and she realized, *that sounds like...footsteps?*

Another massive footfall, another, and something *moved* ahead of them in the darkness of the pass, shoved aside barricades and rocks. There was an incoherent, echoing growl and a thirty-foot high siege engine of metal and stone was suddenly thrown aside like a pebble.

"Ohhhhh, *crap*," she heard Erik say.

From the shadows within the canyon-like pass emerged a monstrous figure. It was humanoid but stood over fifty feet tall, eyes glowing a venomous yellow, skin rough and grey and stony, a shock of black hair cascading greasily across the immense shoulders. The mouth was filled with sharp, misshapen teeth, and tatters of rich clothing were draped across the mostly-naked form, clinging as though they had been stretched across something vastly too large for them.

"YOOP! YOOP! YOOP!"

It raised an immense spiked mace whose head was more than ten feet across and roared, *"YOOOOOOP!"* Then it fixed its eyes on Polychrome's little group.

"*That*," Ruggedo said dryly, "is considerably larger than I had heard Mr. Yoop to be."

"*That*," Erik responded, eyes still fixed on the approaching monstrosity, "is what happens when you were the abusive husband of a Yookoohoo that gains enough power to teach you a lesson. The way he's walking, he's awfully solid, not just pure magic. I can hurt the hell out of him if I *get* there...but that damn mace could do me in."

"Could do *any* of us in, I suspect," Zenga said. "But perhaps his size will slow him down."

Polychrome took a deep breath, preparing herself. She shuddered as Yoop's eyes met hers. His expression had shifted slightly, and the hunger in those eyes was nothing she wanted to imagine.

The Yoop roared again and whirled the gigantic mace in a blur that made Zenga's hopes of slowness seem nothing but feeble, wishful thinking. It paused for a moment, studying them with a dull cunning.

And then the monster charged.

"Great, now I have to fight an armed King Kong. Where's Godzilla when I need him?" Erik leapt up and delivered another earthblow, sending out a shockwave to kick the giant Mr. Yoop off his feet. Polychrome and the others fanned out to take him from either side when he fell.

But with shocking agility, Yoop *hurdled* the earthshock wave, leaping over it like a runner clearing a two-foot bar, landing and swinging down with the massive mace at the same moment. Erik barely dodged out of the way and fell, knocked down this time by the shockwave created by that huge mace. Zenga pitched a boulder the size of Yoop's head at the giant, but he caught the stony missile with one hand, threw it back. The Penitent was down near his feet and Yoop gave a pained growl as the battlestaff *cracked* against his ankle, slowing his next movements.

Polychrome ran up through the clear air and cut at Yoop's head; the parrying blow of the mace nearly knocked her from the sky, and that was a hasty blow, barely in time, without any force to speak of. She was forced to back off, trying to dart in but finding that even with her Sky-Faerie speed she was just not quite able to get through. *Whatever they've done to him, he's no longer a giant, he's not even an elemental or Faerie; he's a monster with powers such as we've never seen before!*

311

The next few minutes were a whirlwind of confusion, fear, and pain. Yoop leapt in a thunderous ballet, bringing feet down to crush, swinging mace in a path of destruction, stopping and whirling to prevent any from approaching him too closely. Erik was barely able to keep out of the way; even though he was able to cut through the magical mace with his own sword, it carried such impact that the mortal was hammered to his knees by the slightest touch of the weapon. Zenga was no faster than he, and her strength did not make her invulnerable. The Penitent could only evade and strike, hoping — though such hope seemed terribly forlorn — that in time the small painful strikes would wear him down.

And this is the weapon they sent with their smaller force. What abominations are waiting for us at the Grey Castle? Polychrome didn't know what she could do. She had managed three cuts — the merest scratches against something like Yoop — and those only when the monstrous Giant focused its attention on one of the others. Never could she get near any vital areas.

And then it happened.

Zenga, hefting another gigantic missile, stumbled the slightest bit. But it was enough to slow her, to make her unable to drop and dodge, as the giant spiked mace whipped around towards her.

And — as Polychrome knew all too well — the supernal strength granted by the Pearl did not come with invulnerability.

At the last possible split second, another figure barreled in, shouting *"ZENGA!"* With a desperate shove, he sent the dark-haired Princess tumbling to safety twenty feet away.

But that put Erik Medon directly in the mace's path, and with not even a fraction of a second to do more than see the weapon come down.

For a moment, everything seemed to exist in a dreamlike slowness; she saw the monstrous spike-covered weapon hammer down on top of Erik, crushing him into the very rock beneath like a fly being smashed under some immense fist. She heard herself scream his name, felt horror rise in her, and looked up to see a wide, gloating smile on the face of Yoop.

At that smile something else rose, a storm of cold silver fury. She heard a choir of voices deep and hard around her and the call

312

of horns and drums resounded from the Spheres. It swept up the horror, made it part of fury and pain and *drove* her forward. Running on air as she had never done before, she *kicked* the giant's knee so hard that he roared in pain. Then she dodged his grasping hand, ran *up* his arm, and delivered a roundhouse swing of her shield that smashed alongside his head as though driven by the giant's own strength.

He staggered, his roar now confused, but there was no thought in her of mercy, it was far too late for that. It was time only for Judgment, and the cold silver voices echoed the fury that redoubled every time she saw the crushed stone beneath the mace Yoop no longer held.

She was off his shoulder, behind him, and drove her sword in, deep, deep, and his roar was a scream now, a cry of fear. Fear spun him around faster, hand lashing out, catching at her.

Now she heard laughter, cold and bitter, and a part of her shivered to realize that it was *her* voice, so chill and cruel. But the rest of her echoed that laugh, and her blade cut deep, cut *through.*

Even as the Giant looked in slow-witted disbelief at his hand as it came away, she was up, up. She hammered into Yoop's chin with all the strength this frightening, unstoppable rage had given her, then around as he reeled, with one final screaming kick, tears streaming from her eyes.

With that blow, Yoop was driven face-first into the ground. He lay still, the blood pooling from his hand and then slowing, slowing.

The Usurpers' armies broke then, withdrawing before the charge of the Armies of Faerie, and she was herself again. Polychrome staggered out of the sky, running to the spot where Erik had been, crying, as Zenga rose looking at the same spot.

The mace suddenly quivered. Polychrome's sobs caught in her throat, halted by impossible hope.

Something catapulted the gigantic mystical weapon away like a chip in a torrent, and a silver and blue crystal armored figure heaved painfully out of the crushed rock.

Erik Medon looked around, slightly unsteady, but smiled at her. He *smiled!*

313

She didn't know, for a moment, whether she wanted to run and hug him, or slap him for *scaring* her so. "Oh, thank the Above... you're alive. I thought..." she breathed, and heard Zenga saying something very much like it at the same time.

"Ha," Erik said weakly, but still with a pained grin. "Sorry about that, both of you... but remember, this place is about as magical as anything gets. And Yoopie there was using a really magical mace. So that looked pretty ugly to you guys out here, I'm sure — and looked pretty *damn scary* to me, let me tell you! — but since I made sure I was focused on my True Mortal defense, it really was sort of like being hit by a really big puffy hammer of styrofoam while standing on a very deep featherbed. Hurt some, from sheer impact, but didn't break anything."

He stared over at Yoop's corpse. "Who the hell did *that?*"

"Princess Polychrome — single-handedly, in the end," Nimbus said, coming up to them.

Erik turned to stare at her. She blushed and shifted; inside, she felt an amazing, roiling, totally incompatible mixture of pride, embarrassment, nausea, shame, and confusion. "What... How the hell did she pull that off?" Erik asked Nimbus, and then immediately turned back to her. "I'm sorry, I didn't mean to make that sound...it's just that I was so worried about you getting hurt..."

Those words brought a smile to her lips. "I was worried about that, too. And you. And I don't know how I did it, I just...saw you and Zenga go down, and I got so...angry."

Erik muttered something under his breath with a grin, something that ended in what sounded like "...-hulk," but Nimbus was speaking. "I told you, Princess; the power of the Above is in you and with you, if you find the key to unlock it. And, at least for those moments...you did. Nothing on that field could have stood before you, save perhaps only our Hero himself. It was well done; we have our undeniable victory, the enemy's morale is badly broken, and there will be more than sufficient witnesses to make sure that they now understand that we have a True Mortal and other forces besides."

She tried to grasp what Nimbus was saying. The power of the Above? *Hers?*

314

Nimbus nodded with a satisfied air. "Few were our casualties, given the circumstances. Our first engagement has gone well. Now the enemy must make their moves, but we have already dictated the course of actions, though they know it not.

"All is arranged; only the final act of this dark play remains."

Polychrome Glory

Chapter 45.

"All went as expected?" Amanita asked brightly.

Cirrus bowed to her, and Ugu restrained an ironic grin. He knew which part of the plan truly interested her.

"All indeed, my Queen. Our forces — small though they were — fought respectably, but were well and truly routed, as we expected." He glanced at Ugu. "Majesty, I must say again that your selection of Guph as our advance General was inspired. His reputation as a strategist is known, and they will attribute most of our later work to his doing."

"Precisely my intention. You are our most powerful weapon, Cirrus, but you only remain so as long as your existence remains a secret. But go on, tell us of the battle; we need this intelligence."

"They have given the overall command of the assembled armies, in terms of strategy, to Nimbus. Unsurprising, but formidable. However...he is not the true leader of the assault."

Oh no? Interesting. "Indeed? So who is the true leader?"

Now Cirrus' well-hidden nervousness became clearer in the stiff way he held himself. "Princess Polychrome Glory."

"*Polychrome?*" Amanita repeated incredulously, a disbelieving smile on her face. "That dancing little snip of a girl? The one I once kept as a pet canary for months? The one who barely escaped here with her life?" That high, chilling laugh rang out. "What in the *world* are they thinking, Cirrus dear?"

Cirrus' lips tightened, but only for a moment. "It devastates me to disagree with you, my Queen, but in the centuries it appears some...change has been wrought in her, perhaps even more recently, in the past year or so. For she spoke as a leader — no, as a *ruler* — to her troops, and they responded as though they were all of one will. This was one of the few true surprises of this engagement, reported to us by our select spies."

Amanita raised an eyebrow, then shrugged prettily. "Well, well, the little girl has grown up then? How charming."

317

"Go on, Cirrus. What other surprises?"

"The leader of the Nome forces — under Nimbus' overall generalship, of course — is the one we knew as the Penitent."

Ugu frowned, as did Amanita. The Penitent had been a thorn in their sides for centuries, and startlingly hard to pin down... "You say that *we* knew him as the Penitent. Does this mean we now have a name to put to that shadowed face?"

"Yes, Majesties. General Guph met them face-to-face, and recognized the Penitent as none other than Ruggedo the Red."

"*WHAT?*" Now both exchanged much more serious glances. The average denizen of Faerie might not understand, but Ruggedo was the true King of the Nomes. Exiled he might be. Disavowed by his people. But the true and rightful ruler of a Kingdom of Faerie had powers of his own that, if he was to regain his place... "This is a much more serious matter. If Ruggedo survives, and has been given such respect...he may be close to regaining his kingship, and *that* would make the Nome Kingdom twice as formidable as it already is."

"I understand that, Majesties. However, if the remainder of our plans proceed, is it not true that this will be rendered utterly irrelevant?"

"True enough. Go on, then."

"Perhaps not the least surprising was that yet another truly formidable warrior is with them: the girl who was travelling with the mortal."

It seems my enemy has been thinking in broad as well as deep strategy. What new move is this? "The Gilgad fighting-girl?"

"That was our assumption — perhaps reinforced by his own words to others that were expected to reach our ears. Her true name is Princess Zenga...of Pingaree."

Comprehension. "His journey to that island kingdom had a *twofold* objective, then, one hidden within the other. It had not occurred to me...but now the strategy is clear. Pingaree throws in its lot with the Prophecy, and — in true royal style — prepares to capture the greatest prize of alliance possible by pairing their daughter with the greatest Hero of the age. Bold moves on both parts."

"Why, naturally, that makes so much sense now!" Amanita said with another laugh. "The royal and secret treasures of Pingaree would not be just handed out to others...but given to a Princess to accompany a hero, of course. You know," she continued, in a contemplative fashion, "I always rather fancied the idea of a necklace of those three pearls, and here one's being delivered. How thoughtful of them."

"Indeed, my Queen. We will request the other two for you... later." It was a good idea to keep her believing that he was willing to please her — possibly from fear, possibly from still believing he might win her favor. *This need only endure a few more weeks, perhaps even days.*

"After the finale? Yes, I think we will be in a position to make many...requests at that time." She settled back in a self-satisfied manner.

"Go on, General."

"She appears to have the Pearl of Strength; no, I would say she definitely has that Pearl, but gives no indication of having either of the others. This would fit with wise policy; give her the most powerful weapon, leave the realm its most potent defenses." He glanced up. "Majesty, this does concern me in one way –"

Ugu thought he knew what Cirrus was thinking. "The Pearl of Wisdom."

"Yes, Majesty. It surpasses belief that such a decision would not have been undertaken without consulting the Pearl; and it is well known that the Pearl has verged on oracular in its ability to foresee events and chart the best course."

"Your concern is well-founded, General, and it is wise of you to bring this to our attention. Yet it is of no major concern; My Lady, would you explain?"

"How kind of you, My King." Amanita crossed her legs and smiled seductively down at Cirrus. "Powers have limits — this is one of the basic tenets, yes? Well, the Pearls are creations of the Sea Fairies — perhaps their greatest creations — and thus quite formidable. Anything that happens within or immediately within reach of the sea is known to the Pearl, and much beyond it...as long as they remain unknown, or no power opposes them.

"But here," she swept her arms wide, "we are in Oz, far indeed from the sea, separated from the ocean by the most impassable desert and the great Barrier, and we — both myself and King Ugu — were quite aware, oh, very much aware, of the potential of the Pingarese. So for long the power of Oz has been set to fog the Pearl's vision, and it cannot pierce that veil with any clarity, for even the Sea Fairies are not the equal of the power of Oz...or of the power of its rulers."

"I now understand, Majesty, and I thank you for making this clear." He turned back to Ugu. "The vanguard of their true assault was but four: the True Mortal Erik Medon, Zenga of Pingaree, the Penitent, and Polychrome herself." He looked, with only slightly disguised fear, at Amanita. "I... I am afraid it was she who slew Yoop."

For a moment Amanita looked utterly shocked. But then, to Cirrus' obvious surprise, she laughed. "Oh, now, that *is* a surprise... but a very pleasant one, a very pleasant one indeed, my General. I had hoped Yoop would die in this battle, but I had rather expected him to die at the hands of the Mortal. At the hands of a beautiful young girl? Ahhh, that is so very much more wonderful. Almost poetic. A shame his transfiguration made it impossible for him to appreciate the justice and the irony."

"As you say, my Queen," Cirrus said, relief written large on his face, "yet it does make her a most formidable adversary as well."

"Surely, surely...but we are very much prepared for powerful adversaries." Her smile was meant to be light and pretty again, but Ugu saw far too much of the shark in it. "And the more powerful she is, the more...use I will have for her."

Ugu saw Cirrus twitch the faintest bit at that; knowing how supremely well the other man played his roles, that reaction spoke volumes of Cirrus' relationship to Polychrome...a relationship only peripherally discussed before. *I must remedy that...but not in Her Majesty's earshot.*

"Still, in the end, all has gone well. They have had their victory. They have shown off their True Mortal, to draw us into their trap, not realizing that now the trap is entirely of our own devising."

"In essence...yes, Majesty. Their victory was somewhat greater than expected, but that is not relevant to our actual goals."

"Excellent." Ugu nodded slowly. "The pieces are all in place. The strategies have all been devised.

"Only the endgame remains."

Chapter 46.

The Rainbow Castle was silent now; he had even sent the servants away with the rest of the people. On Caelorum Sanctorum was space and enough, and safety assured; the Above would not mind, he thought, if he used it as a refuge for his people, so long as he kept the veil of cloud high and deep between the Mountain and the Heavens.

If only I could call upon them. But I gave that up long ago, when I chose this place, this world.

His footsteps echoed endlessly through the high vaulted corridors, and the Music of the Spheres was sad and muted. Once more he cast his gaze to the pool, but only shadowed shapes moved within. *They have passed through the Great Barrier around Oz, and I can see nothing clearly through that, unless I were to put forth my full strength...and I may need that soon enough.*

He moved then and stood on the battlements, looking out. His vision was keen beyond mortal, or even ordinary Faerie, imagining, and he saw all about the castle now for a hundred miles and more. *A gift of my heritage, yet a pale shadow of my father's sight.* He would have given much for his father's vision now.

Nothing. Not a Tempest, not a soldier, naught but ordinary clouds and the brilliance of sky in all the directions below, and below.

Iris Mirabilis glanced upward with a sudden surge of fear. *Even* they *would never dare an assault upon the Holy Mountain!*

He relaxed as he saw no sign of movement beyond his people, but a tension remained. *It has been days, now, since all my armies passed into Oz. I have sensed a clash of armies, my daughter's first battle. Surely they know I can have few, if any, here to defend the Rainbow Kingdom. If Amanita and Ugu are as powerful as they must be, then they also know this cannot be a battle of armies, it is a battle of Powers. Why do they not* come?

He slammed down one massive fist, and the entire wall quivered under the impact. Here, with none to see him, he need not

Ryk E. Spoor

be restrained. With no others in the line of fire, he could use his powers as he had not done since ages past, when first he founded the Kingdom. That was why he had sent all away, left himself the sole and lone defender of all he had built.

Yet none came to challenge him. The air was clear and empty of all but questions.

In his heart, he knew his hopes for a battle, perhaps a *final* battle, were nothing but distractions, a way for him to ignore the truth. The Prophecies of the Bear were enigmatic in ways, but deadly clear in others, and it was not here in his Kingdom that the fate of worlds would be decided. It would be decided by the actions of one man who owed the Rainbow Kingdom even less than he thought, and of one girl who was owed far more than she could imagine now.

Even so, the Usurpers would not pass up this chance. He had listened to the news that had come from Faerie, the course of action taken by the Usurpers, their choices and strategies as manifest in their deeds. Early on they had been...*crude*, would be the best way to put it, in their approaches. But as time had gone on, at least one of the rulers of Oz had become more far-sighted and cautious in their strategies — Ugu, he suspected — and to that one the opportunity to at least test the defenses of the Rainbow Kingdom when they were at their lowest would be something that could not be ignored.

Unless there was something else that Ugu knew that he did not. Iris looked out again, the sense of foreboding laying even more heavily upon him. Nothing.

"They will not come."

Startled, he glanced down. The Little Pink Bear stood, almost invisible, in the shadows at his feet.

A chill ran down his spine as he took in the meaning of the words...and the fact that they had been spoken by this comical-looking Oracle. "What do you mean?"

"They will not come; they are not coming." The high-pitched voice was as jerky and semi-mechanical as ever, the voice of a passionless child as a judge and seer. "There is no need."

Now the chill turned to a dawning, vague realization and horror. "Why? If they time their strike right, there would be no

324

better opportunity, and little risk; they could withdraw and return their forces to Oz before the full forces under Nimbus and my daughter could reach the Grey Castle!"

"Because they know what you have planned, and use that to their advantage."

He snatched up the tiny stuffed creature, shaking with anger and fear for everything he held dear. "How could they know?"

"Once in motion the Prophecy was, then in their hands the Prophecy fell."

He was speechless with shock and found himself on his knees, staring at the emotionless black-bead eyes. *They have had the Prophecy since Erik Medon arrived in the Kingdom?*"

The crank turned slowly. "Yes."

It took nearly all of his control to keep from crushing the Bear in his hand. "*Why* did you not *tell* us this, Bear?"

"You did not ask. I am built to answer questions." The Pink Bear's voice carried a slightly wounded tone under its usual mechanical sound.

"But you *can* act and speak now on your own. As you did just now." He rose slowly and placed the Bear on the wall, and the lightnings gathered about his hand. "Now you will explain why you did not speak long ago, and explain well, or by my father and the Above I shall reduce you unto ashes and scatter those so far that not all the power of Above and Below could gather them again."

"Fate."

Nearly he released the Power. "*What?*"

"Fate," the Bear repeated. "Destiny. Wyrd. The thread is spun, the words are spoken, Clotho, Lachesis, Atropos, Urdr, Verdandi, Skuld."

He went cold, cold inside. "You knew it would happen from the beginning."

The little Bear looked at him, and its voice carried a force and power he had not heard before. "The future is not *known*. It is only *made*. But the *way* to the future is guarded by many, and there is no victory without cost, no Prophet who carries not the weight of the Prophecy in the knowledge that many things must be allowed to happen or there *is no choice*."

Suddenly what stood before him was no stuffed and somehow amusing Seer; though its form changed not at all, he saw something else, a vast and shadowy Presence that was more ancient than Iris Mirabilis himself, even older than his mighty father. "Is *that* what you wish, Iris Mirabilis, Bifrost-Child, Sign of Promise, Kamanabillu? To have all safety in knowledge, and take all of choice away?" The power held him in terrifying thrall, seething with the absolute certainty that it now held before him. "Would you, then, choose to have no choice?"

He fell to his knees, stunned and appalled. "No!"

"Then there must be possibility of spies, chance of betrayal, unknown and unknowable things that still chart the course of prophecy, that the choices of Man and Faerie and God may still be of meaning and their strivings not the echoes of a clockwork they see not." The presence began to fade.

"No. I would not have that," he said, more quietly. "Never that.

"But...she is my daughter, and still so very young."

Chapter 47.

We crested the final hill and looked down. "Oh...my...God," I heard myself say slowly, feeling the horror creep its way down my spine. Before us lay the Usurpers' Army. And behind them, the Grey Castle.

It was a gargantuan edifice, a mountain of grey stone walls that might be three miles or more on a side, towers reaching hundreds of feet into the air, enclosing — or so they said — the entirety of the Emerald City within those walls.

But what was worse was the *land*. Almost at our feet, in a line as sharp as though cut with a razor, the grasses turned from brilliant green (with a touch of lavender) to dead, cold grey, the color of the darkest, deadest dust of the Moon, the color of spent, cold ashes. The Grey Castle lay at the center of a perfect circle of sterility, a symmetric monochrome memory of life that was.

The only color on the dead, rolling, petrified meadows was the Army. And color there was, but all of it *wrong*; the bruise-harmful green-black of the Tempests, fever-bright flame-orange of Infernos, frozen-hatred ice-blue of Torrents, poisoned-earth swamp-brown of Temblors, and the myriad other delirium-intense hues of the soldiers, their armor, their weapons, the siege engines, stretching across our entire path and many, many ranks deep.

I looked over to the others. "I guess this is it."

Nimbus, Ruggedo, and Polychrome's eyes reflected the knowledge that the others lacked; this was a battle we might fight, but did not expect to win.

"So it is. One last parley, and then — the battle," Nimbus said.

"I guess you don't expect them to surrender now."

"It would seem...unlikely."

Once more the five of us strode forward; once more, General Guph and the select four Dark Elementals met us.

"General, we have brought the battle to your very doorstep. You have now seen that we have forces in hand that you cannot hope to match, even if the might of your individual warriors surpasses that of our own," Polychrome said without preamble. "We do not wish any more slaughter of the people of Oz, for most of these warriors — as you know — are not men and women of war, but merely victims of the magic of the Usurpers."

Odd, though. I thought as she spoke. *There's still a lot of people out there* not *impressed into their armies...and not all the words they've had to say about the Usurpers were bad. Well, not quite; I haven't heard anyone say a good word about Amanita, except when they looked terrified about someone repeating what they said and then stammered something about how wonderful she was. But Ugu...there's been people saying how he actually made some things* better. *Solved disputes, arranged repairs of bridges and things, a lot of other little and big projects that weren't all focused on this war.*

Polychrome had gone on. "If the Usurpers will not surrender themselves, then I ask you — I *beg* you — to stand aside and let this conflict be between those who have stolen the heart of Faerie, and those who would restore it."

Guph raised an eyebrow. "Prettily said, and your first battle was conducted well, Princess. Yet in the end you know that there are limits to even your True Mortal weapon, and sheer numbers with the powers we have are, in fact, that limit. You seek to cloak as mercy what is, in truth, fear of defeat." He gestured her away. "Look to your weapons and make your peace with the Above, for when this battle ends, 'tis I and King Ugu and Queen Amanita who will stand triumphant."

"So be it," she said grimly. "But have a care, Guph; for your speech places you as equal to the Usurpers, and they have no love or tolerance for any rivals. They will see to your heart, and your reward for victory will be not power, but death."

Before he could muster a retort, we were already moving away. I leaned closer to her. "*Zing!*" I said with a grin. "That was a good parting shot."

Her smile flashed out for a second before fading. "I fear it is only the truth."

"And the truth hurts," I said, returning her smile.

We reached the crest of the final hill again and turned. For a long moment, nothing moved save the live and dead grass, and the banners of each army, in the faint breeze from the still-rising Sun.

And then the horns sounded, and the charge began.

This time we were not to be in the vanguard, but a reserve force and coordinators. My anti-magical capabilities were perhaps the most powerful single force on the battlefield, able to shatter coordinated mystical assaults, blunt the charges of magical warriors, make holes in defenses; at the same time, Zenga and Polychrome together were most capable of helping me *get* to the widely separated targets without getting caught up in intervening messes, by the combination of Zenga's strength and Poly's ability to dance on air. The two girls coordinated well — though not, oddly, as well as Poly and I had in the first battle, and I felt a warmth spread through me for a moment as I remembered. It had almost been like dancing with her again.

The clash of armies was even more deafening now, for our seventy thousand and more were now facing sixty thousand, an army even larger than we had first believed. Nimbus had pulled our force into a sort of serrated double-flared arch whose units would shift in a coordinated fashion, arranging it to minimize what amounted to exposed surface area, allowing our weaker forces to concentrate maximum force on the attackers.

My military knowledge being weak, I didn't know exactly how to describe it, but it looked in action something like a grinding attachment, funneling attackers around the perimeter and to the center where more and more of ours could attack fewer and fewer of theirs. This meant the strongest of the Army of Faerie's defenders were at the outer, more exposed edges, with the more adept at assault being near to the center.

The key to keeping that working was, of course, to not let them flank on either side. Superior numbers were currently in our favor, but the proportionate power was on their side.

Now the gloves were off and all the powers either side could use were being thrown into the fray. Nomes and other Earth-spirits merged with the ground and came forth elsewhere, mirrored by their brutal Temblor counterparts. Sea Faeries unleashed waterfalls and

Torrents deflected them or Infernos vaporized them, filling vast areas with mist and steam that blinded both sides; Sky Faeries and Storm Guards clashed above with Tempests and shadowy, terrifying wraiths that seemed manufactured of the stuff of nightmare. Siege weapons pounded each other and opposing troops with stone and flame and light and dark.

With both sides now throwing all their magic into the fray, even the battlefield became both opponent and ally. The ground shook and danced, groaning uneasily under the forces of Faerie at war. Stormclouds boiled overhead, winds whipped unpredictably, funnel clouds started to drop in one direction and were then sent dancing elsewhere. Polychrome had to start focusing her attention more and more on that aspect, using powers I could see were very new to her to redirect winds, shunting storm and cloud aside.

Nimbus was forced to use a squad of Sky Faeries to move me from point to point on the battlefield. *Up* and off to the left, beat back a flanking charge, another flight to the right, now dropping into the center to break up a knot of Temblors that threatened to break the entire formation, Sky Faeries falling as I came in to rains of arrows and bolts of power, and I felt sick. *I might be a hell of a weapon, but the cost in men to use me... these people are dying just playing* taxi!

I landed, feeling not only furious at the *waste* of this war, but shaky, tired. "Nimbus, this is not good."

He shook his head, flashing signals to one of his commanders even as he answered. "It is bad, Lord Medon. These creatures of the enemy are hard to control and direct, yet someone does so. I am beginning to suspect that it is not Guph."

"What? Why?"

"I am...not sure," he answered after a moment. "But even the clumsy directions they will follow seem too...precise. Almost as though our adversary understands each shift of my strategy even in the moment I make it. I have ordered a change of motion now, and — see!"

The two curving lobes of the grinder-army flowed slightly back then merged into a charging wedge, defenders layering and interlocking with assault-heavy forces to try to split the enemy army in half. It was a maneuver of absolutely astonishing precision and speed made possible only by the training, morale, and close command coordination of our army.

Yet...

A mass of Dark Elementals seemed almost to have blundered to the correct position, straight ahead of the oncoming wedge, a force so strong that I was going to have to be sent there just to give the wedge a chance — to regroup and reposition, if not to break through.

"I think I see what you mean," I said, my gut tensing as the Sky Faeries prepared to take me aloft again.

And the battle went on. If most of these troops had been human, I don't know if that dragging sense of eternal battle could have been sustained; exhaustion would have set in, and there would have been pauses as the troops regrouped, gathered their dead, prepared again. I seemed to remember that was the way of things in ancient battles; hand-to-hand combat was like boxing (except with really sharp pointy gloves, little differences like that), and no one could keep that up for hours on end without rest.

But there was no weariness that could touch the Temblors, the Tempests, the Torrents, the Infernos, and not much could touch their ensorcelled shock troops, either. And while our troops may have been weaker, they were no less magical, no less able to continue.

For my part, as a resource run from one side of the battle to the other as needed, I got plenty of little rests, so while I was tiring, I, too, was far from finished.

And still there was no clear victor, and the battle raged on, and the sun was beginning to set, and across the length and breadth of the grey plains were bodies.

And then it happened. An emerald-green bolt suddenly lit up the entire battlefield, and a part of the lefthand arch of our Army was obliterated.

"Holy *crap*, what was *that?*" I pulled out a spyglass Nimbus had given me and looked. "Nimbus, they've got something on the main castle, looks for all the world like a Navy cannon, a sixteen-inch gun. It's starting to glow again, too!"

331

"Lord Erik, you are the only one who can deal with such a weapon. Go, go now!"

The Sky Faeries snatched me up and we streaked through the boiling sky towards the battlements, where that massive cannon was building towards another shot. The storm roared into full power and we felt the winds dragging at us — only to stop, suddenly. I looked back, saw Polychrome standing in a momentarily clear space, arms thrust upward as though shoving the entire storm aside. We were almost there –

And out of the cloud in coordination so perfect it seemed mechanical dropped twenty Tempests, curling down and around in a four-pronged pincer that closed directly on the Faeries carrying me.

I plummeted towards the ground below, and despite the mystical nature of that ground, I wasn't sure I would survive. *This falling-from-great-heights thing is* really *getting old*, I thought. But out of the corner of my eye I saw other movement, several other movements, other assault forces erupting in clockwork timing from the ground and air, and one Sky Faerie, bleeding, but diving, closing in on me, the Tempests screaming in behind, her hand catching mine, spinning me around; I kicked out and the Tempest that was just upon us exploded into nothingness, its fellows fleeing from my power, but we were close to the ground, her power failing, *impact!*

I had barely managed to force us to turn again when we hit, and so instead of mashing my rescuer under me I took the brunt of the hit and forced the earth apart before me. Even so, I was stunned, barely able to force myself upwards. *Dammit! I have to get to that stupid gun before –*

"*ERIK MEDON, HEAR ME!*"

The voice thundered across the plains, so deep and powerful that it rumbled in my chest and vibrated through my boots. The entire battle paused.

"*Look back upon your Armies, Mortal.*"

I looked.

Even at that distance, I could see that Polychrome stood in the center of a ring of Dark Elementals, holding her as still as death with blades of fire and lightning at her throat. My gaze tracked farther, saw Ruggedo on the ground with two Temblors standing ready to break him in half, and Zenga and Nimbus surrounded.

"Throw down your weapons, Mortal, and surrender, or I, Ugu the Unbowed, shall most surely order the execution of your friends."

Now I could see a single figure high above on the battlements. I looked up into deep-set dark eyes in a lined face, with white-streaked black hair.

And so we win by losing...maybe. I felt terror trying to rise up in me, for now my death was so very, very close — even if we won, probably.

But at the same time, I felt immense relief. The battle and the slaughter was over, and now the only one who would have to pay the price would be me.

I raised my arms and dropped the crystal-metal sword to the ground. "I surrender."

Chapter 48.

The next few minutes were a blur. The armies stopped fighting
— though some detachments wanted to continue, and would
have if both Nimbus and Ruggedo hadn't basically shouted
them down. Soldiers came forward and stripped me of my glittering
armor and sword, leaving me in the mundane clothes I'd chosen to
wear on this, my final day of life, the clothes I'd worn the day
Polychrome found me and brought me into wonder.

The hardest part of it was the shouts and cries from our own
army, calling me coward and traitor. Many of them understood the
costs of the war — being in the front lines, better than I did — and
to them such a hostage situation was intolerable. Even their
commanders would have expected them to continue. True, the
Rainbow's Daughter was unique...but still, many of them felt
betrayed.

And they had been, in truth. Just not in the way they thought.
Fortunately I had much practice in ignoring name-calling from my
youth, and I had much more important and pressing worries now.

Finally they dragged me forth, through the dark corridors of the
Grey Castle and into an immense courtyard, within which stood the
petrified remains of Ozma's Palace. We'd come through the walls
and the grey, dead streets of the Emerald City, buried now beneath
the stupendous ash-colored pile of masonry which was the Grey
Castle, and I had not been able to restrain my horror at the
hundreds of people caught frozen in the last instants of their lives.

Before the dead grey of the Palace, a huge open space had been
made, cleared from the stony skeleton of the City, and I wondered
how many of those people, now statues, had been callously shattered
to dust in the work. Around that space there were stands, as for
some great gladiatorial arena; on one side, sitting just above the
entrance to Ozma's Palace, was the Royal Box, a roofed-over
observational platform with two thrones to the front, and other
shadowed places within. There sat Amanita Verdant and Ugu the
Unbowed, the Usurpers, rulers of Oz.

Ugu rose as I was brought in. Unlike Neill's portraits of him, the real Ugu was a man of presence and striking appearance. His voice and face and demeanor reminded me strongly of Christopher Lee's Saruman as he would have been when younger: the same deep, resonant, commanding tones, the intensity of the gaze, the arrogant patrician look, black hair streaked with white.

Amanita rose a moment later, lazily, as though she found this a play on the stage and not a real event at all. She was as beautiful as rumor had implied, silky waves of leafy green cascading over creamy shoulders, framing a heart-shaped face of perfect symmetry with brilliant emerald eyes, and a body of exquisite perfection. But the smile and glitter of the eyes told me this was a woman at the edge of insanity, or possibly well over it but with great control.

"Welcome to Oz, Mortal. Welcome to our domain." Ugu's voice rolled about the colosseum. "Your deeds have already become a wonder, and perhaps one day will be a legend. A cautionary tale, true, but legend nonetheless."

I grinned up at him, feeling at this point there was nothing much for me to lose. "The day is not over yet."

"Indeed. But its ending is near, as is yours." He gestured.

In the center of the arena, I saw a small pyramid, perhaps six to eight feet high, seeming to be made of polished crystal; the sides pulsed with colors that chased themselves around its perimeter, red, yellow, green, blue, violet, and back to red again. Within I thought I could see a small, motionless figure.

Ozma.

The pyramid stood at the center of a set of elaborately carven circles, with a curving four-pointed design reaching to the outer perimeter. At each of these points was another circle, and within that circle stood something monstrous. One a giant of flame and cinder, another a cadaverous, insubstantial monstrosity echoing an eagle from some forgotten age, the third a serpent of oozing liquid corruption, and the last a great misshapen dragon of solid stone.

The pyramid itself lay within a perfect circle that just touched each point...and before one face was another circle that just touched the edge of that face.

A circle just large enough for me to stand in.

"Yet you do have one decision to make, Erik Medon," Ugu went on. "The final ritual which requires a True Mortal also requires that the Mortal cooperate — that while he may be bound, he must have consented to the binding in the ritual." His arm swept around to the stands.

While most of the stands were filled with citizens of Oz, soldiers of the armies, and many of the Dark Elemental Faeries, on one side nearest the Royal Box was another wide platform, taking up many spaces and levels of the stands, with guards ringing the platform.

There I could see Polychrome, chained and under guard, blades hovering at her throat. Zenga and Ruggedo, chained together in such a way that if Zenga were to try to use her strength to break free, she'd have to pull Ruggedo apart — assuming the alert Temblor and Tempest guarding them didn't kill them upon the instant. Nimbus, alone and proud, chained and unable to move.

"You will cooperate with the ritual," Amanita said, her voice light and yet penetrating, "Or your lovely little friends will be killed. One at a time. In front of you."

Careful. I have to make this convincing. "And what possible assurance do I have that you won't kill them as soon as you've *finished* your ritual?"

Ugu nodded. "A fair question. In truth, you have no *assurance*, Mortal. All that can be offered for the future are promises, and promises can be broken. Yet there are those whose promises have value, and those who do not, and I, Ugu the Unbowed, would give you my word that this will not happen."

"Not good enough." The guards tightened their grip on Polychrome and I raised my hand. "Wait. Just letting them live is not enough. That could mean as slaves or prisoners of your domain for all time. If I participate in this...ritual, which your words indicate will kill me, then I want more."

Amanita glared at me, but Ugu nodded. "Speak, then. What more do you ask?"

"That they go free. You send them home, all of them — all the remaining armies, our allies, and my friends up there. Without me they couldn't penetrate the Great Barrier, you know that, so they're no threat to Oz once you've sent them away. Yes, that means they'll not be entirely defenseless against you. So now *you* make a choice, Ugu. How valuable is this ritual to you and the Queen? Do you gain enough from it that this will be worth it? For *that* is the price for my cooperation." I looked at my friends, and finally at Polychrome. "Enough people have died for this. I would be the last."

For a long moment Ugu gazed down at me, gauging my resolve. Then he nodded. "So be it. You have my word."

"*No!*"

To my surprise, it was both Amanita and Polychrome, speaking almost in unison. Polychrome's I'd expected. There was a short, heated exchange of whispers between the two rulers.

"Erik, our lives are not *worth* this! You cannot let them do this!" There was an earnestness, an intensity in her voice that brought a stinging lump to my throat. This was not just an act to convince them. *She doesn't want me to die.* "We all knew the price!"

As she said that, Ugu gestured sharply, finishing the conversation — though from Amanita's expression, I doubted very much whether she was done, or would abide by his decision for long. "Enough, my Queen. For our purposes this will serve very well. The Mortal is correct; if this we accomplish, all their victories here are naught but hollow boasts, empty of any meaning save the cold comfort their contemplation might bring in the darkest hours of the night. While by this bargain, we seal his obedience as well; for know well, Erik Medon, that True Mortal though you are, here, in this place, at the center of all Faerie, if this bargain you make, to it you are held by Fate and Law."

He looked down, fixing me with his dark gaze, and in those eyes I saw more than the mere tyrant I had expected. "So choose, and choose wisely. Will you swear to cooperate with this ritual, to struggle not against us, and allow it to be completed, if I, in turn, swear to you that I shall not merely spare your friends' lives, but to return them without further harm to their homes — so long, I will add, as they offer me and mine no further resistance?"

I looked up, and saw Zenga shaking her head, so furious or upset that she could say nothing, Ruggedo's face as expressionless as stone, Nimbus' eyes closed, body tensed, and Polychrome, storm-violet eyes wide and filled with tears that could not be mere acting. "My friends... Polychrome... I'm sorry. I've talked about how a hostage situation is intolerable, about how you can never yield to it or you give those who use those methods permission to use it again... but now, faced with it, I know it doesn't matter what I think. I can't do it. I can't let those I care about die in front of me when a word from me will save them."

I kept my eyes focused on the one face that mattered to me more than anything in the world...or beyond it. "Yes, I make this bargain, King Ugu," I said, using for the only time his title, "because even my death is a very small price to pay, if only she is safe."

I said it. Maybe not as directly as I would have liked...but this is no time or place for that.

Her eyes went even wider and her hand went to her mouth as Ugu said, "So be it. They shall be witnesses, and then sent to their homes, all of them, their armies and servitors alike. It is done."

I felt a shock of something in that pronouncement, and knew the bargain was sealed, even as Ugu turned to Amanita and bowed. "My Queen... The Ritual of Transcendence awaits your pleasure."

Chapter 49.

What's *wrong with me?* Polychrome thought, feeling the tears streaming down her face. *This was the plan, this was what we knew we came here to do!*

And then he said those last words, and something in her seemed to break.

Because she suddenly heard other words, as clearly as though he had spoken them aloud: *"I love you."*

She stood frozen, unable to move, as a terrible abyss seemed to gape wide beneath her.

"Even my death is a very small price to pay, if only she is safe."

She closed her eyes and stilled her trembling. *It is too late now. Too late for so many things. He has made the bargain. He is consecrated to the ritual.*

They led Erik out to the center of the great ritual circle, and stood him there, in the smallest circle before the shimmering pyramid. "Shall we bind him, lord?" asked a great Temblor, one of his escorts.

"That shall I do myself," Ugu said. Erik's clothing was suddenly torn from him, leaving him barely enough for dignity, and reshaped. Bonds of strong cloth wrapped themselves around his arms and legs. "Mortal material, not Faerie, so that even if you try to pit your will against that of destiny, you will not find it so easy to break these bonds. And..."

A thick, blue strip of denim forced itself suddenly into Erik's mouth, tying itself in back. "...There shall be no names spoken here this day save by ourselves."

Oh, no. Father and the Above, no!

Erik, hampered only slightly by the bonds, whirled, gazing up at Ugu in mute disbelief, as Amanita walked to the edge of the circle.

"Oh, yes, my friend, we know of your little Prophecy," Amanita said with a laugh at his stunned expression. "We have known it for quite some time now. After all," and she extended her arm towards the Royal Box, "we had such a wonderful source to rely upon."

Slowly, reluctantly, another figure emerged from the shadows, and light glinted brilliantly from his snowy hair. Polychrome felt almost as though she would faint from this final horror, even as she heard Nimbus roar in shock and betrayal, "*CIRRUS!*"

Cirrus Dawnglory's expression held none of the triumph one might have expected. He would not meet her gaze, and looked down instead.

Polychrome did as well, and realized that everything was lost. The ritual had begun.

Amanita began to dance. It was a simple dance, one-two-three, triple step; she sang words in a language Poly didn't know as she continued, then triple step, one, two, three, and began again. With every step, the air seemed to dim, so that by the time she completed the circuit of the entire array, the amphitheatre was in twilight.

Then, as she continued, each of the monstrosities began its own self-contained dance, and deep, atonal, discordant voices began to be heard, the Music of the Spheres echoing the hatred and destruction inherent in that ritual. Polychrome knew something of Faerie magic, but she could make out little of the symbolism or language...and what little she could understand sent shudders down her spine.

Amanita's dance curled inward, spiraling slowly towards the center, and in her hand was a knife, straight, black, carved with runes, made of pure dark glass. Black shapes like shadows followed her, a hellish sort of parade dancing in lockstep with its mistress.

Oh, Father! Oh, Erik! We've failed you! One of our own has betrayed us, and Erik, poor Erik, is going to die for nothing!

Behind Amanita, echoing the steps of the dark spirits that followed her call and repeated the ritual, black flames ignited from candles set at intervals along the entire array, lighting in darkness as Amanita Verdant passed.

She heard the names of the four Abominations and understood all too well the madness and hubris they implied, and her heart shrank even further within her. *Surtur, Niddhogg, Jormungandr, Hræsvelgr... She is mad with power, and yet I sense the power that builds might even shake the foundations of the world, enough to make hubris into truth.*

She stared down, seeing Erik standing rigid, trying to hold on at least to dignity and pride if not to hope, and keeping his eyes away from hers. *He spoke a farewell to me...*

"I love you."

And suddenly she saw it all. Everything she had denied within herself, everything her father had left unsaid, all that had happened from the very beginning, it was all clear. It had all been meant to come to this very moment, and for the first time in her life she cursed her father, cursed his name.

Then curse yourself, for you are very much his daughter, and you will do what has to be done.

And you know what that is, and why.

Amanita was closing in now, a single short circuit of the last and smallest circle around the Pyramid, and the black blade was rising, sufficient in magic to slay a Faerie, sufficient in sharpness and substance to kill a mortal outright.

I must not fail. He cannot act — by the oath he has given — and so I must. The movement, the timing, must all be precise... or all truly is lost.

The procession halted, a final deep note droning, rising, rising in a crescendo as the blade arced backwards.

Now!

Polychrome *moved.* She drew upon all the power of her Faerie heritage, that had kept her beyond the reach of others that tried to capture her, on the silver-burning power she had touched when Yoop had nearly killed them all, and on sheer desperation. She tore free of her startled captors, moving faster than even Tempest eyes could follow, streaking on rainbow light and destiny towards the center of the ritual.

And she was just in time.

Chapter 50.

I tried to keep myself under control as Amanita approached, the beautiful emerald eyes glittering with greed and insanity; but to stand still while someone put a knife — a really long, sharp obsidian knife — into me wasn't something I had quite been able to prepare myself for. At the last moment, as the four monsters sounded a thundering drone that rose like a trumpet of doom and Queen Amanita brought up the knife... I closed my eyes.

There was an impact that drove me backwards and for an instant I wondered that I felt no pain; but even as I opened my eyes I knew with rising horror what I was going to see, because in the instant before I smelled a wash of summer rain and spring flowers eternal.

She had been driven against me and was beginning to fall, fall, and I got my bound hands under her, sagging to the ground not with her weight but with the realization that the great knife had struck her fully. Somehow I broke the cloth on my wrists, stronger far than I'd been when I left Earth, and yanked the gag down.

"POLYCHROME!" I screamed, and cradled her in my arms. "No, no, no, no..."

The stain was spreading, all across, and the glorious eyes looked stunned and afraid.

"Well, *that* ruins the ritual completely. We'll have to start over from the beginning," Amanita said. I felt a fury burn within me, but distantly, for all my attention was riveted on Poly, trying to staunch the bleeding. *It didn't hit her heart, not quite, she came in from the side, it's not instantly fatal, maybe, maybe...*

Amanita started to gesture to the guards, but then I heard Ugu's voice. "Nay, Amanita. You have parts of the circle to prepare again; the candles needs must be doused and re-prepared, other small things that only you can do. It is his death we prepare for him; at the least, I shall give him this time to mourn."

But I barely registered any of this, all that mattered was the Faerie Princess who had brought me to wonder and now was going

345

pale before me. "No, Poly, no, God, Polychrome, *why?* All that mattered to me was that you were going to live, that's all, why did you do this, *why?*"

Then she smiled softly, as though she felt no pain, and answered in a voice that only I could hear. "Because I love you, Erik, and all that mattered to *me* was that *you* would live."

"You...love me?" I repeated, and for a moment I could not imagine the meaning in those words. And then the meaning burst in and I found myself sobbing. "Oh, no, Polychrome...Poly...Oh, God, I'd have given anything, anything at all to hear you say those words...and now I'd give anything never to have heard them, if it means –"

Her hand came up and touched my lips. "Shh. Shh, Erik. I've been so very blind, love. You were telling me you loved me almost from the moment we met; I just didn't hear it behind the words you used." I tried to speak, and the fingers touched me again. "No, no, Erik, we've *both* been fools, and..." She winced. "...and we've wasted so very much time. Please...don't waste the time we have left."

Her hand rose, curled behind my head, and I felt as though my heart was about to shatter as I understood. And then we kissed.

And it lasted for an instant, and for what seemed to be beyond forever, and for just that timeless eternity I knew that she did love me, that Polychrome Glory, Daughter of the Rainbow, had somehow fallen in love with *me*, and that there was no other wish or desire I could imagine having.

Except for it not to come to an end, and it *was* over, and her lovely hand sliding down, falling, the violet-stormy eyes clouded with pain and her breath coming in quick gasps. "And...now, Erik... Please...do what we...came here...to do."

Her hand dropped to the ground, and her eyes shut, and one last breath escaped.

I screamed again, for there was no pulse, no breathing, nothing. "Please, Poly...please..." I could barely speak, and what was the point, for there was no one left to hear. "Please, no...I can't do it, Poly. They... They still have our other friends, Zenga, Ruggedo, Nimbus... and even if they didn't, how *could* I, how, how could I do that now, when they've just ripped out my –"

346

And *then* I understood. For one terrible moment I hated them all, Iris, the damned Pink Bear, Nimbus, all those who must have *known*. A laugh escaped me, an ugly sound, and more like another sob than anything else.

"The preparations are complete," Ugu said quietly, and looked down at me. "Come. Let us...end this."

Oh, we'll end this. But not the way you think.

Slowly I lowered Polychrome to the ground, feeling wetness across my chest as well as my face as I did so, and took a deep breath.

"Ozma," I said, my voice barely a whisper, and the words came to me, as though I had known them all along, "I, a Mortal Man, bathed in the blood of my *heart* call to thee. Give me the power to set right what is wrong," and I let my voice rise to its full volume, "and wipe these *monsters* from the face of Faerie!"

Ugu shot to his feet, shock and dawning understanding on his face. "What –"

I reached back and slammed my hand onto the face of the shining pyramid.

"COME FORTH!"

The world exploded in light. It dissolved everything around me, a seething, burning multicolored fountain of corrosive luminance so hateful that I wanted to shrink back. But I stood my ground, and the light flowed past, and shimmered more softly, and slowly, slowly, within the light, beyond the light, a figure was coming forward. I stood in an abyss of brilliance on a path of pure darkness, and the darkness rose up, radiating from me, I realized, as light from a candle, dispelling the roiling light as the sun wipes away the fog, and the figure became clearer, a girl, with hair the color of midnight and the depth of dreams, a single crimson flower twined in her hair, and a face as lovely as the one I had just laid down.

For a moment she was as stern and proud as any queen, emerging from a prison, prepared to face her enemies. But then her eyes found mine, her expression softened, her arms were held out, and I realized, somehow, that she *knew* me. "Oh, Erik," she said, and her voice was as a ringing of bells, "I have seen your loss, and I grieve."

I wanted nothing more than to take that embrace, and cry, and run away, take refuge from what I did not dare face, what I had just won and left behind at the same time.

And I could not do that. Not yet. And just knowing that was nearly enough to break me.

"*No!*" I said, and took a step back, my voice cracked and desperate. "No, Ozma. No sympathy, no pity, no comfort, none, or I'll lose all the control I have, and all of this will be for *nothing!* Maybe later — if there is a 'later' for me. But for now," I bared my teeth in a grin that had not a trace of humor, "*finish this.*"

She nodded gravely, eyes filled with crystal tears, and took my hand.

And as white-hot fire burned through me, I opened my eyes and *screamed.*

Chapter 51.

Ugu felt no joy in this ritual. *Finally we come to the end. The powers will be bound. And then — if all goes as planned — the threat of my Queen will be ended, as will all threats to my power.*

He winced as Amanita revealed Cirrus' existence. *Damn her. Now, by my word, I am bound to return them to their homes, and they will know.* Not that this would entirely remove the usefulness of Cirrus' knowledge, but it would surely blunt the effect, for Nimbus Thunderstroke would undoubtedly immediately begin the process of changing all procedures, entrances, and so on.

As Amanita proceeded, becoming more and more involved with the ritual, he caught Cirrus' eye and nodded. The young General, still shaken from his unveiling, gave a small bow, and then departed — with an expression of relief that he would no longer have to suffer the burning regard of his old commander or — as Ugu now knew — his former fiancée.

How difficult must that be. I am glad it has not come to the final options.

And then came the penultimate moment, and a streak of rainbow light shattered all his calculations. *What has happened?*

But as he saw the Mortal collapse to the ground, sobbing, heard the broken tone of his voice, he felt a long-dormant part of his own heart twinge, send an echo of loss and sadness that led him to understanding; he allowed Erik Medon that time, the last he would have, and watched gravely as the dying Princess and her Hero kissed a first – and final – time.

But all of Amanita's preparations were complete, and there was no more time for delay. "Come," he said, as gently as he might manage to one he had led here to die. "Come. Let us...end it."

The Mortal gave a last, sudden sob and was still for a moment. Then he lowered the body of Polychrome to the ground, whispering something, as Ugu gestured for the guards to restore his bonds.

And then the blond head came up, and the whispered words became a shout: "...and wipe these *monsters* from the face of Faerie!"

He knew something was wrong, then, but for a frozen moment of time he did not understand. And then it was too late, as Erik Medon touched his hand to the Pyramid of Imprisonment and called Ozma forth.

A tremendous detonation of power blasted outward, a shockwave that knocked all around — even Amanita's abominable four — to the ground. Amanita's magic protected her, brought her in a shimmer of green to his side. "Wh... what is happening?"

Ah, it is now clear. And I have been entirely out-maneuvered in this Prophecy. "He was in love with the Daughter of the Rainbow. And you, *my Queen,* have bathed him in the blood of his heart!"

The Music of the Spheres was gathering now, calling, calling not to Ugu or Amanita...but to a Mortal Man, bathed in the blood of a Princess born of Faerie and perhaps the Above itself.

She stared openmouthed in shock and outraged comprehension. "He can't *do* this! He swore to *cooperate* with the Ritual! The Powers should tear him apart, Mortal or no!"

Ugu smiled thinly. "Ah, yes. But you completed *that* Ritual. True, it was rather spoiled because you killed the wrong person at the end, but it did go to completion — something, again, neither of us considered." He looked up. "And we shall pay the price for that error."

Now the ring of light that had flown outward slowed, reversed, began to return, and as it passed over the Armies, Ugu could see from the High Seat that thousands of his troops were collapsing, falling, reverting to what they had been. Other changes were beginning to be evident, none more than in the dwindling sense of connection he and Amanita had shared for three hundred years and more.

"All the power we have taken from Oz is returning to its source — and through her, into *him,*" he said grimly, and rose to his feet, grasping his staff, calling forth all the enchantments he had prepared against this one impossible chance. "Ward thyself, Amanita; *this* is our moment of reckoning."

350

The power funneled back into Erik Medon, an explosion in reverse, and disappeared.

For a moment — just a moment — there was silence and stillness. Nothing moved. Nothing spoke. The entirety of Faerie held its breath, to see if the Mortal would survive this final moment.

And then once-blue eyes flared open, blazing pure green fire, and Erik Medon let out a cry that shook the foundations of the Earth. It was a shriek and a roar and a growl, a scream of pain and ecstasy and fury and triumph, of loss and vengeance and betrayal, of sorrow and courage and unbending will, and the power *blasted* from him, kicking the few remaining guards aside like toys. A rampage of force crackled out, shattering stands, throwing Dark Elementals to the winds, and sundering the steel bonds of his friends, scattering those holding them.

The cry went on and on, and the earth *danced* beneath Erik Medon until it seemed that the entire Grey Castle would be brought down by his fury in the very moments it was awakened. The Spheres sang in icy precision, a rhythmic chant of ancient words:

"*Ultio!*
Vindicatio Vir!
Termini Tyrannorum!
Libertas!"

And suddenly it stopped, and there was only the figure standing in the ruins of the Pyramid, gazing up at him. The Mortal chuckled, a laugh on the edge of sanity, and the Chant of the Spheres remained, softer but no less grim, no less the sound of bared steel.

Ugu shook his head. "I shall give you no time to learn this power you have gained. *Frozen Soul!*" A blue-white bolt streaked from the staff, freezing the very air between them, racing at the speed of thought towards the once-Mortal with the glowing eyes.

The mouth quirked upward, and for a moment a phantom image surrounded him, a dark-haired man in a red shirt. "Deflector shields up, Captain!" he said, almost at the same time as Ugu's spell, speaking in an accent that was not his own.

351

An insubstantial barrier intercepted the Frozen Soul, turned it to a harmless spray of frost and snow.

Ugu felt his mouth drop open. "*What?*"

Erik Medon's laugh was humorless but loud. "I already *know* how to use it. Imagination, Will and Power. The first two I have had all my life, and now I have the third." He clenched his fist, and it *blazed* like a newborn sun. "And there is *nothing* you can do against me now!"

"Surtur!" Amanita called. "Slay me this man!"

The titanic flame-spirit smiled and strode forward, raising a sword of flame and doom.

Erik turned and raised his arms over his head; a hint of longer gold-blond hair, a shimmer of fantastic silver-blue armor, and the arms came down, directly at Surtur. "Aurora... *Execution!*"

A blue-white ray, somehow akin to Ugu's own, thundered outward, but as Surtur parried it, the monster suddenly realized that this had been a terrible mistake. Ice began to form, ice clear and hard as diamond, spreading as swiftly as frost across an icing pane of glass, hardening, sealing, extinguishing the eternal flame and leaving only blackness behind, until before them was no fiery giant, but a huge block of ice with something dead and black at the center. It teetered and slowly, slowly fell, shattering to ice chips and foul-smelling dust, and Surtur — one of Amanita's greatest creations — was gone.

"Understand this," Erik said, his voice echoing across the land. "This is the land of Faerie, the land that sparks the dreams of Mortals...and which is born, I think, of human dreams, human will, human imagination. And so...Imagination: whatever I can think of and imagine doing, this I can do; I need no spells, save those which raise the sense of wonder and courage within my heart, those which symbolize that which I call forth. Will: The strength I can wield is limited only by how much I am determined to do, by what I will risk. Power: I have all of Oz to draw upon."

Light now began to radiate from his body. "My world was *built* on imagination, my reading was filled with it, my entertainment was nothing *but* imagination, and though on my world this was nothing, the life of a man who has nothing else, *here* it is the one and only thing that matters, the sole weapon any Mortal could hope to wield against you."

He looked directly into Ugu's eyes, and that cold, emerald gaze was like looking into his own death. "I have the dreams and hopes, all the monsters and weapons and spells and powers imagined by a thousand men and women, of a dozen countries, of more books than you could read in a dozen years, all, here, in my mind, ready to answer any of your riddles with unanswerable power."

His arms rose and came down; towards Ugu and Amanita came the same force of absolute cold that had extinguished Surtur — and his eyes narrowed as the energy faded and vanished.

"Powerful indeed, and dangerous, but you have yet to win the day, Erik Medon," Ugu said. He was grimly aware that his words were at least half bravado. Despite all his preparations, the power of the Mortal's sacrifice, of the Princess of Oz bound within a mortal shell, was something truly beyond any of his calculations, and Erik Medon himself was fey and dangerous, a man uncaring of his own survival, intending only destruction of those that had deprived him of things more precious than power or gold. Still... "One enchantment I prepared for decades, against the possibility I might be forced into conflict against such power." *Though it was* meant *for Amanita.* "The Eye of the Soul watches, and sees all that you do. I cannot stop any action you may take...unless it is the *same* action as a prior one.

"So show us this imagination, Erik Medon. Show it well. For if once it fails, little indeed shall you have to protect you against ours."

Chapter 52.

At that moment there was a rising shout, and both Ugu and I
turned.

The Armies of Faerie were on the move.

I looked up, and realized that the half-formed wish in my mind
— when Ozma had infused her power into me — had come true.
Zenga, Ruggedo, and Nimbus were no longer bound, and they had
regained command of the Armies. Now, with many of the powerful
creatures gone from the Usurpers' forces, they had a chance.

That knowledge, and Ugu's unexpected and brilliant
countermove, shocked me back to some form of sanity. The power
was burning in me, with a sensation that could not be described. It
was agony, as though my very bones were afire — and it was ecstasy,
as though there was nothing I could not do. And I knew the longer
it went on, the less of me there would be. *How long? How long can
my soul withstand the power? I have to be careful. Go too fast too
soon and I'll die before I can win. Go too slow... and they'll kill me
sure. I'm both Mortal and Faerie now, and I have to use both
exactly right.*

I concentrated, remembering — with a sharp and sudden pang
of renewed loss — the sheer speed Polychrome had shown. *Ugu can
negate combat powers, probably, but I doubt his little trick can stop
me from using things on myself; that'd mean he could directly
affect me.* I found myself streaking across the ground so fast I was
leaving an arrow-straight cloud of dust behind me. The Usurper's
forces, regrouping — with both Cirrus and Guph shouting orders —
were just in front of me.

I *tore* into their ranks, tossing bodies aside like confetti. One of
the mighty siege engines loomed up and I grasped it, hefted it like a
softball, and spun around like a hammer-thrower, lofting it directly
for the Usurper's stands. With sight and hearing multiplied as well,
I could see eyes widen, hear their gasps, though I stood half a mile
away.

Ugu shattered it with a word and a gesture; I realized that he must have spent many, many months preparing, and even the inhuman speed I'd gained wasn't going to be able to beat him alone. I would have to start pushing what I had...and hope it would last long enough.

Amanita cast out a handful of powder, and the ground began to erupt with stone warriors, the transformational power of Yookoohoo magic making unliving ground into real opponents. These charged towards the still re-forming ranks of the Armies, even as her other three monsters rose and came for me. "You have done well, Mortal Man, but see! I have more forces for the asking, while you — powerful though you are — are but one man. You cannot confront us and protect your friends at the same time."

Oh, can't *I?* A flash of thought, blond hair and simple headband and an unyielding will, fingers of my two hands crossing just *so*, and in a blaze of light and smoke there were three, five, twenty, a hundred of me. We grinned our nastiest grin at Amanita as her face went slack in astonishment. *The others might not last long, but it'll sure slow things up. And if...yep, I see ten of me keeping near each of my friends; that should keep them for a while.*

"An illusion?" Ugu gestured, then frowned. "No. Truth. Perhaps all not equally powerful..."

But while he was chewing on that, I saw a shadow, dropped and rolled, as Hræsvelgr dove upon me, chill-bladed claw cutting a gash along my body. *Oh, damn, I'm almost naked, too.*

That was fixed even in the moment I thought it, and I realized I had other options. Even having thought about this power beforehand, it was different actually *using* it. I came to my feet, dressed, and something shimmered into existence, a long wide tube with a handle, I swung, pointed it as the half-substantial Roc-sized eagle began its second dive, and pulled the trigger. "Let's lay down the *LAW.*"

A projectile of flame blasted from the mouth of the mystical bazooka and detonated on the creature's head. Magical flame warred with airy cold and Hræsvelgr flew erratically, desperately trying to shake off the clinging fire, and finally plummeted to the ground with an earthshaking crash.

Flaming projectiles screamed at me from Ugu's staff and my weapon became an ornate spiky orange shaft of steel, spinning so fast it countered the arrows. I charged back towards them, but the ground was moving, rising, a great hand reaching out, crushing down on me, but I imagined red and blue and the power of legend, and up, up, and *away!* Through the hand I went, shattering the dull-witted elemental before it could realize what had happened.

But things were happening faster now, Ugu and Amanita working together and far, far more quickly than anything mortal could ever have managed. I rebounded from a crystal shield and something shocked me, thunder-bound power so intense that its pain momentarily eclipsed my burning soul, and I escaped, fingers to ghostly-green crested forehead and instantaneously moving, behind them, calling energy and the soul of the oceans forth in a rising dragon of water accompanied by the shimmer of long black hair and the calm of discipline I'd never known; the dragon strike slammed into the crystal shield and it began to crack, but the King and Queen leapt from the Royal Box and landed safely below, a barrage of steely bolts filling the air from Ugu as the ruins of the stands were transformed to a savage flock of wood-and-stone gargoyles set to rend me apart.

I disappeared from them in a puff of blue smoke and brimstone, but I hadn't thought ahead too much, just *over there!* Regaining my bearings took too long; Niddhogg's tail smashed into me.

That very nearly finished everything.

I fell from the sky, tumbling over and over, fetched up against a broken wall of the Grey Castle, stunned, unable for a moment to move. *What...that felt...like stone.*

I realized suddenly that my combination of Faerie and Mortal power was a two-edged sword. While wielding the full power of Faerie, I no longer had the True Mortal invulnerability; if, on the other hand, I pulled in Ozma's gift, hid it for a moment within my Mortal shell, I could not use the power; it had to be released, driving me forward, or it would do me no good at all.

But as Niddhogg slammed down a talon the size of a two-bedroom house, I yanked the power inside somehow, withheld it from my form. The concussion was like Yoop's club, only even softer. These things were almost purely magical creations, elementals, unlike Yoop who had at least *started* out fairly solid. As it lifted its paw and looked with glazed-yellow eyes, I released the magic, reached out to the chaos of the war that was now raging full-bore, and for just a moment the sounds faded, all sound disappearing into silence, and inside an echo of a singer, a fighter, a blonde-haired outcast. My body blazed brighter, into a detonation of pure light that blinded and dazzled the stony creature. It roared in confusion, staggering, and I ran up its leg and onto its back, as Hræsvelgr, wounded but once more airborne, came at me. I stopped, waving, hurling insults, and then dove aside.

Amanita's injured demon of the air collided with her infuriated and blinded monster of the earth. Immediately Niddhogg turned its fury onto Hræsvelgr, and half the south tower went down on top of them as they rolled over and over into the Grey Castle.

More exchanges of power, even faster now as they unleashed monsters, dancing swords of power, true tempests and transformed creatures. I battled my way through them with borrowed sword and symbolic power and spells created by a hundred imaginations, Druid-fire and Freeze-Arrow and "you cannot pass!," a sword of pure light and an orchestral fanfare so mighty that it echoed awe and wonder through my entire life.

I was closing in on them. I felt the power still burning within me, but it was not close to the end – I thought. But would I know? Or would I go on fighting until – in one fiery instant – it all came apart, never sensing that my soul was almost gone?

Ugu's face was showing the strain of the combat, sweating, no longer so sure, realizing that I had not been making some empty boast. He could counter every trick I showed him, and had many of his own, but... "My Queen," I heard him say grimly, "He is coming, and I think all our efforts may not hold him more than another minute or three."

Amanita's laugh floated over the battlefield, and I felt my heart constrict. *She doesn't sound worried at all.*

"A minute or less – perhaps less than half that – and he is done."

I paused, shielding myself. "What?"

"Ah, he has heard." Her smile was poisoned candy. "They told you, no doubt, that your power burns your soul. But did they tell you *how* it does so, little Mortal? For as you so truly say, 'tis your *Will* that drives you, that holds you to this world with such power as could shatter a world held within you. But what drives the Will, save the knowledge of your loss?

"The power erodes you, wears you away, as a river cutting through a canyon, a candle burning down. And the layers of your soul are *time*, Mortal, the length of your soul the depth of your life." The cold smile widened. "How long ago did you come to Faerie, Erik Medon? A year? A year and a half? For know this: you have burned nigh unto a year of your life already, and when your soul is worn away to the point at which your purpose began — when that which drives you was truly a part of your heart — in that moment you shall *forget* what drives you, and your will is gone, the power with it...

"And in that moment, Mortal Man...you will die."

Chapter 53.

For a moment, Erik Medon stood still, the aura of his shield flickering, as he stared at Amanita, and Ugu began to feel a faint hope.

And then Erik Medon laughed.

This laugh had none of the bitterness of his prior words; it was pure surprised humor, the laugh of a man told an excellent jest. Ugu watched as Amanita looked first surprised, then furious. *She never liked being laughed at.*

The laugh cut off suddenly, and the radiance of the power with it, and only cold, ice-blue eyes gazed into his and Amanita's; but the mouth still smiled, with a sharp and dangerous smile.

"How do you think I knew Polychrome the moment I laid eyes on her?" he asked quietly, and Ugu suddenly knew they were doomed. "I fell in love with her before I even knew what that *meant*, as pictures and words in a book!" The power of Faerie flamed up again, but brighter, much brighter. "And the last part of the puzzle is answered, because now I know why *I* had to be chosen. Pray to whatever gods you believe in that my body gives out fast, because you've just shown me how much farther I can *push* this!"

The once-Mortal's body was almost a pure blaze of light, and he seemed to shimmer within that power like something seen through the heat of a furnace. *"I HAVE FORTY MORE YEARS TO GIVE YOU!"*

He *lunged* from the Earth, and the force of that leap sent a concussion through the ground, left a crater the size of one of the castle towers. Against Ugu's shields he slammed a single punch, and *shattered* the spell as though it were crystal and not pure mystical force.

Were I not a Herkus, I would be ended in this moment. Only the superhuman strength and toughness of his people kept him upright as the shield-spell shattered and the remaining force of that blow took him directly in the chest. As it was, he skidded backwards and tumbled fifty feet before he stopped and regained his footing. *I can afford to reserve nothing now. We either defeat him in the next few minutes, or this once-Mortal will have our hearts in his hands.*

He reached deep within himself, unleashed a stupendous column of force driven by the power of a thousand Faerie souls he had taken in the first days of his power. Even as he did so, he felt another part of him go cold, reviling his former self. *But there is no turning back; they were no longer Faerie, merely power, for long since had I stripped them of anything that made them otherwise.*

Now it was on its way, and even Amanita threw up her arm to shield herself from the malignant radiance and absolute power of that stroke. Erik Medon did not dodge; instead he held up his hands, middle fingers down, as a strange peaked cloak shimmered ghostly about him, and golden light streaked out, branching, forming a series of insubstantial circular shields that took the brunt of even *that* attack, every shattering disc robbing Ugu's bolt of substance until the final shield, not more than inches from the Mortal, merely cracked and disappeared with the last vestige of power.

"Now catch me, you. Guesses for grabs where I am next!" As he spoke those nonsensical words, he was gone, and *here*, hands grasping for both of them, hurling them apart, the reinforcement of the other's power now gone. Ugu was on his own now, as was Amanita, unless they could rejoin. They were twin poles of power; this was the foundation of their conquest, and what had kept either from betraying the other in the early days. Never had Ugu needed her support more — nor she his.

But neither was helpless, and Amanita proved it with a shrieked invocation, gesture and mystic powder-shot scattering across the shambles of the courtyard. Hundreds of stone soldiers, Tempest-spawn, and lesser Torrents materialized and charged the Mortal.

He could destroy one, a dozen, even a hundred, but he was, now, just one man, though of supernal power, his impossible duplicates gone back to the vapor from which they had come, and sheer numbers would overwhelm him, even as a mighty warrior might fall beneath the wrath of a hive of ants.

For a moment he disappeared beneath a tide of fang-mouthed, taloned horrors, and Ugu thought they had won. But the Music of the Spheres sounded a note of doom, blue-gold light suddenly blazed out from within, and a detonation of power blew the mob away like leaves in a hurricane. *"AWAY FROM ME!"* the Mortal's voice thundered, and the power raced out in a perfect sphere of destruction, scything down all save Amanita, Ugu, and Jormungandr; the impact finally shattered Amanita's wing of the Castle, and the central dome collapsed like a malignant flower opening, exposing the seething, roiling mass of black vapor and lightning that lay within: the Great Binding.

Jormungandr charged at Amanita's order, and Ugu reached into his robes, took out a final handful of charms and suspended spells, the most powerful and final resorts of defense and offense he had ever devised — aside from the Eye of the Soul, without which he and Amanita would have been dead long since. He needed this time to prepare.

The acid-green serpent of corrupted water's essence slithered, an undammed flood, for Erik Medon and opened its mouth, spewing corrosive slime everywhere. Somehow, the Mortal evaded the fountaining death, leaping and bouncing with acrobatic skill and speed beyond comprehension. Jormungandr missed in its strike, but reversed — not by turning, but by simply changing malleable front and back to their reverse.

But Erik was standing before it, hand upraised, phantom image of black hair and white glove, and snapped his fingers. With a doomsday roar, the very *air* ignited around Jormungandr, water's nemesis — fire – burning it away, flame without source or cause until naught but grease-black smoke remained of Amanita's last creation.

The dark-air eagle and the grey-stone dragon had destroyed each other.

Erik turned towards Ugu, and now the wizard could see that the shape within the vengeful light was growing less substantial, evaporating like his soul due to the terrible exigencies of the power he had taken. The eyes still were visible, now green like avenging emerald, now blue, but the rest was indistinct, hair mingling with light as though boiling away, body more light than substance. But he showed no sign of stopping.

"Here I come," Erik Medon said, as the light around him gathered in a sparkling aura.

And he burned a path across the ground as he came.

The shields Ugu had spent a dozen years preparing were shattered in instants. The spells that could have slain a hundred men missed their target or were brushed aside, the foolish attempt of a child to harm a warrior born. Bright-flaming fists battered into him even through his greatest defenses, kicks stunned him, and a final double-handed strike slammed through his staff, broke one rib, left him prone and defenseless in the ruins of the wall he had just been slammed into.

"And that's all," the Mortal said. "You have nothing left. And though it's taken a lot from me, I have more than enough power to finish both of *you.*" The fury and loss in his voice was under control, but no less because of it; merely colder and more calculated.

Amanita laughed, and *this* laugh was very much mad. "Oh, you want *power,* little boy?"

And before even the lightning speed of Faerie could stop her, Amanita Verdant leapt lightly into the heart of the Great Binding.

Chapter 54.

I stared as Amanita disappeared within that roiling black mass, neither I nor Ugu moving. For a few seconds, nothing happened.

Then the black, lightning-shot cloud — that seemed to scream in anguish and hatred to my augmented senses — began to spin, funneling inward like a whirlpool, but from the center something began to *grow*.

It grew, towering higher and higher, condensing shape and substance from smoky power, a hundred feet, two hundred, five, a thousand, a head the size of a castle tower, scale-armored, black and poison-green and silver, house-high blades of teeth, a Dragon on a scale undreamed of. And it was laughing, a voice deep as thunder yet with overtones I knew. "Now let us test your power, little Mortal, for I have become the Binding, taken to myself all the power of Phanfasms and souls I have sacrificed these centuries. Not...precisely...my plan, but now I wonder that I hesitated." The Verdant Dragon's eyes opened, blazing a venomous crimson and as mad as the voice that spoke.

"Ohhhh, *crap*," I heard myself say. I glanced down and saw Ugu pale as a ghost. *This* hadn't been in any of his game plans either. I pointed down to him. "Stay," I said, and launched myself into the air. *Have to see how dangerous she is.*

As soon as I left the ground, she spat out a column of black-edged green that slammed me back down like a sledgehammer. Even all the power of Oz seemed unable to overcome that absolute force. *No wonder. The Phanfasms were said to be the ultimate in power, the greatest of the dark Faeries, and she's apparently fused all of their power into one being — herself. Maybe it's not more powerful than I am as the channel of Oz itself –*

"But how long will your power last, little boy?" that storm-deep voice said tauntingly, echoing my own thoughts. "Oh, perhaps if you could fight me with your True Mortal capabilities you would win, for surely nothing more magical than I is, or has ever been."

But it didn't take a genius to see what she meant by "if"; the titanic Dragon flew, thousands of feet overhead. I couldn't leap and bounce that high, and I couldn't *fly* without the power of Faerie. I couldn't use the power of Faerie, though, and still have my True Mortal power, which was the *only* thing that might penetrate that monster's defenses.

"So fight as you must, please, fight and die screaming! But my magic is strong enough, strong enough to survive anything you can deliver for a time, and a little time is all you have; and then shall *I* remain, and all of Faerie will become mine!" She smiled down, a savage threat and hunger. "Oh, my King, I am afraid...I shall have no more use for you, either. But then, after your failure today, I'm sure death will be a welcome release!"

Her head rose. "First...I will deal with your friends and your army, little Mortal boy. That should hurt you a great deal!"

I looked with extended senses, memorizing what lay near my friends, twenty-decimals of similarity, and I was there, next to the Army. *No time for reserves, the big guns are needed.* And as she drew in her breath for a devastating attack, I concentrated. "You want to play with the big boys? Let me show you the biggest of them all!"

And I *grew*, changing, feeling invincible armor covering me in grey scales, claws forming, a great sheet of spines growing between my shoulderblades, dwarfing even the castle below me, titanic, uncaring, unstoppable, and I roared a challenge to my opponent, whose eyes were no longer so arrogant, her breath drawn in, mine as well, and we both *breathed* at the same time, the blaze of electricity and nuclear fire from my back channeling into me, through me, and outward, streaking out just as the Verdant Dragon breathed.

Black-green power met a column of blue-white energy and the two stopped, contesting, as I fought her life-destroying breath with all the strength and will I had left. The point of contact *blazed*, a sphere of seething radiance that made the sun itself look dim and distant. She redoubled her attack and I threw more of myself into my own, jagged-edged scales blazing red and blue behind and sending atomic holocaust onward, until suddenly both of us lost control and the energy exploded, shattering the last towers of the Grey Castle and knocking everyone but myself to the ground.

But even in that moment, the transformation reverted. *Ugu's Eye of the Soul is still working, tied to them both. Once, and once only.*

She laughed again, a mad laugh that confirmed what I suspected: her will might have allowed her to retain control, rather than becoming just one of an amalgam of all the minds that were once there, but there was nothing sane left. If I didn't beat her here, Faerie would be ruled by a monster without restraint or care, a sadistic, unpredictable sociopath with the power of a god.

But that clash of power had also shown me she was right. We'd both thrown our full power into that contest, and hers was the equal of mine. And she was equal to me in another way: she was no longer just a giantess or transformed human, she was a living container of Faerie power, with all the flexibility that implied. Perhaps she lacked my imagination, but I didn't have that Eye of the Soul power to understand and negate everything she did.

"How funny. You'll protect them instead of attacking while I am focused on them. You know that *is* the only chance you'd have, don't you?" She shook her giant head mockingly. "The next time you would be wise to attack me, for afterwards shall I concentrate on *you*. Do not disappoint me; I expected an adversary of intelligence, not a fool."

She began to draw in her breath, and I knew she was right. I could sacrifice my friends and possibly get in a strike that would take her down...or I could stand here protecting them until the power that even now burned like acid through me finally wore away the last of my soul. To do anything else would be stupid –

And that triggered a memory, and the memory told me what I had to do. I prepared for my last moment, the only strike that might both save my friends and destroy Amanita Verdant. It terrified me – but I remembered her cruel laugh, saw *her hands* on the knife plunged into Polychrome's chest, and my own fury flared up with the power of Faerie.

I called upon the ultimate reserve, the one I'd never used, strange twin to the blue and red I'd used before, dark hair flaming

367

golden in extremity. *Ore wa... Ore wa densetsu no choujin.* "You're right, that would be the smart thing to do. Villains try to be smart, find the safe and wise path." I grinned, even as she, with a draconic smile, began to open her mouth, as the golden power exploded about me and shook the earth once more. "But in the words of Marvel's Thor: Heroes... heroes have an *infinite* capacity for stupidity!" And I blazed up from the ground, straight for her.

The ravening column of emerald-ebony fire blasted forth again, and with a scream of agony I focused all the power of Faerie ahead of me, splitting that gargantuan flame down the center. *Just a little farther, a little closer, faster, faster! Kaiyo-ken!*

The fire raged around me, eroding defenses, burning, scorching in a sick and twisted agony nothing like the purifying incandescence of Ozma's power. But I could spare no more, I had to drive faster, faster, red-gold aura blazing like the burning of my soul, feeling the air itself screaming louder than my own voice.

Even through the searing dragon-fire I could now see the immense black-scaled head, looming ever closer, closer –

And I yanked in all of the power of Faerie. I was an unguided missile, a bullet of True Mortality with winds tearing at my blistered skin, and the dragon-fire vanished about me, the dragon eyes widened. My speed threatened to rob me of breath and consciousness but I hung on, and snapped out my arms into the bone-breaking airstream, envisioning the Mortal Power streaming outwards in both directions as I plunged straight down her throat.

Chapter 55.

Even *more mad than I had imagined, and this a move I cannot counter.* For a moment Ugu forgot his opponent, forgot even his pain, as he looked upon true horror. *She was mad, and she may still have been right in her arrogance. She is the very race of Phanfasms in a single being, a monster of destruction and hatred given indomitable life and power.* He looked over, heard the muttered curse under the breath of the shimmering avenger. *Even he knows he has met his match, and perhaps more.*

The order to "stay" was as though spoken to a dog, but Ugu did not protest. *The wisest policy is to watch, here. One and one alone will survive this...or, perhaps, both shall perish. In either case, I will gather what remains to me and decide whether to risk myself against the victor.*

A part of him also thought that, perhaps, he should simply flee. But that, too, he was denied, for though his throne was shattered and his armies embattled, still was he King in Oz, if only for moments more, and he would see how this would end. He owed...he owed Oz that much. And in truth...perhaps he had no more stomach for this fighting any more. It had cost the lives of so many, the souls of others.

Erik Medon launched himself upward and the Verdant Dragon smashed him down, and Ugu understood the cleverness of her plan. *Insane, but far from stupid. He has no allies left who could save him from a fall, and he cannot use his Mortal power while flying. He cannot reach her without magic, but the magic will not avail him against her.*

And then Ugu gasped, a silent curse on his lips, as Erik Medon became...something *else*, a monster fully the equal of Amanita's Dragon, yet different, a massive bipedal form that loomed like a mountain and gave vent to an alien, echoing roar that screeched like tearing metal and boomed like thunder, and sent forth a column of blue-white fire that stopped the Verdant Dragon's power cold in its tracks.

But even that five-hundred-foot titan could only stop the Dragon once, and it was gone, gone, leaving only the man behind, and Ugu could see the desperation and growing despair on Erik Medon's face.

But then...a realization, an idea, and the phantom image of a warrior transforming, transfigured to a gold-blazing avenger only slightly less substantial than the burning man of Faerie power that remained at the core, launching himself at a Dragon that covered the sky. The Dragon-fire enveloped the auric flame, but it seemed to bore *through* the black-green destruction, cutting forward, ever closer, ever nearer the great head –

And the light disappeared, and there was only a tiny dot hurtling the last few yards, the Verdant Dragon's fire gone, gone with True Mortal power, and the great jaws snapped shut even as the dot streaked inside. There was a flash of light, a line drawn down the draconic figure from end to end, that then flickered downward to strike earth in a flare of brilliance that died away almost immediately.

The Dragon that had been Amanita Verdant convulsed, bellowed, and plummeted from the sky, smashing down atop the same point like an avalanche, piling up, an impact that sent a shockwave through the ground that just kept *going*, breaking the last of the Grey Palace, leaving only the original Castle of Ozma, also grey stone yet more solid than anything he had built, and finally the last massive coil struck ground and the shockwave died away.

Is it...over?

Even as he thought the question, the Brobdingnagian head stirred, rose, opening cold ruby eyes.

And just before the head, another figure rose, tiny, but glowing, staggering, cradling a broken arm, standing on a leg that bent wrongly. Yet... the leg was straightening, the arm as well, though they seemed less pieces of a living thing than shimmering outlines, a sketch of a man done in sunlight and fire. He strode away from the Verdant Dragon, his back to the monster.

"A...clever stroke, Mortal Man... One that hurt me. But alas, it, too, has failed, and now..." The Dragon smiled, and rose higher, preparing to strike once more, "...now shall I destroy you, if indeed enough is left of you to destroy!"

"Hmph." The face was a study of lines and contours, an impression of a human countenance, but Ugu could see the one-sided, contemptuous smile. "You are...already dead."

The Verdant Dragon began to draw in her breath, building the power of her strike... and stopped, as though choking. "What...what have you *done?*"

Erik Medon did not even turn around, but kept moving, eyes the only dark part of his burning form, and his voice was a mixture of pain and ecstasy that made him sound like the very embodiment of retribution. "Extended myself as a knife of mortality, across your entire body. I have cut through your soul, whatever you had of one, severing its connections to all that you have become."

A brilliant golden line suddenly shone out along the Dragon's length. "No...!"

"For a few moments your...pieces remained in contact, wires severed yet still touching, unaware they had been cut. But as soon as you sought to use the power, you placed pressure on the breach... and you have now torn yourself apart."

"*No! NO! I WILL NOT DIE!*"

The scream of denial echoed across all Oz, as the monstrous thing that had been Amanita Verdant rose up, blotting out the setting sun with clouds of black storm, crackling lightning about her form, a terrible and awesome sight — but the light burned more brightly, a line, a seam, a crack, a splitting wound that burst open, releasing energy like a fountain of blood that could drown a world, with a shriek of agony and loss that left even Ugu, for a moment, on his knees, covering his head, tears in his eyes.

And when he looked up, it was gone. The sky was clear. And a single strand of green hair drifted away on the wind.

His armies broke then, fleeing. General Guph led the retreat, Tempests and Infernos provided speed and the remaining Temblors performed rearguard action, disappearing as fast as they could into the forests beyond.

He began to turn, and with speed he could not follow Erik Medon was there. Erik's hand, flickering like fire, almost

371

transparent, closed about Ugu's throat, burning iron, and effortlessly lifted him from the ground. Ugu pulled at that deathgrip, hammered at it with all his Herkus-born strength, but it was useless.

A strange peace came over him then. *So...it does end here. Amanita has died, and I, who helped make her, who helped do all those things in her name, will follow her.*

The blue Mortal eyes glared fiercely up, and he felt the hand trembling, starting to contract. There were footsteps, and from the corner of his eye he saw three other figures: Nimbus Thunderstroke, Zenga of Pingaree, and Ruggedo the Red, the Penitent. They were staring at the tableau before them, with mingled expressions of disbelief and triumph.

"Victory, Lord Erik! Finish this one and we have won!"

In that glowing countenance, insubstantial lips skinned back from crystal teeth in a snarl. "Ugu. Release the enchantment on Oz. Free the Castle and the Emerald City." The words were forced from Erik, clearly the work of a man holding onto himself for dear life.

Of course he would ask the one thing I cannot do. "I...cannot." He forced the words out, painfully, past the grip on his throat. "To willingly...release...required both."

"Ah." Ruggedo said softly. "A safety mechanism, to ensure that both held the keys to the realm."

"Then the only way to save the Emerald City — to unbind that enchantment — is to finish the job," Zenga said coldly, and Nimbus nodded with grim agreement.

"Finish this now, Erik," Nimbus said quietly. "It is the last thing left undone."

The hand on his throat tightened... but slowly relaxed. "Is that the only way?"

I...find I do not mind, any more. "As far...as I know." He managed an ironic shrug. "Without us fighting you...there may...be other ways."

"We cannot risk that!" Nimbus said decisively. "Lord Erik Medon, hurry! Finish what we came here to do! Do not let her sacrifice be in vain!"

That nearly ended it. The hand squeezed, crushing, as molten tears started from Erik Medon's blue eyes. The world began to go grey around Ugu, and though he felt much fear at what might await him on the other side, a part of him...welcomed it. *I have done enough evil here.*

But then the hand slowly began to relax. "I...can't do it."

"Erik –" Zenga began.

"I *CAN'T!*" This was the voice of the Mortal man again, though the power still burned through him, a voice of simple pain and tragedy. "In the middle of a battle, against something like Amanita, that's one thing, but ... Nimbus, you know me."

"But –"

"*No.*" Erik straightened, and Ugu – incredulous – felt himself being slowly lowered. "I will not kill in cold blood. Not with Ozma's power." His voice dropped to a whisper. "And never in Poly's name."

He tossed Ugu into Zenga's grip, stronger even than a Herkus. "Take him away." Still blazing, he collapsed to insubstantial knees, tears welling up in his voice, falling to the ground like stars. "I'm... done."

The world went white.

The light streaked into the sky, a column of sunfire that became a pure leaf-green, coalesced into a perfect sphere, a shining ball the color of life itself.

It flew out, near the horizon, and began to run, roll, skip, jump, along the ground. And wherever it touched, grey turned to living green. The light split, became two, danced along the dead circle, the broken battlefield, and scarred land was healed, was waving grasses and bright flowers; twisted bodies vanished, injured rose healed. The lights spiraled inward, and the great stone wreckage of the Grey Castle evaporated before them like morning mist in the sun, the houses beneath beginning to emerge, sparkling with emeralds and aquamarines, jade and nephrite, green-polished granite and emerald marble. The broken was rebuilt, and the Spheres *SANG*, a call of joy that even lifted the now-all-too-solid Erik Medon's bedraggled head, caused his sobs to cease and a momentary catch of wonder in his breath, for the Emerald City was rising, the

Castle of Ozma was no longer all grey dead stone, the towers were flying the banners of green and gold, gemstones were catching the light as they had not in centuries, and the lights spun with laughter, and Ugu suddenly understood.

"All will hinge on the choice of one;
A choice only made before it has begun."

"Of course," Ugu heard himself say, and Nimbus turned from incredulously staring at the miracle.

"Of course?"

"He is a man. A Mortal man. But he is not a killer. He sought to avoid killing, even in our battle, for much of it. Had he killed me then, it would have been an act of deliberate evil, using the power of Ozma in ways..." he smiled bitterly, "that only *we* have ever attempted. He would have become that which he fought, and in doing so would have destroyed what he came to defend. Only by being true to his own nature — only by *having*, as his true nature, mercy in his heart rather than hatred — could he release the spell by releasing the power that otherwise was bound to him unto death."

The lights coalesced again as the Emerald Palace was restored, coming together at the entrance. And from within that light came a figure, a woman, a girl really, with coal-black hair around a delicate face for which *beauty* would be a poor and inadequate word, in royal robes and with a dainty crown upon her head, a great emerald scepter in her hand. Nimbus dropped to one knee, followed by Ruggedo, Zenga, all of the men and women emerging from the newly-freed houses, the soldiers only now approaching. Ugu, too, dropped to his knees; Zenga looked mildly surprised that she had not had to force him down.

I have lost. I shall take this defeat, at least, with somewhat more grace than my first.

Only Erik Medon did not move. He remained on his hands and knees, immobile, as though even this miracle was not enough to give him hope or care.

Ozma looked down at him with sorrow, but did not intrude. Instead she came to them and gestured. "Nimbus Thunderstroke, we thank the Rainbow Kingdom for their faith and all you have given, and give our inadequate sympathies for what you have lost."

Nimbus bowed, and Ugu could see that he was making a great effort not to cry before the Ruler of Oz. *I knew this...Polychrome not at all, yet I see how she has touched them all. Where is my legacy, whom have I touched that would care to remember?*

Other figures were emerging from the Castle — figures of legend he had passed many times in their stony prisons, now come to life, and at their head a tall girl, a young woman of fair hair and merry blue eyes, not as beautiful as the Princess-Queen but at least as formidable a presence, wearing the great jeweled Belt.

At that, Ozma turned to the Penitent. "Ruggedo, you have come to save my kingdom, that once you would have taken. You have my thanks."

Ruggedo bowed so low his forehead touched the ground.

"And though you say nothing, and neither does he who saved us all, I was one with him. In a way, all of us of Oz's heart heard him when he truly awakened to himself, and I was at his center. I know what was promised."

Ruggedo shook his head, and Ugu wondered. "I know he had no true right to promise such things. I went with him anyway."

"And because of that, the promise will be kept. I will not have my rescuer — the savior of Oz — foresworn. Dorothy..."

Dorothy Gale raised an eyebrow. "Are you *sure* 'bout this, Ozma?"

She smiled. "Look at him, Princess Dorothy. Is this the Ruggedo we knew... Or the one we thought he was, once?"

Dorothy studied Ruggedo the Red for a long moment. Then her hands went to the Magic Belt and with a simple twist unfastened it, and laid it in Ruggedo's hands. "There. Just as well, really, I never really did figure out everything it did, an' it didn't go with *anything* in my wardrobe."

Ugu stared in disbelief. *They have just given away one of the most powerful artifacts of Faerie to a former enemy.*

Ruggedo was staring down at the Belt, and when he raised his face there were two tears trickling down the seamed face, tears backed by a rising smile. "My...my dears... I do not know what to say. I gave up hope of this when I gave up hatred, I think, and..."

Ryk E. Spoor

"You need say nothing, Ruggedo, save that never again will the Nome Kingdom and Oz be anything other than friends and allies," Ozma said gently, and the old Nome nodded, clearly unable for the moment to speak. "But if you would do anything..." She glanced towards Erik, and spoke very quietly. "The Hero deserves at least *one* Wish, don't you think?"

Ruggedo smiled, and nodded. "The cost may be...high. But no higher than he has paid." The Belt *clicked* into place, and Ruggedo placed his hands upon it and closed his eyes.

With the sound of shattering goblets, half the gems of the Belt exploded into sparkling dust. *What has he* done? *The powers of that Belt are...*

And from behind them all, an uncertain voice said, "E...Erik?"

Erik Medon snapped upright, and on his face was a look of utter terror — the expression of a man who dares not look, dares not hope, because he knows that if that hope fails it will shatter him completely. Eyes wide, voice trembling, he turned his head slowly, almost unwillingly. "Poly?"

Rising from the ground, even her stained garments once more unmarred, the golden-haired Daughter of the Rainbow stood, pale, unbelieving, her gaze only for the man before her.

Erik's eyes grew even wider, and for a moment his face lit up until he looked not near fifty, not near forty, perhaps not even past one-and-twenty, shining with a piercing elation that transfigured him, and in a whisper so heartbreakingly joyous that it echoed across the land like a shout, he breathed, "*Polychrome.*"

The two were suddenly in each other's arms. Their lips touched and would not let go, even as the Daughter of the Rainbow began to dance. Her Hero followed her, with every step a glitter of polychromatic light that sent their joy echoing through the Emerald City. Ugu felt a stinging at his own eyes that he could not, for a moment, comprehend.

"*Ho ho ho hooo!*" Ruggedo laughed, a deep booming laugh that did indeed, as legend held, sound for all the world like the very essence of Saint Nick's.

"Ahhh," said the small, neat, balding old man with a clever, sharp face that had just come to join them, "so it *is* a happy ending, after all."

Dorothy was smiling, tears in her eyes, and Ugu realized that what Ozma had said was literally true; these people, those imprisoned in the Castle with Ozma's power, had *felt* Erik Medon's pain, had come to *know* him...as, Ugu now understood, Erik had in truth known *them*, without ever having met. "Well, I'd say he deserves it, don't you?" she asked, even as the others from the Castle arrived to watch Polychrome Glory and Erik Medon dancing across the courtyard.

"He showed *great* courage," agreed the immense Lion.

"And he used his brains!" The indomitably cheerful Scarecrow nodded, painted smile seeming even broader than normal.

"*And* his heart," said the glittering figure of polished tin beside him, with a gentle voice and a face of metal that still could smile.

A brightly-colored figure of patches and yarn-hair tumbled into view and plopped down to watch as Polychrome and Erik, still in embrace, danced up stairs without missing a beat. "Yeah, he was pretty clever, but, you know, I don't think he's hearing a *word* any of you are saying!"

The Wizard chuckled. "None in his position would," he said, following the golden hair as it swirled about the dancers amid the light of all colors. "He's a lucky man."

Ozma smiled and tilted her head. "I am not so sure it isn't *Polychrome* who's the lucky one."

Dorothy nodded. "He did it all for her, you know."

"Not just for her," Zenga said, with a brilliant smile through her own drying tears. "For all of us. He loved her more than anything, but...he loved Faerie too."

"Then," the Wizard said with a little bow to Ozma and Dorothy, "shall we agree they are *both* most fortunate?"

"Indeed, my Lord Wizard," Glinda the Good said. "Wisely put."

Ozma's eye was suddenly fixed on him, and Ugu raised his head and met her gaze. "And what say you, Ugu?"

He looked across at Erik and Polychrome, and felt a sad smile on his face. "It is not the ending *I* sought," he said slowly. "But...it is the ending that should have been."

Ozma raised her head and stared at him for a long moment. Then she closed her eyes and gave a short nod. "Then perhaps you have gained some wisdom after all, Ugu. And for that wisdom, I shall leave your final fate in *his* hands."

Ugu looked at her with dawning hope, and then at the Mortal, who had separated from Poly for just a moment, just at arm's length, to see once more that she was truly there, truly whole, truly smiling and joyous and happy to be with *him*, and Ugu knelt before Ozma and bowed his head to the ground. "Then truly you are merciful, Ozma, for on this day and for many to come he will have naught but mercy to give to any, I think."

There was a movement in the crowd of the armies, and a figure was hauled forward, in armor, bloodied, red staining pure-white hair, and Nimbus' face darkened. He strode forward, drawing his sword. "The Usurper's fate is a matter between kings, but the life of a traitor is in *my* hands!"

Ugu did not know how or — at first – why, but suddenly he twisted from Zenga's loosened grip and sprinted forward, throwing himself between the upraised sword and Cirrus Dawnglory. "*NO!*"

Nimbus' arm hesitated, but by the trembling in it Ugu could see that only his surprise kept the Marshal of the Storm Guard from ending both Ugu's and Cirrus' lives in that moment.

"Take my life if you must," Ugu told him. "But spare him, for he was no traitor, but the most courageous, faithful, and honorable of my own legions." He saw Nimbus' confusion and felt his own surprise...and yet knew he spoke truth, and straightened proudly. "For he is *not* Cirrus Dawnglory, not exactly."

"What lie is this?" Nimbus growled, and the sword was now at Ugu's throat. Ugu did not move. "I know Cirrus Dawnglory well — or I *thought* I did."

"And so you did. But," he looked apologetically at the confused man behind him, "the *real* Cirrus Dawnglory died centuries ago, in the patrol of which you believed he was the sole survivor. Instead what returned was a creation of mine and

Amanita's, the perfect spy for the Rainbow Realm, called back only after he had lived among you for centuries.

"What even *he* did not know," Ugu continued, "was that he was not merely a Tempest and the soul of a Gillikin given the form and false memories of Cirrus Dawnglory. He was, in fact, made *from* Cirrus Dawnglory, from what memories and fragments of his soul remained once Amanita was done with him."

Cirrus looked at him with dawning horror and, at the same time, understanding. Ugu looked back into Nimbus' eyes. "But as a Tempest — as a spy — he was in *my* service at all times. In the most dangerous of all positions, and he was faithful to us. *Even* though," he raised his voice as Nimbus began to speak, "Even though he came to care for you, and your King Iris, and especially his daughter Polychrome, and think of you as friends and comrades. When called he returned, and that was hard, hard for him, yet he did it because that much of the true Cirrus Dawnglory was a part of him — faithful, true, and loyal. Slay him not for being exactly the sort of man he was supposed to be. I may be defeated, but I am still *his* King, and none shall touch him unless first they slay me."

Ozma's hand came down on Nimbus'. "He is right, Nimbus Thunderstroke. And there has been more than enough killing this day." She looked at Ugu with new respect. "It is said that power corrupts, Ugu the Unbowed. Yet I do not see this in you."

Ugu did not know what to say. "I...regret many things I have done, Ozma." He held up a hand. "I do not regret, nor retract, many of the things I felt or believed...but I do sincerely regret the foolish and evil ways that I attempted to follow those beliefs and feelings. I should have found some other way. And had I done so earlier...perhaps even Amanita might not have become the monster she did."

"I kinda doubt that," Dorothy said tartly. "She was a downright *mean* woman from the start. But you *have* changed, Ugu, even if it did take a lot more'n changing you into a Dove."

A sunshower, rain falling from a nearly clear sky, suddenly fell over them, and he could see Polychrome and Erik Medon laughing as they danced in the rain. Ugu heard himself chuckle, and it was a strange sound indeed, one without malice or the heaviness of intrigue. "It required that I change *myself*, Princess Dorothy, and that is a harder task than a mere Belt might accomplish." He glanced at Ruggedo and the somewhat-diminished Belt.

A greater light shimmered above, and they all looked up to see a great Rainbow descending from the heavens. "We have reached the ending of this story, I think."

"Not quite," Ozma said. "The last words have yet to be spoken by the Hero and the Princess. And we all should be there for that moment."

And Ugu understood, as the Rainbow grew even greater, and all of them — of Oz, of the Armies of Faerie, himself, Ruggedo — began to ascend the Rainbow, led by the dancing figures of the Mortal and the Faerie Princess.

Chapter 56.

She *is* alive. *She is alive, and she is beside me on the Rainbow,* and she loves *me. She loves ME. SHE LOVES ME!*

For a time I could not measure, I had no room in my mind or heart for any other thought or feeling except the utter incredulous and perfect joy of a literal dream come true, of a fantasy held for decades that had proven, in the end, to be far more than I had imagined.

I remembered a line from one of the Narnia books — *The Voyage of the Dawn Treader* — about the smell and the song at the End of the World: "It would break your heart." "Why? Was it so sad?" "Sad!! No." I had never quite understood what sort of feeling that could be; now I did, for I was filled to bursting with a joy that I could not imagine I could contain, and tears kept flowing from my eyes because there were no smiles or laughter that could adequately express what I felt.

But at last I looked up from those perfect violet-storm eyes and beheld the glory of the Rainbow Castle, and realized that we had travelled the entire length of the Rainbow without my even realizing it. And by her startled look, I realized Polychrome, too, had lost all track of time, and I laughed aloud for the sheer amazement and wonder of it, that I could in any way, in any imaginable way, be the focus of such attention.

"By such a laugh I know you are healed, Erik Medon," Ozma said, gently laughing herself. "It is well; truly would it have been a steep price to pay, that our savior be broken in the moment of his triumph."

I turned, and suddenly stopped dead in my tracks, staring. I hadn't realized how many were following us, and *who* they were, and I knew then that I had been wrong, that it *was* possible for me to feel more wonder and joy than I already did, for they were there, all of them: the Scarecrow and the Tin Woodman, Dorothy and Glinda, the Cowardly Lion and Scraps the Patchwork Girl, the Wizard of Oz himself, some not *quite* like their illustrations — but more *themselves*, even as Ugu had been more than the simple caricature of an impotent villain.

And for a moment I simply could not speak. There were so many things I wanted to say, and do, and think, and I found myself on my knees again, crying and unable to stop, and Poly asking me what was wrong, and I just took her hand and shook my head and though I was blushing crimson I couldn't stop the tears.

Another hand covered hers. "Nothing's wrong, Poly," Dorothy said, with a smile and tears in her own eyes. "B'lieve me, I know what he's feelin', at least some of it. Couldn't talk very much myself, when I knew I'd come back to Oz to stay. Add that t' you comin' back to him? Poor man's just *got* to have too much happiness for one person t' say!"

I met her gaze, and saw she did understand, as she'd say, jus' 'bout *'zactly*. I smiled and nodded again, and took a deep breath. "Princess...Dorothy Gale." I stood and bowed. "You're right. It...was all just too much. Still *is*. I love Polychrome more than anything," I looked to her again, just reassuring myself that she really was there, alive, "but I've loved all of Oz, all of Faerie, for just as long."

"And *I* understand, perhaps, more than even Princess Dorothy," the Wizard said with a smile — and, I thought, a suspiciously bright sparkle in his own eyes. "You no doubt understand that my return to Oz — to confront the Princess I had betrayed — was nowhere near as simple as Baum painted it... and so you can realize my own joy when I was, in the end, welcomed home." He leaned a bit closer, and in a lower voice said, "And as a man, I can *very* well understand the rest."

I hoped Polychrome liked the sensitive blushing sort of guy, because it seemed I was awfully prone to that.

Suddenly another voice, a deep voice like thunder, shouted out, "*Polychrome!*"

And Iris Mirabilis was there, sprinting from the mighty gates of the fortress, somehow smaller but still immense as he caught up his daughter and swung her around, his own face not entirely dry. "Thank all the Above. You are alive."

Then he turned to me and — in front of all assembled on the Rainbow — knelt and bowed to the very ground. "My thanks — all the thanks of Faerie — to you, Erik Medon."

I looked down at the top of his head, and waited a moment. "Thank you, Iris Mirabilis," I said finally, and he raised his head. "Yes," I said, in answer to the unspoken question, "I was royally pissed at you when I finally understood what was going on. And if she were *not* alive..." I realized my eyes must have gone terribly cold, because I saw understanding in his. I pushed my hair back from my face — for some reason it seemed to be dropping over my eyes more — and drew another breath. "But that is what *might* have been, and I won't waste more time on it. We all paid prices for this war — none more than the soldiers on both sides who died, and they are gone -" a thought struck me, and I turned to Ozma. "Unless whatever...brought back Poly...?"

"Alas, no." It was Ruggedo, and I turned to him in surprise. He raised his eyebrow, then chuckled. "Ah. So deep in your grief were you that your powers of observation failed to even note that it was I, not Ozma, who was able to return life to Polychrome."

Iris' eyes narrowed. "That is...virtually impossible. It requires the power and the tolerance of the Above, and the price is -"

"I know the price — none better, Iris — and the power was returned to me by those who had taken it — and most justly so — in centuries past."

Now I realized that Ruggedo was wearing the Magic Belt, the Wishing Belt, the Belt that had held the vast majority of the powers of the Nome Kingdom. But as I looked, I could see that while it still blazed with gems of all sorts, fully half of the settings were empty, their gems shattered and dull. "That...was the cost?"

Ruggedo nodded, but his smile did not fade. "A small price indeed; after all, I had long since given up any hope of ever holding my Belt again; what matter, then, that it has lost much of its power now? I still have far more than I did when first we met — far, far more, I think, even had the Belt been destroyed entirely for my temerity in using the gift of the Above to flout their law."

"Thank -"

The old Nome shook his head violently. "I will take no thanks or intimations of a debt from you, my friend. I paid what I owed, as best I could — and as I said, I think I still have had a bargain." He looked at Iris Mirabilis. "Now *your* thanks I shall accept, Lord of the Rainbow."

"And you have them, and more besides." He looked back to me, having risen now to his full height, and saw as Polychrome took my hand again, and smiled. He raised his arms in a welcoming gesture. "Enter the Rainbow Kingdom, friends and allies, for today Faerie is free."

His gaze flicked across the crowd, and I saw it suddenly halt, and his face go first pale, then dark. "What is the meaning of *this?*"

I didn't have to turn — though I did — to know what he was looking at. I didn't remember exactly what had gone on afterwards, but I knew that I hadn't killed Ugu, and no one else was likely to have tried.

Ozma stepped between Ugu and Iris as the Rainbow Lord started forward. "Ugu the Unbowed has been defeated, and in his words I have heard some faint hope that he is not beyond reason; his life was spared by your very champion, and in doing so he fulfilled your prophecy to the very end. So it is that his final fate is neither in your hands, nor in mine, but in those of Erik Medon, for it was he, not you nor I, who defeated the Usurpers and freed us all."

I noted Ugu's surprise — which I rather echoed — that Ozma used Ugu's self-chosen title. I was also startled that they were lobbing *that* ball back into my court, and despite the euphoria that still sang through my veins, I recognized a deadly serious issue waiting for me. *I will not make that decision immediately, that's for sure. I need a clear head to judge someone like that.*

Iris opened his mouth as though to argue, then looked down at me, closed his mouth, and finally gave a short bow. "As the Princess of Oz directs, so shall it be. Still, I would have someone be responsible for his actions, and watch over him."

"I will do that." Zenga stepped forward. "His strength isn't the equal of mine, he's just about out of magical tricks, and I really don't think he's looking for any more trouble."

Ugu said nothing, though he did nod at the last. I suspected he figured it was best to keep his mouth shut, even when it came to agreeing, and he was probably right. Three centuries and more of fear will make just about anyone irrational.

"So be it," Iris agreed finally. He turned to the assembled masses and spread his arms wide again, gesturing us forward. "Welcome again. And well done to you all — and especially to our Hero. We will thank him in true Royal style tonight — all of us!"

And the responding roar of agreement nearly deafened me. "Oh, jeez, I'm in trouble now," I whispered to Poly. She giggled and pushed that annoying lock of hair out of the way as she leaned closer.

"You certainly are. Nomes *and* the Storm Guards throwing a party in the Rainbow Castle? This won't be over for a *week* — and you'll have to be there *all the time!*"

I shuddered, but kissed her cheek, marveling once more that I *could* do that. "Is it too late for us to say I fell heroically in battle?"

Chapter 57.

Polychrome felt Erik rise from his seat next to her and turn towards the throne, which was near to hand at one end of the immense banquet table. The celebration had already been going for hours, and the vast majority of the guests — though still toasting the Hero and his party whenever the mood struck — were mostly talking and laughing with each other, less attention finally focused on the nominal reason for the party.

"Iris, I would speak with you more privately, if I might," Erik said, just loud enough for her father to hear.

The Rainbow Lord looked down and nodded, as though he had expected this — which, she guessed, he probably had. "Alone, or merely away from this mob of partygoers, Lord Erik?" he asked.

She noticed Erik's cheeks were momentarily red, but that faded, and he glanced around at the others. "There are several things we must discuss...and they do concern Faerie as well as myself. So...with these others, if you allow it."

Iris smiled ironically. "Erik Medon, though you are in my realm, on this day I do not think there is much that I would dare *not* allow."

Erik's gesture had included his own party — Zenga, Ruggedo, Polychrome of course, Ozma, Dorothy, the Wizard, Glinda, and Nimbus. With Zenga, of course, came Ugu, and Cirrus.

Polychrome wasn't quite sure what to think of Cirrus. On the one hand, he wasn't really one of the Sky Faeries of the realm, except in some macabre way from his origin, but at the same time he really was the person she'd come to know and been betrothed to, and he seemed to be exactly the same as when she had known him. Which meant he was so ashamed that he refused to meet her gaze.

The little party followed Iris to his throneroom, where the Rainbow Lord caused another, smaller table to appear, with matching chairs for all. "Very well, Erik Medon, you have called us here. Speak."

Erik drew a deep breath and stepped forward. "First things first. This isn't the way we do it where I come from...but I'll bet it's the way it works here. Iris Mirabilis, would you approve... Gah, that's not the way..." He trailed off, and Polychrome noticed there was a tiny upturn to her father's mouth, as though he was restraining a grin. "Never mind, I'll just say it. Iris, Polychrome and I are going to be married, if she'll have me, and I hope you approve. Not that it'll stop us either way."

Iris burst out laughing. "Indeed, Erik Medon, that is not quite the way it should be done here; yet to expect you to ask *my* permission would be to expect you to be other than you are. And, in truth," he looked fondly at her, and she felt the warmth of his affection wash over her, "I never could either tell her what to do, or deny her anything she truly wanted." He rose. "Polychrome Glory, do you truly wish to marry this Mortal man?"

Erik looked at her with wide eyes, and she realized that part of him *still* could not believe what had happened, as he said, "Yes, Poly — it's your choice, not anyone else's. I... don't know how long I'll live, and as I'm pushing fifty I know I'm not much to look at already, so I –"

She stared, then burst out laughing, shaking her head. She danced up, and suddenly delivered a gentle slap to his cheek. He blinked, startled. "You are...so adorably *idiotic* sometimes, Erik, I almost think it's an act. I didn't fall in love with a face, even if *you* did — at first."

His face flamed crimson again, and his gaze dropped.

"And one of your worries...he doesn't *know?*" She addressed the last to Ozma.

The Princess of Oz looked surprised, then nodded. "Of course, he would not. To the celebration directly, cleansed by magic... When has he had the time to really examine himself?"

"What the heck are you talking ab—" Erik broke off suddenly as a shimmering mirror appeared before him, and he stared at the man in the mirror — a young man, much less than thirty, perhaps no more than twenty. "What... How?"

"You burned your soul away, Erik Medon, for the sake of Faerie. You did this knowing it might — almost certainly would —

mean your death, and you did it gladly and without stint or hesitation, for the sake of your fallen lady and for my realm, my people, and all of Faerie. What that means for you now — whether you have extended your life by in effect turning back the clock, or simply thrown away those years, whether you remain mortal at all, or are something new never seen, we cannot say," Ozma answered gently. "But I was determined that at the least you would gain one thing; your body now mirrors the age of your soul, as it did before you began. Your soul is younger; so, now, the face and body."

He brushed at the hair that hung down in his face and laughed suddenly. "Well, that explains my sudden sheepdog problem. My hairline's moved forward two inches!" He was suddenly serious again as he looked at Polychrome.

She took his head in her hands and drew his lips down to hers. "I would marry you, my love, if I knew we both would die the moment after, and never regret it unless we were separated in the Eternity to follow."

Iris bowed. "Then so it shall be. To you goes what, in the old way, is the greatest treasure of my kingdom; yet I am well pleased, for I had thought to lose it all, and never have I been so happy to find a prophecy had been wrong after all."

Erik raised his eyebrows, and she recognized the analytical look he gave Iris. *He's thinking again.* "As you mention it...what *were* the missing verses, Iris, the ones you knew and that I didn't?"

Iris smiled faintly. "You all deserve to hear it, I suppose. Following the verse warning of the consequences if you failed to show my daughter a mortal glory and beauty, that ended:
For mortal heart has withered, and Faerie has no friend.
There was this verse:
Hero's ways he now must learn, of strength and sword and will
Bring to the fore what lay within, and both will pay the cost;
For Rainbow's Daughter teaches, the Prophecy to fulfill
And though she knows it not, her heart is forever lost."

Iris' smile faltered for a moment. "And just before the final verse, was this:

With him then the Rainbow's Daughter
Sees love where once was friend;
But win or lose, your favorite child
Shall come home not again."

Erik nodded, then laughed. And in a voice that was an uncanny imitation of another voice, one that — Polychrome realized with a chill — Erik could never have heard, the mortal said, "He *never* makes a mistake!"

Several of the others present recognized both the voice and the words, and stared at Erik Medon. "How... Erik, you *couldn't* have met the Lavender Bear, you jus' *couldn't*, so how could you know his voice...?" Dorothy said after a moment.

Erik looked mildly surprised. "That's the voice I always used when I read him out loud. Just like I always used to give the Wizard a slight English accent — as he appears to have." He nodded slowly. "But that might be significant."

"How do you mean that he — by which you must mean the Pink Bear — never makes a mistake?" Iris said finally.

"You could ask him yourself," Erik pointed out, "but it's simple. Prophecies play games with literal and figurative — as everyone here knows. That's what finally bit poor Ugu on the ass," he nodded at the erstwhile King of Oz. "Your favorite *child* will not come home again. Polychrome might have been, in a way, described as a child when she came down to get me. She's not a child in any way, shape, or form now."

Iris blinked, then whirled to face the tiny pink shape that sat in the shadow of his throne. "So you tricked even *me*."

"You tricked yourself, Iris Mirabilis. Yes, I knew it would be so. But those words could have been more literally true — and nearly were."

"I have a question, if I might."

Polychrome was startled, for the deep, resonant voice was that of Ugu, who had been completely silent — and thoughtful — throughout the party.

"Go ahead," Erik said after a moment.

"During our battle, when you unraveled Amanita's hopes that you would burn yourself out immediately, you said you understood exactly why you *had* to be chosen. Would you be able to explain that?"

"Well, you obviously got part of it, but sure. The requirements for the Hero — once we got to the end of the Prophecy and saw all the things that had to happen — got to be terribly specific. It had to be a man — since Poly isn't interested in girls as far as I know."

Polychrome blinked and blushed. *What? Is that ... possible? Or... well, I suppose it is. How would he even think of ... I'll have to ask him. Later.*

"So right there you cut the candidates in half. Then you have to really cut it down because you need the True Mortal blood. That has to be really, really rare.

"After that, you needed someone who was already a fan of Oz, because if they weren't, they couldn't recognize Polychrome when she arrived, and thus wouldn't speak her name. Now you're *really* cutting the numbers down — Oz just isn't as popular as it was, and most people know it from that darn movie. Then — as it turned out — you needed someone who didn't really have the heart to kill anyone if they could help it, but who *was* willing to fight. And they had to be someone who would fall in love with Polychrome — not that that's hard — and who could afford to do that. I mean, if I had been married, I couldn't have been your hero; the kind of man who'd dump his wife and possible kids to follow her, even to save Faerie, isn't a hero type you want.

"And then, finally, you had to have someone who was all of these things...and who had been a fan of Oz for *many* years, decades, so that he had a lot of years to burn, and yet who still wasn't so old that he couldn't somehow survive the training he needed in order to fight his way through what he'd run into." Erik grinned and tried to look self-deprecating as he gestured to himself. "Follow all of that, and even starting with six billion people your field of choices has just gotten really, really small."

Ugu pursed his lips, then shook his head. "And still you leave out one of the most vital points. The Hero would have to win against such vast powers and could only do so by having a mind of great quickness, personal inventiveness, and — as you made clear — the ability to recall, and visualize — not merely with your mind, but with your heart and soul — the weapons of the imagination that your society provided. A rare talent indeed. Now, truly, do I understand."

"Which brings us to one of the important questions *I* have of you, Erik Medon," her father said. He looked grimly down at Ugu. "He is here because he has given his...parole, I suppose you would call it, and because Princess Zenga has taken responsibility for him, and for...Cirrus, I suppose we must call him. It is *your* duty to decide his ultimate fate, and I do not wish to wait long for that decision. The longer he remains alive yet neither punished nor set free, if that be your will, he is a potential focus of unrest and even violence from those whom he has wronged."

Erik's face grew serious, and he walked up to study Ugu for a long moment. "They say you apologized to Ozma voluntarily, and you protected Cirrus here at the risk of your life."

"I apologized to the Princess and Queen of Oz for many of my actions," Ugu said after a moment. "Not for my beliefs in some ways, but for the ways in which I sought to redress what I saw as wrongs. And I did protect Cirrus from what would have been a terrible wrong."

The blond-haired man looked into the older man's dark eyes, and she could tell that he was measuring what he saw there. "I understand, I think. A shame it took this long to sink in, but at least you've figured it out."

Ugu's laugh was humorless. "A self-righteous anger can make one proof to nearly any reason."

Erik turned, and she saw something new in his stance. He was straighter, head held just a slight bit higher. *He looks...like Father. Like King Inga, like Princess Ozma. He's taken the responsibility for a decision that affects us all.* "Iris, Ozma...Ruggedo," he nodded to the old Nome, "for I suspect that when you return home, Kaliko will happily hand the crown back. My Lords Assembled, in our travels across Oz we learned some few things about the Usurpers, and one that struck us all was that there were many who did *not* speak ill of Ugu. Many, indeed, who had words of praise for his fairness, for his considered efforts to control his Viceroys and direct the efforts of the countries. Yes, there were also many who had grievances...yet the reports were not of the oppressive tyrant we had expected.

"And when I confronted him...I was struck by the difference between Ugu and Amanita. His Queen was insane; Ugu...was not. And even in our confrontation, he showed human feeling, even — I realize now — a consideration for his defeated enemy. Most people know the old saying that 'power corrupts,' but there is another version that says that power *reveals*. There are two moments when you will come to know what a person is really like: the first is when his back is to the wall and he has nothing left but desperation. The other is when he has everything, and need fear nothing, when he can gain anything he wishes simply by reaching out. Some people this makes worse. Others — like Ugu — it can make better, because no longer are they driven to action by fear that others will prevent them from acting. Without fear, they act according to their basic natures."

Ozma looked confused, which echoed how Polychrome felt. She noticed, however, that Glinda was thoughtful and grave, as was the Wizard. "But...what did Ugu have to fear in the beginning?"

Erik shook his head. "Wait on that for a moment. Ugu the Unbowed!"

The once-King of Oz dropped to one knee, realizing judgment was on him — and clearly accepting that this man had the right to judge.

"You have shown the potential for good. You have taken some steps in that direction. Yet none, not even you, could argue that by your actions — and your assistance of Amanita Verdant — you have done great evil, caused much destruction, many deaths, disrupted in one way or another the workings of all of Faerie."

Ugu nodded.

"I spared your life, and the others here have allowed that choice to stand. I would not waste the potential you have shown. It will be your task to assist in the rebuilding of Oz, to help track down and defeat those of the rebel forces that remain — your Viceroys, General Guph and the remains of your army, any other forces you may have had. You have vast magical knowledge, perhaps equal of any others in Faerie; this you will put at the disposal of those you deposed, and what remains of their treasures you will find and return to them." He paused, then continued, "I will be watching."

Ugu nodded again. "You are merciful."

"Hardly." That sharp grin was on his face again. "You will be forced to confront every one of your mistakes, to correct those which can be corrected, to apologize for those which cannot. As you have gained a conscience, Ugu, the pain you shall inflict upon yourself will be far more than any others could ever manage."

Ugu acknowledged that truth with a bitter smile. "You speak truly. Yet...I still count this as a mercy, for by the time you had arrived, I realize I had wished for the chance to do just that. Still... there are...questions remaining for me."

"I think I know what you mean," Erik said. "And I have a few more questions of my own. Give me a day or two to read certain archives which I only got to skim while I was being trained, and I think I will have answers...though not the answers some of you will expect."

"What do you mean, Erik?" Polychrome asked.

He touched her arm gently. "I'll explain later. And to everyone once I'm sure." He turned back to Iris. "And as all the guests are already here...can the wedding be soon?"

At the sudden turn of the subject, Iris laughed anew. "A practical reason to rush so important an event! You are a man of contrasts, Erik Medon. Yet what you say is undeniably true, and the year you spent here was, as I already knew, your courtship of my daughter, though neither of you realized it. So shall it be; in two days shall you be wed, and I shall myself perform that ceremony, on Caelorum Sanctorum, for the Above themselves should witness this, as they watched your struggle and victory."

Two days? Polychrome wanted to protest, say she hardly would have time — but she looked at Erik, and knew that at the same time she would almost rather it were now. *He may be Faerie more than human now...or he may have only a few years left to live. Not even Princess Ozma or my Father can say for sure yet. I want to spend as many days with him as I can.*

Polychrome

Two days. Let them go by swiftly.

Chapter 58.

"Lords of Faerie. Mortal allies. All peoples of the Rainbow Kingdom, all those assembled here upon the Mountain of the Heavens before the eyes of the Above, we are here for one of the most joyous of events," Iris Mirabilis said, his voice echoing across the mountaintop, through the vastness below and above.

I glanced to my side, and the beauty there could have blinded me. *I still can't believe it. It has to be a dream. I'm going to wake up any minute now...and then I will cry myself back to sleep.*

Because it was more than just her beauty — although for her face and form alone I'd have done anything at all. It was for who she was, and that she did love me as I'd come to love her, ten times more than I could have imagined even when first we had met. That year together — when I hadn't dared speak of what I felt and thought, and when she hadn't imagined the possibility of what was now about to happen — that year, that incredible, terrifying, grinding, precious year, had made us more than a dizzily-infatuated couple drunk on the first surge of attraction; it had made us *friends.* And my father had told me that what had kept him together with my mother for all their years was very simple: "I married my best friend."

If I wake up now...I won't just lose a teenager's fantasy. I'll lose a friend, a companion, someone who risked everything for me, as I was risking all for her and all her people, who put herself through just as much as I. For a moment, I shuddered at the very thought. *If this is a dream, I very seriously mean it when I say never let me wake up.*

"Lord Erik Medon has asked my daughter, Polychrome Glory, to marry him, and she has agreed, with joy and certainty," Iris continued. "Though it may seem abrupt, know all assembled that they came to know each other well in the year he spent in my kingdom, for Polychrome guided him in his learning of our world, aided his seeking in understanding, and in the end followed him to the final battle to do what must be done.

"And so I call them forth, the Hero and Heroine of the realm, the Mortal Man and the Heir to my Kingdom, to speak their vows before us all."

We stepped out of the royal tent to the accompaniment of cheering that nearly deafened me. *It's a wonder my cheeks aren't suntanning from the inside, with the amount of blushing I'm doing.* I kept my eyes focused on the mighty form of Iris, because I knew if I looked at Poly right now I'd just stop and stare like an idiot until someone kicked me.

We reached the very peak of Caelorum Sanctorum, facing Iris who stood somewhat below — so that his great height brought his eyes just slightly above mine. We stopped and waited until the cheering died down.

"Polychrome Glory of the Rainbow, do you come here to marry this Mortal Man, Erik Medon?"

The most perfect voice in the world answered, "I do."

"And you do this without doubt, without reservation, without question, knowing that once this bond is made your lives and souls are bound for all eternity?"

"Without doubt, without reservation, without hesitation, yes, Father."

His eyes turned to me. "Erik Medon, of the Mortal World, do you come here to marry Polychrome Glory, Princess of the Rainbow Kingdom?"

"I do." My voice was slightly hoarse with the tension of the moment.

"And you do this without doubt, without reservation, without question, knowing that once made, the bond between you shall remain for all eternity, in life and beyond?"

"Without doubt, reservation, or question, with all joy and willingness, Iris Mirabilis."

He smiled. "It is well." He turned to the assembled crowds. There I saw all our companions, the masses of the Rainbow Kingdom — many of whom I recognized, for after a year I had come to know them — and others of the Faerie realms. Jack Pumpkinhead stood near Ozma, his creator, and nearby was Dorothy, Trot, Betsy, and I grinned as I saw the eternal Lost Boy Button-Bright, and nearby the Shaggy Man; he was one of those who looked exactly as Neill had painted him, curling shags and all. Kaliko was there, and to my surprise I saw that Zenga stood with her mother and father and brother, with old Rin Ki-Tin and Inkarbleu, and a dozen dozen others from the surrounding countries. *The Rainbow must have been busy.*

"If there be any reason, if any question exists, as to whether these two shall be wed this day, then I command — as Lord of the Rainbow Realm and as one of the Children of the Above itself — that you shall speak now, or never."

And to my shock, Polychrome spoke. "Father...there is...one thing."

I turned, my heart feeling as though it was turning to ice, and even Iris looked shocked and pale. But it was part of an ancient ritual, and he spoke his part, even as he gazed at each of us in surprise. "Then speak, Polychrome."

She turned to me, and her eyes were filled with tears. "Erik... Erik, my love...there is something I have to say, something you *must* know, before you marry me, for it is something I'm ashamed of, and..." she took a deep breath, "... and once you know it, you may change your mind about marrying me."

I blinked. "Poly, I..."

She shook her head. "When I saw you to be sacrificed, when you stood in that circle and Amanita was readying her knife for your heart, it was then that I knew. I knew why Father had seemed so distant from you at first, I knew what he had to have been hiding. And I understood, oh, my love, I finally understood what you were saying to me all the time we had known each other."

"Yes, I know, Poly, but –"

"Please! I have to finish." She swallowed. "I knew, then, you were in love with me. And I knew — by the Prophecy and its riddles — how it was possible that you could be bathed in your heart's blood and still speak, how you could be sealed into your promise for that ritual and still fight, how all we hoped for could be achieved.

"I knew that you had to lose me. And so I made sure that you would." Tears were pouring down her cheeks now as I stared. "Do you *understand*, Erik? I made that decision *just like Father*, I knew what it would do to you, and I knew that it had to be done in exactly that way. I didn't fling myself in front of that blade just because I loved you, I did it because it was the one way to save Oz, save Faerie, save...my father and our friends, and that one way was to make *you* into the weapon we needed to destroy our enemies. And even when we said our goodbyes," I heard a choked sob, realized it was my own, as the agony of that moment echoed back to me, "even then, Erik, yes, even then I was speaking those words and choosing them oh, so very carefully, to make sure you would be the pure and unstoppable avenger that we needed."

She bowed her head, and waited.

I stared at her. *She* planned *that speech? Her own sacrifice? To make sure I...berserked? Had no doubts, no hesitation in using that power even if I burned my soul to nothing?*

I understood why she felt shame. But at the same time I felt a smile on my face. "Poly," I said, and her eyes looked up, even though her head stayed down, eyes afraid and ashamed. "Polychrome Glory, I need to know only one thing.

"You say you did these things knowing what they would accomplish, knowing that your death and your words would make me the weapon that would break the Usurpers."

She nodded, wordlessly.

"What I need to know, then, is whether you *lied* to me — in deed or word — in those moments, or if every action and word *also* came from your heart."

Her head came up then. "I have *never* lied to you, Erik."

I smiled then, my heart beginning to beat again. "Then there is nothing to forgive, Polychrome, my first and truest love. There is no shame at all in finding that deep and cold policy must be followed... if it is also in accord with your heart. And..." I shook my head, and heard my voice almost break, "and it would not matter to me in any case, so long as you have told the truth when you have said you loved me. I was ready to die for the fact that you *existed*, Polychrome; for the very *idea* that you could care for me, that you could *love* me? There is nothing I would not do, and nothing you *could* do that I could not forgive so long as you were still...who you are."

"Oh..." she reached out and took my hand and I almost forgot where we were, looking into those violet-stormy eyes.

Iris Mirabilis' voice brought us back to facing him. "Then as no objections exist, Erik Medon, Polychrome Glory, give me your hands."

His huge hands swallowed ours, but held them gently. "May the Will and Wisdom of the Above watch over us all. Erik Medon and Polychrome Glory, be you now joined together, not as one, but as two who are now made greater by each other. May your bond exalt you in triumph, support you in trial, comfort you in loss, ease your pains, and echo your love and belief in one another for all eternity. May the Above, in whatever guise you may see it, bestow upon you their ineffable and sacred blessing, that in the day when your time in this world has ended you shall not pass into the Void or be taken Below, but instead shall walk together, for all eternity, in the realm which cannot perish and in which you shall be as you were, and more besides."

He placed our hands together, and about them twined two golden chains. "The chains of gold are as imperishable as the binding of your souls, and so long as you are true to each other, never shall they fade or break. Do you, Erik Medon, take Polychrome Glory to be your wife? Will you pledge to her your body, your breath, your blood, your mind, your will, by Earth, by Air, by Water, by Fire, and by Spirit?"

I could barely speak. "I will."

"And do you, Polychrome Glory, take Erik Medon to be your husband? Will you pledge to him your body, your breath, your blood, your mind, your will, by Earth, by Air, by Water, by Fire, and by Spirit?"

She looked into my eyes, and there was nothing else in the universe to me. "Oh, yes, I will."

"Then the chains are bound, and by the power of the Rainbow and the Above that bond now sets you free of all others. Let no power attempt to separate you, for none shall avail against you," and here I saw him smile, and knew he was adding his own words, "any more than any have done so in life.

"It is done."

We looked to him as he spoke; and in that moment — for just an instant — I saw beyond him the great golden city, and the shining figures within, and one that stood above them all, whose piercing blue eye met mine.

There was approval there, and a blessing, and a fierce and undeniable feeling of command. And as the vision faded, a warrior's smile.

And then it was over, and another vision was before me, and I was kissing Polychrome Glory, First Daughter of the Rainbow, our hands still entwined by the golden chain of our marriage.

Chapter 59.

I looked up as the door of the Throne Room opened, and the others entered. "Ozma, Ruggedo, Zenga, Ugu — thank you for coming." I glanced behind me and higher, to Iris. "And thank you for waiting."

"I admit to a bit of impatience, Erik," Iris said with some humor, and Nimbus echoed his smile. "But that is perhaps foolish. After all, you shall always be here, now."

I glanced at Polychrome, who raised her eyebrow and smiled at me; we had already talked some about this. "That... is not entirely correct, Iris," I said.

"I would expect that both he and Polychrome will be visiting Oz," pointed out Ozma with a smile, "for they are of course most welcome, and if I do not mistake him, Erik would very much enjoy seeing Oz from the point of view of a guest and not an invader or a sacrifice."

I laughed. "You are completely correct, Princess. Yet I speak of something far more serious." I turned to Ugu. "Ugu the Unbowed, you mentioned certain questions that remained to you, and that while you abhor your methods you do not entirely repudiate your prior feelings. In this, you are entirely correct."

Ozma looked at me closely, and Iris leaned down; to have both looking at me that intensely was, to be honest, slightly intimidating. Maybe I was mostly mortal still, but some lingering touch of Faerie gave me the ability to sense the vast power in Ozma; I didn't see a delicate little girl, really, but rather I saw something more like Iris Mirabilis in a female guise.

"How do you mean, this, Erik Medon?" Ozma said finally.

"First, let me speak of what I've learned here — and what I've guessed. Which will require me to confirm some things I've guessed, in order to go onward. Iris, long ago — even by some Faerie standards — your people, your world was one with ours, and it then

403

began to separate. I believe this was no accident; it was according to a directive of what you call the Above. Am I right?"

Iris nodded. "You are."

"And the purpose of this was to allow humanity to follow the path it had begun, one of self-determination, and to prevent the presence of the Gods and the Faerie from being either too great a help, or too great a hindrance, in that development."

That surprised him, and he sat back in his throne. "Now by my Father, how did you know *that?* For I shall take an oath that not a hint of that is written anywhere in the Hall of Records."

I smiled my favorite sharp grin. "Don't underestimate us mortals, Lord Iris. That kind of thing is an old, old idea, and one that makes sense with the timing of events.

"But the problem of course was, and is, that the Above — the Gods, if you will, and the Faerie — were, and are, connected to humanity, and we are connected to them. The worship and belief, the faith and will, the strength of our spirits connects somehow to your very essence, and the battles and triumphs, the hopes and fears, of this world are echoed, even across the great gap separating us, into my own. Thus many of the things we have remarked upon — how things that I could not have known still seemed to be true, from the voice of a ruler I had never known to the ways of magic that had been lost to my world." I turned back to Ozma.

"My Lady — your Majesty, you must forgive me for what I am about to say, but you made a terrible and grave mistake in your rulership. An understandable one, even a laudable one — but a terrible one with grave consequences nonetheless."

For a moment she looked affronted — and then her coal-black eyes closed, and opened again with a rueful sparkle. "Speak, then, Erik Medon. We would still be imprisoned, and our realm enslaved, were it not for you and your imagination. We would be both ungrateful, and dangerously foolish, to disregard your insight now."

I sighed with relief. *Whew. I hoped she'd be reasonable about this, but there was always the risk...* "You sought to make Oz as close to a paradise as there has ever been. Seeing the evil done with magic in the wrong hands — having suffered a terrible transformation and violation of your own body and mind as a child," and I saw both acknowledgement of that wound, and thanks that I had chosen *not* to bring the Wizard into this discussion, "you determined that *none* would practice magic without your direct leave. More, you sought ever and ever to replace argument with negotiation, anger with peace, any pain with joy, through the power of your Above-mandated position as Ruler of Oz, the very heart of Faerie."

She nodded slowly. "This is true. Even the books speak of these things — though of course not so clearly or directly."

"But in doing this you created your own destruction — and perhaps that of my own people as well," I said quietly.

"What?" Iris' voice was shocked. "What can you mean by that?"

"Your citizens are *human beings*, Ozma. Perhaps with a trace of Faerie blood, perhaps a bit more, some animals touched by the magic of the realm, but in the end not *that* much different than those of my world. They feel anger, they feel hatred, they feel love and pain and fear and joy and all the other things that I do or that I could feel. By exerting your will to make these things less and less common, you fought the very nature of what people *are*. That... darker essence could not be destroyed, not here in Faerie, where the metaphysical is as real as the physical. But you rejected it, and your people with you. All of Faerie, in fact, for the most part, because when you make a decision — as the Ruler of Oz — it is not just a simple command, a directive like those a mortal might make. By your very nature and the position you hold, your will becomes manifest throughout all Faerie, and calls upon its power to make your will into truth. Only those of the meanest and most savage natures — or those with the strongest wills and — perhaps — most selfish and self-justified reasons for their negative emotions — were able to hold on to them. The rest...went elsewhere."

"Where?" Zenga asked, her voice showing that she was starting to understand the implications.

"To *his* world," Ugu said, his deep voice echoing about the throneroom with grim understanding. "We all have heard the tales of the world of men and how it has become increasingly...frenetic, dangerous, dark, strange, alien. And..." his brow furrowed, and he continued slowly, "and...if what he says is true...why, then, this echoes back to us, creating confusion, instability, unrest."

405

Ryk E. Spoor

"Bringing together those who are unaffected or resistant to the effect, yes," I continued. "Such as yourself and Amanita. Were it not you, it would have been others, I believe."

The diminutive Ozma stared at me in horror. "Do you mean to say that...that I *caused* all this to happen?"

"Not willingly. Not planned it. But I believe, very strongly, that this sequence of events has its roots in your attempt to make Oz something it could not truly be — for the best possible motives. Ozma, the fact is that people here really are the same as people from my world, in their most basic essence. The first glimpse we saw of Oz — before you returned — showed just that, a land of great promise, of evil and ugliness and of goodness and beauty. After you returned, it became more and more a place of minimal danger, where even death was reduced or eliminated. At first I'd thought this was just Baum's choice...but once I came here I started to wonder."

Iris looked at Ozma, and then down at Polychrome. "My daughter, what have you to say?"

"Father, you know he's right," she said bluntly, without hesitation. "Everything...became more...oh, I don't know... extreme, perhaps... after Ozma became ruler of Oz. And yet somehow none of the great tensions were released while she was there. Then when Oz...fell..."

Iris closed his eyes and nodded. "It was devastation. As though all the unrest of hundreds of years had been unleashed in a matter of hours."

"An astute interpretation...and an accurate one, I suspect," Ruggedo said finally. "What do you intend to do about it, then?"

"We've mentioned the Above. But the fact is there's another side that you speak of much more seldom, that you call the Below. They, too, play their part in this. Do you think the disruptions and chaos are unguided? I don't. They've taken this opening and tried their best to cause utter destruction. We've averted it...for now. But that won't last if things continue as they are."

"What would you have us do?" Ozma asked.

"For Oz? You need to let it be what it truly is — the center of Faerie, a place of high beauty, high adventure, of great danger and great mystery, of the grotesque and horrific as well as the whimsical and heartwarming. Ugu might have been a terrible threat...or, without your directive threatening his family's tradition, he might never have even become known to you. Magic is *part* of Oz." I chuckled. "Hell, look at the books. The most interesting things *in* them only happen when someone *is* playing around with magic, so Baum had to rely on either the stories of renegades, or in making up some himself."

"That, however," Ugu said, "will hardly reverse the consequences of centuries. Not swiftly, and perhaps not at all, if the Below has chosen to move."

"And that brings me to the other point. Poly and I won't always be here, because I have a responsibility for two worlds, not just one — and now that we're married, so does she."

Iris shot to his feet, and his height made him three times as intimidating. "It is *forbidden!*"

I took a deep breath. "I'm un-forbidding it."

"You would challenge the *Above?*" He looked at me as though I was insane — and no doubt that possibility was on his mind.

"It's more that the *Above* has challenged *me*," I answered with a wry grin.

"What do you mean by that?" Ozma asked.

I remembered that moment on Caelorum Sanctorum. "I... saw the Above again, as Poly and I were married. And the look that... well, their leader, not to use any one name, gave me wasn't just one of congratulation. He was looking at me in a way that said, as clear as if he'd spoken it, that I wasn't anywhere near done *yet*."

Iris stared at me for several moments. Then slowly he reached down and brought up the Pink Bear, and looked down at it. "I am... loath to ask many questions of you, Bear, for too much pain have we endured after the last time, no matter the reasons. Yet I would know if he saw truly."

The Bear looked up and spoke in its mechanical, jerky, high-pitched voice. "He saw as well as a mortal may, Iris Mirabilis, and read in the gaze of the All-Seeing that which it was desired he should read."

Iris narrowed his gaze. "Desired by *whom?*" he said, clearly determined to leave no assumption untested this time.

"By the All-Seeing."

Iris hesitated, then sighed. "Then it is as you say. But do you understand what you imply, Erik Medon?"

"I think I do. We've had a long time to grow, Iris. Humanity's got a lot of problems, but we're not children any more, and I don't think...I don't think it's *good* for us that we are separated any more." I took Polychrome's hand, felt the warm accord between us. "We were meant to be together, and I don't think the Above meant this separation to be for all time."

"And when," he said after a moment, looking to Nimbus, "will you be going?"

"Soon," I said simply. "The time advantage here has helped — I've only been gone a few months from the mortal viewpoint. But it would be too easy for me to stay, lose track of time, and suddenly run out of it."

"Run out?"

"I left instructions when I left that would keep things going for a year, but once that's over, I'd have nothing left and I'd have to start from scratch — which isn't easy in the modern world. I'll have a hard time explaining everything even *with* all my resources still intact." I grinned. "Believe me, you've never had to fill out the forms I have."

I went back to looking serious. "And yes, I could also run out of time myself. Both you and Ozma admit that you haven't any idea what I am now, or whether I'm going to break apart in the next ten minutes or live as long as a Faerie. So I can't afford to waste time."

"That is true," Ozma admitted. "The few times something such as you and I have done had been attempted... well, the mortal did not survive. Perhaps you are still a True Mortal — that we could, I suppose, test. But even such a test would not prove that there are no other effects, merely that you have not entirely changed. Yes, your soul could be deeply damaged and on the verge of dissolution, or you could be something far more than either Faerie or Mortal.

None can say, nor shall we be able to unless and until something happens to give us that insight."

Iris closed his eyes and his shoulders slumped for a moment. "Nimbus?"

"I have little to add, Majesty. If we accept the words of Lord Erik and the Pink Bear, there is no choice for it but that we must turn back towards the Mortal world, prepare for a change in both realms such as has not been seen since we both were far younger, since Polychrome herself was a child in truth." He hesitated, then turned to the rest of us. "You should understand, Lord Erik, and the rest of you, as well, for of all of you only Ruggedo was full-grown in those days, and he absented himself from most of the proceedings."

The old Nome King gave a snort. "Indeed, for I cared not at all for mortals then. Grasping, scurrying ephemeral rats, I used to call them. What fools we all were in youth, even we of Faerie."

"At least you have come to this knowledge while still able to appreciate it, Ruggedo," Nimbus said with a wry smile. "But to explain: much of the weight of the Separation fell upon Iris Mirabilis, for he is the master of the Rainbow that bridges the worlds. To bring them together will, also, fall upon him, and such a burden is a hard thing to bear."

Polychrome nodded. "I remember that Father was often gone, and when he was not, he was...tired, distracted, for a long time."

"Meaning that once this task is begun, Iris will be able to do little else for us," I finished slowly. "It will be up to the rest of us." I thought for a moment. "Ugu?" He nodded. "While I think your basic responsibility remains unchanged, I'd amend the manner of carrying it out. Ozma will need a strong right hand who will act, who is respected by both the people of Oz *and* by forces much darker, able to both converse and combat those he confronts. She also needs insight from one who has seen the consequences of her policies, and who understands what it is to rule. I can think of no better choice than you."

Ugu stared at me, and then almost fearfully at Ozma, an expression startling on that almost imperturbable face. "Majesty?" he said finally, as she returned his stare with an unreadable look on her flower-perfect features.

She was silent for a moment. "Erik Medon, you truly ask me to accept as a trusted advisor the one who bound my country, *myself,* who unleashed Amanita Verdant upon the world, who planned and led the revolution that nearly destroyed all of Faerie?"

I looked back steadily. "I do indeed, Ozma. In this, I can point only to your own beliefs. This man has repented of his acts, and wishes to make amends for his evil. You forgave one who acted against you out of selfishness before, and he has become one of the most beloved and celebrated men of Oz. Can you do so again? Will you give him that chance, as you gave the Wizard?"

Then she smiled, with a smile so wide and bright that it lit the room. "And I see that truly you understand what I sought to be, and I cannot argue with myself. All deserve that chance at redemption if they truly seek it. Ugu the Unbowed — for indeed that is your name, and shall remain your name, for though beaten you have kept a pride that is not bravado — you shall come with me as advisor, and...troubleshooter, as I think Erik Medon would say. And so, too, if he wishes, will Cirrus Dawnglory, for I have seen that he finds too much pain here to be truly happy."

I saw a shadow pass over Nimbus' face, and Poly gripped my hand a little tighter, but Nimbus nodded, and Ugu bowed. "I accept with gratitude, Princess Ozma."

Zenga stepped forward. "I'd like to come too."

"You don't want to return to Pingaree?" Ozma looked surprised.

Zenga shrugged. "I wasn't just sent out to fight the Usurpers. The idea was political alliance. Well, the first one seems not to have quite worked out," she threw a grin and a wink at me, "but that doesn't mean there aren't other...possibilities." Her gaze flicked boldly from Nimbus to Ugu, both of whom looked suddenly taken aback, and then to Ruggedo, who coughed and was suddenly red as his name, and even to Iris, who tried and failed to conceal a look of combined amusement and minor affront. "I'm in no hurry, though, and I'm not planning to marry *just* for the advantage." I could tell that last phrase was there for me, and I smiled at her. "So helping out in Oz, in the Rainbow Kingdom, the Nome Kingdom —

traveling like the Penitent, even — sounds to me like the right thing to do."

"You may have an alliance with Oz without need for such... drastic measures," Ozma said, with a smile of her own, "but you have shown how formidable you are — in more ways than one, it would seem — and surely you are welcome in Oz to help us in these troubled times."

Iris turned back to us. "And so you shall leave us...soon?"

"Tomorrow, in fact. Honestly, it's also a tradition."

The Lord of the Rainbow blinked. "A *tradition?*"

"Sure. Where I come from, when people get married, they often go to some faraway exotic location for a honeymoon." I smiled at my wife — *wife! What an alien...yet wonderful...word!* — as I continued, "well, the Mortal World's really faraway and exotic for Polychrome, and for me...it's been a long time since I went home."

The immense Lord of the Rainbow gazed down, and slowly a smile spread across his face, and suddenly he threw back his head and laughed. "So be it, Erik Medon. And indeed, it is fitting. The Faerie and Mortal worlds are to be joined again, and in the moment of that decision, a Mortal and a Faerie have been joined with the blessings of the Above, after together saving the realms of Faerie; now, together, they will go to *his* world, and perhaps for the same reason.

"So rest well, my son, my daughter, for tomorrow my Rainbow shall span the length of the Heavens, and you shall walk on the soil of the mortal world once more."

Epilogue.

Carl Palmer looked around the kitchen again. *It's all neat, the heat's working, checked the vents, the contractor will be here tomorrow for the repairs...*

He shook his head, catching sight of his own narrow face with hazel eyes in the stainless-steel surface of the refrigerator. *It just seems so futile. Sometimes I wonder if they're right.*

Coming to the little house by himself had been a mistake, he decided. Usually he brought someone else — his wife Katrina, one of his other friends like Joe or Rob — but this weekend everyone else had been busy, and Carl felt he'd put off the prep of the house as long as he could. Freezing weather was starting, and it had to be ready.

But ready for what?

He'd left the note on the table where Erik had left it when... whatever happened had happened. The police had looked at the note of course, there'd been a lot of running around and questions the first couple of weeks, but eventually things had settled down; the note was hastily written, with Erik's usual sloppy handwriting, but it was clearly his, written with the phrasing his friends would expect. Aside from the fact that he *had* disappeared, there wasn't anything to indicate that his friend had lost his mind or been the victim of foul play.

He found himself picking the note up again and reading it, as though reading it again would somehow give him a clue as to what had happened and why.

To whoever finds this note (probably Carl, I bet):

If you're reading this, I've had to go away very suddenly. You might say I've been...called away. I'm not going into details on this, I don't have time.

This is a legal document; if I don't return within one year, you should treat me as dead and execute my will as will be found in my safety deposit box at Key Bank. For that year, however, I want

413

everything maintained here for my return. Carl Palmer, of 3 Rowland Court, Delmar, is hereby given a full power of attorney to use the resources of my current estate to maintain my home, car (the latter you will probably find empty on Route 4), and other possessions. This includes paying all heating, power, telephone, and other bills of normal operation, and any maintenance or repair as may be needed. My brother David is named as a secondary power of attorney and oversight on the use of these resources.

Please forgive any failures of proper legal procedure; I have no time to consult a lawyer or rewrite this exactly. Basically, make sure things are ready for me to return anytime in the next year; after that, I'm dead.

Hope we will meet again.
Erik L. Medon

The note was both signed and had a blue blotch which turned out to be an improvised fingerprint; as near as the police could tell, Erik had rubbed a ballpoint pen quickly over the surface of his thumb and pressed it down, creating a readable fingerprint that verified his presence when writing the note.

Unfortunately, reading it again hadn't added any more enlightenment. Try as he might, Carl simply couldn't imagine what could possibly have gotten his best friend to up and disappear at something like four in the morning, with no warning, no build-up, no hints of what was happening or why.

"He was *comfortable*," Carl heard himself say. Which was, really, the problem. Erik might not have been *perfectly* happy — he had regrets, of course, and Carl knew about most of them, but overall he was a pretty relaxed, cheerful, and — if you were being honest — slightly lazy geek who was satisfied to play RPG campaigns on most weekends, read books, write fanfic and stories for his own amusement, play videogames, and pretty much *not* expend much physical effort.

Dashing off in the middle of the night to an unnamed mysterious location for some unknown purpose? That was just about the *opposite* of Erik Medon's usual behavior. Normally you couldn't wake him *up* before nine even on a workday.

Carl sighed again. *I'm getting depressed again. Damn him anyway!*

The late afternoon sunlight streaming through the windows suddenly...shifted, and Carl looked up in confusion. It wasn't the usual golden-pink color of the sunset, and it wasn't the change in light of a cloud passing by. It hadn't faded; it was *brightening*, and not with just one color, but many; the walls and floor danced with color, red, yellow, green, blue, as though rippling, flowing torrents of spotlights of all hues were cascading down in front of the house.

Carl got to one of the windows, looked out — and gasped.

A tremendous Rainbow stretched down from the heavens, reaching out of the nearly cloudless sky from some unguessable height to rest — or so it seemed — on the far side of the house, near the front door. There was not the slightest trace of rain, the grass was dry, the leaves tumbled in a faint breeze, yet that luminescent vision remained, illuminating everything with colors so strong and pure that they almost brought tears to Carl's eyes.

Even as he registered this, really grasped that a rainbow had come to Earth in some impossible fashion, the Rainbow lifted, fading at this end as though picked up by some inconceivably mighty hand, dwindling away into a final flare of prismatic radiance in the heavens.

Carl sank back into one of the nearby chairs, staring out at the now perfectly ordinary fall afternoon. *Did I really see that? What the heck was it?* And with more than a bit of self-annoyance, *and why the hell didn't I snap a picture of it with my cell?*

The front door rattled.

He jumped out of the chair and strode towards the door. *I'm not expecting anyone else, so I wonder if someone's trying to break into the vacant house. Bad timing for them, if so.* His car was parked off to the side, so it wasn't immediately obvious to a potential thief that he was present.

Just before he reached the door, it opened.

Two people stood on the doorstep. The one in front, opening the door, was a tall young man wearing what looked like some incredible cosplay outfit, a sort of crystal-armor thing, right down to the Ludicrously Oversized Sword. Then he looked up from the doorknob, from which he was withdrawing a key.

"*Carl?!*"

Carl knew, vaguely, that his jaw had dropped, that he was staring like an idiot, but he simply couldn't help it. It was Erik Medon in front of him — but it wasn't. Or rather, it was an Erik Medon who couldn't have existed for the last twenty years. The lines of the face had faded, the wrinkles about the eyes smoothed — the hair that had been in full retreat had returned. And under that ridiculous yet impressive armor, there were muscles that his friend had never had except in his most active imagination, muscles that couldn't possibly have developed in two or three months.

"Carl! So you *did* get my message! Thank God, I had a terrible vision of everything being seized and sold off, coming home to a vacant lot or something."

"Erik?" he managed finally. "Erik? What the hell *happened?* Where have you — how did you — what are you wearing that — *arrgh!*" He shook his head furiously to clear it, since all the questions were crashing into each other and making a total mess of things.

Erik laughed, but not unkindly. "I'm sorry, Carl. I really am, but I just didn't have a chance to tell anyone." He turned slightly. "Poly, this is Carl Palmer, my best friend for, oh, twenty years or more. Carl, this is Polychrome...my wife."

For the first time, Carl really *looked* at the second person, who now stepped forward, and for the second time found his jaw dropping. *That's impossible. No girl really looks like that. Not in real life.*

But the impossible vision was taking his hand and shaking it. "I'm very pleased to meet you, Carl," she said.

Carl forced his mouth closed, then gave the automatic response, "And I'm glad to meet you too. Um... excuse me for a moment." He turned back to Erik. "*WIFE?*"

"Yeah." For a moment his friend looked toward Polychrome *(that's a weird name, too...sounds almost familiar,* Carl thought*)* and he looked almost awestruck, as though he still couldn't believe it himself. "Yes, we're married."

Then Erik snapped himself back to the present. "Look, let's go to the kitchen. I think we'd better order some delivery. This is going to take a little while."

"*That* is an understatement," Carl said, still trying to take in the changes. *It's Erik, no doubt about it. But he's so changed. Yet... not changed, in a way. Almost as though he was... more himself than ever.* He shook his head and grinned as he picked up the phone. "Okay, Erik, but I warn you — you got some *'splainin'* ta do!"

And Polychrome looked absolutely confused as her husband burst out laughing.

FIN.

418

The Prophecy of the Bear

[The italicized verses are the ones that Iris Mirabilis withheld from
Erik and Polychrome]

Two paths before, and the way never clear.
One brings you joy, the other filled with fear.
All will hinge on the choice of one;
A choice only made before it has begun.

The one a Hero, True-Mortal born
Whose heart awaits call of Faerie horn.
Unbirthed as yet, and you must wait
Until the day decreed by fate.

Where three cloud-castles stand and face the sun
There the Rainbow Princess ends her run;
Cloud-wall ahead, dark storms behind
At last the fated place you'll find.

Down the Rainbow all is changed, there is no familiar ground;
Only when your name is spoken shall you turn yourself around
And when you see the speaker know your hero has been found.

To the Rainbow's Daughter a beauty will be shown
Might and mortal glory as she has never known
Set her feet to dancing, until they've skyward flown
Through the skies and homeward to stand before the Throne.

If no joy by dawning, if no dancing glory felt
Hope is gone now, shattered, lost, like first snow's fading melt.
Return you to the palace and prepare you for the end
For mortal heart has withered, and Faerie has no friend.

419

Ryk E. Spoor

Hero's ways he now must learn, of strength and sword and will
Bring to the fore what lay within, and both will pay the cost;
For Rainbow's Daughter teaches, the Prophecy to fulfill
And though she knows it not, her heart is forever lost.

Across the sky and sea, wisdom he shall seek
That which he sought shall he refuse
And in rejecting wisdom gains he strength;
With one companion he sets out; another he must win
To brave the perils still to come and find his way within.

Within find danger, maybe doom
And then the saga's done;
But safely pass where perils loom
And half the quest is run.

Wasteland to be crossed remains
Where only walk the dead
If the other side he attains
Follow where he's led.

Army faces army
Fifty thousand strong
Both of Faerie, neither yielding
The battle will be long.

Forward always be the path
To city, once of Emerald, gray
Win you through the wizard's wrath
To face your judgment day.

With him then the Rainbow's Daughter
Sees love where once was friend;
But win or lose, your favorite child
Shall come home not again.

Now he comes to the end, few his friends, alone

Held by words and chains before the Warlock's throne.
Sorely wounded shall he be, and then his fate be known;
If struck through the heart and silent, unable he to call
Then Ozma's power sealed forever and darkness shall rule all;
Bathed in his heart's blood but still with voice
Ozma's name he calls;
Her power lifts him up, burns his soul away
But in those final moments he may win the day.

Patron Page

The following people contributed greatly
to the publication of *Polychrome*.

Wanda Beers: *For Xander and Maddox - May your imaginations take you over the rainbow!*

Ron Critchfield

Raja Thiagarajan: *with thanks to Julie, and to Jason–who may enjoy it when he's older.*

David Churn

Paul (Drak Bibliophile) Howard

Bill Ryan: *Wherever, whenever and however you write the result is always the same. Magnificent!*

Rich Pieri

Thomas Talley: *Very good book!*

Chris: *Keep writing!*

Kevin Reid

Rob Masters

Chris Baumgartner

Terry Austin, God King of Trolls

Sean Haley: *If it ain't broke, I can fix that.*

Sue Fisher

Caden, Ethan, & Isaac Osborne

Rob Hampson

CPSIA information can be obtained at www.ICGtesting.com
Printed in the USA
LVOW04s1216240615

443675LV00002B/334/P